VOODOO
BALL

C.P. MORTENSEN

© 2019 C.P Mortensen

C.P Mortensen
Voodoo Ball

All rights reserved. No part of this publication may be reproduced, stored in a retrieval system or transmited in any form or by any means, electronic, mechanical, photocopying, recording or otherwise without the prior permision of the publisher or in accordance with the provisions of the Copyright, Designs and Patents Act 1988 or under the terms of any licence permitting limited copying issued by the Copyright Licensing Angency.

Published by: Red Key Press

Cover & Interior Design by: Peter Langdon

ISBN-13: 978-1-7333353-0-0

*For
Carol.*

"The question is how to swing like
you've already swung.
The Answer is what everyone is
trying to find."

Dr. Warren Sleeves D.D.S.

"It's impossible to beat Snog at the
game that bears his name."

Snog

The Turbine Field

He was the color of sand, a beige ghost with a set of golf clubs hanging from his neck. He had materialized out of the storm, coming over a rise, backed by a sea of spinning propellers, trudging with his head bowed, one shoulder raised, against the wind and the driving rain.

When he reached the spot where I stood, he raised his eyes and seemed to look right through me. Then speaking slowly, as though each word occurred to him at the very instant he uttered it, said: "Mind… if… I… play… through?"

His eyes were as black as the sky we'd just fallen from. Confronted by this phantom, I should have been afraid —I was afraid. But fear seemed somehow beside the point, pre-empted by the staggering wave of déjà vu that swept through me. I knew this creature—was sure of it. Somehow, somewhere, we'd met before. Just like this. But I couldn't place the where or when of it. I stood there frozen in place and time straining for a connection that hung just out of reach, thinking I'd go crazy if…

"Charley!" That's when I heard Dave call me. The ghost heard him too. He didn't turn or look toward the sound but raised his chin and closed his eyes, listening hard, as if trying to conjure an image to go with the sound or remember where he'd heard it before.

When he opened his eyes again, I recognized him.

Dave said later that he heard me scream and saw me take off running. I only got about thirty yards when, looking backward, I ran smack into a turbine and knocked myself out.

Floyd and the Golf Trip

Floyd Birdwell was what happens when golfers and bikers cross breed indiscriminately. He was a fierce-looking guy with his mangy beard and sweat-stained visor that bundled his unkempt blonde hair upward like a cluster of sprouts. The front of his visor read: Floss More, which I assumed was a crude knockoff of Flossmoor, the elegant country club outside of Chicago, until I found out that Dr. Sleeves, Floyd's golf guru, was also a dentist.

Astride his Fatboy Harley, golf bag slung from his shoulder like a quiver of arrows, Floyd personified an Avenging Angel of golf. He played Titleist Professional balls, aces and eights, and had his handicap (five) tattooed on his right forearm. When he couldn't play to it, Floyd declared he'd have the arm cut off. None of the range rats doubted this.

Floyd worked at Mallard's Driving Range where his main duty was to drive the little caged cart that picked up the balls. He'd load them into milk crates, and haul them back to the shed behind the office where he fed them through the washer, poured them back into wire buckets, and stacked them on the worn wooden shelves opposite the cash register beneath the sign that read, "No Extra Handfuls." From there the balls were snatched up by a relentless bucket-brigade of golfers, hauled back to the stalls, and swatted out onto the range for Floyd to pick up again.

When the monotony got to him, which was most of the time, he'd careen around the range, venting his fury on the customers, taunting them, telling them their swings stunk or what candy-asses they were until it seemed every shot was aimed directly at Floyd in his little cage. That was fine with him. Floyd liked being the center of attention.

Mallard's range wasn't much by way of a golf facility. It offered a single row of stalls with artificial turf tee boxes separated by little mesh barriers. Behind these were some benches to sit on while you changed your shoes or took a breather from the quest.

The range measured two hundred and fifty yards to the back fence and a little less than a hundred yards side to side. Large cutout numbers designating one hundred, one-fifty, one seventy-five, and two hundred yards served as targets. In addition to these were painted barrels situated at sixty and eighty yards. Or, if you preferred a moving target, you aimed at Floyd. Which happened to be what we were doing that afternoon when the bankers first proposed the golf trip.

"Two days in Palm Springs," Ron Baxter said. "Two championship courses, thirty-six holes a day."

Dave, the mechanic, customarily dressed in his oil-stained coveralls, hit another in a series of lengthy worm-burners that skittered down the range, coming to an abrupt halt in a mud hole. "What's it gonna cost?" he said.

"The weekend's all free," Mike said without looking up from the loan applications he'd spread all over the bench. He was in shirtsleeves, tie loosened, the jacket to his pin-stripe banker's suit draped over the back. Mike Kelly had just passed his thirty-sixth birthday, but if you ignored the prematurely gray hair and dark cross hatch wrinkles under his eyes, might have been the same baby-faced fraternity brat I knew in college. A jet-black mustache contrasted dramatically with his silky gray hair, adding to the riverboat-gambler image he cultivated. He'd begun his banking career loaning candy money at usurious interest to school mates. Decades later, he was still at it, huckstering loans to unqualified borrowers.

"All you pay for's booze and golf balls," Mike said. "Think you can manage that?"

"How's that work?" I was in a stall next to Dave, lobbing wedges at the sixty-yard barrel.

Mike jerked his head toward Ron. "Tell 'em, Ronnie."

Ron worked for Mike at the bank where his job, as I

understood it, was repossessing the things people bought with the money Mike loaned them. A fastidious dresser, Ron had shown up at Mallard's straight from the bank—it might have been St. Patrick's Day—with a carnation in his buttonhole. Floyd had watched from his cage as, prior to hitting balls, the young banker folded his suit jacket over a bench and combed his thinning hair. This simple act was more than enough to convince Floyd that Ron was gay. No amount of arguing would convince him otherwise. Even when you pointed to Ron's wife and three kids as material evidence, he wasn't buying. "Ringers," he said. "Probably pays 'em a salary."

"Golf," Ron said now, "is courtesy of Mr. Wendell Gilmore of Gilmore Development."

"Courtesy?" Dave frowned, as if unfamiliar with the word.

"He belongs to Tamarisk, Thunderbird, and I believe Mission Hills."

I had to whistle. It was a very impressive list. "Where do we play?"

"Wherever we want," said Mike, flashing the little smirk you saw when he raked in a poker pot. "We bailed old Wendell out when he went belly-up on that shopping center. Now we're his pals."

Ron adjusted his suspenders, mopped his brow with a monogrammed handkerchief, and switched to his five wood. "Oh, yeah," he said. "We're his boys now."

"Sounds good," said Dave.

"It is," said Mike, "which means you'll be riding in the trunk of the car. And, by the way, they have a strict dress code, so you'll want to take a long look at your wardrobe."

"Yeah," said Ron. "And then burn it,"

Dave was a good guy and one of my best friends. A gifted mechanic and half-owner of a luxury-imports garage over in Walnut Creek, he'd discovered golf a couple years ago and now spent less time at the garage and more time on the course. This, had caused some strain between Dave and Herb, his partner, but Dave explained he needed golf to counter the stress of dealing with the whiny and demanding import-car owners who made up the bulk of their clientele. The dispute threatened to destroy the partnership, but then a funny thing happened. The way Dave explained it, his absences had created a back-up in scheduling, and word got around that appointments at Third Street Auto were tough to get. Human nature kicked in and, soon, luxury import owners from all around the area were honking their way onto the lot. Herb and Dave had to hire a college kid just to answer the phone and make appointments. Herb raised prices and started smiling again. "Maybe you should practice more," he told his partner. Dave's game did improve. But not much. He was a twenty-handicapper and likely to stay one—unless something impossible happened. But that wouldn't be for a while yet.

"Transportation," Mike said, prompting Ron to continue.

"Provided by Mr. Ed Nenniman. To and from the desert"

"What kind of wheels?" said Dave.

"Wings," said Ron. "The Cessna we financed. Uncomfortably seats six. He'll have us in the Springs in just over an hour."

Dave was impressed. "Not bad. How do we get back?"

"Walk," Ron said and hit a sharp pull hook into the parking lot fence.

"Nenniman will fly us out Friday night," Mike said, "and come back for us after dinner Sunday night. Everybody in?"

"Sounds good," said Dave.

"Charley?"

"Better count me out," I said. "Cathy's made plans for a family weekend. We're taking the kids up to Santa Rosa. See the grandparents."

Mike opened his eyes. "Hey, this is shaping up to be a big weekend. Gilmore's got us lined up with games. You can't afford not to go. Tell her your winnings'll pay for the kids' college."

"Well, I'll ask her," I said. "But I can tell you right now what she's gonna say."

Mike made a face.

"Oh, good idea," said Ron. "Why don't you ask? That's real bright."

Dave bailed out of an ill-conceived backswing. "Hey, Charley," he said. "You don't wanna be asking. You've got to just be going. Like there's no question."

"Wait a minute," said Ron. "Check it out. Floyd's got engine trouble."

Out near the one-seventy-five sign, marooned in his little rolling cage, a red-faced Floyd struggled to turn over the engine.

"We may have something here."

Trying not to draw attention to himself, Floyd eased out of the cage, pulled a seat cushion from the cab and held it in front of him as he crept around and lifted the hood up over the engine.

Mike jumped up, sending papers flying. "Gimme a club."

Ron, in his stall, performed a hurried preshot routine, settled into his stance, wound up, and struck a high, spinning shot toward the truck. It landed a good ten yards beyond Floyd and kicked sideways.

"Too much club," he muttered, and reached for another ball.

Mike was waggling in the next stall.

"What club was that?"

"Five."

"I'll punch a six."

Mike played a little knockdown fade—his bread-and-butter shot. It started left, then leaked back to the right, bouncing off the tire well with a sharp bang.

Floyd looked up from under the hood. "Hey!" he shouted. "Hold off. I got engine trouble!"

Big mistake. Up and down the range, golfers looked up now and saw a sight they dared not hope for—Floyd the Bully, Floyd the Tormentor, Floyd the Merciless Heckler, exposed and unprotected.

Within seconds, it was open season on Floyd. Balls rained on him from every angle. Line drives, lobs, knee-cappers, and worm-burners caromed off his tractor or smacked into his clutched seat cushion with a resounding thud.

"Hey." Floyd's shrieks of protest had risen a full octave. "Hold off. Cease fire, goddamit."

After a well-struck five wood, apparently hit by Mrs. Yee, landed between his legs (her lessons with Shortgrass appeared to be paying off), Floyd took off on a dead run to his left, dove headlong behind the hundred-and-fifty-yard sign, and tried to scratch himself into the turf. This was another imprudent move, since the sign's cutout numbers provided minimal shelter. It was also closer to the firing line, placing him now within the range of just about every club-wielding man, woman, and child—a mistake brought home to Floyd when a loping grounder hit by a vengeful retiree struck him midthigh.

"All right," he roared, scrambling to his feet. "Who did that?" Then took off again, cutting a zigzag pattern toward the eighty-yard barrel.

"Why doesn't he get back in his cage?" Dave laughed, reaching for his sand wedge.

"He knows we won't let him out," said Mike. "He'll have to stay in there all night."

The barrel was an oil drum painted red, white, and blue and tilted at a forty-five-degree angle with its open end facing the firing line. Floyd crouched behind it now with his head resting on the outside of the drum. The range rats grasped his predicament and sent a torrent of balls slamming into the metal drum, each collision striking a great bass note that reverberated across the range, one after another, seeming to escalate in volume like the grand finale of a fireworks display. Somewhere around the third salvo, Floyd lost it. Deafened by the sonic assault, he threw aside his seat cushion and rose, howling and spitting from behind the barrel.

"Uh-oh," said Ron.

"He's pissed," said Dave.

Shoulders drawn up to his ears, fists clenched, impervious now to the surlyn hailstorm, Floyd advanced toward the line of stalls like a stiff-legged Frankenstein monster. All firing ceased as the mad retreat began. Clubs got shoved into bags, frantic hands fished for car keys. Panicked range rats scrambled over one another, shoving and clawing their way to the parking lot where all the engines firing up at once sounded like the start of the Indy 500.

"Time to pack it in, boys," I said.

"I'm outta here," said Mike, fumbling for his paperwork. "Don't forget, Charley. This weekend. Make it happen." Then he was outta there.

Ron stumbled after him, visor askew, golf bag clutched to his chest. "Just tell her you're going." He shouted the words but didn't need to. I was right behind him.

Floyd chased us to the lot gate, then stood there, ranting. "I see you assholes. I'm gonna remember every one of you. Your asses are mine." Pointing at me, he said, "I see you too, Cotter. Don't think I don't."

I confess it gave me a cold chill to hear Floyd single me out for retribution. It was also a trifle unjust—none of my shots had come close to hitting him (my middle irons obviously needed work). Still, by tomorrow, I'd be the one he'd most remember taking pot shots at him. You see, I knew how his mind worked.

Even then.

That night, I had the dream again where I'm standing on the first tee at this legendary golf course. It's never clear which one. It might be Pine Valley or Riviera or Shinnecock Hills, but it's always some incredibly famous and challenging track. Also, very exclusive. But somehow—they must think I'm somebody else—they're going to let me play.

And like always, I've got my clubs and a case of nerves, but not too bad, and I'm ready to tee off but there's a bunch of people, could be tournament officials or gallery members, milling around on the tee box, and I look around for an open spot to tee up my ball.

Eventually, I find one but, by the time I push my tee into the ground and get ready to hit, somebody is standing next to me, blocking my swing. I don't want to say anything because I'm afraid I'll get noticed and they'll realize I'm not supposed to be there. So, I go looking for another spot. But then it happens again. I no sooner get the peg in the ground and get ready to swing, when there's somebody else standing there, blocking me.

It goes on like this, until eventually I wake up. I never get to hit the ball. I don't know what the dream means or if it's supposed to mean anything. I usually just forget about it until the next time. One thing though, I used to think it was different people blocking me, but I'd started to believe it's just the one guy. I'd never gotten a good look at his face and, maybe it's because I've had the dream so many times, but... he was starting to look familiar.

Possibilities Past

We had plans to drive up on Saturday to Santa Rosa for a visit with Cathy's parents. Grandpa Bob and Nana Shelly lived on a couple acres of ranch land, populated with miscellaneous pets and livestock, including a pair of "kid friendly" horses, a chestnut gelding named Southwind, and a sweet, undersized paint named Tammy. Sean and Sara loved going up there almost as much as the grandparents enjoyed having them. The plan was for Cathy and me to spend Saturday and Sunday and then drive back to Walnut Hill, leaving the kids up there for a week of riding horses, chasing chickens, and roving around in Grandpa's restored Chevy pickup. Maybe even an excursion over to Bodega Bay for some whale watching. It was more a vacation for the kids, but I knew Cathy was looking forward to going.

As the weekend approached, I found myself thinking more and more about the golf trip. Here was a once-in-a-lifetime chance to play three of the most historic and exclusive golf courses in the country—for free. Opportunities like this don't pop up every day. I knew there was close to zero chance Cathy would let me off the hook. Especially since, in her opinion, I already played way too much golf for a grown man with a young family and career responsibilities. I also knew that, just by floating the possibility of going, I could be facing weeks— even months—of recriminations and non-person status. My wife was on the whole an understanding and sympathetic partner—maybe to a fault. But, beneath the compassion, in there somewhere, lurked a red-headed temper you almost never saw, but never forgot was in there.

Everything depended on catching her at the right moment and then putting the golf weekend out there in the most positive light. Thunderbird… Mission Hills… Tamarisk—are you kidding? This was the opportunity of a lifetime and, hell, her parents weren't going anywhere. We could visit them any time. I'd also want to be sure there were no blunt instruments or throw-able objects within reach.

That evening, after I'd gotten the kids scrubbed, storied and tucked in, I came downstairs to find Cathy on the living room sofa flipping through a battered, black school binder that looked familiar.

"What's that?"

She held up a half-column scrap of yellowed newsprint. "Reading about your exploits," she said.

"God, where did you find that?"

"I forgot how skinny you were. What size were those pants?"

"Same as now."

She giggled. "Yeah, right."

"What? Let me see that."

She brushed my hand away. "Who're these guys you're with?"

The photo was a clip from the school paper, the year we'd lost in the NCAA semi-finals to a tough Oklahoma team. It was taken that first morning—why we were still smiling, the five of us: Sean, Dusty, Arthur, Rico, and me. I'd lost touch with them after graduation when I moved to the west coast. That was a dozen years ago.

"Wow," Cathy was saying now. "The semi-finals. You never told me."

"You knew I was on the golf team."

"Yeah. But I didn't know you were this good. This is big—almost national champs."

"Not even close. We got our butts kicked that week. At least two of the guys on the Oklahoma team turned pro right after that."

"What about you?"

"What about me?"

"Did you want to be a pro?"

"Maybe for about a minute, but you need more than talent. You've gotta devote your whole life to it. Guys out there on the tour are super-dedicated. They practice all the time."

"Oh, my God! More than you?"

"Yeah, all right."

"But you can be a pro and not compete, right?"

"Sure, I could've probably gotten a club job but then you need the patience for teaching or the tolerance-for-abuse to be a country club pro. Anyway, I was young. There was a lot going on in those days. Lot of possibilities. Didn't want to limit myself."

"Possibilities?"

"Yeah. There's more to life than just golf, you know." This is good, I thought. Cathy had brought up the subject of golf all by herself. Here was my opening. I took a deep breath—"Speaking of gol—"

"What did you see yourself doing back then?" she said. "In your heart of hearts."

"Like now, I guess—communications. It's what I majored in."

"Do you ever wonder what would have happened if you'd gone the other way?"

"Not really."

"Any regrets?"

"No."

"Really? Career…life?"

This was headed in the wrong direction. I picked up the TV remote. "What're you in the mood for? Sex or violence."

"Charley—"

"Sorry… forgot the question."

"*Possibilities.*"

"What about 'em?"

"Are they out there? Still out there."

I leaned toward the window. "I don't hear anything. Want me to go look?"

"*Charley…*" She was trying to be angry but couldn't help laughing. This was the Cathy I loved most—the one only I was privileged to see—at her most desirable: sans make-up, face flushed, auburn curls in a tangle, doing her best to frown—and failing. I was laughing, too, while at the same time marveling, once again, that such an exquisite, sweet-hearted, creature had demonstrated such bad judgment by marrying me.

"Okay…" I said, "is this about the job again or—?"

"Everything… "

"Everything, wow. We can't narrow that down just a—?"

"Are you happy with things the way they are, or do you wish they were different?"

"I wish they were different."

Her eyes narrowed. "Different how?"

"Not having this conversation."

"Oh, just forget it."

"All right…I'm sorry… what do you want to know? Am I happy with…what? My job? "

"With your life. Your whole life."

"Jesus, Cathy…"

"Are you?"

"Of course, yeah."

"Are you sure?"

"Yeah…' I flicked on the TV and started surfing for programs. "Why are we talking about this?"

She picked up the binder and went back to thumbing through the clippings, frowning now. "Sometimes, it doesn't seem like it."

"Hey, Barnett's been hounding me at work, that's all. If I've been bringing it home… sorry."

"You're not bringing it home. You're bringing it to the golf course. It's like when are you even here anymore? And even when you are, you're someplace else."

"I don't know where you're getting this. I'm here."

"I know how you are, Charley, and I love you. You're a good dad and a good guy but… I want all of us to be happy and that only works if you're happy too."

"Cathy, for God's sake… I'm happy, okay? Look— happy." I flashed a toothy grin that got ignored.

"You can't be—not if you're spending every day doing something that makes you miserable."

"Who said I was miserable? And, anyway, it's a little late in the game to be talking about changing careers."

"You're not even thirty-five. You could look around, see what's out there."

"Another agency job. What'll that change?"

"It doesn't have to be advertising. There's lots of stuff you could do."

"Start from scratch? C'mon, get serious."

"I've got my job at the hospital, and we don't have to live like this."

"Sure, move back to our old studio in the city. Kids can sleep in the tub."

"Why does it have to be one or the other?"

"Look, can we stop? I don't even know how we got started on this."

"Don't you?"

"Nobody said things were gonna be perfect, Cathy. This is life we're living here. It's not always gonna be like in a movie."

Cathy got up and started arranging pillows, giving each an extra whack. "Okay then," she said. "So, it's not about the job. What, then? What's the problem?"

"What problem? "

"Maybe it's us, then. Me and the kids? Or just me?"

"Jesus—what?"

"Oh, forget it." She started for the kitchen.

"Hey—"

I followed her out into the hall. "Cathy, what are we doing? I don't even know why we're arguing—hey—"

The kitchen door swung shut behind her. Standing there, I caught a glimpse of my reflection in the hall mirror. I turned and stood there for a long moment, looking at what I'd come to regard as my 'despite self.' Still young despite the dark circles under the eyes. Still athletic—sort of—despite the slight bulge under my tee shirt. Absently, I watched myself make a couple of practice swings and thought, damn, I'd have to lie to her.

Personal Golf

Sometimes on a Saturday in good weather when the range was jammed, you'd look down the row of stalls, see all the different swings—gyrations is a better word—and have to laugh. People can figure out all sorts of crazy ways to take a swipe at a golf ball, and Mallard's Driving Range offered a comprehensive sampling. Every kind of self-taught, store-bought, or hand-me-down swing. Every lurch, lunge, lash, or lunacy. Mallard's was the showroom, the laboratory, the chopper's proving ground.

Mallard's drew a cross section of people too. Male, female, young or old, businessmen, garbage men, high-handicappers and low, you could go right down the line of stalls and not find two golfers with anything in common other than the one thing that had brought them there—they were all searching for the Answer.

Oh, maybe on a summer night you'd get the young couple on a cheap date or after school see a bunch of kids taking turns with a metal driver, trying to hit Floyd's cart. But they're civilians, not golfers.

You're not officially a golfer until the day you hit that *one* shot—that sucker shot. When, suddenly, in the midst of chaos, there's harmony. Head, hands, hips, knees, feet, wrists, and clubface all—regardless of what convoluted or roundabout paths taken to get there—arrive back at the ball at precisely the same instant. The shot is miraculous. Instead of the quarry-tool-striking-acattle-skull sound you've come to associate with a golf shot, there's a simple click. Your hands experience an exhilarating, effortless feeling as the ball compresses against the clubface and springs into hyperspace. Rising gracefully against the sky, maybe even drawing a yard or two, correcting to dead center, the trajectory a brush stroke drawn across the sky. The ball lands soft as an August zephyr in a place you've never been.

And you're hooked.

No matter that you go and shank the next one into the snack bar. You've had the feeling. And, ever after, all you want to do is feel it again. You've sipped from golf's golden chalice, and now you want to guzzle the whole damn thing. From that moment on you're a golfer—a hacker actually, from Floyd's point of view—and, day after day, night after night, while the wife despairs and the kids forget you, you fill ranks with all the other hopeless cases, prisoner in a range stall, flailing away the hours.

Searching, searching.

The question is, how to swing like you've already swung. The Answer is what everybody's trying to find.

For those who required guidance in their quest, Mallard's driving range provided no shortage of false prophets. All you had to do was *look* like you were struggling, and a host of proffering pundits would descend on your stall, dispensing hoary swing tips and tired dogma about keeping your head down or your left arm straight.

Or, for forty dollars, you could spend an enlightening half hour with any one of a dubious assortment of 'teaching professionals' ranging in style and substance from messianic to simply unqualified.

Shortgrass, for instance, was a black man in his mid-forties, named for the fairways he frequented. His real name was Earl Jackson, but if you said that name around Mallard's, no one would know who you were talking about. Shortgrass's claim to fame was being able to hit the ball a long way. Between lessons, he'd delight the range rats by lashing drives over the back fence with his rubber-band swing. Hitting the ball out of sight was, for him, the most natural thing in the world. So, naturally, he had no idea how he did it and consequently couldn't teach it. Frustrated, Shortgrass resorted to shaking his head and stamping his feet. His students soon felt inadequate, got upset, and the lessons dissolved into hard feelings.

Hollerin' Hank, another Mallard's fixture, turned up the volume to get his message across. In his prime, Hank had been a long-driving champion. Now, well into his seventies, he taught—yelled, actually—at Mallard's. Hank was a folk hero to those who worship the long ball but, like Shortgrass, he had few answers to share with his students, and now that he was old, could scarcely demonstrate anymore what he was shouting about. His lessons consisted of a half hour of high-decibel verbal abuse, for which he charged forty-five dollars. When the occasional courageous student complained about his charging five bucks more than the other pros, Hank would ceremoniously produce a yellow, tattered press clipping from a long-defunct newspaper that generously described him as a "local legend."

"I am," he'd bellow, "the only true bargain you'll ever find in your entire miserable life." Despite these assurances, Hank enjoyed little repeat business.

Fred Montalcino or "Handsome Freddy" as he was known on the range, was a semi-handsome guy with bleached hair in his late forties who specialized in female students. Fred believed in hands-on teaching, wrapping himself around the ladies until you couldn't tell where he left off and they began. His lessons looked like molestations committed in broad daylight.

Floyd had a particularly low opinion of golf instruction, especially as practiced by the pros at Mallard's, so I was surprised to hear he was seeing a coach. One afternoon at the range, I'd found myself in the next stall watching as he dreamily smashed six irons into the distance. After one of his shots bounced off the seven in the one seventy-five sign, I asked him if it was true.

"What do you care?"

"Just curious. Somebody's got you swinging pretty good. Do I know him?"

Digging for another ball in his tray, he said, "Ever hear of Dr. Warren Sleeves?"

"Who?"

Floyd shook his head and sighed. "It figures you wouldn't know the name, Cotter, 'cause you don't know squat about golf." Floyd loomed over another ball, chin raised, forearms held tightly together, almost touching, the silent assassin waiting to spring. "Check the fade," he muttered, and launched it toward the one-seventy-five, except this shot flew higher and waited almost until the top of its arc before drifting quietly to the right and floating to earth five yards behind the sign.

"Golf shot," I said, and meant it. When Floyd was on his game there were few around Mallard's who could play with him. His swing was strong and aggressive. Borderline frightening.

"Dr. Warren Sleeves is our greatest living golf scientist," he said.

Golf scientist?

Questions tended to provoke Floyd, and I knew better than to ask: "What's a golf scientist?" But I did.

"What it sounds like. What am I, a moron?"

"You mean like somebody who studies the physics of golf? Measures club-head speed and stuff?"

"That's horse shit," Floyd said, scowling. "I'm talking about somebody who knows about golf. Not just how. But why."

"Why golf?"

"Yehggh."

This utterance came at the very instant he struck another six iron. The ball started off to the right, but then he glared at it, and it corrected back to the one seventy-five marker.

"Dr. Sleeves," he declared, "is the greatest golf teacher who ever lived."

"What about Ben Hogan?"

"Who'd he teach?"

"I want to say everyone. The entire modern golf swing is patterned after Hogan's swing."

Floyd threw his head back and cackled. "That's what you think, isn't it, Cotter? After the Hogan swing, right? That's what he taught, wasn't it? The Hogan swing. I hate to tell you this, but you're a real moron."

I, of course, having initiated this conversation, already knew that.

Floyd chuckled as he dropped the five into his bag and selected a short iron. "Think, Cotter," he said. "Why would they call it the Hogan swing?"

"Ah… because it was Hogan's swing?"

Floyd exhaled through clenched teeth. He liked explaining things even less than answering questions. "Look," he seethed, "the Hogan swing is great if you're Hogan, but it don't do jack shit for anybody else."

"Why not?"

"Because they're not Hogan."

"Okay, forget Hogan. What about Bobby Jones? Or David Leadbetter or Butch Harmon or any or those other guys? What about Jack Nicklaus? Ever read Golf My Way?"

Floyd duck-hooked one into the parking lot fence. He put a chill-stare on the spot where it landed as if to say, "I'll remember you next time, ball," but said instead, "Do I look like Jack Nicklaus to you?"

"No," I was forced to admit. If Floyd resembled anyone famous it would be Nick Nolte—in the DUI mugshot.

"Do I swing like Jack Nicklaus?"

No, again. Floyd was an original, and that extended to his golf swing. If you had to compare that to something, you'd have to go all the back way to maybe the Cyclops in the Seventh Voyage of Sinbad.

"No," said Floyd. "And neither can anyone else. Only Jack Nicklaus can swing like Jack Nicklaus. Why? Because Nicklaus is a different *person* than anyone else.

Nobody else has the same brain and spleen and appendages and shit. How they gonna swing like him? What's the name of that book?"

"Golf My Way?"

Floyd sneered. "Golf His Way! That's what they should have called it. Golf *His* Way. He's the one should be readin' it."

"So, what does this doctor say?"

"Why should I tell you?"

I was stuck for a reason, but then he said, "Dr. Sleeves is the world's foremost authority on Personal Golf."

"Personal Golf?"

"Cotter, do you have to repeat *everything* I say?"

"Sorry. I'm just not familiar with the term."

"Personal Golf," Floyd said, "is where you tailor-make the swing to the guy who already has it."

Floyd went back to harming golf balls, leaving me to reflect on the profundity of that concept.

"Why does he need it?" I asked finally.

"Who?"

"The guy. Why would he need a swing he already has?"

Floyd performed an exaggerated sigh and bit into the rubber grip on his iron. "Because he doesn't know he has it, all right? Or maybe he does know, but he doesn't know where it is."

"Why wouldn't he know?"

"How do I know? Maybe he's a moron. Maybe he doesn't want to know."

"Why wouldn't he want to know?"

Floyd rolled his eyes. "You really oughta listen to yourself sometimes," he said, "because you sound like a real idiot. The reason these dipshits don't want to find their swing is because they're afraid. That's why they're out there trying to copy somebody else's swing. Because they're too chicken-shit to swing the one they already got."

So that was it. You'd expect Floyd to be the last one to embrace this kind of new-age psychobabble, but here was this doctor telling him exactly what he wanted to hear, that the swing he already had was the ideal one. Don't change a thing, baby. You're perfect just the way you are. For a guy like Floyd, with an extremely high opinion of himself, this was the Answer.

"He's also a dentist," said Floyd.

"Who's a dentist?"

"Who we talkin' about? Dr. Sleeves."

"This is your *dentist* giving you golf tips?"

Floyd's expression darkened. "So, what're you sayin', Cotter? You sayin' you got a problem with Dr. Sleeves being a dentist?"

Uh-oh. "Not at all. Why would I have a problem with anybody being a dentist? I mean, we all got teeth, right?"

"I don't know. Just sounded for a minute like you think Dr. Sleeves couldn't possibly be a brilliant golf scientist and also an outstanding dentist."

"Not at all. I'm just… in awe of somebody who can… multi-task like that."

"I guess then, you never heard of Dr. Cary Middlecoff either."

"Middlecoff, he was back in the fifties. I think he won the Open."

"That's right, he did. Twice. Doctor Cary Middlecoff. Won the Masters too. And you know what? *He* was a dentist."

"I think I knew that. What else does Dr. Sleeves say?"

"Make an appointment and ask him yourself," said Floyd. "Maybe you haven't noticed, but I'm trying to hit balls here."

Good Solid Advertising

"Crumb cake on the golf course?"

John Barnett's crimson face clashed with his burgundy necktie—an unfortunate lapse in an ad man. Across from his desk, seated in what we'd come to refer to as the "accountability chairs," Susan, my art director partner, and I faced the music.

Susan dabbed at her drippy nose with a tightly clenched wad of tissue. The same respiratory ailment she'd been battling for weeks had once again regrouped and counter attacked. She maintained it was a head cold. I saw it as an allergic reaction to Barnett. And lately, there'd been plenty to sneeze about.

Barnett's ham hands shuffled clumsily through our storyboards. "We presented this?" he asked in mock wonderment.

"They said they wanted to get the product out of the kitchen." I said, resorting under stress to the account-speak I privately ridiculed.

"I'm aware of that. I'm aware the client wanted to get the product out of the kitchen. That part is very clear. What I'm unclear on is how we went from the kitchen to this clown's golf bag with no stops in between. Does that seem like a logical progression to you? Because it mystifies the hell out of me."

The 'clown' was the drawn character on the storyboard we'd inadvertently shown the week before to the Mrs. Beeble's clients, Bill Harder and Mariel Bonebroth. Barnett, president and CEO of The Barnett Agency had been out of town, leaving Susan and I to "honcho the sit" (more ad-speak) along with Richie, an empty suit from the account staff.

"We thought it'd be a cute twist," I said. "They seemed to like it."

Barnett looked up at me. "That's not what I heard."

"Who've you talked to, Richie?"

Barnett nodded. "Richie says that Bill and Muriel were disappointed with your presentation."

"What presentation? It was a 'work-in-progress.' Richie had no business bringing them in. If we'd known we were going to be nailed to the wall, we wouldn't have shown them anything."

"And, John," said Susan. "That wasn't the only idea we came up with."

"Richie said it was."

I threw up my hands. "How would he know? He was playing with his phone the whole time."

"Charley," said Barnett, "I would think that by now I wouldn't have to explain to you how important it is we present choices to a client."

"John—"

But Barnett was just getting started. He leaned back in his chair and ran his fingers through his well-barbered white hair.

"Mrs. Beeble's products are traditionally—and correctly—shown in the kitchen. Coming out of the oven, cooling on the counter, being served. You want to get the product out of the kitchen? Put it in the dining room. Change of pace? Try the family room. You want to get crazy? Take it on a picnic."

"John, the plan was to position Mrs. Beeble's as a snack food as well as a dessert. We accepted that mission and what we're trying to get across is that people don't eat snacks in the same room where they eat their meals. They take them to work or on a hike or when they're out doing something active—boating or camping or something."

"Why don't we have any of that? Boating, camping?"

"Golf is an *activity*. It could just as well have been a hiking trail or—"

"Yeah, but why'd we have to have a golf course?" Barnett looked at Susan. "I take it this was not your idea."

Susan threw me, an I-told-you-so look.

"Let's get you on the record here. Do you consider this good advertising?"

"Well," she said. "It's fresh… a… departure."

"It certainly is."

Susan's fingers fidgeted as she jerked a fresh tissue out of her handy-pak. "And…golf is… an activity."

"John," I said, coming to the rescue. "It wasn't Susan's idea."

Barnett slumped back in his chair as if the air had been let out of him all at once.

"Charley," he said. "You've been playing a lot of golf, lately, haven't you."?

"I don't know whether you'd call it a lot."

"Well, we seem to have a lot of golf creeping into our ads around here and I'd just like to know if there's some connection."

"C'mon, John, that's ridiculous."

"Is it? How about this one?"

He shuffled through some papers and picked up a one-sheet. Susan squirmed in her chair.

"This one for the Hamlet Restaurant. Copy by Charley Cotter. 'Only a five iron from Meadowbank Country Club.'" He stopped and looked up, smiling mirthlessly. "How far is that?"

"John, Meadowbank is a local landmark. Everyone knows

where it is. It's like saying "across the street from City Hall or something. It just happens to be a golf club."

"You say the Hamlet is next door to the country club?"

"Yeah—pretty much."

"Then why don't you say, 'next door to the country club'?"

"John, it's a famous golf club. Don't you think it's more creative to say a five iron away?"

"Yes," piped in Susan. "It's more golfy."

"Golfy?" Barnett looked to be having trouble containing himself. "How far is that, Charley? A five-iron away?"

I felt myself flush. "Somewhere between a hundred-fifty and two hundred yards, depending on the wind."

Barnett nodded, smiling ruefully. "Depends on the wind, eh? This may come as a shock to you, Charley, but there are a lot of people out there who don't play golf. They don't know a five iron from a curling iron. And wouldn't it be swell if they could find our client's restaurant without having to hire a caddie?"

"John, in fairness to Charley…" Susan said.

But Barnett wasn't having any. "And whatever he's got seems to be catching. I notice where my senior art director staged her fashion layout for Kelb's department store on a putting green. That was pretty golfy."

Susan went pale.

"C'mon, John," I said. "We were trying to save money. Make the location work for both presentations."

"It was actually lovely out there," Susan added.

Barnett put his hand down flat on the desk in front of him. "Yes, well, hear this. We're having lunch with Bill and Mariel tomorrow. That should give you time to come up with some fresh ideas for Mrs. Beeble's. We're going to want plenty of options. Lots of choices. I would think a minimum of—why don't we show off? Say half a dozen TV spot outlines and ten or twelve print ad ideas.

And let's keep it non-golfy. What do you say? Sound like a plan?"

Susan and I got up to leave. "By the way," Barnett said. "I want to hear what you've got before we leave for lunch. And if it's even remotely golfy, you can be sure neither of you will ever play the five iron again."

Back in the office we shared, Susan collapsed on the sofa. I picked up a wedge and began chipping balls into a stuffed chair.

"Could you not do that just now?" said Susan. "My stomach is in a knot."

"It's not a big deal. We just think of some ads that don't have golf in them." I feathered a nice one into the center of the chair cushion.

"I can't relax when any second I think I'm going to get hit."

"You know what we could do...?" I said.

"I know what *you* can do."

"We make it a where thing. Like—where are all the different places you can eat Mrs. Beeble's crumb cake?"

"The crumb cake goes places?"

"Not the cake—the *person*. Mrs. Beeble goes places."

"She's got the cake with her?"

"Yeah. Of course. She's always got the cake with her. She's Mrs. Beeble."

I picked up the phone and hit the speed dial button for Bank of Walnut Hill. When Ron came on the line, I told him I'd have to beg off the game we'd penciled in for that afternoon at Stickley. When I hung up, Susan was ready with a pad and pencil. "Okay, so where does she go?"

"Wherever discriminating people demand crumb cake."

"Not a golf course."

"She doesn't play."

"A picnic."

"That'll work."

Brain Surgery

Strangely enough, the next time I ran into Floyd after the range 'turned on him'—his description—he was almost cordial. It was at Mallard's, right at sundown, maybe my favorite time of the day, when the range lights first come on and there's still daylight in the downrange sky. I was working on my short irons and some plausible stories for Cathy when he puttered up in his cage. "How ya hittin' 'em?" he said.

"No cause for concern. How about you?"

"Pretty outstanding. Kicking ass with the driver. Got it going about three, three-ten. Irons are solid through the bag. Got my short game pretty much where I want it. Figure I'm all set."

"All set?"

"Yep." He leaned over the steering wheel, chin resting on his arms. "Ready to take it to the next level."

"Yeah?" I said, trying to sound interested. I knew what Floyd was ready for. Get two family members to sign the papers.

"You know," he said, adopting a confidential tone, "I was one-under at Meadowbank last week."

"Meadowbank?" My interest level spiked. Meadowbank was a championship layout of heroic proportions, a perennial fixture on the short list of prospective hosts for major tournaments, including the US Open. But the members had consistently rejected these overtures. Too much trouble, they said. And too stressful for the golf course with all the barbarian galleries tromping around. And where would they all park? Nope, all the spectacle and hub bub would be just too 'goldarn' inconvenient.

Now, here was Floyd, looking like the medalist at a toad stomping contest, claiming to have not only trod the hallowed and forbidden fairways but to have broken par in the bargain. Normally, I'd have said "bullshit," and gone back to hitting balls, but saw no need to court violent death twice in one week.

"That so?" was all I could muster.

"Yep. It's a great track. Suits my game perfectly. They've got this one short par three next to a waterfall that just sort of falls away from you."

"Number twelve."

"You played it?"

I shook my head. "Read about it."

My few glimpses of Meadowbank had been snatched from the pages of golf magazines. The majestic layout showed up on just about everybody's list of the world's great golf courses. And any discussion of great individual golf holes had to include the twelfth, which one article described as "a delicious tumble toward a bitter conclusion," or the fifteenth, a narrow dogleg par five, which another article called "the most timorous walk in the woods since Hansel and Gretel."

I'd dreamed of playing Meadowbank for as long as I'd known the name. Hearing Floyd talk about it left me with me a pining hollowness, as if he was graphically describing a tryst with someone I secretly cherished but didn't stand a chance with.

"Thought Meadowbank was a private club."

"That's right," he said, with a smirk that radiated through the bars of his cage. "You gotta be a member or a guest."

"Whose guest were you?"

"Wouldn't you like to know."

I took a big swing with my eight iron and hit a towering pitch toward the one-fifty sign.

"Hey, Cotter," Floyd said. "Maybe one of your rich pals'd be interested in sponsoring me on the tour? It's pretty much a no-brainer they'd make a shit pile of money off their investment."

"Can't think of anybody off the top of my head, but if I do, I'll let you know."

"All I'd need are some entry fees and gas money. Don't need to stay in hotels. Probably just camp out in the parking lot until the checks start rolling in."

"Have you tried Mike and Ron?"

Floyd snorted. "Those bankers? Bankers are the last people in the world gonna loan you any money."

"Thought that's what they did."

"Oh, yeah, sure they'll loan it to you if you've got it already. Or if you're from a foreign country and wanna put up a mini mall, no problem. But if it's for anything anybody wants—somethin' real—you're shit outta luck."

"I didn't realize that."

"Wake up, Cotter. Why do you think they got all these foreigners investing in mini malls? Do you know anybody in their right mind'd wanna work in one of those? Stay open all night in case some moron wants to buy a pack of gum at three in the morning? No matter how many signs they put up saying they don't have any money, they get robbed all the time. And the really sad part is these foreigners don't know any better. They get off the boat, and there they are, the bankers, waiting for them with their line of horse shit about how everybody in America shops in mini-malls, and how they can get rich by working twenty-four-seven, selling toilet paper one roll at a time."

"You're saying there's people working in mini-malls against their will?"

"Okay, think about it. Have you ever seen a mini-mall in a foreign country?"

I had to confess I hadn't, but that was partly because I'd never been to a foreign country, outside of one sodden spring break weekend in Baja. And if there were any mini-malls, I wouldn't have been in any condition to spot them.

"If they wanted to work in one, don't you think they'd have them in their own country?"

I was reasonably certain that, aside from his annual biker pilgrimage to Sturgis, South Dakota, Floyd had never ventured much beyond the Bay Area. But his logic, however lunatic, was inescapable.

"Let me tell you something about bankers and mini-malls, Cotter—"

That's when a ball ricocheted off Floyd's cage with a bang. Floyd glowered at a cluster of teens over near the snack bar.

"Gee!" he shouted down the line. "I hope nobody's aiming at me on purpose. Otherwise I'll have to come over there and kick some ass!"

By the time he returned his attention to me he'd lost his train of thought, and I wasn't about to help him find it. I'd heard all this before and knew Floyd was quite capable of tracing his banker/mini mall/foreigner conspiracy theory all the way back to the Kennedy assassination.

Now, after thirty seconds or so of glaring off in various directions, he gave up and struck up another favorite refrain. "You still seeing that nurse?"

"You mean my wife? Yeah, I'm still seeing her."

"I love nurses. They're so hot in those white dresses, you can practically see through them. Does she wear those?"

"Not too much. She usually wears the kind with the pants. Scrubs."

"Are they white?"

"Blue and green. Purple sometimes."

"That's too bad." Floyd seemed genuinely disappointed. Then he brightened. "Hey, Cotter, maybe your nurse could fix me up with one of her nurse friends, and we could all go out sometime."

"I wouldn't get your hopes up," I said. "They're pretty

finicky about who they go out with. Snooty like that."

Floyd was crestfallen. "Who do they go out with?"

"You know, rich guys…doctors."

"Oh, yeah? Well if you're so rich, what are you doin' hitting balls here? Why don't you join a country club?"

"Who said I was rich?"

Floyd looked puzzled. "Well, then… wait a minute. You're not trying to tell me you're a doctor?"

I didn't say anything, just lobbed a little pitch toward the barrel.

"No way, Cotter! That's bullshit! If you're a doctor, I'm a—whatever."

"Okay, fine. I'm not a doctor." I shrugged and hit another pitch while he mulled this over.

"Then how come I never hear anybody calling you doctor?" he said at last.

"Hey," I shushed him, glancing around. "I like to keep it quiet."

"What for?"

"People find out you're a doctor, they start right in telling you everything that's wrong with them. Next thing, they're asking for consultations and free samples in the middle of your backswing. I'd appreciate you keeping this just between us."

Floyd was looking at me with new interest. "No problem."

"I appreciate it." I pulled a longer iron out of my bag. Out of the corner of my eye I could see Floyd stewing over this and practically hear his brain working.

Finally, he said, "What kind?"

"Surgeon."

"Heart?"

"Brain," I said, expecting him to laugh. But he nodded, frowning. "Uh huh," he said. "Lemme ask you something."

"Shoot."

"How come you see doctors playing golf all the time?"

"Simple," I said. "Don't suppose you've ever held a human brain in your hands?"

Floyd gave it some thought and then slowly shook his head.

"Believe me," I told him. "It's not something you wanna do every day."

"No shit. I heard that."

Unlike most of my encounters with Floyd, this conversation was having a positive effect on my swing. My four irons were flying high and straight toward the right-hand corner of the range.

"What club is that?"

"Four."

He watched another shot and, for a minute I thought he was about to pay me a rare compliment. But then he said: "I guess Kelly and those other guys you play with know what you do?"

I put a finger to my lips and shook my head.

"What do they think?"

"Told them I was in advertising."

"No shit?" He leaned back, eyes wide, and began to laugh. Rocking back and forth in his cage, he looked like some kind of maniacal fun-house clown who, if he got out, might just decide to stop laughing and eat you.

Then, abruptly, he stopped laughing and affected a kind of cartoon shrewdness. "Sure, Cotter," he said. "No problem. I'll be happy to keep your little secret for you. But I'm going to need a little something in return."

"What's that, Floyd?"

"You fix me up with a couple nurses, and I won't say a word about you know what."

"Yeah, but I told you, they only go out with—"

"Hey, no problem. We tell 'em *I'm* a doctor."

"Who's going to believe that?"

"Fuck you, Cotter. My ass looks more like a doctor than you do."

Mallard walked out of the range office next to the snack bar, saw Floyd loafing in his cart, and yelled "Balls!"

Nearby, at a snack table under an umbrella, old Mrs. Gimble choked on her tuna melt.

"Uh-oh," said Floyd. "Gotta get to it." He started up the engine and ground the cart into gear. "Figure out what kind of doctor I should be," he said. "Make it have something to do with tits."

Ad Lunch

"Phone call for you, sir."

I glanced around the table. All eyes were on me—John Barnett, Susan Schager, my art director partner, Mariel Bonebroth, Bill Harder the Mrs. Beeble's clients, and the sea bass on Harder's plate.

"Are you sure it's for me?" I said.

"They asked for Mr. Cotter."

We'd cabbed it down to this seafood grill in the city where we'd been pitching our new, non-golfy, ad ideas for Mrs. Beeble's Crumbcake.

"Could you take a message?"

The waiter looked at me blankly. Waiters don't ordinarily take messages, especially in financial-district grillrooms at lunch hour. It's an accomplishment if they can manage to find someone in the din of a San Francisco lunch crowd.

"Don't you have a cell phone?" Barnett asked me.

"It's turned off."

"Take a message," Barnett told the waiter, anxious to get back to the business at hand: variations on a crumbcake theme, solos by Charley Cotter to the minor accompaniment of Susan's supportive oohs and ahhs, Mariel's nervous tics, and Barnett's relentless chewing.

The fresh-faced, twenty-something waiter was still green enough to not be entirely sure whether or not waiters took messages. He hesitated, then frowned.

Barnett repeated, "Take a message," along with a look that means "scram" in any language. "And bring some more

Chardonnay. The same."

"I wonder who knows I'm here," I mused, then saw Barnett glaring at me.

"They'll take a message," he said, and nodded toward the clients. We were in a condition yellow. Fred had stopped chewing, and Mariel had escalated to twitches.

Plunging on. "Our fourth approach begins with Dad. It's a Saturday morning. The kids run through the kitchen heading for the backyard. Mom has just finished the breakfast dishes and is already thinking about lunch. And Dad is, well, he's finished his Dad chores. You know, little repairs and things around the house, and now he's getting ready to go out and play a little—"

"Picnic." Barnett nearly shouted. Mariel jumped in her chair, emitting a sharp yelp. Harder looked up from the dinner roll he was troweling with butter. "He's going to play picnic?"

"Well, actually," I said, "I was going to say 'catch.' Dad's going to play *catch* out with the kids in the yard."

Barnett feigned astonishment. "That's even better than picnic."

The waiter was back. "It's your bank," he said.

"What is?" I wondered.

"The phone call is from your bank. They said it was important."

"Why are they calling you here?" said Barnett.

"I have no idea."

Susan was gaping at the waiter as if trying to remember who he was. Barnett nudged her arm. "Why don't you take the call?" he said. "See what they want."

"You want me to talk to his bank?"

"A word of advice, Charley," Harder said, spewing crumbs. "Always take calls from your banker. Am I right, John?"

"Oh, most definitely." Barnett shared a business laugh with Harder. "Better hop on that one, Charley," he said.

"Sorry," I said, getting up.

Barnett's grim nod told me to make it quick. The phone was an old push-button job at the end of the bar. All the lines were blinking.

"Line two," the hostess said, not at all happy to have her reservation lines tied up.

"Charley," Ron's voice. "Can you get away?"

"Jesus, Ron, you pulled me out of a meeting."

"Mike's got us a match set up for later."

"I can't. I'm in the middle of a client presentation."

"That's okay. We got time."

"I'm going to be tied up till at least six."

"That'll work."

"What are you talking about?"

I could see Barnett in his chair on the other side of the room, craning to watch me.

"Not today, Ron. Maybe tomorrow."

Back at the table, Susan was regaling the clients with the story of how her credit cards had disappeared at the Rome airport on her one and only trip to Europe. Susan was an artist in Barnett's eyes and not expected to contribute to mundane business discussions, yet he dragged her to client meetings because, in addition to being smart and attractive, she personified the image he wanted for his agency—all the things he wasn't: creative, stylish and young. She also functioned as appreciative audience at large and general bellwether, ready at the raise of an eyebrow to jump in with a conversation-bolstering anecdote from what Barnett considered her hilarious personal life. "Susan, tell Bill and Mariel about the time your parakeet was dead, and nobody knew it," he'd say when the business had been concluded. And, like a child hustled down in pajamas to sing "Noel" for company, Susan would dutifully launch into her story while Barnett leaned back and inventoried the room.

"And all I can say is thank God my passport wasn't in the—"

"Oh, good, here's Charley," interrupted Barnett. Susan, accustomed to—if not grateful for—having these turns cut short, retreated to her iced tea.

I sat down. "Everything's fine. Just a computer glitch. Now, we were on, I believe…"

"Approach number four," Susan prompted.

"Right. Dad's playing—"

"Catch," Barnett said with conviction.

"In the back yard with the kids," I agreed. "And then, right after one of the kids makes a terrific catch, the other one comes up to Dad and says…"

The rest of the lunch was pretty much uneventful. Me presenting the mind-numbing litany of commercial concepts Susan and I had conjured up in a creative frenzy since yesterday; Susan reacting in stock displays of appreciation and amazement as if hearing them for the first time; Barnett eyeing the proceedings with the vigilance of a pit boss; Mariel, antsy, glancing at her watch; and Bill Harder, in an impressive display of professionalism, consuming anything and everything placed before him.

When the check came, Barnett signed the credit voucher with a flourish, then went trolling for compliments. "Well, I'd say we're back on track with Mrs. Beeble's, wouldn't you say?"

"Yes," Susan said.

Barnett ignored her, eyeing Harder and Mariel. Mariel offered a pained smile, nodded, and huffed on her glasses. Harder was preoccupied with wiping food stains from his polka-dotted tie, uncertain which was which.

"How about it, Bill?" Barnett tried again. "Wouldn't you say we're headed in the right direction with these approaches?"

"Oh, yes," Harder agreed, dipping his napkin in a water glass. "I think Charley and Susan have done a fine job of heading us back in the direction we want to be headed."

Barnett beamed as if we'd won the Nobel Prize for Crumb Cake. "Wonderful," he said.

Susan clapped and squeaked. Mariel mumbled something and bolted for the restroom.

Minutes later, outside the restaurant, we made our good-byes, then stood around, irrelevantly grinning, while a pair of valets stuffed Harder into a cab. They pulled away leaving us on the curb, waving like Munchkins.

"Well," Barnett said, "there they go. Off to give Harris and Saperstein the account."

"Oh, John, don't say that," Susan said. "I thought we were a hit."

"What table were you sitting at?"

I felt bad for Barnett. He'd come up doing business over a rare steak and a dry martini. In John's era, the deal was the thing. The details—the actual advertising—were worked out afterward by (unfortunately) indispensable creatives like Susan and me. But times had changed. Barnett's contemporaries had mostly retired and were either "clogging up golf courses"—to use Floyd's terminology— or swinging in a hammock on a porch somewhere. The days when Barnett could get loaded with a CEO and come home with the business had long passed. Companies had in-house advertising departments now, staffed by midlevel, non-decision-makers, like Harder and Mariel, whose main function was to pass along the information and wait for a consensus from higher up. Decisions were made, if at all, by committee. John Barnett, self-made ad man of the old school, was no match for a committee. He was a one-on-one guy. And there were damn few around anymore to take him on.

"I'm afraid I let you down, John," I said.

"No, you didn't, Charley. Your concepts were fine. Good work, both of you." He sighed, then looked off after the clients. "Those two wouldn't know an ad campaign from a meatball."

"Bill Harder would," Susan said.

Barnett managed a chuckle. "That's right," he said. "He definitely would."

A car horn sounded behind us, where a large, white stretch limo sat parked at the curb. The rear window slid down, and a familiar prematurely gray head emerged.

"Charley," Mike called, waving me over.

"Who's that?" Barnett wanted to know.

"My banker," I said. "I'll just go see what he wants."

I trotted over to the limo, feeling Barnett's gaze on my back. Mike was grinning like a man who'd just inherited a brewery which, coincidently, was what the inside of the limo smelled like. Next to him, Ron was reading spreadsheet figures into a cell phone.

"Hop in," Mike said. "We gotta talk."

I crouched down next to the window. "Mike, you see that guy over there? That's my boss. And right now, he's in a mood to fire somebody."

"I'm going to say two words to you, and after hearing the two words, you tell me you don't want to listen."

"Mike, really, I gotta—"

"Meadow… bank."

"That's only one word." Dave's voice, coming from the front seat.

"What about Meadowbank?"

"Thought you might want to play there."

I stared at him in open mouth surprise. "You got us on Meadowbank?"

He nodded.

"When?"

"Now."

"Now?"

I looked back and saw Barnett and Susan climbing into a cab. The front door stood open, waiting for me.

"Tell 'em an emergency came up at the bank," said Mike.

"Yeah," said Ron. "We found money in your account."

"But, really, I—"

"*Meadowbank*, Charley," said Ron.

I took a deep breath, walked over to the cab, and leaned in the open door.

"Listen, John, there's a problem at my bank. This could take a while."

"They sent a limo for you?"

"Yeah, I guess they did."

"What bank is that?"

"Bank of Walnut Hill."

"You have a lot of money tied up with them?"

"Just a checking account."

"I'm a stockholder in my bank. They don't validate my parking."

Behind him, Susan was miming something that looked like, "This better not be about golf, or I'm going to cut your heart out with your own two iron."

"Go ahead," said Barnett. "Do what you have to do." He sighed, then nodded to the driver. The taxi pulled away and blended into the afternoon traffic.

Back in the limo, a mini-tailgate party was in progress. I climbed into the jump seat, opposite Mike. Ron, cell phone still pressed to his ear, tossed a beer into my lap.

"What's this?" I asked, meaning the limo.

"Bad ride, eh?" Mike leaned back, stroking the leather upholstery. "Lenny's Livery Service had a little problem making its auto-loan payments, so we were forced to repo this bad boy."

"Don't you have to sell it to get the bank's money back?"

"End of the month. Meanwhile, we're enjoying the fruits of our labors."

I'd seen Lenny a couple times over at Mallard's. He was a lesser luminary in the constellation of would-be entrepreneurs and assorted dunderheads that made up the bulk of Mike's client base.

"So, how's Lenny feel about this?"

"He's fine. We placed him in a little coin-operated laundry in Gilroy."

"You got him a job in a Laundromat?"

He shook his head. "Loaned him the money to buy one." He smirked in Ron's direction. "Got him a handsome rate."

"What's he gonna do with a Laundromat?"

Ron covered the mouthpiece. "Drive it into the ground like he did with the limo service," he said.

"Hey, Dave," Mike yelled toward the front seat. "Put the hat on."

Behind the wheel, in his garage coveralls, Dave held up a middle finger to the rearview mirror as he steered the big car away from the curb.

"Who do you know at Meadowbank?" I said.

"Nobody," said Ron out of the corner of his mouth.

Mike was playing with the intercom, buzzing Dave in the front seat.

"What?" Dave yelled through the glass divider.

"Stop at the BART station first. Charley needs to pick up his car and his clubs."

I looked at my watch. It was nearly two-thirty. Walnut Hill was a good forty-five minutes away, even without traffic on the Bay Bridge. By the time I drove home and changed and got over to Meadowbank, it'd be close to five. The sun had been going down around six-thirty. At that rate, we'd be hard pressed to get in nine holes. When I told this to Mike, he winked at me and pressed the intercom button. "Hey, driver, what time did our 'host' say to be there?"

"Floyd says we gotta wait till at least seven-thirty," Dave shouted back through the glass. "We need to give the clubhouse staff enough time to clear out."

"Use the intercom, for chrissake," said Mike.

I stared at him. "Floyd? What's he got to do with this?"

"He's the one getting us on. Actually, the Beaner's arranging it. Only catch is we can't tee off until after seven-thirty."

"It'll be dark then."

"That's the whole idea," said Mike. "We're gonna *snog* it."

Speed Night Option Golf

Floyd, who'd invented the game, said snog was short for Speed Night Option Golf. And, that night, without the club's knowledge or permission, we were snogging Meadowbank. Floyd, Dave and I were doing the actual snogging. Mike and Ron had opted to ride in the truck with the Beaner, keeping time and brokering the wagers.

The Beaner was Floyd's close associate and golf buddy—actually the only guy who would willingly play golf with him. He also happened to be Meadowbank's night watchman. An ambiguously swarthy character of indeterminate age, ethnicity, and species, the Beaner would have been well cast as your generic terrorist. If he had a proper name, none of us knew it. Floyd called him the Beaner, so we did too. Not to his face, of course, because whenever Floyd did, we noticed the Beaner's pupils dilate and turn even blacker, as if he were cataloging these slurs against some future day of reckoning.

The plan was for us to park out on Hibbard Road, then locate and climb through a hole in the hurricane fence that bordered the property. Traffic was normally thin along Hibbard at night. The fence was hidden behind a thick hedge, and the homes across the street were set back and spaced far apart so we felt confident— at least Floyd did—that we could get in without attracting attention. He'd pioneered the route on previous evenings and assured us it was a piece of cake. Everything seemed buttoned up and do-able. Only one nagging question remained.

What in hell was I thinking?

I was a thirty-four-year-old taxpaying father of two with a mortgage, car loan, and a worried wife who should have been channeling his energies in responsible directions, jumpstarting his stagnant career or socking away money for the kids' college, but was instead engaged in a blatant act of illegal trespass with a motley assemblage of golfing psychopaths, sophomoric bankers, and a guy named Dave.

Why? Two words—actually one—Meadowbank.

Meadowbank. The name conjured up images of gorgeous, glorious, coffee-table-book golf. Classic golf. The venerable course ranked high in Golf Digest's listing of top private clubs in America, as one of the most challenging and physically beautiful tracks in the game. It stood also, along with Cypress Point, Shinnecock Hills, and Augusta National, among the last great bastions of exclusion with a membership so snooty they reputedly blackballed their own family members. Membership was limited to old money— in the gazillions. Napa Valley wine barons, captains of California industry, media (excluding Hollywood, of course) and commerce, retired military and diplomats, past and present heads of state.

Personally, although I considered myself a 'man of the people,' I had no problem with Meadowbank's exclusionary policies. As a boy, I'd spent many a happy hour on a scruffy little muni course back in Illinois, pretending it was Meadowbank, blocking out tufted fairways and mossy greens and replacing them in my imagination with serene and elegant images lifted from the pages of golf magazines. The pictures never showed golfers playing the course, just the holes perfectly modeled in early or late light. Mine alone, waiting for me. Whenever I heard or read about some organization, interest group, disenfranchised race or gender—no matter how deserving, noisy, or politically correct their petition—demanding admittance through her austere and hallowed gates, I sided with the dinosaurs of the membership committee and silently cheered. Meadowbank was mine and mine alone. Until I got in, nobody should.

Although I lived only a few miles from the front gate, I'd never gotten more than a glimpse of her elegant acreage, this through the occasional bare spot in the formidable hedge that rimmed her perimeter. Lesser mortals, including myself and everyone I knew, had to settle for Stickley Municipal, a crowded, mostly flat, patchy track with rubber mat tees and unpredictable greens. Located just a few blocks from Mallard's range, Stickley got so much play they'd recently begun sending out players in groups of five, a move that, although necessary, pleased no one. But cheap golf was hard to find, and Stickley was the only public golf course within a twenty-mile radius.

When Ron and Mike said they'd lined up a game for us at Meadowbank, I'd been initially thrilled, naïvely assuming our host to be some well-heeled bank customer, forgetting that the Bank of Walnut Hill didn't attract old money so much as found money and that Mike and Ron had more in common with Tenderloin loan sharks than with the sort of San Francisco financial institutions patronized by Meadowbank bluebloods.

As our host for the evening, the Beaner's duty was to illuminate each hole with his truck headlights. There were two other guards posted at the front gate and in the clubhouse parking lot, but they rarely, Floyd assured us, ventured out onto the course—or woke up, for that matter. There was, we knew, a slight chance that some bat-eared homeowner might hear us out there and call the cops, and that, the more time we spent out there, the greater our chances were of getting caught. That's where the 'speed' part came in.

Floyd had measured the amount of time the Beaner spent on a typical evening patrolling each hole, checking out the sprinkler heads, etc. If we limited our playing time to no more than ninety minutes total, the odds were better than good against the neighbors in the homes bordering the course noticing anything out of the ordinary. Not a leisurely pace, but if you offered me ninety minutes on Meadowbank against a lifetime of free rounds—day or night—on Stickley, I'd certainly have to think about it.

Floyd had explained the rules to us earlier that evening at Mallard's. I hadn't listened too closely, as I was still dealing with the disappointment in learning that we'd be playing under the cover of darkness. I suppose I shouldn't have been surprised. There's no way in hell that Floyd Birdwell gets anywhere near a shrine like Meadowbank in the daytime, unless the grounds crew mistakes him for a shrub and plants him there.

The sun had been down nearly an hour when I cruised down Hibbard Road and pulled onto the shoulder a cautious distance of about fifty yards past where the Beaner had tied a white towel on the hedge to mark the hole in the fence. I'd insisted on driving my own car. Excited as I was to be snogging Meadowbank, in the back of my mind I had no illusions about the disaster potential in all this. If a quick getaway became necessary, I wanted to have my own means of escape.

My old Ford might be charitably described as a "station car," the clunker I kept to go back and forth from the house to the train station. Cathy needed our good car—the Volvo—to transport the kids. I was afraid the Ford might be conspicuous, parked out there at night, as it was definitely down market for the neighborhood, but then realized that could actually work in my favor. A guy walking with golf clubs on a dark street next to a private country club might draw suspicion, but I could claim my car had broken down and I hadn't wanted to leave my precious equipment in the trunk. One glance at the vehicle would verify my story. The wonder was that it ever ran at all.

As it turned out, not a single car passed by during the time it took me to walk from my car to the towel, and I was pleased to find the branches in the hedge already bent back, leaving just enough room to slip through. No doubt Floyd had passed this way on more than a few occasions.

There was very little moon that night, and though it was right in front of me, I could scarcely make out the hurricane fence, let alone find any hole. After a few minutes of fruitless groping, I was ready to chalk the whole thing up as a bad idea, except now there was another, bigger problem. Thrashing around to find the hole in the fence, I'd lost track of the hole in the hedge and was now stranded somewhere in between.

Exasperation turned to anger, then anxiety, as I blindly swiped and swatted. Perfect. This is what I deserved—stuck in a hedge, until—what? The sun came up? Until some kindly groundskeeper happened along and cut an exit for me? Tears of frustration welled in my eyes. I wanted to shout or scream, but then stopped, took a couple of deep breaths, and laughed instead. There was comedy in this and not a little bit of poetic justice. I took another deep breath, leaned back against the fence.

And fell through.

It was a slit, not a hole. Lying on the chilled ground, feet still sticking through the fence, clubs heaped across my chest, I could see where the wire cross-hatching separated. It was plenty large enough to get through, as I'd just demonstrated, but unless you held it open, you couldn't see it. I pushed the clubs aside and did a slow, backward summersault to free myself, then stood and looked around.

Meadowbank.

My fears, guilt, and self-recriminations evaporated in an instant. I'd passed through the looking glass, and even in the low-hanging darkness, could make out the familiar shapes and planes of the golf course.

I spent a moment getting my bearings. The fence bordered the second hole, which would put the green somewhere off to my right. We were supposed to meet on the third tee, which figured to be directly adjacent.

There was less than a quarter moon. "Not much change back from a quarter," Cathy liked to say. She'd be home by now, making dinner for the kids, waiting for my call saying whether or not I'd be working late. The image kicked me lightly in the gut—just a small taste of the monster guilt I knew was lurking. "She'd be okay with this," I lied to the creature. "She'd laugh."

As my eyes adjusted to the darkness, I could make out the second green, no more than a hundred yards away. I was concerned I hadn't run into anybody yet. Mike,

Ron, and Dave had all left the range before I did. I hadn't seen any other cars out on Hibbard Road, but assumed Dave would have dropped Mike and Ron off, then gone and stashed the limo on a side street.

Moving in kind of a half-crouch, clutching my golf bag close to my chest to keep the irons from jangling, I'd almost reached the second green and still hadn't found anyone. "Mike?" I called softly. "Anyone here?"

My answer was a pair of high-beam headlights, switched on, blinding me, causing me to stumble and pitch headlong into a sand trap. There, lying in the cold sand, I fought to control panic.

The headlights certainly belonged to a police car. There was no match. It was a set-up—Floyd's payback for the range incident. He'd sworn to get even, and I'd literally fallen into his trap. My mind raced to essay a plausible cover story for being out here after dark. "Hi there, I'm Charley. I'm here for the Grimaldi wedding. Wrong night? Oops, my bad."

That's when a grimy shadow appeared and tossed a rake at me. "You gonna have to rake that trap." The Beaner stood, backlit in the waning moonlight. I could have hugged him.

The rest of the group had assembled behind the green where Floyd was taking belligerent practice swings. "About time, Cotter," he growled.

Moments later we'd found ourselves staring into the foggy abyss of what Floyd assured us was the third hole. Floyd said we needed to start there because, even if they couldn't see us in the darkness, the security guards up at the clubhouse, might hear us and come out for a look. I'd been reading descriptions of the third at Meadowbank since I was a kid. One of them described the stalwart par four as "a distant and remembered meadow jealously guarded by a squadron of scarlet oak." Right now, it was looking like a black hole as viewed through a furniture pad—until the Beaner moved his truck into position behind the tee and turned on his headlights and, I remember thinking, this… might… actually… work out.

But then, just moments later, Dave pull-hooked his drive and we heard a loud crack from off to our left. His ball had collided with a glass or aluminum door from the sound of it. This was followed immediately by a piercing alarm, deafening even from two hundred yards away. A chorus of dogs joined in. Floodlights snapped on, bathing the surrounding yards in a harsh white light.

Uh-oh.

Behind us, the Beaner killed his headlights and ground the truck's gears into reverse. Floyd snatched up his clubs, ran over, and jumped on the running board. The truck listed heavily to one side as it made a tight turn and bounced off through a stand of trees into the darkness.

"Hey," yelled Dave. "Wait up." He sprinted after the truck with me right behind.

I had my carry bag tucked under my arm like a football, but it was awkward like that, and I dropped it, scattering irons in the grass. Dave stopped to help, but I told him to go on and try to catch up with the guys in the truck. I could hear angry voices shouting at the dogs to be quiet. By the time I got my clubs together, Dave and the truck had vanished.

Slinging my bag over a shoulder, I took off, cutting a diagonal, I hoped, back toward the second hole and the Hibbard Road fence. Guiding on the rough and the tree line, I circumvented the third green, listening for signs of pursuit. It was unlikely that a homeowner would come chasing across a dark golf course after an unknown intruder, but the dogs sounded like they'd definitely be up for it.

I could hear the Beaner's truck engine off somewhere to my left but getting the hell out of there seemed more prudent than trying to hook up with those guys. And they obviously weren't too concerned about me.

I made it back to the fence where I'd come in and was relieved to find the slit right away, there being no foliage on this side to block the moonlight. There was even a strip of blue cloth marking the opening, and I wondered how I could have missed that the first time, until I saw it was a piece torn from the sleeve of my windbreaker. Oh, well. A torn jacket was getting off easy. I ducked through the fence—without incident this time—then patted my way down the line of bushes until I found an opening to the street. I'd been anxious about the car and was thankful to see it still sitting where I'd parked it—had it been less than an hour ago?

I walked the fifty yards to the car feeling very conspicuous and very stupid. It was such a relief to get my trunk open and dump my clubs into it, that I didn't notice the patrol car pull up behind me until they turned the bubble light on.

Sloppy Kisses

Cathy had found Dr. Farrow through the psychology department at St. Helen's Hospital, using her connections to get an appointment on short notice. The doctor was a tall man with a pale complexion that contrasted with his dark beard, looking to be playing the backside of middle age. His darkened office, too, offered a study in contrasts, decorated as it was, in a sort of contemporary schizophrenic. One side of the room—Dr. Farrow's side, with its heavy oaken desk and black leather Eames chairs was decidedly male. The patient's side, with its overstuffed chair and sofa and white patterned slipcovers, might have shown nicely in a suburban tearoom.

On the wall, between, and at right angles to, this aesthetic stalemate hung three small black and white photographs. Two of them were depictions of murky scenes or objects that evidently defied photography. The third was a portrait of either Sigmund Freud or someone who looked a whole lot like him wearing a tweedy outfit similar to the thinking-man's get up Dr. Farrow sported now.

Given the choice between the stuffed chair and the sofa, I took the couch, skeptical of the whole arrangement but determined to get my money's worth. Sitting down, I noticed Dr. Farrow write something in a stenographer's notebook. He watched while I shifted around for a bit, not knowing whether I was supposed to sit or lie down. "Whatever's comfortable," he said and made another note while I settled into a half-sitting, half-leaning, position at the end of the sofa.

Then followed an increasingly uncomfortable period of silence. Dr. Farrow sat, pen poised, watching, as I glanced around, trying my best to transmit a sane-as-the-next-guy vibe but feeling like a worm in a dish. Being new to head shrinkage, for all I knew, the therapist didn't talk at all but just sat there and took notes while the subject blurted their innermost thoughts. If that was the case, there ought to have been an instruction sheet in the lobby. My mind riffled through a list of potential openers. I was leaning toward something along the lines of "Do you validate?" when Dr. Farrow at last spoke—was it a trifle impatiently?

"Why have you come?"

As welcome as the question was, it seemed a bit belligerent—like inviting a guest into your home and then demanding to know what they were doing there. I was stuck at first for an answer but managed to choke out: "My wife's idea."

Dr. Farrow looked up at his picture of Freud. Their eyes seemed to lock for a moment. "So, you're here at your wife's suggestion?"

I nodded. "And the city attorney."

Farrow opened a file on his desk. "Oh, yes. I see that here."

"He thinks if we tell the club manager I'm seeing a shrink he might not press charges."

"I see. And the charges…?"

"Huh?"

"The reason you were arrested?"

"Oh… illegal trespass."

"Trespassing." Dr. Farrow nodded thoughtfully. "Where was this?"

"A golf course. Meadowbank Country Club."

Farrow pointed out the window. "Right over here? That's a nice club."

"You've played it?"

"No, I don't play golf. But I've heard it's very nice."

"Supposed to be."

"What were you doing out there when you were, ah—"

"Well this guy I was with calls it snogging. It's like—"

Dr. Farrow looked up from his note pad. "Snogging? You mean like… *snogging?*"

"You've heard of it?"

"Yes, I'm familiar with it. I've spent some time in England. It's a common term over there."

"That's wild because I wouldn't have guessed that. I just assumed this nutcase I know made it up. You're not treating a guy named Floyd Birdwell by any chance?"

"You know, I'm not. But I couldn't tell you if I were. Doctor–patient privilege."

"Oh, right. Sorry."

"So, you and this Floyd were snogging?"

"Yes."

"At night, on a golf course."

"Sounds pretty stupid, I guess."

"You've done this before?"

"God, no. Definitely a one-time thing."

"I see. And… how was it?"

"I'm sorry?"

Dr. Farrow cleared his throat. "Did you enjoy the experience?"

"Well," I said. "We'd hardly gotten started when the cops showed up."

Dr. Farrow's smile was sympathetic. "I see."

"Where we made our mistake was letting Dave join us."

Dr. Farrow frowned and made a note. "This is

someone else now?"

"Yes, this guy Dave. Friend of mine."

"Dave wanted to snog too?"

I nodded. "So, we let him."

"How did… the other fellow… what's his name?"

"Floyd."

"How did Floyd feel about Dave participating?"

"I don't think he cared. I mean, he would have if he'd known Dave was going to get us chased out of there."

"Something Dave did?"

"Yes."

Dr. Farrow put down the file, then came around and sat on the edge of his desk. "Charley, I want you to know that anything you say here in this office is held in the strictest confidence."

"Okay…"

"Nothing you say here is ever heard outside these walls."

"Okay."

"So, I want you to feel completely at ease and open."

"Okay."

"What did Dave do?"

"Excuse me…?"

"What did he do that got you arrested and brought you in here to see me today? I'd like to hear it if you're comfortable sharing it with me."

"No, it's okay. It's not a big deal. He hit a house."

Dr. Farrow stared at me for a moment, then frowned. "When you say, 'hit a house—'?"

"With his tee shot. Dave hit a house."

"I guess I'm not following you. By hitting a house, you mean…?"

"You asked me what Dave did. He hit a house on number four. The fairway's lined with houses. It set off an alarm and the people called the cops."

Dr. Farrow blinked a few times. "You were playing golf?"

"Yeah, night golf…snogging."

"Snogging. Maybe I'm not—"

"Snogging is golf played at night."

"Night golf?"

"Yeah—speed night option golf—S.N.O.G.—Sorry, I thought when you said you knew what it was…"

Farrow chuckled and shook his head. He went back and sat down behind the desk.

"That's very funny," he said. "I've heard the term used before but in an entirely different context. I studied in England. When you say snog over there, you're talking about making out—when I was young, they used to call heavy petting. You've never heard it used like that?"

Now that Farrow mentioned it, snogging did sound familiar. Back in college, a guy in the dorm who'd grown up in London, used to talk about slipping out for a "snog" with his girlfriend. Once, when we pressed him for the concise meaning of the word, he'd defined snogging as sloppy kisses—the kind of necking that young people do in parked cars or the back row of a movie theater. I had to laugh, imagining Floyd's reaction to Farrow's definition.

"You know what, Doc? That context had completely slipped my mind."

Farrow laughed right along with me, and I found myself beginning to like him. He poured us both a cup of water from a dispenser in the corner.

"Okay, so let's start over," he said. "Basically, you guys were charged with sneaking on a private club at night to play golf. Is that it?"

"Pretty much. Except I was the only one charged."

"Why's that? "

"There were six of us altogether. I was the one they

caught.”

"Is there a reason for that?”

I shrugged. "Bad luck. They ran one way. I ran the other.”

"These are men your age?”

I nodded and sighed. "I don't know what we were thinking of.”

Farrow looked down at the file on his desk. "You work in advertising?”

"Yeah. An agency in the city.”

"What's the attraction in night golf for a guy like you? You must have opportunities to play during normal hours.”

"Sure, but not Meadowbank. It's one of the world's great courses but only a handful of people have ever even seen it. I figured it was the only chance I'd ever get. So, I went along.”

"How do you see your ball?”

"They have these little day-glo inserts that make the balls light up. Whole thing sounds pretty juvenile, doesn't it?”

"You couldn't imagine playing as somebody's guest

or—?”

"Not Meadowbank. Not in this lifetime.”

"Well… how was it?”

"Stupid. Couldn't see anything. Then, we got chased off before we finished the first hole.”

"That's too bad.”

"It was a dumb idea.”

"You don't come across as someone given to foolish behavior.” Dr. Farrow picked up his cup and took a few sips. "You know your wife and I have spoken. She says golf takes up most of your free time.”

I shrugged. "I play a fair amount. I don't think it's a problem or anything.”

"You think she sees this as more of a problem than it actually is?”

"Absolutely.”

Dr. Farrow made a note. "How much golf do you play?"

"Well, Saturdays…"

"Saturdays," he repeated, making another note.

"We have a regular game."

"And so, your wife objects to your playing on Saturdays?"

"Well, Sundays too."

"Okay, Saturdays and Sundays."

"Then maybe during the week, once in a while, I'll try to duck out of work early and squeeze in nine holes before the sun goes down."

"How often?"

"Couldn't tell you."

"Best estimate."

"Couple, three times a week."

Dr. Farrow nodded and made another entry in his book.

"Not every day," I clarified for the record. Dr. Farrow smiled thinly.

"And then some mornings, I'll get up early and play a quick nine before I catch the train."

"Um hmmm."

"Cathy thinks I'm playing golf all the time but I'm not."

"You're not?"

I shook my head. "A lot of the time, I'm just hitting balls."

"Hitting balls?"

"Yeah. At Mallard's driving range over on Randall Road."

I see… couple, three times a week?"

"At least."

"Whenever you're not playing golf?"

"Or working," I reminded him.

There was a pause while Dr. Farrow made a long entry in his notebook.

"I guess this must sound like a clear case of responsibility shirking."

Dr. Farrow ignored my question. He was looking closely at my file. "How long has this been going on?"

"My playing golf? Since I was a kid."

"Your wife says it's only been a year or two."

"That's because for first eight or nine years we've been married—we're going on ten years now—I never played. I mean, once or twice on a business outing or charity thing, I'd drag the old clubs out of the garage. But, other than that, you'd never think of me as a 'golfer.' But then, some of my friends started taking up the game. You know, you get past thirty and you're looking for a sport you don't have to stay in shape for. We started hanging out, you know, playing around, and then it just escalated from there. Next thing you knew... here we are."

"So, it started as a social thing, for you."

"Partly. My dad was a golfer. He got me started early, eight years old. First time I ever played, we won the father and son championship at his club. That's how good he was, trade shots with an eight-year-old and bring home a trophy. After that, I played all through school and in college."

"What made you stop?"

"Well, I graduated."

"From school. Not from golf."

"It was time to get on with my life."

"You didn't consider golf a part of your life? You'd been playing for how long—?"

"Fourteen, fifteen years."

"You must have been good at it by then. College team?"

"I wasn't bad."

"But you quit…"

I shrugged and didn't say anything. Dr. Farrow let the sentence hang in the air.

"I guess," I said finally, "I didn't think it was something I could make a career of."

"Weren't good enough or didn't want to try?"

"Probably little of both. Didn't think I had what it takes."

"And what is that?"

"Talent for one. Dedication… persistence… patience. Along with a lot of other traits I didn't have."

"So, you went to work in the ad business… because… you felt—what—more suited?"

"Right. That was my major, communications, advertising."

"And you felt you needed to give up golf entirely?"

"Well, it wasn't like a conscious decision. I just— starting a marriage… a career… starting a family— there just wasn't enough time."

Farrow looked up at his Freud picture while he drummed his fingers on the file. "But now you're back, golfing again—with a vengeance, it sounds like—and your wife—"

"Cathy."

"Cathy doesn't know what to make of it. In fact…" he said, going back to the file. "…she calls you a 'born again golfer.'"

We sat in silence for a moment, while Dr. Farrow went back to looking at the file. "Creative director?" he said. "What does that entail?"

"Basically, I write ads for a boutique agency in the city. The Barnett Agency."

"T.V. ads?"

"Print too."

"You find that satisfying work?"

"Yeah, I guess so."

"Uh-huh." He turned a page in the file. "Your wife says that all the golf has put your job in jeopardy. She says she gets calls from your office in middle of a workday, co-workers looking for you."

"Cathy's a worrier. I'm not going to lose my job." I shook my head. "Jesus, who else would they get to do it?"

Dr. Farrow looked at me over the top of his reading glasses. "Sounds like you have a low opinion of your job."

"No. The job's okay. I just meant they'd have a hard time replacing me."

"Why is that?"

"I had several clients follow me over from the last place I worked. John Barnett—he's the CEO—John knows what side his bread is buttered on. Lose me and say goodbye to some hefty commissions."

Another pause while Dr. Farrow leaned back in his chair, studying me. "So what's behind this sudden re-emergence of golf in your life?"

"I don't know, I just…"

"Go ahead."

"One day I'm at my desk, struggling over some copy. I don't even remember the product—probably something you wouldn't buy unless somebody held a gun to your head. And I'm trying to figure something nice to say about it and then it was like…all of a sudden… I remembered golf."

"You remembered it?"

"Yes. I remembered how it used to feel when I was on a golf course, how calm it was. How calm *I* was. I could think. There's something about walking on the land. We don't get to do it that often—just *walk* on the earth. Not concrete or asphalt or indoor-outdoor carpeting but on the land. Terra firma. And then have to *think* about it—*consider* the wind and the length of the grass, the slope of a hill and the placement and height of a tree. Feel what the wind is doing and judge distance by your eye. I don't think a lot of people get that."

"People like Cathy, you mean?"

"Her too."

"Did you ever try to tell her how you feel about it?"

"Believe me, she doesn't want to hear it."

Dr. Farrow took off his tweed sport coat and draped it over the back of his chair. In his vest and shirtsleeves, scratching his beard, his wide shoulders filling out his striped oxford shirt, he looked sturdier. Leaned over his desk, big hands planted on either side of the blotter, studying my "profile," he could have been a Civil War field commander studying intelligence reports before a battle.

"Tell me about Cathy," he said. "How'd you two meet?"

"At a friend's wedding, the year after college. We dated for a while and then moved in together. Got married the next year. In the fall."

"She doesn't play golf, I take it."

I had to laugh. "Cathy wouldn't go near a golf course. Not unless somebody was going to demolish one. That she might show up for."

"What else?"

"About Cathy? She's my sweetheart and my partner. Mother of my kids. Beautiful, smart, great sense of humor. What else do you want to know?"

"All right. Let's for the sake of argument, say that Cathy comes to you and says: 'I've decided to take up golf. It's something I've always wanted to do, and it'll be a good way for us to spend more time together. What would your reaction be to that?"

"First of all, there's no way she would ever say that."

"You're certain?'

"Not in a million years."

"But if she did—"

I shook my head. "It doesn't apply—you know, like you see on questionnaires: N.A.? Not applicable. Cathy hates golf. Besides, she's not what I would call athletically inclined. I mean, she's capable of playing any sport you want—got a great, athletic body. She's just, these days, all about the kids, that's all."

"All right, forget golf for a minute. What do you like to do as a couple?"

"Well… we go to movies. Eat out, usually with the kids. What do you want to know? We got married as a couple. We had two children as a couple. We live, eat and sleep as a couple. We're not exactly strangers."

"Okay."

I was ready for this session to be over. "Look, Doctor, believe me. There's no hidden reason behind my playing golf. I love my wife. I love my family. Golf is just… something that I enjoy doing, okay? And as for being out there at night. I'm not crazy. I did it because I figured it was the only way I'd ever get to see the course. Plain and simple."

"All right."

Dr. Farrow saw me glance at my watch. "We still have a few minutes left if there's anything else you want to talk about."

"No," I said. "I'm good.

The doctor hesitated like he wanted to say something, but then went back to writing in the file.

"So," I said. "What will you say in the report, if you don't mind my asking?"

He looked up in surprise. "I'm not submitting a report."

"You're not?"

"I told you, what's said in this room is entirely confidential. The authorities will be notified that we met. That's all."

"Really?"

"I thought you understood that."

"Okay, thanks." I started for the door but then something

occurred to me. "In that case," I said. Do you do dreams?"

"You mean, do I analyze them? Sometimes…"

"Well… this might not have anything to do with… anything but there's this dream I've been having…"

Weekend Plans

The fact that I had gone—albeit grudgingly—to see Dr. Farrow seemed to placate Cathy and, for at least the next twenty-four hours, we managed to avoid the sore subjects of golf and what I'd been thinking of crashing Meadowbank at night with my "nitwit friends." Not to mention her stress and humiliation at having to pack Sean and Sara into the car and drive over to the police station in the middle of the night to spring Daddy from jail.

The plan was for the four of us to drive up to her parent's farm in Santa Rosa on Saturday morning. Guilt and cowardice had caused me to put off dropping the golf-trip bombshell for as long as possible, telling myself I'd try Wednesday night after the kids went to bed. But then, we'd had such a pleasant dinner, and Cathy was in such a good mood afterward, curled up on the sofa watching one of her favorite TV shows, that I didn't have the heart—okay, the guts—to ruin her evening. I knew it was irresponsible and selfish, considering the Meadowbank fiasco, to even consider going, but I'd told the guys I'd go and, well, that's how far gone I was.

When I came downstairs the next morning—Thursday—Cathy was in the kitchen making lunches for the kids. Sean and Sara sat at the table, dressed in their bright blue, day-camp uniforms of T-shirts and shorts, eating cereal. Sean had the box propped up in front of him, studying a puzzle while he ate. I kissed him with a loud smack. He made a face and wiped it off with his sleeve. Sara was selecting Cheerios and carefully lining them up on the placemat next to her bowl.

"Where's my breakfast?" I asked the room at large, then bent down to nibble on a spot between her neck and shoulder.

"Daddy!"

"Is this my breakfast? Yummm, this is good," I said.

"It's me!"

"Are you sure? You taste delicious. Don't worry, I'll only take little bites."

Sara scrunched herself into a little ball, shrieking happily. It was one of our favorite games.

"Wait a minute," I said in mock-indignation. "I ordered waffles. Are you waffles?"

"No, I'm a *girl*."

"A girl? Are you sure?"

A nod.

"Well, okay, but just to be sure, I'm just going to pour some syrup on you and see if you taste like waffles."

Another shriek.

"Charley, let her eat her breakfast," said Cathy, sounding tired. "The camp bus will be here in a minute."

Sean looked up from his cereal box. "Dad, can we go to the A's game on Saturday? Jason and his dad are going."

Cathy, her back turned, was spreading peanut butter on bread. I figured this was as good a time as any.

"We can't this weekend, Sean."

"Why not?"

I took a deep breath, but then Cathy beat me to it.

"Did you forget? We're going up to see Grandpa Bob and Nana on Saturday."

"Yay!" Sara clapped her hands.

"Maybe we can go to the game first, then go," said

Sean. "Can we, Dad?"

"Not this weekend," I said. "Daddy has to go away."

Cathy whirled around, a lunch sack in each hand. "What? Go away where?"

I'd told myself I'd only lie if I had to. Now, at that moment, I couldn't see an alternative. "L.A.," I said. "Hotchkiss is sending a team of marketing people to check out the distribution operation. Barnett thinks we need to be there. We do a little handholding, and we can avoid a review. He's convinced they're talking to other agencies."

"Why didn't you say anything?"

"I just found out yesterday. That's when everything was finalized."

"*Finalized.*" She laid the word out for both of us to think about. "So, you waited, what, twenty-four hours to let me know?"

"I was hoping things would change," I said weakly. "But… they didn't."

"You know how much we've been looking forward to this weekend. My parents—"

"I know. I'm really sorry."

"Can you at least get back for Sunday?"

"Doubt it. They've got meetings lined up both days. I think I get in around nine Sunday night. You won't need to pick me up. I'll leave my car at the airport."

Cathy didn't say anything, so I said, "Hey listen, what's the difference? You guys can still go, and we'll be going back up next weekend to pick up the kids. We can have a nice visit with your folks then."

She picked up a marker and started writing the kids' names on the lunch bags.

"It's work, Cathy. Nothing I can do about it. Responsibility, remember?"

"Uh huh," she said, without turning around. "And I suppose 'work widow' is better than 'golf widow,' right?"

Regrets

That night, I drove over in the late evening to hit balls at Mallard's. Cathy hadn't bothered to ask where I was going. At that point, I doubted if she cared.

It was cool for June—they were predicting storms for the weekend—and the wind was up. It blew through the big eucalyptus trees that lined the perimeter of the range rattling the leaves and dodging dark shadows across the yardage markers.

Generally, on cooler weekday evenings, hardcore range rats had the place to themselves, and on that particular night only a few lonely figures occupied stalls. I knew them by name, but we only exchanged nods. It's been my experience that, when you come to a golf range late at night, you're not looking to practice your swing so much as be alone with it. For the lonesome few, hitting balls is a proactive form of introspection—a more desirable and healthier alternative to a recliner or barstool. You're hitting balls, but you're thinking too— about life, loves, children, the things you might have done, the things you wish you had. In that setting, at that hour, I'd no sooner disturb a duffer in a range stall than if they were sitting in a church pew.

Floyd, of course, had no such compunctions. I'd just set up in my favorite stall, second from the left end of the range, next to the parking lot, when he rolled up in his cage.

"How you hittin' 'em?"

"Only time will tell." I pulled my sand wedge out of the bag and took a practice swing.

Floyd flashed his sexual-deviant grin. "Heard you got busted the other night."

"Yeah, I wanted to thank you guys for hanging around and making sure I got out of there all right."

"We ain't your mommy, Cotter. Anyway, we had a truck full of bankers. What'd they charge you with?"

"Trespassing. Stupidity's not a crime yet, I guess."

"Probably just got you a slap on the wrist, huh?"

"Probation and a fine."

"Okay, so no harm done. Beaner and I are thinkin' 'bout driving up to Silverado tonight. He's got a friend on the grounds crew can get us on after they close. You up for a rematch?"

"Nah, my snogging days are over, I'm afraid."

"Tomorrow at Stickley, then."

I shook my head. "Gotta work."

"I guess they need you at the hospital?"

"Huh?...Oh, yeah, the hospital." I'd almost forgotten.

"The weekend then?"

"Wish I could. Going out of town." I hit a nice flop shot toward the sixty-yard barrel. When I looked back at Floyd, I could see his eyes staring at me through the bars of his cage.

"Where you goin'?" he said.

"Desert," I answered, and instantly regretted it. While it was highly unlikely he'd run into Cathy over the weekend, or anytime soon, I wanted as few people privy to my weekend plans as possible. And, with Floyd, you never knew. He was a wild card capable of turning up anywhere at any time. And with his propensity for high decibel blurts it was conceivable that one of them might somehow make its way to Cathy's ear. This was no doubt paranoia on my part—she and Floyd certainly didn't travel in the same circles. But that's the way my mind was working, already paying the price for the big lie.

"Okay, when you get back, then. When's that?"

I shrugged, not wanting to be specific. If I said, for example, Sunday at noon, he'd want to play at twelve-fifteen. "Not sure. Might be a *while*."

"What you gonna do out in the desert?"

"There's some stuff I need to sort out," I said, surprised at the honesty in my words.

"Nurse goin' with you?"

I shook my head and hit another shot toward the barrel.

"Whoa, Cotter." That gargoyle leer again. "I don't know about you, but I'd think twice about leaving something like that on her lonesome."

"How's that?"

"Well, shit, Doc," he said. "You of all people ought to know what nurses are like."

Ed's Plane

Friday evening, I drove over to the airport and found the boys already gathered on the tarmac next to the Cessna. With them was a shortish, puffy, middle-aged guy named Ed Nenniman. Ron introduced him to me as "our fearless pilot." Some guys just look like pilots. They can be old or young, fat or slim, but they generally have a look about them. Maybe it's a military bearing, a strong countenance or competent manner, a glint of steel behind the eyes. Ed Nenniman looked like a guy whose wife hangs a note on him in case he gets lost at the mall.

Apparently, I wasn't the only one having second thoughts about our fearless pilot. Standing off to the side, Dave was alternately gaping at Ed and the plane as if trying to reconcile one with the other.

I took Mike aside. "How long has Ed been flying?"

He yelled over to Ron. "Hey, when did Ed's loan go through?"

"April, maybe?"

"April?" I said, gripping the sleeves of Mike's jacket. "Last April? Like two months ago?"

Mike nodded, seeming to have no idea where I was going with this.

"But this probably isn't his first plane?" I said.

"No. No. I think he had a Bayliner before."

"How many engines did it have?"

"I dunno. At least one."

Ron came over, all business. "Ed wants us to come

aboard. There's a storm brewing, and we can beat it if we hurry and get out of here."

Minutes later we were poised at the end of the runway ready for takeoff. Ron sat up front next to Ed in the copilot's seat. Behind them, Mike sat in a single seat opposite the hatchway. And one row back, Dave and I sat across a mini aisle from each other. The rumbling engine made conversation almost impossible, but then nobody felt like talking. All eyes were on Ed, watching him bumble through his preflight checklist, tentatively flicking toggles and tapping gauges while thumbing through his flight manual like he was hunting for a plumber in the Yellow Pages. When Mike leaned forward and touched his shoulder, Ed yelped.

"Jesus, don't bother him," Ron said.

"How we looking, Ed?" Mike said.

Ed stared at Mike and then at the rest of us, as if he'd only just noticed there were passengers aboard. He managed a plucky smile along with a thumbs-up. That's when the radio crackled with the information that Cessna 379 was clear for takeoff.

"That's us," Ed shouted. "Here we go."

Dave leaned back in his seat, monitoring the engine's whine with a professional's ear. "Nice plane," he shouted.

"Yeah," I said. "He had a Bayliner before."

Ed swung the Cessna onto the top of the runway and opened up the throttle.

When I glanced back at Dave, he was looking at me.

"A Bayliner's a boat," he said.

Then we took off.

We were airborne no more than fifteen minutes when Ed steered us into the heart of the thunderstorm we'd hoped to avoid. For the next hour and a half, we pitched and dropped as heavy winds, combined with explosions of sound and light, concussed our tiny craft. Through it all, Ed clutched the wheel, mouth half-open, squinting through thick glasses as fusillades of rain pelted the windshield. Ron fidgeted in the copilot's seat, alternately staring at the altitude indicator and keeping a sharp lookout for anything else Ed might fly us into. Mike held on to the back of Ed's seat with both hands, eyes tightly shut, as if any movement on his part might tip the plane over. Across from me, Dave dozed, blissfully unconcerned. Between thunderclaps, I heard the brittle pitch of near panic in Ron's voice talking to Ed.

"Can't we get above the storm?"

"There's no way to know how high the ceiling is."

"Why don't we try going up and see?"

"That could suck up a lotta fuel. Wanna make sure we have enough to get there."

"Can we go around it?"

"Yeah, if we knew which way it was headed. But it keeps changing direction."

I leaned forward. "What do you do when visibility's bad like this, Ed? Do you fly on instruments?"

"Nope."

"Why not?"

"Don't have any."

Mike's eyes were open now—wide.

"What do you do when you can't see anything?"

"That's never been a problem. I don't see too good anyway."

This cracked him up, but he stopped chuckling when he looked back and saw the stricken looks on his passengers' faces.

"Hey, listen, the one thing I found is that flying's just like driving a car. All you wanna do is keep your wits about you and watch out for the other guy. See this gauge? That's the altimeter. It's all you really need. Shows you where the ground is, helps you avoid CFIT."

"What's CFIT?" I asked, yelling over a thunderclap.

"Controlled Flight into Terrain. It's the aeronautical term for crashing."

"What about GPS or radar or anything like that?"

Ed shook his head. "Ron advised against them," he shouted. "And it made a lot of sense. It would have meant a bigger downstroke, and then the monthly would have been outside my comfort zone."

Ron wouldn't meet Mike's gaze.

"And…" Ed continued, "…when you consider the fact that electronic instruments depreciate at an accelerated rate, the numbers just didn't work. It boiled down to cash flow versus a write-off I didn't really need." Ed threw Ron an appreciative glance. "Right, Ron?"

"Fly the plane," Ron said.

It was only a few minutes later when Ron thought he spotted something ahead in the clouds.

"There!" His cry of alarm was almost a shriek. "Where the clouds are thinner. See that?"

Mike strained forward until his chin was nearly resting on Ed's shoulder. "What is it? Is it a plane?"

"There's something up there. I saw it. Go around it! Go around it!"

"What is it? Ron, is it a plane?"

"I don't know, but we gotta turn now, or we're going to hit it!"

"Hang on!" Ed shouted.

The Cessna banked hard to the left. Dozing in his seat next to me, Dave's head flopped from one shoulder to the other.

"See anything?" Mike said.

Ed turned around long enough to say, "Not a thing." That's when I noticed the little arrow on the altimeter pointing at a mark between one hundred and two hundred. We couldn't possibly be only a hundred and fifty feet off the ground, could we? Now, I was no expert on reading altimeters—this was the first one I'd ever seen, and there was more than a good chance I was reading it wrong. But then, an enormous propeller loomed out of the cloud directly in front of us.

"Look out!" Ron screamed, reached over, and heaved back on the stick. The Cessna roared into a steep climb. Ron fell back across Ed's lap, clutching the stick in a death grip.

"Let go!" Ed shouted. "Lemme do it! You're gonna— shit! You're gonna stall us!"

"We're gonna die!" Ron wailed, holding fast to the stick, locking us into our too-steep climb. Within seconds we found the ceiling, breaking through the clouds into an ink-black sky filled with stars. That's when we stalled, sliding silently back, dropping like a stone into the storm.

Tied into my seat, I was a helpless witness, yet strangely removed from the action around me. Ed had managed to wrestle the stick from Ron and was frantically trying to restart the engine. Mike shouted instructions I couldn't hear, and Ron gibbered about airplane-loan amortization. But none of that seemed important to me. My life was passing before my eyes, just like you hear about. I saw my mom feeding me, buttoning my coat, and taking me to my first day of kindergarten. I saw my dad, in the fall, raking leaves into piles, then me jumping into them. I saw Cathy on our first date and then, another time, at a baseball game, sunlight in her hair and then how she looked right after she had Sean, sucking on a glycerin lollypop while they wheeled her off to the recovery room.

Meanwhile, as if from a distance, I heard Ed telling Mike to look for someplace to set down, then Ron shouting that he could see an airstrip. Then, for some reason, I thought about Floyd and what he'd said about Cathy: "You know what nurses are like," suddenly furious with myself for letting him get away with it, for not smashing his stupid, ugly, grinning face in when he said it—each time he said it. Where did he get off saying something like that? Well, it was too late now. I was going to die a coward.

Then Ron was screaming, "That's not the airport! That's not the airport!"

Mike was shouting, "Pull up! Look out!"

Right at that moment, Dave woke up. He looked over at me and said, "Is there any more beer?"

"That son of a bitch," I said. "Who does he think he is?"

"Who?"

"Floyd."

Just as the Cessna hit the power lines.

Through the Looking Glass

I woke up in a hospital room to the sound of giggling and moans. The curtains were drawn around the bed next to mine and I could hear bedsprings squeaking. I cleared my throat and the sounds abruptly stopped and were replaced by whispering. Then, a guy about my age peeked out from behind the curtain.

"Oh," he said, "I see we're awake."

He ducked back behind the curtain. I heard more whispers and muffled giggling and then, after a few moments, he came out, straightening his white medical jacket, a sheepish grin on his face. Behind him, a red-faced nurse in a starched white dress appeared and made a beeline for the door, stopping just before she went out to smile and give me a little wave.

The doctor came over and picked up the clipboard mounted on the foot of my bed.

"Sorry about that," he said, nodding toward the door, "But, you know what they say about nurses."

I stared at him. There was something familiar about this doctor. Yet I was almost certain I'd never met him before. He looked to be in his mid-thirties, tall with the dark good looks you'd associate more with a TV medical drama than a real hospital.

"I'm Dr. Kiley, Mr. Cotter," the doctor said. "You've had a nasty blow to your head. You have a concussion and we had to take a few stitches but, aside from that, there's nothing really to worry about. We'd like to keep you under observation for a day or two."

"Excuse me, where am I?"

"Oh, sorry. This is Coachella Valley General. Do you remember the ambulance bringing you in last night?"

"No. Not really."

"That's all right. It's nothing to be too concerned about. You were unconscious for several hours so it's completely normal to experience a little amnesia."

"What happened?"

"What's the last thing you remember?"

"I don't know—we were on the plane, in a storm— how are the other guys?"

"I'm afraid I couldn't tell you. There are some people in the waiting room who might have some information on that. I'll send them in when we're finished."

Dr. Kiley spent the next few minutes taking my pulse, looking into my eyes and ears and poking around my head and neck. When he was about to leave, I asked him what was true that they say about nurses. He stopped in the doorway and raised his eyebrows in mock surprise. "What nurse?" he said.

Dave came in then, dressed in golf shirt and slacks, looking more subdued than I'd ever seen him. I almost didn't recognize him without his coveralls.

"Hey," I said. "You okay?"

"I guess."

"Who else is here? Are the guys all right?"

"What guys would that be, Mr. Cotter?" A heavy-set, tired-looking man with a drooping mustache stepped into the room. He wore a uniform and a gold badge.

"Charley," Dave said, "This is Deputy Sheriff Mullin. He needs to ask you a few questions."

"Morning, Mr. Cotter. How's your head feeling?"

"Like a brick fell on it."

"Well, maybe one did."

I felt an odd chill at the base of my spine. The deputy wasn't smiling, and neither was Dave.

"Okay, now Mr. Cotter, if you're up to it and you have no objection, what I'd like to do is record our conversation for the file. That all right with you?" Mullin didn't wait for an answer but pulled a small black digital recorder out of a heavy leather briefcase, placed it on the bed table and then swung it over in front of me. Dave frowned, watching him.

"This interview is taking place at Coachella Valley General Hospital on Saturday, the twenty-ninth of August. This is Deputy Sheriff Paul Mullin. Respondent is one Charles Cotter of—where is your home, Mr. Cotter?"

"Walnut Hill."

"Street address?"

"2168 Bluff.

"2168 Bluff," Mullin repeated. "Is that Street, Avenue?"

"It might be street, but we just call it Bluff."

"All right." The deputy sighed. "Just Bluff then. 2168 Bluff, Walnut Hill, California."

"You want the zip?"

Mullin shook his head. He spread some papers out on the bed in front of him. "All right, Mr. Cotter, why don't you tell us what you and Mr. Tucker here were doing in that turbine field last night?"

"What were we doing there? That's where the plane crashed."

"What plane was that, Mr. Cotter?"

Dave was looking at me, shaking his head. His skin looked clammy and ashen like he had just got finished being sick.

"Our plane—the Cessna—the one we crashed in," I said. "How many crashes were there last night?"

"None that I'm aware of. Not last night."

"You mean besides ours?"

"I mean including yours. There were no plane crashes last night. Period."

I looked at Dave. "What is he talking about? Where're Mike and Ron?"

Dave just stood there looking pale. And scared.

"Oh, shit," I said. "What happened? Tell me they're alright."

"They're fine, Mr. Cotter," said Mullin. "Home safe and sound."

"They're home—already? How'd they do that?"

"You'll have to ask them. But my guess is that they never left"

I looked at Dave. "What's he talking about? What's going on here?"

"Well, Mr. Cotter, that's what I need you to tell me. What is going on here?"

"Dave, what's this about?"

"I'll tell you what it's about, Mr. Cotter. It's about reckless endangerment. It's about trespassing and filing a false police report. It's about dragging a search and rescue detail out in the middle of the night—in a storm—for what? For laughs?"

"I'm sorry—what?"

"Okay, fun's over, fellas. Now, if there's some kinda reasonable explanation here, I need to hear it right now or else I'm going to have to assume that you two are just a couple of jackasses getting' your kicks at the county's expense."

"Look—I don't—"

"Sheriff," interrupted Dave, "Would it be okay if Charley and I had a minute?"

The big cop looked at him, disgusted. "Wanna get your story straight. Sure, why not? I got all the time in the world for this bullshit." He turned his recorder off and trudged out of the room.

When he had gone, Dave pulled a chair over close to the bed.

"Charley," he said softly, "Help me out here. I had a few beers before we took off, but I remember being on a plane. Right? I mean, we flew here. Right?"

"Of course, we flew here. You know we flew here. What's he talking about, no plane crash?"

"You see, that's the thing. There's no plane out there. Not anywhere around that I could see. I looked for a good fifteen minutes. I saw you run into that wind turbine. That's when I called 911. Then, when the cops showed up, they looked too. There was nothing."

"We must have wandered away from it. It could be anywhere out there." I sat up, leaning on my elbow. "Mike and Ron could still be out there."

Dave shook his head. "They searched with helicopters last night and then again this morning. Nothing—no plane. And they called Walnut Hill Airport. Nobody filed a flight plan out of there for Palm Springs or anywhere else last night."

"That Ed guy probably didn't file one. I'll bet he doesn't even know how."

Dave was shaking his head. "*Nobody* filed one… because no planes took off from there last night. None."

My head was throbbing more than ever, and I let it drop back on the pillow. "Look, Dave," I said. "Tell me again what you're trying to tell me because I don't think I'm hearing this right. We were in the plane and then we crashed, right?"

"Yeah—I mean—yeah. I thought we did. But there's no plane. And now they're sayin' there never was a plane."

"That's ridiculous. Somebody's trying to cover up something. If Mike and Ron—"

Dave reached over and clutched my arm. There was no color in his face. None.

"Charley—listen to me. This morning, they called Mike's family to tell them he was missing." He stopped and drew a breath.

"Okay..."

"He answered the phone."

"Who answered the phone?"

"Mike did."

"Mike was there?"

Dave nodded.

"How'd he get home?"

"I don't know. Ron was home too."

"Son of a—they left us out there?"

Dave squeezed my arm. "You know what they told the Sheriff? They said they didn't know anything about any plane crash, or any trip to Palm Springs either."

"Those—!" I tried to sit up, but a surge of pain knocked me back on the pillow. "It's gotta be some kind of scam. I'll bet that Ed guy doesn't have insurance either. I mean he doesn't even have instruments, right? I'll bet you anything those two are covering up for him."

"Sure, okay, but how'd they get the plane out of there?"

"Obviously, they had it towed or something before the rescue guys got there."

Dave's cheeks flushed now that he had somebody to be pissed at. "Selfish assholes didn't even try looking for us."

"Can you believe it?" I said. "Just like at Meadowbank. This is twice in one week they ran out on me."

After a few moments spent vilifying bankers, we turned to our immediate problem, coming up with some plausible answers for Deputy Sheriff Mullin. Anybody who has done as many frenzied, last minute re-writes in restrooms and hallways as I have will tell you that fear is a very effective muse. But try as we might, we couldn't come up with any logical reason for us to be wandering around in a turbine field looking for the wreckage of the plane we'd been riding in that hadn't taken off.

When Deputy Sheriff Mullin came back in, the best we could offer was that we'd somehow been the victims of an elaborate practical joke at the hands of some incorrigible bankers—the details of which were too painful and embarrassing to recount—and offer to reimburse the authorities for last night's misunderstanding.

We were hoping he'd be inclined to cut us a break, write us off as a waste of time and resources. And, for the most part, thankfully, he did, saying he wouldn't hold us but that we'd be receiving an invoice from the county to cover rescue expenses.

As for our apologies, sorry he said, didn't cut it. His deputies had way too much to do, putting their lives on the line every day to waste time dealing with this kind of high school horseshit. It was a message, Sheriff Mullin said, we should relay to our "banker buddies." Next time we all decided to play cute with his department, we ought to think twice lest we find ourselves in a shit storm of trouble. And, if we thought a thunderstorm was bad, wait till we saw what a shit storm was like.

Freefall

Next morning, the doctor cleared me for release. Dave and I caught a late afternoon flight to San Francisco—commercial this time. Then we hopped a shuttle bus to the east bay. I drew a lot of stares owing to the bandage that draped my head at a cockeyed angle and pushed down over my left eyebrow making my left ear stick out.

Since waking up in the hospital, I'd dreaded the inevitable showdown with Cathy. My plan was to come clean with the whole misguided, episode and hope she could find it in her heart to forgive me. Maybe I was growing up at last, admitting to myself that this kind of deceit and denial creates karma bad enough to bring down an airplane—or wreck a marriage. Anyway, even if I wanted to double down on the lie—which I didn't— it'd be tough to explain the nasty bump on my head and the bills from a Palm Springs hospital and Sheriff's department.

Dave asked me for about the tenth time if I thought there might be some truth in the story we told Sheriff Mullin, that it had all been a practical joke—on us. I told him I didn't think so, but I was sure as hell going to find out.

The shuttle dropped us off at the municipal airport, where we'd left our cars. I'd clearly remembered parking my old Taurus by a fence next to Dave's Blazer but now neither vehicle was anywhere to be found.

"All right," I said. "This is way past being funny."

We spent another fruitless fifteen minutes searching before we gave up and called a cab. When I got home, it appeared Cathy and the kids weren't back from the weekend yet. All the lights were off, and her Volvo was absent from the driveway. And here was another mystery waiting for me: the Taurus was there, in the carport, next to the house. Last time I'd seen it was Friday night in the airport parking lot. I couldn't imagine how it could have wound up here unless Mike or Ron had driven it back. I had convinced myself by now that the bankers were somehow behind whatever this was. I mean who else but those two would have known where I'd parked? But then… how had they managed it without the keys that were still in my pocket?

I walked over for a closer look and saw that the entire car was covered in a thick layer of dust. There were some dirty cardboard cartons stacked on the trunk and a pair of rusted lawn chairs leaned against the driver's door. It looked like it hadn't been driven—or even touched—in quite a while. How had they pulled off this trick?

The Sunday paper sat on the doorstep, the frontpage tinted yellow from a day in the sun. When I got inside, there was no note waiting for me on the kitchen table—our usual family message drop. Cathy had never actually said whether she'd be taking the kids up to her parent's without me or how long she planned to be there. More than likely she'd left a message on my cell. But then I realized I'd tucked the phone into my golf bag before we took off Friday night. Phone and bag now numbered, along with plane, as missing or unaccounted for. But I knew that Cathy was scheduled to work the Monday morning shift so, with or without the kids, I expected her to walk in at any minute.

Cathy had evidently performed one of her gonzo cleaning operations before she left. There were a couple of beers in the fridge but, otherwise, the shelves were strangely empty. I opened one of the beers and gulped down half of it before taking a breath. What a weekend! Then it occurred to me to call Mike and find out what the hell was the idea leaving us out on that wind farm. Our kitchen phone normally hung on the return wall next to the refrigerator. But, when I reached for it now, it wasn't there, replaced by a desktop unit on the counter by the microwave. I remembered using the wall phone some time during the last week or two but there was no hook or hole or mark on the wall to indicate there ever had been a phone mounted there and the paint didn't look fresh.

And there was something else odd about the kitchen, although it took me a while to realize what it was. The refrigerator door—normally festooned with photos, notes, reminders, blue ribbons, pizza discount coupons, all stuck on with magnets painted to look like little fruits and vegetables—was now as clean and uncluttered as if the fridge had been delivered yesterday. Not a single note or photo remained.

That was strange. Cathy liked to say our whole life was pictured in collage' on that refrigerator door. She called it the Cotter family shrine. I couldn't imagine her taking it down for any reason.

My head was throbbing again. Had the doctor said something about avoiding alcohol? I truly couldn't remember but, anyway, poured the rest of the beer down the sink. It was getting close to dinner time and still no sign of Cathy. I imagined she'd want to stay up in Santa Rosa for dinner with the kids before heading back and considered calling up there but knew there'd be questions about my 'business meeting' in San Diego and didn't want to have that conversation over the phone. I decided to postpone calling Mike or Ron at home for the same reason. If either of their wives should answer, there would bound to be a barrage of questions for which I'd have few answers—at least not until I had a chance to debrief their respective husbands. Besides, my head was pounding harder now, and I figured the best thing I could do was try to get in a little nap before Cathy got home. But first, I picked up the Sunday paper and thumbed through the front section looking for any mention of a private plane going down. I couldn't find any mention of it, but another article caught my eye:

SNOGGING A GROWING PROBLEM

Walnut Hill, Calif. - A recent "snogging" in Walnut Hill, California drew more than a hundred participants. The snoggers assembled on the fairway of a swank suburban country club, then whacked their way over an approximate two-mile course to the center of town and a confrontation with law enforcement officers.

"These snogs are becoming more brazen," Walnut Hill Mayor Kevin Dunphy. "This is a problem that is not going to go away by itself."

The Snogging Movement routinely stages snogging "events" to draw attention to their "no-growth" agenda intended to promote the construction of new golf courses, prevent the destruction of existing sites and curtail the development of East Bay real estate for commercial purposes.

I read the article once and then again. I'd assumed snogging was just some invention of Floyd's but here it was in black and white on the front page of the *business section*.

It was late, and the beer hadn't done me any good. My head pounded, and my body longed for sleep. In my ragged condition, I pronounced myself in no condition for any kind of reckoning with Cathy. I'd get a good night sleep and hopefully, the morning would bring fresh light—and answers.

The upstairs doors were all shut except for the one leading to our bedroom. I walked in and sat down on the bed. It was comforting to be home, at last. I started to stretch out but then, on impulse, picked up the phone and punched in Cathy's cell number. After four rings, the message clicked in.

The greeting was new—one I hadn't heard before. Nothing unusual about it, just the normal 'leave a message and I'll call you back' but her voice sounded somehow different, huskier, sultry even. 'Provocative' I guess you'd call it. Kathleen Turner or Bacall teaching Bogie how to whistle. "Hey," I said after the beep. "It's me. Just got home. Where are you? Are you driving back tonight? Anyway… I'm worn out from the weekend. I'm gonna turn it. We can catch up in the morning. Love you… night." I hung up and fell back on the pillows, too tired to undress.

In my dream, I was on the first tee at Meadowbank. There was no crowd around me, and no one standing in my way. But the wind was up, blowing hard. This is it, I thought. Nobody around to stop me. This is when I finally get to hit the ball. I teed up my ball and was about to hit but then a strong gust knocked me off balance. I set up to the ball again but then another gust nearly sent me sprawling. I kept trying but the gusts kept coming, stronger each time…

Then, all at once, I blew away.

I tumbled down fairways and soared up high over the treetops. Golfers on the fairways below looked up and waved, shouting words I couldn't hear. None of them seemed especially concerned that I was up there. I rose higher and higher and, in a few moments, was soaring above the clouds.

At first, I wasn't frightened—the billowing, cotton cumulus seemed a splendid safety net. But as I flew higher, and farther, the gusts became a steady wind, the clouds darkened and flattened out and the sky turned gunmetal gray.

No longer lighter than air, I felt myself falling, and saw with alarm that my safety net had hardened into a slick floor of murky ice. Beneath it, lit by lightning flashes, an angry ocean roiled. I felt a bottom-dropping-out sensation like on a rollercoaster or in an old, manual elevator. I steeled myself for the crash, but now the ice was gone, melted into a rainstorm through which I plunged, gathering speed, unable to draw a breath.

Rushing up below me was the wind farm. Tightly clustered turbines formed an impenetrable barrier of frenzied, spinning blades threatening to slice me to pieces. I drew my legs up and covered my face with my arms, then was stunned to land lightly on the ground. But, having braced myself for a crash, I toppled over anyway.

I was back in the turbine field, looking around now, relieved to find myself unhurt, and not frightened or disoriented this time, knowing I'd find my way out and get back home—had done it before. But then there he was, a desolate figure with a golf bag trudging over a rise a hundred yards away, walking toward me, silhouetted, then and again, in lightning flashes, each strike seeming to vault him closer and then closer.

I was determined to speak to him, find out what he was doing—out in this turbine field, golfing in this terrible storm. But at ten yards, I saw him clearly and caught the spark of recognition in his eyes. And, like before—God help me—I turned and ran. He didn't try to chase me, but I heard him cry out. It wasn't a man's voice or even a voice at all but more of a sound—like the whirring skreet of insects on a summer night or the scream of a jungle bird.

But I heard it, all right.
He definitely called my name.

What Nurses Are Like

"Charley, wake up."

Cathy was getting dressed in front of the closet, I got just a glimpse of white silk stockings clasped to a garter belt before she stepped into a crisp white shirt dress and buttoned it up the front. The clock radio said eight-forty-five am. Her side of the bed was untouched.

"I don't have time to talk now," she was saying, "But, if you're going to stay here, I don't want you in my bed. And I'd appreciate it if you didn't leave beer cans all over the living room."

"Where'd you sleep?" I asked her.

"Downstairs on the sofa, but tonight I'm going to be in here—alone." She disappeared into her closet.

"I don't blame you for being pissed," I said. "If it's any consolation, I feel like a real dick. I'm sorry about the weekend. I never, ever should have gone."

She came out of the closet with a pair of white mid-heel pumps. "What weekend?"

"This weekend. I know how much you were looking forward to doing something as a family. It was selfish of me. And lying only makes it worse. A lot worse."

She sat down on the edge of the bed, slipping on the

pumps. "What happened to your head?"

"That's what I'm trying to tell you and believe me, it hurts for me to have to tell you this, all right?"

She got up and went over and stood, back to the closet door mirror, checking the seams on her nylons. "Tell me what?"

"What I'm trying to tell you. "

"Charley, I'm really late. Can we do this later?"

"No. I need to get this off my chest. It'll just take a minute. So, can you just sit down and listen to what I'm going to tell you? Please. I'm trying to do the right thing here."

She sighed, rolled her eyes and looked at her watch. "Oh, for God's sake." She came back over and sat down on the bed. "What?"

"I need you to know the truth about this past weekend." Close to her now, I saw for the first time a slender gold ring dangling from her nostril. "What's that? When did you get your nose pierced?"

"This? A while ago, why?"

"I never saw it before."

She made a face. "I've gotta go."

"Wait a minute, I haven't said what I want to tell you."

"Well, hurry up. I'm late."

"Okay… okay… I feel really bad about this, but—what do you need a nose ring for? Didn't it hurt? It looks like it would've hurt?"

"Charley, tell me what you're going to tell me because I've got to get to the hospital."

"Okay…I want you to know I'm sor—are you chewing gum? It's like eight in the morning."

"Jesus, Charley—just say whatever it is!"

"Okay, okay… Cathy…"

"What?"

"I didn't go to San Diego."

"You didn't."

"No. I went somewhere else…"

She just sat there, waiting.

"Aren't you going to ask where I went?"

She shrugged. "Okay, where did you go?"

"I went to the desert…"

She was nodding, impatiently. "I know."

"…to play g—you know?"

"Yeah."

"How'd you find out?"

"You told me."

"No, I didn't."

"Yes, you did. Just before you left."

"No. I never told you about the desert. I said I was going to San Diego for a meeting."

"Did you? I don't remember. That was so long ago."

"It was last Thursday. Four days ago. It was last Thursday when I told you."

She was looking at my bandage. "When was the last time somebody looked at that head?"

"Yesterday."

"Uh-huh, well you might have a concussion and that bandage is starting to unravel." She reached for the little starched nurse's hat on the bureau and started out of the room. "They can do it for you in the E.R."

"Hey—wait a minute. We're not finished talking."

She turned in the doorway. The starched white uniform caught the sunlight from the window and bloomed. The color in her hair and eyes turned to primary red and blue. She was a daytime phantom I had to squint to see. "Look," she said. "I'm glad you're okay. I was worried about you. But you should know, there's been a lot of changes. So, don't expect us to just start up again like before. It's different now." She turned and walked out.

"What's different? ...Cathy? What are you talking about...?" I could hear her footsteps on the stairs. "Hey," I shouted. "Don't you want to know what happened to my head?"

After she left, I showered for a long time, taking pains to keep the bandage dry. I was confused and annoyed by the scant sympathy from my wife. Now I was going to have to deal with the whole emergency room hassle just to have the dressing changed. I considered skipping the whole thing and making do with the old bandage till the evening but then I got a look at myself in the mirror. The bandage—probably twice as large as it needed to be—had slipped to where it sat crooked, making my ear stick out even farther. By anyone's definition, I looked nuts.

I pulled a blue oxford shirt and some clean khakis out of the closet in the hall that served as my wardrobe. Cathy had claimed the master bedroom walk-in from day one and had kept it running at capacity ever since. The house was quiet with the kids away. I went downstairs to the kitchen and put on a pot of coffee. Cathy didn't drink it and had given up making it for me because I'd complained so often about it being too weak or strong. Usually I was kidding, just trying to get a rise out of her but that had backfired because she'd quit making it.

I went out to the hallway looking for the newspaper. Cathy normally left it on the hall table by the front door under Sara's duck painting—a murky little oil featuring a pair of ducks in an antique gilt frame, the kind of innocuous decoration that escapes notice until someone points it out. Cathy had been tickled to find it at some flea market or garage sale, calling it "a real find," saying it was perfect for that spot in the hallway and I suppose it was. She'd hung it a few months after Sara was born and there it had remained, unremarked-on, until the day two-year old Sara, in her mother's arms, pointed to it and pronounced "Duck," just as clear as could be. She must have recognized them from excursions to the City Park duck pond where the kids often delighted in agitating the local flock with a bag of breadcrumbs.

But now, as I reached for the paper, I noticed the ducks

were gone. In their place hung a delicate little watercolor seascape. I couldn't imagine Cathy moving the duck painting unless Sara had convinced her to move it to her bedroom. Walking back to the kitchen with the paper, I was struck again with the feeling that I was a stranger in my own house. The rooms, though familiar, felt foreign as if I'd lived in them a long time ago in a different life and had come back to visit. The house hadn't changed but I had. Somehow, I was different.

Back in the kitchen I scanned the local paper over my coffee. We subscribed at home to the Walnut Hill Gazette. Cathy read it to keep up with events around town, activities for the kids, movie schedules, etc. I'd never found much in there that interested me. It was my habit to pick up the Chronicle at the BART station and read it on the train. But today the front-page headline seized my attention: "Snoggers Return." Here was another article describing how the police were responding, on an almost nightly basis, to widespread incidents of snogging at local country clubs.

Snogging? I put the paper down and stood at the kitchen counter trying to recall if I'd ever heard the word 'snog' used in a golfing context by anyone other than Floyd. It certainly was catching on fast. In an adjacent column, another, smaller headline caught my eye: "Stickley to Allow Sixsomes." In an effort to keep up with rising demand, the story began, Stickley Municipal Golf Course had revised its policy and was now permitting groups of up to six players.

Sixsomes! I threw the paper down. Fivesomes were bad enough, but this was utter bullshit. If you're going to do that, why bother with groups at all? Why not just allow golfers to tee off whenever they felt like it? Let 'em roam the layout in packs! Sixsomes! No wonder desperate golfers were sneaking out after dark for a little snog.

When I called the office, Susan wasn't in yet, so I left a voicemail saying I'd be late for the San Anselmo meeting. I pictured her shaking her head when she got the message, certain I was playing golf. She didn't know it yet but that was the old Charley. From now on, family and career came first. My near-death experience in the desert had left me determined to re-focus my life. Or it might have been the hurt look on Cathy's face last Thursday morning when I told her I was going. When—I realized now—we both knew I was lying.

It was nine-thirty. I needed to get moving if I was going to have my head re-bandaged, catch a train and make it to work before lunch. Late Friday, as his last official act before the weekend, Barnett had ordered a "full frontal"—Susan's description—on the San Anselmo account for Monday. That meant I needed to hit the ground running. Barnett would be on the warpath and nasty-bump-on-the-head excuses wouldn't fly today, especially if golf was suspected.

Even in its present sorry state—and to my surprise—after I'd moved the boxes and hosed off the dust and cobwebs, the Taurus started up without much difficulty. At the first stoplight, I caught a look at myself in the rearview mirror and was once again amazed at how crazy a large bandage wrapped around your head can make you look.

St. Helen's is a medium-sized hospital located on Ridge Road in the northernmost section of Walnut Hill a good five miles from the BART station. It was nearly ten a.m. by the time I pulled into the crowded visitor's lot and was lucky to find a parking place in the farthest row from the Emergency Room door. The waiting room was filled with patients. When I went to sign in, the duty nurse informed me there'd be a two-hour wait for treatment. At that rate, considering the three quarters of an hour train ride to the city, the San Anselmo meeting would be long over before I made it to the office.

I rushed off to look for Cathy. She was a staff nurse in the orthopedic wing on the third floor but, there was no sign of her around the nurse's station. A nurse I didn't know told me Cathy had taken a patient down to x-ray and ought to be back soon. I hung around for a few minutes, leaning on the counter, watching the clock, but also checking out the nurse I'd spoken to as she sorted charts and filed them away in a steel cabinet. She was a knockout, early twenties, blonde, and possessed of a positively heroic figure that threatened to burst at any moment from her tight sheath-style white uniform. At one point, she looked up, caught me watching her and smiled.

"Filing's pretty boring."

"One of those necessary evils?"

"Totally. It's sure not something you picture yourself doing when you're applying to nursing school."

"I suppose not. How long have you been at St. Helen's?"

"Just a few weeks. I'm still pretty green." She laughed. "That's why the supervisor's got me doing this. I'm sure they're afraid I'll kill somebody."

"What made you want to be a nurse?"

Her eyes lit up when she said: "Doctors."

I laughed and saw her cheeks flush. "What happened to your head?" she said.

"Got a concussion. They took a few stitches."

She wrinkled her nose at my bandage. "Did they do that for you in the E.R.?"

"Oh, no. This happened Friday night. I was hoping I could get it redressed up here."

Now a polite little grimace. "This is orthopedics. You really need to get someone from the E.R. to look at it."

"Yeah, I know but they're all jammed up and I thought maybe I'd come up and see if I could get my wife to do it."

"Your wife?"

"Cathy… Cathy Cotter."

"Cathy Cotter's your wife?" The way she said it, it was more a stunned statement than a question.

"Yeah," I said and then grinned at her look of bewilderment. "Is that okay?"

"No—I mean yeah…" She turned redder now. "I just… had no idea—" She caught herself. "Could you excuse me a minute?" She walked to the other side of the station and picked up the phone. I could hear a voice on the other end answer: "X-ray," and then the nurse asking for Cathy. There followed a short, muted conversation punctuated by bursts of giggling. The young nurse hung up and walked back over to me.

"Cathy says she's going to be down in X-ray for a while so why don't I see if I can re-do that for you."

"That would be great," I told her. "I really appreciate it. I'm kind of in a rush to get to work."

The nurse, whose name she said was Robyn with a 'y,' sat me down on a stool near a supply cabinet and went to work unraveling the old dressing.

"Gee, they really went to town on you," she said.

"Yeah. I think they were in a hurry to get rid of me."

"They must not have known who you are."

"It was kind of a misunderstanding all around."

Robyn giggled. I could feel her breath on my ear as she pulled the gauze away.

"I'm sorry. I didn't recognize you when you came in. It's probably the bandage."

"Don't worry about it," I told her. "No reason why you should. We haven't met, right?"

"Oh, no. But I've certainly heard a lot about you."

"Really? From Cathy?"

"Um-hmm, and everyone. You're pretty famous around here."

"I am?"

Robyn stopped unraveling and looked at me.

"Are you kidding? The kind of work you do, why wouldn't you be?"

"You've seen some of my work?"

"Well, I'm aware of it and how difficult it must be. You do so much to help people. That's actually another reason I went into nursing—so I could be there for people."

"Well, I'm flattered. What are some that you've seen? San Anselmo? Mrs. Beebles?"

"Gee, I don't know them by name. They must be very

grateful."

"Yeah," I said wryly. "You'd think they would be."

She secured a pair of clamps. The new bandage felt tighter on my head. She stepped back, using a hand to smooth out her starched skirt. Watching her, it occurred to me it had been years since I'd seen a nurse dressed like that—or it might have been in a period movie. Nurses didn't wear tight, crispy white dresses anymore. Did they? I mean outside of porno films? Other nurses had passed by while Robyn was working on me. What had they been wearing? At least one of them had worn a shirt type dress with buttons up the front, hadn't she? And then—wait a minute—what had Cathy been wearing this morning? The odd, fish-out-of-water feeling swelled up again.

"There you go, doctor" she said, laughing like we were at a party. "Now we don't look so much like 'Return of the Mummy.'"

"Thanks," I said, and was about to shake her hand when I realized what she'd just said. "You called me *doctor.*"

"Uh-huh."

"Why did you do that?"

"Because… you are one?"

"No, I'm not."

"You're Dr. Cotter, chief of neuro-surgery."

I smiled and shook my head. "You've got me confused with somebody else. I'm in advertising."

Now she burst out laughing.

"Why is that funny?"

"Oh—I'm sorry. You just looked so—when you said, 'I'm in advertising'—you know, with your head all bandaged like that. It just made you look kinda crazy."

"But I *am* in advertising."

Robyn frowned.

"You're not Dr. Cotter?"

I shook my head.

"But you're Cathy Cotter's husband."

"That's right."

"Cathy Cotter is married to our chief of surgery."

"No, she's not. She's married to me."

Robyn was nodding. "Dr. Cotter."

"No."

Robyn folded her arms. "Okay, if you're not Dr. Cotter then what are you doing in this hospital?"

"I'm having my head… uh—"

We passed a long moment in silence. I felt disoriented, sick to my stomach. Keep it under control, I told myself. You have a concussion. Perception is bound to be skewed.

Seeing my distress, Robyn reached out and stroked my bandage. "Don't worry, Doctor Cotter," she said. "You've had a nasty blow to the head. You probably just need rest."

"Well, I…"

"You know," Robyn said, "it's only natural that sometimes we need to get away from who we are and the pressures we face every day. We learned that in psychology class. I mean, goodness, especially somebody like you. What a responsibility—I mean to work with the human brain—*actually hold it in your hand*. Just thinking about it gives me goose bumps."

"Okay," I jumped off the stool and backed toward the wall. Robyn let out a little squeal as if a mouse had run across her feet.

"What's going on?" I could hear the alarm in my voice. "Where is he?"

"Where is who?"

"You know who—*Floyd*."

Robyn was measuring the distance to the phone with her eyes.

"Dr. Cotter—"

I strode quickly over to an unmarked door across from the nurse's station and jerked it open. Inside was a bunch of mops and a bucket on wheels.

"Where is he?" I demanded.

"I don't know who you mean."

"Did Floyd tell you I was a doctor?"

"Floyd?"

"Yes, Floyd. You've been talking to Floyd."

"I don't think I know anyone named Floyd."

"Come off it, Robyn. There's only one person in the entire world dumb enough to think I'm a brain surgeon. You must have heard it from him."

"I didn't realize it was supposed to be a secret."

"Oh, Christ," I said. "Who else have you told?"

"No one—I…"

"Robyn, look at me. There is no way in hell that I'm a surgeon or any other kind of doctor. I got a D in biology—flunked chemistry. I pass out at the sight of blood. Robyn, believe me when I tell you there are people out there whose asses are more qualified than I am to be a doctor. I write television commercials for God's sake!"

That's when the loudspeaker over the desk blared out: "Dr. Cotter, line four. Dr. Cotter, please, line four."

Robyn was staring at me. "You want to take that?" she said.

Recriminations

Through all the weekend's craziness and uncertainty, I'd convinced myself that all I needed to do was get home. There I'd find logical answers for everything that had happened, I'd square things with Cathy, ask forgiveness, and hopefully everything would get back to normal. But that was all out the window. All I'd found were more questions—frightening ones. In my frantic state of mind, San Anselmo or not, going in to the office seemed like a bad idea. Instead, I drove the Ford over to the Bank of Walnut Hill and parked in the lot the bank shared with the paint store.

Downtown Walnut Hill had little to distinguish it from a thousand other American towns, which is probably what the founding fathers had in mind. The sign out on Cumberland Road, listing the population as 46,014, hadn't been updated in years but I suspected the total was still relatively accurate.

A bank guard opened the door for me, and I cut through the lobby past the strident woman in the customer service kiosk who hoped I was having a nice day. Mike had a corner office behind a glass partition with "Loans" stenciled on it. Ron had his own cubicle, but he spent most of his workday in a chair across the desk from Mike—where the action was.

"Charley Cotter, as I live and breathe."

I turned and found myself staring at Ron Baxter—at least it looked like Ron. He was basically the same guy I'd last seen wrestling with Ed the pilot for the controls of the airplane. But there were changes. His hair, dark brown and slightly wavy—he'd always kept it short and parted on the side—

had been tipped and streaked with blonde highlights and aggressively styled into a sort of show dog frizz. The wire frame glasses he normally wore had been replaced with a trendy pair of lavender plastic rectangles. And was that… eye shadow?

"Ron?"

"We were wondering if we were ever going to see you again." It was the same voice, but the delivery was broadly effeminate, almost camp.

"What happened to you?" I said.

He grinned. "You mean my hair? I'm having a new person do it. Do you like it?" He did a little turn in front of me. His striped suit was more form fitting than any I'd seen him wear. His build had always bordered on stocky, really not the type of body you want to show off, but this jacket was tapered to the waist and short enough to see just how tightly his slacks were drawn across his rear end.

"Well?" he said.

"Did that happen in the crash?" I asked him.

His face fell. "What crash? I paid top dollar for this cut."

"The plane crash, remember? Palm Springs? Your friend Ed's Cessna?"

"Ed from Palm Springs?"

"What happened to the plane, Ron?" I said, grabbing him by the necktie. Ron shrieked like a co-ed in a slasher flick. "Watch out—that's Hermes' for the love of God!"

Over his shoulder, I could see heads turn and a bank guard move in our direction. With my free hand, I clapped Ron on the back and laughed as loud as I could. "That's great," I said. "You're a funny guy, Ron." The guard saw it and slowed down, unsure. Ron stared at me, none too sure himself. "What is wrong with you, Cotter?"

"Wave to the guard," I told him.

"Let go of my tie."

"Is there a problem, Mr. Baxter?" The guard was past middle age but looked like he could handle himself.

"Nope," I said. "No problem. I was just telling Mr. Baxter a funny story about a plane crash in the desert and how the survivors were abandoned by their friends."

"Mr. Baxter?" The guard eyed the bandage on my head.

Ron gently tugged the end of his tie out of my hand and waved it at him. "I think we're all right. Thank you, Carlos."

Carlos gave me one more long, measuring look before heading back to his post.

"What is your problem?" said Ron. "What is this mysterious plane crash everyone's talking about?"

"Don't do this, Ron," I said.

"Don't do what? Dave called Saturday morning from Palm Springs babbling something about a crash like I'm supposed to know what he's talking about."

I had to close my eyes. The situation coupled with his bizarre appearance was making me lightheaded. "Please Ron, I can't do this."

"You poor dear. What happened to your head?"

I was standing right in front of him, but his voice sounded distant with an echo on the end of it. Like he was calling to me down a well.

"I think I need to sit down."

Ron brought me into a conference room, gave me a cup of water and then went to get Mike. I swallowed the water in one gulp. The feeling was back, stronger than ever. Fish-out-of-water-meets-déjà vu is the best I can describe it.

The conference room was plain and unremarkable even for a bank. A long glass tabletop sat on a chromed metal base surrounded by metal chairs with upholstered seats and backs. There being nothing else to look at in the room, I found myself staring at a large colored chart propped on an aluminum easel. After a few moments, I felt better and went over for a closer look. It appeared to be a schematic diagram of a golf course. There was a clear sheet of plastic rolled up over the top with some sort of grid on it. I pulled it down so that it overlaid the schematic. The grid divided the golf course into rectangular sections that looked like home sites. There was no writing on the chart, no golf course or project name except for the initials: S.M.G.C. in the upper right-hand corner. I stood there looking at it for a minute or two. The layout of the holes looked familiar.

Mike came into the room all smiles. I was relieved to see no change in his appearance. Ron followed him in and closed the door.

"Well, stranger—decided to come back, huh?" Mike walked over and hugged me. "What happened to your head?"

"Now, what do you *think* happened to my head?"

"I don't know. I got this bizarre phone call from Dave over the weekend. He said you guys were in a plane crash?"

There seemed a genuine concern in his eyes I didn't care for. I glanced over at Ron. Same thing. These guys didn't appear to be lying. My anxiety level spiked to new heights.

"And I suppose that was the first you heard of it?"

Mike frowned. "Well, yes."

"You don't know anything about a Cessna... the storm?"

"Only what Dave told me. That the two of you had been in a crash."

"Did he mention there were rescue teams out looking for you and Ron?"

"Why would they be looking for us?" said Mike.

"Look, Mike, cut the shit. Just tell me what happened to the plane."

"It crashed."

"So, it *did* crash?"

"Yes."

"So, you knew about it."

"Yes... Dave told us."

"I mean before that. You knew the plane had crashed."

"I don't think so. Was it on the news?"

"No! It wasn't on the news!"

"Well then, how would I—?"

"Because," I shouted and kicked a nearby chair leg, "you were in it when it crashed!"

"Hey," said Mike. "Take it easy." He looked over at Ron who was frowning. "Charley, you're not making sense... how could we have been in a plane crash and not know about it?"

"That's what I'm asking," I said.

They were staring at me with what looked like genuine concern. This couldn't be an act. But, at the same time, I needed it to be an act. If it wasn't an act, then... what?

"Look, guys, square with me. I don't know what this is about, what you're trying to cover up or why. Whatever it is, I'm sure you've got your reasons. I'm okay with that. And I guarantee my lips will be sealed. I promise. But, for the sake of my mental health and... general peace of mind, it'd really help me out to have some answers. Okay?"

Both bankers nodded.

"The truth now, okay?

More nods.

"Okay, good... now... what happened out in the desert Friday night? Did we crash or not?"

They stopped nodding and stood there, looking at me. After a long moment, Mike said, "Shouldn't you be asking Dave? Sounds like he's got the information."

"Mike, I'm asking you, begging you. What happened to the plane?"

Mike threw up his hands. "What plane?"

"What about Ed from Palm Springs?" said Ron. "Have you asked him?"

After another extended pause, Mike had us sit down at the conference table. Ron poured me another glass of water.

"Charley," Mike said, "when was the last time somebody

took a look at that head?"

"Few minutes ago, at the hospital."

"Well, good. So, you're getting the care you need."

"What'd they tell you?" said Ron. "If you don't mind my asking."

"Nasty blow to the head."

"Happen in the crash?"

I could only shake my head.

Mike leaned close to Ron and whispered something. Ron's face brightened, and he nodded. "So, anyway," he said. "What brings you back?"

"What did you expect me to do? Settle down on that wind farm?" I noted a slight, hysterical edge to my voice that Mike, if he heard it, chose to ignore. He leaned across the table and folded his hands. "We were just wondering if you'd had a chance to do some thinking and might now have had some second thoughts about our little match."

"Match?"

Mike nodded, smiling. "The one we offered you. The one you were all set to play?"

"The one you ran out on," said Ron.

"Let's not be judgmental," said Mike. "I'm sure Charley had his reasons." Then he grinned at me. "Cause if you're interested, we might be able to set it up again."

"Oh, yeah." Ron winked at me. "I'm betting Larry will go for it. In a heartbeat."

"Larry who? What are you talking about?"

"The phone on the table buzzed. Ron picked it up and listened for a few seconds then hung up. "The Little Sisters of Mercy are in the lobby," he said to Mike. "Here to make a mortgage payment."

Mike frowned. "You told them cash or money order, right? No more rubber checks or baked cookies."

"They know," Ron said. "They've been told. Cash or the street."

"The plane, Mike," I said. "What about the plane?"

"Sorry, Charley," Mike said, getting up. "You'll have to tell us about it later. Meanwhile, let us put out some feelers, see if we can't line something up. Give us twenty-four hours."

Ron was nodding. "That should be plenty."

"Feelers?"

"By the way," said Mike. "How've you been hitting them?"

"Well, not too ba—you mean *since Friday*?"

"I'll bet he hasn't lost a step," Ron said with a wink. He rubbed his hands together. "This is going to be great."

Mike came over, clapped me on the back and led me to the door. "Meet us for lunch tomorrow," he said. We should have something to talk about by then."

"I can't have lunch tomorrow. I have to work."

"All right. Let's push to Wednesday."

"Wait a minute," I said. "I'm not leaving here until I get some—know what? "

"Wednesday," he said. "We'll talk about everything Wednesday. And we want to hear more about that plane crash. But, right now, you need to go and rest that head."

"No—I'm not leaving until—"

"How about we say one o'clock at Meadowbank?"

"Forget it. I'm not—Meadowbank?"

"One o'clock in the men's grill?"

"In the daytime?"

Ron grinned. "You'll be our guest."

"Hey, tell you what," said Mike. "Why don't you bring your clubs and we'll see if we can get in a quick round afterward? Knock some rust off that game of yours."

"Maybe Charley's feeling too banged up," said Ron.

"No!" I almost shouted. "I'm fine. But—"

"Perfect. Then for sure, bring your clubs. See you Wednesday."

"Yeah," I said. "Okay. See you Wednesday."

I walked out of the bank in a daze.

Meadowbank. We were going to play Meadowbank. I was leaving without answers but, I'll confess that, at that particular moment, losing my mind seemed a reasonable trade for the opportunity to play a round at Meadowbank. In daylight. Without Floyd.

Then, moments later, getting into the Taurus, I noticed the graffiti scrawled on the paint store wall:

'It's impossible to beat Snog at his own game.'

Phoning It In

"John Barnett Advertising."

"Susan Schager, please."

"She's in a meeting. I can put you through to her voicemail."

"Fine."

Beep.

"Susan, it's me. Look, I hate to do this to you, but something's come up—some very important personal business—and I'm afraid I'm going to be later than I previously thought. I know the San Anselmo people are in town and John's probably gunning for me but I'm afraid I don't have a choice. I'll explain everything when I see you. If you could kind of smooth things over with John, I'd appreciate it. Thanks. See you soon."

Beep.

"Me again. Listen, it's important that John understands that my not being there is not golf related. It has to do with personal problems that have only recently ari—been brought to my attention. You see, I'm afraid he's going to assume it's about golf, but you've got to let him know in no uncertain terms that he's completely mistaken about that. No golf, no way. Thanks, Susan, I really appreciate it. I'll make this up to you."

Beep.

"Oh, my God, Susan, you know what you can tell him? I can't believe I forgot this—you can tell Barnett I was in a plane crash. Can you believe that completely slipped my mind? I was in a plane crash and now I've got this huge bandage on my head, and I'm supposed to keep stopping by the hospital so they can put on fresh ones. I don't know why I didn't think of that when I called before. Just tell John the plane crashed and that I'm okay but I'll have to miss the San Anselmo meeting, but I'll be in first thing in the morning—I mean first thing Wednesday morning. All right? Great. Wow."

Beep.

"Susan, if John wants to know what I was doing on a plane, tell him you're not sure but you doubt whether it had anything to do with golf. Got that? You doubt if it had anything to do with it. That way, if it turns out later that it *did* have something to do with it, you're covered. You didn't say it didn't—you just doubted it. I'm sure you get the distinction. And if he starts asking why it wasn't on the news or anything, just say it was because they never found the plane, okay? They couldn't find the plane. I'll fill you in when I see you, okay? Thanks, Susan. I really appreciate this and I'm really going to make this up to you. Have faith."

Beep.

"Yeah, that part about them not finding the plane doesn't make a lot of sense. I mean, if they couldn't find the plane, how'd they find me, right? Or why don't I just tell them where it is? See what I mean? Except it's not that simple. I'd tell them where the plane was if I knew but—you know what? Forget about the plane altogether. It's too confusing. Tell John it's a matter of life or death—that's why I can't come in. You don't have to be specific. Just say it was a matter of life or death and now I'm dealing with the aftermath, you know repercussions, insurance claims, all that. But please make sure he knows that I'm okay. It was a miracle, but I came away with just a nasty blow to the head—although I'm thinking it might be worse than first thought because I haven't been myself since the crash—come to think of it, neither has anyone else—been themselves I mean. Okay? We'll talk later.

Beep

"Okay, we straight on this now? Matter of life or death. Nothing to do with golf. Got it? Great. Thanks, Susan. You're the best.

Mecca

I suppose I should have gone to work but, instead, drove over to Mallard's range where I intended to confront Floyd. The bankers had successfully if temporarily—deflected my attempt to extract answers about the plane, but there was also the confusion about hot nurses and brain surgery that needed to be sorted out.

It should have been obvious the first time I saw Cathy in the R-rated nurse's uniform that he was somehow involved in… whatever this was. Only in the context of Floyd, did any of this begin to make sense. He could have run into Cathy—perhaps while stalking her—and started chatting. She'd inadvertently spilled the beans about me not being a brain surgeon, and by way of getting even, he'd told her about me going to the desert and now both were conspiring to teach me a lesson.

The sexy nurse's uniforms were a nice touch although it was hard to imagine Cathy and the other nurses on the orthopedic floor willing to cooperate in Floyd's fantasy. Somebody was going way out of her way to teach me a lesson. I should have known I was being had the first time I heard one of Floyd's favorite sybarite-nurse catchphrases coming out of the mouth of—who was it—the doctor in Palm Springs?

Uh-oh…

I could feel my stomach knot up again. My theory was not even fully launched and already taking on water. There was no way Floyd or even Cathy could have gotten to the doctor in Palm Springs. They wouldn't have known about the plane crash or that I was in a hospital. Besides, wasn't I kidding myself with this conspiracy centering around Floyd? Floyd on his own—or even with help—couldn't mastermind the digging of a hole let alone an elaborate prank like this. Farting in your backswing was more his style.

Mallard's parking lot was strangely crowded for a Monday noon hour. I drove around the block a couple times and wound up parking on the street. As soon as I stepped through the gate, a big guy in a windbreaker with "Security" printed down each sleeve appeared and asked me if I had a reservation.

I begged his pardon.

"May I help you?" he said.

"What did you have in mind?"

The guard gave my bandage and me a long look-over and then he lifted a walkie-talkie and spoke into it. "This is Bernard at the parking lot gate. We may have a problem."

Off to my left, next to the hurricane fence that separated the range from the parking lot, a guy clutching a golf bag shouted: "Hey, buddy, the line's over here." There had to be at least three dozen golfers waiting with him.

"You got some kind of event going on?" I asked Bernard. But he was looking over my shoulder.

"Watch your back, sir," he said.

I turned around in time to be nearly bowled over by another security guard escorting a contingent of middle-aged Asian men in expensive golf clothes.

"Welcome to Mallard's, gentlemen," Bernard said.

I moved to follow them, but he placed a hand on my chest. "Sir," he said. "If you don't have a reservation, I'm going to need you to wait in that line over there by the fence."

"What do I need a reservation for?"

"Sir, as you can see, we're very crowded. There are only so many stalls." Bernard stopped talking to me and listened to a voice in his earpiece. "Roger that," he said into his radio. Then he yelled over to a guard at the head of the line. "Send two." The guard lifted a chain and a pair of middle-aged ladies in pastel golf outfits hurried onto the range.

"What is this?" I asked, looking around at the milling crowd and the eager faces pressed to the fence.

"This is Mallard's, sir. It's a driving range."

"I know it's a driving range. Why do you suppose I'm carrying golf clubs?"

But the guard was listening to his radio again saying, "Yeah, copy that."

"Look," I told him. "I just want to hit some balls."

Bernard cracked his gum and pointed at the herd of golfers by the fence. "Dude, you see those people over there? They just want to hit balls too."

I walked over and joined the end of the line. I didn't see anyone I recognized and that struck me right away as strange. When you spent as much time at Mallard's as I did, you got to know the faces.

I peered through the fence, craning for a glimpse of whatever had drawn this overflow crowd to a sleepy driving range. Golfers stood shoulder to shoulder, in rows two and three deep behind each stall struggling to hold position against a buffeting surge of bags and humanity. A scuffle broke out over a stall up near the snack bar. A couple of security guards appeared, shoved their way to the scene, and pulled the combatants apart. They dragged them out through the clubhouse shack and presumably out to the sidewalk. They were no sooner gone when another brace of golfers rushed to claim the vacant stall. Within seconds, another fracas began, and the guards were back sorting it out.

Out on the range, golf balls rained like hailstones to nearly obscure the grass. The ball cart motored at full throttle, tracing a haphazard pattern of green in a sea of dimpled white. Even from fifty yards away I could see that the driver was not Floyd.

In a stall near the center—finally a familiar face— Handsome Freddy, the golf pro—employing his hands-on teaching method on an attractive redhead. She was hitting it pretty well and, each time, he'd grin and try to hug her. One of these days, I thought, a jealous boyfriend is gonna step in and send Freddy into early retirement.

114

By the time the guards ushered me in, the sun was nearly down, and the glare of the range lights heightened the carnival atmosphere. I was in no condition to fight for a stall, so I leaned my golf bag against the tall hedge behind the benches and worked my way down the firing line looking for Mallard or anyone else able to explain this madness.

Another scuffle broke out near the snack bar. I recognized Mrs. Yee in the thick of it, swatting a short man with her cap. Hollerin' Hank was there too. It looked like the short guy was his student. Hank was hollerin' his case to the guards. Mrs. Yee was shaking her head, pointing at him. There were other participants I didn't recognize, a red-faced senior in a pair of too-short, sky-blue shorts and a country-club-looking guy in a cashmere sweater and pleated slacks who must have said something because, all of a sudden, Hank had him in a headlock—the poor man's horned rimmed glasses dangling from one ear. One of the guards came up behind Hank and got him in a chokehold while another tried to pry his arm from Country Club's neck.

"Hank," the guard was yelling. "For God's sake, you're killing him!"

I felt a tap on my shoulder and turned around. Shortgrass stood there grinning at me. "Well, brother Charles. The man returns."

"Hey, Grass-man."

"I'm delighted to see you, my man. How long has it been?"

"What do you mean?

"Must be a while now. What'd you do to your head?"

"Uh—ran into a—it's nothing."

"When'd you get back?"

"Last night."

Shortgrass threw his head back and did his hearty, James Earl Jones laugh. "And you just had to come straight over and check out the old range. Couldn't stay away, huh?"

"Guess not. What's going on anyway? What's with all these people?"

Shortgrass looked at me. "You mean the tourists? Hell,

son, we been discovered."

"By who?"

"Damn, you have been out of touch. Mallard's is the spot of the moment, man. We having our fifteen minutes of fame. You in the shrine of Birdwell."

"Huh?"

This is the house that Floyd built."

I stared at him.

"You don't know what I'm talking about, do you? They don't have TV out in the desert?"

"You knew I was in the—?"

"So then, you don't know about Floyd?"

"What about him? Something happen to him?"

"I'll say it did. He went and won the Open."

"Who did?"

"Floyd Birdwell."

"What about him?"

"I just told you. He won the Open."

"What open? What are you talking about?"

Shortgrass shook his head. Then he leaned in close to my face. "Chuck, read my lips. Floyd won the U.S. Open. Final round was yesterday. Over at Pebble Beach."

Shortgrass saw the look on my face and laughed.

"Man, Charles, you want to close your mouth before a bird flies in there and craps on your teeth. What'd they do to your head out there in the desert?"

"The U.S. Open?"

He nodded. "By nineteen shots, over Spieth. Koepka was twenty-two back, took third."

"That's impossible."

"It was on TV."

"How'd he do that?"

Shortgrass was grinning again. "Don't ask me. He just did it."

"Floyd can't win the Open."

"There's thirty-five thousand gallery members and maybe ten million more on TV saw him do it. In all the papers."

"Where is he now?"

"Off celebrating somewhere is my guess."

"And all these people…?"

"It's like a pilgrimage, man. This, right here, is Mecca. People want to rub up against greatness—see where the miracle began. That's what I thought you were doing here. Figured you heard about it out in the desert and had to see for yourself."

I blinked a couple times. "How'd you know I was in the desert? Floyd tell you?"

"I don't think so. Haven't seen much of him since the sectionals." He was looking at me with concern. "Say, you all right? Your face about as white as that bandage."

Shortgrass led me by the arm over to the water cooler where I took a long drink and then slumped down on the bench beside it.

"That's a significant looking bandage. You didn't go and have brain surgery out there in the desert, did you?"

I shook my head. "It was an accident—plane crash."

"Plane crash. Didn't hear nothin' about that."

A crimson-faced, Hank stumbled past in the clutches of a pair of security guards. A third guard brought up the rear, shouting into his walkie-talkie. Shortgrass said he needed to make sure Hank didn't sideswipe his Lincoln and followed them out to the parking lot, leaving me to wonder whether the shock of the crash was only just now kicking in, interfering with my ability to process information.

Floyd-wins-the-Open? That unlikely development now vied with the-plane-crash-that-didn't-happen for top spot on my conundrum list. What had Shortgrass said? He won it by nineteen shots over whom? The world's golfing elite? The Floyd I knew would have had a hard time beating me. And—wait a minute—when had he had time to win the Open? I'd just seen him here at the range last Thursday night when I told him about our upcoming weekend in the desert. That was just four days ago. If the Open were held over the weekend, that would mean that, as we stood here talking Thursday night, the first round would have already been played. He hadn't said a word about it. And, never one to let his horn go un-blown, it was inconceivable he wouldn't have.

The conversation with Shortgrass left me with a gut ache to match my throbbing head that I knew stemmed from fear I was losing my mind. I could have come up with a half dozen possible scenarios for the missing plane crash—probable or not—and maybe, one or two semi-plausible explanations for the nurse's outfits or confusion at the hospital about my identity. But Floyd not telling me that he had entered—and then qualified for the U.S. Open—that was way beyond impossible. That was nuts. Somebody was putting somebody on. But… what were all these people doing at Mallard's?

My battered brain was chewing on all this when the sweet-swinging redhead wound up her lesson with Handsome Freddy and bounced off in my direction. As she got closer, I could see her hair was more auburn than red. A thick lock of it hung down straight covering half her face. She wore a nifty little wine-colored leather biker jacket over tee shirt and jeans. It was an outfit you'd never associate with golf, but she humped her sticks like she knew what she was doing. She was no more than a yard away when she stopped in her tracks and looked straight at me. Her lips were lacquered deep red. Her eyes were impossibly blue. Guys like me don't usually get to talk to girls like that. We're only supposed to stare at them. But this one was speaking to me.

"Charley?"

Cathy. But not the Cathy I knew. This one was younger by quite a bit or… did she just seem that way? Had she looked this way that morning—as if her natural, subtle beauty had been somehow "amped up?"

As if over the course of a single weekend, she'd undergone a transformation from self-proclaimed golf widow and soccer mom into a Harley-Davidson pin up?

"Cathy, what are you doing here?"

"What's wrong with you? You look all crazy with your mouth open like that."

"You were taking a golf lesson?"

"Uh, yeah. I had a lesson with Freddy."

"You don't play golf."

"I don't, huh? Who says that? You?"

"No… I mean… yeah. I mean, what the hell? When did this… start?"

"She was shaking her head. "Same old Charley. Show up out of nowhere and start right in criticizing."

"I'm not criticizing. I've just never—what do you mean, out of nowhere?

"Let me ask you a question, Charley. Why did you come back?"

"What kind of question is that?"

"An honest one. Don't you think it's time we started being honest with each other?"

"Yeah, I do. That's why I came right out and told you about the weekend."

"What weekend?"

"Just—this past weekend."

"Why do you keep bringing up the weekend?"

"I told you—because I lied to you and I feel bad."

She sighed deeply and shook her head. "Charley, I really have no idea what you're talking about."

"Remember…I told you I had business in San Diego but, really—"

She was looking at her watch. "I've got to get back to work."

"Wait a minute," I said. "I need you to hear this."

"Why?"

"Why? Because you need to understand what happened."

"I already know what happened. One day, you decide to take off for the desert and now you decide to come back. What else? Is there anything I've left out?"

I stared at her, this stranger, who looked and sounded like my wife but who otherwise bore no resemblance at all. "What happened to you?"

"Look, I'm sorry. I'm just tired and very surprised to see you. It was kind of a shock to come home last night and find you there." There was a catch in her voice, and she looked away. I thought she might be tearing up. But then she took a deep breath and turned back, and her eyes were dry. And cold. "I'm glad you're back and if you need to stay at the house for a while, until you find a place, I guess it's okay. But we can't keep having these conversations. Things are different now. You need to understand that. We've both moved on. You've got to let it go."

A Chilly Reception

Cathy came home late that night and, next morning, was gone before I woke up. She'd claimed the alarm clock along with the master bedroom for her own and hadn't bothered to wake me. By the time I dug myself out of the sofa, I'd already missed my usual train to the city and the one after that.

I drove the Ford over to the BART station and caught the 8:24 for San Francisco. With rush hour nearly over, the railcar was less than half filled with business stragglers, students and suburban matrons headed to town for some afternoon shopping. In the rush for the train I'd neglected to pick up the Chronicle for the ride so, without paper or cell phone, there was nothing to do except slouch down in the seat and watch the East Bay roll by.

When we hit the bay tunnel and ran out of scenery, my gaze switched to the few advertisements mounted inside the car. There was one for Cal Bears football and another for a real estate broker in Concord. Then, on a poster at the other end of the car, I spotted what looked like the logo Susan had designed for the Hamlet restaurant. I couldn't recall seeing bus cards included in the media budget, so I got up and walked over for a look. You could say I was more than a little surprised when I read the copy describing the Hamlet as being "just across the fairway from Meadowbank Country Club."

My first reaction was to laugh. It appeared that someone or something had convinced Barnett to change his mind about golf-related ads. Susan must have gone to work on him after I left. But that been just last week. Even if his about-face had occurred mere moments after he threw us out of his office, that still wouldn't have left enough time for this ad to be approved by the client, get to the printer and distributed. From Barnett's desk to this railroad car was a months-long process, not days. All right, I thought. This part could be a clue. Time was somehow skewed here. Maybe whatever was happening had something to do with time.

There was nothing to see outside the window but the murky blur of tunnel walls and the reflected image of a worried man with a bandage on his head staring back at me. I realized, at that moment, that I might never get back to my family and the life we'd shared. And if the hollowness I felt was what being alone feels like, I wanted no part of it.

When the train stopped at the next station, I found myself staring at another billboard, this one mounted on the tunnel wall opposite my window. It was for a new home development in the East Bay. A happy thirty-ish couple stood in the front yard of a tract home described as a "golf course villa." The wife swung a golf club while her husband proudly looked on. Nearby a son and daughter, each with their own golf bag, stood and admired mom's swing. This one made me wince. Unlike the dad in the photograph, I hadn't shared the game with my family but kept it for myself and allowed it to get between us.

There was another ad, right next to it, for some weight loss product. It was a "before and after" ad showing a fat guy on the left, bulging out of his sweat clothes and then a thin guy on the right swinging a golf club. We're supposed to believe they're the same guy before and after. There was nothing out of the ordinary about the advertisement except for the fact that, like the Hamlet and the housing development, the advertisers had used golf to help sell their product. Well, John, I imagined saying to Barnett. Apparently, I'm not the only "communicator" using golf to get his point across.

I got off the train at Montgomery Street and bounded up the stairs into a bracing San Francisco midday.

The familiar buildings of the financial district loomed tall, blocking the sun and forming gray channels of steel, glass and concrete for the chill Pacific wind. The temperature in the city was easily twenty-five degrees cooler than in Walnut Hill, fifty minutes away. Suburbanites like me were accustomed to the phenomenon of waking up in summer and commuting into fall. That was only one of the things I liked about working in the city. Its energy never failed to invigorate me and stir my ever-reluctant creativity.

The Barnett agency occupied the top two floors of a medium high-rise office building on the northernmost edge of the financial district. Most days, believing that any San Francisco walk is preferable to a ride in one of those sardine-can muni buses, I walked the ten or so blocks from the BART station covering the distance in less than fifteen minutes. Tracing my usual path now through the city streets was familiar and comforting and I didn't hurry but paced myself, drawing strength and a bit of courage from recognizable surroundings.

Through the open door to the Helena coffee shop on Sansome I caught a glimpse of Eddie, the owner, a Greek immigrant, haranguing Stan, his long-suffering waiter and brother-in-law. In another doorway, the neighborhood UPS driver, package jammed under each arm, traded greetings with the elevator man. I dodged sideways to avoid a pair of crooked metal racks, one with umbrellas and another with postcards, gathering street dust in front of the smoke shop window, heartened to see the entire world hadn't gone nuts. Most of it was just as I remembered.

I pushed through the doors into the lobby of 553 Sacramento Street and took the elevator to the fourteenth floor, then crossed through the open glass doors inscribed with the Barnett agency logo. A new receptionist was at the front desk. The polite thing would have been for me to stop and introduce myself but there'd be time for that later. I breezed by the desk and was into the corridor when her question stopped me.

"May I help you, sir?"

"Sorry, late for the morning meeting." Adding, "It's okay, I work here."

The receptionist stood up and peered at me over the dark

rims of her glasses. She looked to be in her thirties but presented herself as much older. Her straight, nearly black hair worn up in a bun emphasized an extremely fair complexion. I had to smile. She looked like a caricature of an office spinster. Where had Barnett found this one?

"I'm sorry," she said, "your name—?"

"Charley Cotter. Maybe we can chat later."

She appeared to recognize my name, and that was a relief. At least they knew me here. But then she began punching numbers into her console.

"Mr. Cotter," she said. "Would you mind taking a seat in the lobby? Someone will be right with you."

But I was already off toward Barnett's office.

"Mr. Cotter—please!"

Barnett's corner office was empty and the door to the conference room across the hall was closed. That told me clients were in there and a meeting was underway. I had no idea who was scheduled but, as creative director, I'd be expected to be present at client meetings. I took a deep breath and absently reached up to brush the hair off my forehead. My fingers touched the bandage and I winced, not in pain, but apprehension. I had no idea what was waiting for me inside that room.

Manufacturing a grin, I opened the door and breezed in. It was reassuring to find a room full of mostly familiar faces. Barnett was in his usual seat at the middle of the long table. Susan sat in a chair to his right, reading some copy aloud. Next to her was a guy about my age I'd never seen before. Opposite them were Bill Harder and Muriel Bonebroth, the Mrs. Beeble's clients. Richie the account executive sat at the far end of the table ready and eager to embrace any emerging consensus.

"Sorry John—sorry everyone."

I glided over and flopped down on the empty chair to Barnett's left. "Don't worry," I said, pointing to my bandage. "Looks worse than it is."

Susan had stopped reading. She and the guy I didn't know were leaning forward, craning around Barnett to get a look at me. Bill and Muriel appeared to be waiting for Barnett to acknowledge my presence. Barnett simply stared for a moment then looked over at Susan who shrugged. He turned back to me, and I guessed he was pausing for dramatic effect before delivering some sarcastic greeting of the "so nice you could join us" variety. But he said instead, "Can we help you?"

His choice of phrase—and his tone in delivering it—spooked me. There was no telltale sparkle in his eyes or chuckle in his voice that said 'relax, kid, there's a punch line coming.'

"I'm sorry, John," I said, keeping my voice low and deferential. "I had an accident. I thought Susan might have passed along the message. Matter of life or golf… er death?"

Barnett started to say something but then the receptionist in her Mary Todd Lincoln get-up appeared in the doorway.

"Is everything all right in here, Mr. Barnett?"

"Who is this gentleman?" he asked her.

I started to laugh. It was so ridiculous. It had to be an act. But why I was the only one laughing?

"That's Mr. Cotter, sir."

"Oh, my God," said Susan. "He's the one who's been calling me."

Barnett looked at her. "You know this gentleman?"

I scanned the faces in the room, feeling my heart sink. Not a smile or knowing wink among them. "C'mon, guys," I said. "Seriously. Cut it out."

Across the table, Harder cleared his throat. Muriel squirmed in her chair. There was no sign of recognition in Barnett's eyes. Zero.

"Where exactly are you from, Mr…?"

"Cotter," said the receptionist.

"John," Susan said in a modulated, let's-not-upset-the-crazy-guy-tone, "Maybe we should call someone."

Considering my other bizarre encounters since returning from the desert, I probably shouldn't have been surprised. But it was a shock just the same. I knew these people, had worked beside them for years, but it was clear this was no joke. They truly had no idea who I was. We sat that way for a long, strange moment until Carl Macy, the office manager, appeared in the doorway.

"Security is on the way up," he said.

Who Are You?

"What exactly is your business here, Mr. Cotter?"

The security guard's name tag said 'Randolph.' A big man with graying temples and skin the color of bittersweet chocolate, he managed the building's security staff. He wore thick spectacles with black frames through which he now regarded me with suspicion. I'd seen Randolph often, down in the main lobby working the front desk or after six o'clock in the evening making rounds, looking into offices. He was a courteous man, experienced at avoiding confrontation. When he'd arrived, summoned by Barnett's receptionist, he hadn't ordered me out or even raised his voice but merely asked if he and I might "enjoy a word in private." We had gone out to the lobby with Carl Macy to talk things over.

"This is just a colossal misunderstanding," I told Randolph now. "You see, I work here. At least I used to."

Randolph nodded once and said, "Uh-huh. You used to work here." Then he turned to Carl. "Did Mr. Cotter use to work here, do you know?"

Carl shook his head, looking pained.

"This gentleman says you're mistaken about that."

"Carl," I said. "Are you sure you don't recognize me. Maybe from a… a while ago? Think back."

"Sorry."

"So," said Randolph. "You don't know this gentleman?"

"I'm afraid not," said Carl.

"Dammit, Carl," I said. "Cathy and I were at your wedding, what—three years ago. You had the bachelor party at that brewery in Oakland. Remember? What was his name—your best man?"

"Donald."

"Right, Donald. Remember he passed out and we had to dig the rings out of his pocket?"

Carl had a strange expression on his face. "I'm sorry," he said. "I don't know you."

"C'mon, Carl—"

Randolph held up his hand. "Mr. Cotter, it appears that Mr. Macy doesn't know you. Now, Mr. Macy, would you state your title here for Mr. Cotter?"

"I'm the office manager and head of human resources."

"And you're saying that, as far as you know, in your capacity as office manager and head of natural resources, you have no knowledge of Mr. Cotter being employed by your company now or in the past. Is that right?"

"He's never worked here. That's correct, right."

"I see."

Randolph turned back to me.

"Well, Mr. Cotter—"

"Something's very wrong here," I said.

"Mr. Cotter, I need you to calm yourself now."

"But he's wrong. I can prove it to you. I can name every client we have and the campaigns we've done for them over the last five years. Go look. There's awards with my name on them on shelves and bookcases all over these offices…"

"Mr. Cotter…" Randolph was saying. "I need you to—"

"Will you at least look?"

"Mr. Cotter, please…"

"Hold it," I said. "Wait a minute…" I reached for the keyring in my pocket. "Look, I've got the key to the men's room, right here." I fumbled through the ring and found the key. "There," I said. "What would I be doing with the key to the men's room if I don't—or didn't—ever work here? Tell me that."

"Mr. Cotter," said Randolph gravely. "Our men's room door has no lock on it. Least not in the sixteen years I've been here."

My breathing became shallow and more rapid. I heard giggling, looked around and then realized it was coming from me. Within seconds, I was hysterical. Tears poured down my cheeks. Bent over, clutching my gut, I stumbled to the sofa and collapsed. When the laughter subsided to the point where I could breathe again, I opened my eyes and saw an alarmed Randolph standing over me.

"You seem to have sustained a head injury, Mr. Cotter. I wonder—is it possible that you walked into the wrong office? This is the Barnett Agency." I don't know whether it was the words themselves or the concern in his voice when he said them, but it was enough to set me off again. I sat there, holding my sides, eyes tightly shut, convulsed in laughter, howling.

"Mr. Cotter," said Randolph. "I'm afraid I'm going to have to ask you to accompany me down to the main lobby."

I looked over at Carl Macy. We didn't see much of each other outside the office, but we'd been acquainted for years. I knew him as a competent and genuinely nice man who'd worked at the agency even longer than I had and felt sympathy for him now having to deal with this "problem" in his lobby.

"Is there someone we can call?" Carl asked gently.

"Could I just ask… your creative director's name?"

"Mathew Bray," he said.

"And how long has he been here?"

"He was here when I started and that's been—quite a while."

"A while?"

"Yes."

"Tell me something," I said. "Have either of you noticed that any time anybody asks how long anything has been going on, they always say 'a while?' Have you noticed that?"

Randolph shook his head.

"No," said Carl. "I'm afraid I haven't."

"And you don't have any idea who I am? You swear it? Swear it, Carl."

"Sorry." Then he said to Randolph, "Maybe Mr. Cotter should rest for a bit before he tries to go anywhere. How did you hurt your head, Mr. Cotter?"

"Plane crash."

"Well, no wonder you're confused. You might even have a concuss—"

"Carl," I said. "I'm sorry. I just—I keep trying to find something or somebody to help me make sense of all this but… I need answers. I need to know where I am and how I got here and…"

"There, there, now," said Randolph.

I was aware of how pathetic I must have looked sitting there bawling in the lobby. Up till then, I'd held up pretty good, considering. But now, I was like a man stumbling off a tilt-a-whirl with no sense of which way is up.

Carl came over to the sofa and laid a compassionate hand on my shoulder. "I'm sorry you seem to be in so much pain, Mr. Cotter. Is there someone we can call to come get you?"

That's when Susan walked into the lobby. She had changed into a monogrammed polo shirt and pastel cardigan over pleated rayon slacks—which could be appropriate, I suppose, for any casual occasion except she'd accessorized with a white PING visor and two-toned Footjoys with soft spikes.

Susan Schager, wearing golf clothes.

"Is everything all right, Carl?" she said.

"I think we're going to be fine," he said, sounding like a grade school teacher after a playground accident. "We're just taking a moment to collect ourselves."

I sat up rigid on the sofa, wiping tears with the back of my hand. "Susan," I said. "Why are you dressed like that?"

She looked down at herself. "What? Do I clash?"

A familiar voice rose from the hallway beyond the lobby. "Where's Susan? We've got to get out of here if we're going to make our tee time." John Barnett strode into the lobby trailed by Bill Harder and Mariel Bonebroth. It took me a moment to figure out who they were because they, too, were now dressed for the links. Barnett wore a pink Izod shirt over oyster white silk shorts, white cotton socks and penny loafers. His legs were a shade of white lighter than his shorts. I'd never seen Mariel in anything but the dourest goth get-ups. But here she was, country club chic, in loose fitting black tank top over Japanese patterned black and brown silk shorts. Harder was another story. His golf shirt was stretched tight over his Rubenesque torso and, judging from his expansive shorts, some poor circus would be doing without a tent that season. With his saddle shoes and lumpy butt, he looked like the fat kid in an old TV sitcom.

"Call Half Moon Bay and confirm our 1:30 tee reservation," Barnett was telling the receptionist. "We want to have lunch in the grill first. Is the car here?"

"It's out front."

"Let's go, children. We're burning daylight."

Barnett was like big kid, happy as I'd ever seen him as he tramped past us on his way to the elevator. Susan smiled at me and said, "Don't worry, Mr…"

"Cotter," said the receptionist.

… "I'm sure it'll all work out."

But I was staring, open-mouthed, at the space Barnett had just vacated. "He plays golf?"

"Who—John? Sure, he's crazy about it. He says he gets more work done on the course than in the office."

"And *you* play?"

"Only every chance I get."

"How long?"

"How long—what—have I played? Gee, a while I guess."

"Hear that?" I shouted at Carl. "She said it. I asked her how long and she said, 'a while.' Everybody heard that right?"

"That's right, Mr. Cotter. We heard it." Randolph taking charge. "Now you need to be quiet now."

"Wait—I want to know why she said it. Why did you say that, Susan?"

"I don't think I know what you—"

"You said 'a while.' What did you say that for? Why does everything take a *while*?"

Susan was looking at Carl. Both he and Randolph were shaking their heads.

"Susan—" Barnett was holding the elevator door. "We don't want to have to snog the place."

"Gotta go," she said

"Wait—what did he say? What about snog?"

But Susan was already on the elevator and the door was closing. I lunged off the sofa and made it to the elevator before Randolph could grab me.

"This—all of this—has something to do with Floyd, doesn't it?" I yelled.

But the door closed in my face and, when I turned around, Randolph, Carl and the receptionist were staring at me.

"Who's Floyd?" she said.

A List of Lunacies

After I'd calmed down enough to where I could assure Carl and Randolph I'd make it home all right, they both shook my hand and wished me luck. Randolph rode down with me in the elevator and walked me out onto Sacramento Street, even patted me gently on the back when we said goodbye. When I reached the corner of Battery and looked back, he was still standing there. I turned right and headed toward Market Street getting about halfway down the block before stopping dead and standing there, quivering like a rubber dart stuck to the pavement.

What the hell was that?

I knew those people, had worked with them for years. I'd met their families, socialized with them. How could they not know me? I mean, since arriving back, I'd been bombarded with one lunacy after another. But at least the people knew me.

The answer to this—and everything—I believed, was close, right there in front of me. If I could just stand there on that piece of pavement and concentrate, not moving a muscle, it would come to me. It had to. And I did stand there, long enough to draw plenty of stares from passersby. But no matter how hard I concentrated, the Answer hung, maddeningly, just out of reach. Like a name on the tip of my tongue or the swing I'd already swung.

On the train, back to Walnut Hill, I wrung out my battered brain trying to make sense out of the maze of puzzle pieces I'd collected since flying off to the desert. I took a pad of paper from my briefcase and made a list.

1). The missing crashed plane on the wind farm

2). Mike, Ron and Ed the pilot disappearing along with the plane.

3). Mike and Ron denying knowledge of the crash—or the golf trip for that matter.

4). Ron going suddenly, inexplicably gay.

5). Changes in Cathy.

6). Robyn, the nurse at Cathy's hospital insisting I'm a brain surgeon and then—

7). Me…subsequently finding my name listed in the department directory under resident surgeons—neurology.

8). All the ads with golf in them.

9). People at my office claiming to not know me…and last but by no means least…

10). Barnett and Susan rushing off with the Mrs. Beebles' clients to play golf!

Had I left anything out? Let's see—Mallards range being jammed on a weekday morning was pretty strange, but that hardly rated mentioning alongside the other lunacies. Then, of course, there were the snoggers themselves—rampaging mobs of unruly golfers. Can't overlook them. Or—wait a minute—how about Floyd winning the Open? How's that for a lunacy?

Yes, these made for a pretty impressive and extensive list of lunacies and taken singly or as a group, I was at a loss for any logical explanation. But I was at the same time convinced of a shared commonality among them and that, if I could somehow connect the dots, I might begin to figure out what was happening to me.

This new scientific approach to my dilemma cheered me to the point that, when I saw some more golf-themed ads in the train car, it almost didn't bother me. One was an ad for Lasik surgery that featured a middle-aged guy lining up a putt with his new enhanced eyesight. Right next to that ad was another for a golf school—well, naturally, that would have golf in it. But then, as we reached my stop and I stood up to get off the train, I saw one mounted on the platform shelter. It was for a mortuary. "Playing the back nine of life?" it read. "Time to reserve a spot in the clubhouse." That concept seemed far more of a stretch than Mrs. Beeble's Crumbcake in your golf bag.

I stood there wondering what poor golf-distracted soul had come up with that one and how in hell they'd been able to sell it to the client. But then I heard the loud exhale of air that meant the doors were about to close and I barely had time to lunge through them and out onto the station platform before they slammed shut behind me. My momentum carried me several yards to where I nearly collided with a steel pillar. I grabbed hold of it to keep from falling on my face and saw some writing on it—graffiti painted a bold legible red:

In the land of the blind, the one-eyed man is Snog.

A Second Opinion

"So, what do you *think* is happening to you?"

Dr. Farrow's putt rolled across the carpet, glanced off the leg of a chair and disappeared underneath the sofa I'd been lying on for the last forty minutes.

"Couldn't tell you," I said. "Ever since I got back from the desert, things have been different."

"You're sure about that?"

"Am I sure about what?"

The shrink got down on all fours and began swiping under the sofa with his putter. "Are you sure things are different? Is it possible that, before the trip, you weren't seeing them clearly for whatever reason and now that you're back, you're seeing them for the first time as they really are?"

He retrieved the ball and puffed to his feet. "For example, your observation that people are obsessed by golf. Haven't they always—I mean to some extent?"

"Well, no. It's like every other billboard or TV commercial has some kind of golf reference. I certainly don't remember anything like that. And I'm in the business so I notice that stuff."

"You're talking about the ad business?"

"Yeah."

He went over to the desk and picked up a file. "Why do I think you're an M.D.?"

"That's another thing—wouldn't you think that, if I were a doctor, I'd remember it? Especially a brain surgeon—my God."

"Well…"

"I mean, seriously, I doubt if I could tell a brain from a cauliflower."

"It's possible you could be in denial. Clinically in denial."

"How do you mean?"

"Well, this is just a theory but… you've suffered a nasty blow to your head. Your brain is damaged and, in order to repair itself, must remain free from stress. Your job is highly stressful thus your brain, in effect, refuses to consciously acknowledge what you do for a living."

"So, you're saying I could be a brain surgeon but my brain—what? Won't admit it?"

"In simplistic terms, that's correct. It's protecting you in the only way it can."

"But you're *telling* me now that I am one and I *still* don't believe it."

"That could just mean it's working. It doesn't matter how many people validate you. They can show you irrefutable evidence—video footage of procedures, patient testimonials—but you won't believe it yourself until your brain allows it. Maybe not until you once again find yourself actually holding a human brain in your hand will you—"

I sat up straight. "What did you say?"

"Sorry…?"

"What you just said… about holding a brain in my hand. Why did you say that?"

"Why did I say it?"

"Was it your idea to say it or did someone tell you to say it?"

"Tell me to say—? No. I haven't discussed our session

with anyone."

"No one named Floyd?"

"Floyd? No. Who's that?"

"You haven't talked to Floyd?"

"I don't think I know anyone named Floyd. And, even if I did, professional ethics prevent me from—"

"Okay." I leaned back against the lime green cushions.

Dr. Farrow was studying me. "Is this Floyd someone we should be talking about?"

"God, no. No. It's nothing. Something you said just… probably just a coincidence."

"You're sure?"

"Yeah, no problem. I didn't mean to interrupt you. You were saying something about my brain not wanting me to know that I was a brain surgeon…"

"I'm saying it's possible you could be in stress-related denial."

"For how long, do you think?"

"Until your brain feels the time is right, I expect."

"And that will be… ballpark?"

"When you've recovered enough to process the information without undue stress."

"Great —what do I do in the meantime?"

"Try and relax and stay as stress-free as possible." Dr. Farrow picked up his putter and stroked a ball toward a chair leg. "You might try getting out for a little golf."

"You think I should play golf? More golf?"

"I don't see why not."

"You realize that, at our last visit, we determined I was playing too much golf?"

"We did?" Farrow walked over to his desk and flipped some pages on his calendar. "When were you here last? It's been a while, hasn't it?"

"Last Tuesday at two o'clock. A week ago. Same time, same place. You're saying you don't remember it?"

"Funny, I don't. My notes seem to have gone missing too. Is this… pretty much what we talked about?"

I sat up on the couch. "No—none of this had happened yet."

He nodded and then stroked another putt that got away from him and skidded back under the sofa. "Damn," he said softly.

"Okay," I said, anxious to get him back on track. "So even if this brain theory explains the confusion about my job, what about all the other stuff? What about Cathy playing golf? Or Ron going gay all of a sudden?"

"Is it possible," Farrow said from under the desk. "That the signals were there but you weren't programmed to receive them?"

"Ron isn't *signaling* gay. He's shouting it. It's like he's headlining in 'La Cage aux Folle.'

The psychiatrist went over and selected another putter from the half dozen or so leaning in the corner. "But the changes in your wife's behavior—you admit you've been less than attentive recently. I wonder if it's been happening all along and you've only just begun to pick up on these changes."

"I suppose it's possible. But that doesn't explain the missing plane crash or a driving range misfit winning the Open or—you, for that matter."

Dr. Farrow looked up from his putt. "Me?"

"Yes. Do you consider this normal behavior? I mean for a psychiatrist to be putting during analysis?"

"All right." Dr. Farrow came around and leaned against the front of his desk. "What do we know for sure? You flew to the desert with your friends for a golf weekend and somewhere along the line suffered a pretty good head injury. Okay so far?"

"Yeah, except I don't think it happened in the crash. It was after that when I ran into a wind turbine and knocked myself out."

"You remember that much?"

"Absolutely."

"But not how you wound up on that wind farm in the first place?"

"The plane crashed."

"Are you sure?"

"It must have. One minute we were in the air and then, the next Dave and I were on the ground."

"But you couldn't find the plane. Even the authorities couldn't locate it."

"Sure, but—what are you saying? You saying it didn't crash?"

Farrow shrugged.

"Then what happened to it?"

"Maybe nothing."

"What do you mean."

"Maybe it didn't crash because it didn't take off."

"What?"

"Now, remember, we're just speculating here but consider this—you say, when you woke up, you couldn't find the plane. What if there never was a plane?"

"No plane? Then how did I get there?"

"Any number of ways. Maybe on a different plane. Or maybe you drove. Then afterward you hit your head and imagined you flew there in your friend's plane."

"Imagined it? Come on, Doctor—"

"Imagined isn't the right word. *Dreamed* is better."

I groaned and slumped back into the cushions.

"Tell me, Charley, do you remember your dreams?"

"Sometimes. Not too often."

"A lot of people don't. You know, it's possible to

dream a particular dream over and over and not be aware of it—consciously at least."

"You're saying I dreamed all this up?"

"Only that it's possible."

"It all seems pretty real to me."

"I have no doubt. Dreams can seem very real. But consider this. Let me draw up a possible scenario for you. The impact to your head—whatever the source—wipes out chunks of your conscious memory leaving you with amnesia. That same jolt dislodges other images—call them replacement images—from the depths of your unconscious mind. You've seen these before, perhaps in dreams, but you don't remember them. And now your brain, in its frantic attempt to sort out the jumble in your head, literally shoves these replacement images into your conscious mind where you're seeing them now—consciously—for the first time."

"You think this is what happened to me?"

Dr. Farrow spread his palms out, face up. "It's an answer, and a plausible one, I think. And because these occurrences or events now reside in your conscious mind, you assume they actually happened and that you lived through them."

"So then… Mike and Ron don't know about the golf trip because… it was a dream I had?"

"I wouldn't be surprised." Dr. Farrow picked up his putter again.

"And I dreamed all this—when?"

He shook his head. "Last week. Last year. No way of telling. Believe me when I say, the unconscious is a real can of worms."

"But, what's a dream and what's real?"

"Go with the facts. The police couldn't locate the plane, right?

"Right."

"Sounds like you may have dreamt that one."

"And you're fairly certain I'm not in advertising?"

"Again, look at it logically. You were recognized at the

hospital. There was even a locker with your name on it."

"That's right."

"All right let's try something," Farrow said. He went over and took a heavy medical tome from his bookshelf, turning pages until he found what he was looking for. "Okay," he said. "If you were treating a malignant primary tumor, would you employ stereotactic surgery, laser instrumentation or ultrasonic aspiration?"

I stared at him. "This is something a brain surgeon would know?"

"I would think so, yes."

"Because I haven't got any idea."

"Okay."

"What you're saying is that I might know but that my brain won't let me remember it?"

"Something like that."

Dr. Farrow looked at his watch. "But, just to be safe, I'd hold off on performing invasive cranial procedures for a while. And now our time is up, and we have to stop. We can pick this up again next week. Two o'clock work for you?"

I was writing Dr. Farrow a check when something occurred to me. "What if I'm still dreaming? Like right now? You think it's possible?"

"Nope."

"You seem awfully certain."

He took the check and dropped it into a desk drawer.

"If this were a dream, I probably wouldn't be charging you," he said.

Ask a Dentist

I spent the rest of that day over at Mallard's following Dr. Farrow's suggestion and getting my swing in shape for Meadowbank. An entire afternoon of practice sounds like a lot until you subtract the time I had to hang around just waiting for a stall to open up. And, even then, I had to be careful not to overdo it—for part of that time I was seeing two balls at address. I drew some stares from the range rats, checking out the guy with an apparently significant head injury out there beating balls.

Floyd was nowhere in sight but his influence was greatly felt. He'd put Mallard's on the map, all right. His newfound fame was like a magnet. It seemed like everybody in Contra Costa County with a golf club was out there swinging. As for me, thrilled and delighted though I was to be playing Meadowbank, in the recesses of my heart and what was left of my brain, I knew that, under the circumstances, with my upside-down sense of reality, playing golf was about the last thing I ought to be doing. Well, I'm sorry folks, but Meadowbank will do that to you.

On the way home, I stopped at Nevada Bob's, rented a new set of Pings, bought a pair of Footjoys to replace the ones I lost in the crash and splurged on an ultra-thin Cabretta leather glove. Then I swung by the grocery store and picked up a couple of Cornish game hens, wild rice, asparagus and a nice bottle of red wine. I'd have Cathy's favorite dinner waiting when she got home.

I hadn't seen her since our bizarre encounter at Mallard's the night before and thought, if I could just get her to sit down and talk to me, it'd help make sense of Dr. Farrow's theory that dreams and reality were tumbling dice inside my head.

It was dark by the time I pulled out of the Safeway lot and cut through the center of town. I was stopped at the light on Main Street, next to the park when I heard what sounded like a rock hit my front fender hard. Then, seconds later, half a dozen shadowy figures dressed in dark clothing came running out of City Park. They all carried golf clubs. Two of them flung themselves headlong across the hood of my car. Another hopped up on the trunk then onto the roof where he began to bounce up and down. Then one of the guys on the hood put his face right next to the windshield and grinned at me. He was college age, late teens or early twenties. I heard him say: "Mind if we play through?"

Then his buddy hauled him off the hood and the guy on the roof leaped to the pavement just as a police cruiser, with dome light flashing and siren whooping, zoomed out of the park, jumped the curb and took off after them. The whole thing was over in seconds. I hadn't moved but just sat gripping the wheel. I was a little shaken, but what disturbed me more than the punks jumping on my car was the one kid asking me if I minded them playing through. The déjà vu was back. Where had I just heard that question?

Minutes later, home in the driveway, lifting the grocery bags out of the trunk, I noticed streams of white liquid running down the rear windshield. Someone had used a spray can to write a single word on the roof: 'Snog.'

Most of the paint came off with a car sponge and the hose. I wasn't too concerned about the Ford. Most of the time it sat rusting in the train station parking lot. It was transportation, that's all.

Cathy wasn't home yet. Her usual shift ran until six p.m. Most evenings she'd be pulling in the driveway just before seven. The routine was for Elvia, our nanny, to pick Sean and Sara up from their respective schools at three—or be waiting when they got home from camp in the summertime—and then mind them till we got home. Typically, Cathy and I arrived around the same time. The kids would rush to greet us (that is, unless Scooby and Shaggy had found themselves in a particularly perilous situation, in which case they'd ignore us completely). Then, after making dinner, cleaning up, bathtime, an episode or two of the 'Wiggles' (Sara) or 'Three Stooges' re-runs (Sean) and getting them, finally, into bed, Cathy and I would meet in the living room, often as not with glass of wine in hand, collapse into opposite sides of the living room sofa and negotiate which TV program we would fall asleep watching.

But now the house was too quiet so I flipped on the TV in the living room, then went back into the kitchen to pre-heat the oven and wash the hens. The asparagus and rice could wait for a while. Every once in a while I picked up snatches of talk show conversation playing to the empty living room. I didn't pay much attention until I heard the words 'personal golf'.

Diane Sawyer was talking to a balding, soft-spoken man of late middle age dressed in green medical scrubs.

"I believe there's no such thing as a universal or perfect golf swing," the doctor guy was saying. "A swing is as unique to an individual as his or her DNA code. No two people have the same one."

"Until we start cloning golfers," Sawyer added.

The doctor laughed politely. "You're right. And that's why it's counterproductive to copy someone else's golf swing. Doesn't it make more sense to perfect the one we already have?"

"But let's say I'm new to the game and don't have a swing yet," said Sawyer.

"Everyone has a swing, Ms. Sawyer," said the doctor. "It's the one you were born with. You reveal it when you take your first whack at a ball. From there, it's just a matter of refinement. Some golfers spend a lifetime working on their swings. Others don't feel the need to excel and therefore never do. It's a matter of priorities—personal choice."

Sawyer turned to the camera and held up a book. "The book is titled 'Personal Golf—Finding Your Inner Swing.' We're talking to the author, Dr. Warren Sleeves. Now, doctor, as a physician—"

"Dentist," Dr. Sleeves said.

"Dentist, yes, excuse me. Still practicing?"

"Oh, yes. I have a full time practice."

"How much time are you able to devote to your own game?"

"Oh, I don't play."

"You don't play?"

"I'm afraid not. Between the demands of my practice and of raising a family, there just isn't time. It's a matter of priorities, you see?"

Sawyer looked a little flustered. "Let me see if I understand this," she said. "You must have played at one time."

"Not really, no."

"But you've written a book on the subject."

"That's right."

"Have you ever played golf?"

"Once or twice. I enjoyed it very much."

"That's extraordinary. I've read this book. It's filled with insight and philosophy."

"Thank you."

"How is it then that you're so conversant with your subject?"

"Well, Ms. Sawyer, I do have a brother-in-law who plays and, now and then, a patient will tell me about their golf games." Sleeves chuckled. "Of course it's a little difficult for them with my hands in their mouth."

"Oh my God, you're cooking?" The voice from the doorway startled me. Cathy stood there with the mail, looking skinny and girlish, hair pinned up, the red leather jacket draped over the shoulders of her nurse's uniform.

"Yeah... hey, come and look at this." I said. "Diane Sawyer is talking to Floyd's dentist."

146

Cathy stood her ground. "So what are you now, the Iron Chef?"

"Believe this guy? He wrote a book about golf and he's never even played."

"Charley, you made a mess in here."

"Hold on a sec," I said, trying to hear the interview. "Hey, put on the asparagus. It's all cleaned and ready to go."

"Sure. Great. Then you run upstairs and get in bed and I'll come and serve it to you."

Diane Sawyer was saying, "Your practice is in Northern California?"

"Yes. I'm in a town—it's really become a small city—Walnut Hill."

"That's in the East Bay."

"That's right. About forty minutes east of San Francisco."

She referred to some notes on her lap. "We've been tracking in the press, over the last few weeks, public—how would you describe it—disobedience or demonstrations I guess is a better word—in your area. The reports call it 'snogging'?"

"Yes, unfortunately that's true. Snogging has become a big problem in and around Walnut Hill."

"Some of our viewers might not be familiar with the term. Can you enlighten them?"

"Certainly. Snogging, in this context, is a form of golf."

"Okay," said Sawyer. "A *form* of golf. How is it different from regular golf?"

"All right. There are two main differences. Both are played with a club and a ball but snogging isn't always played on a golf course. And it's usually played at night."

"You say it's not always played on a golf course. Where else would you play it and please tell us what the object of the game is."

Cathy came back in long enough to tell me she wasn't running a bed and breakfast and that I'd better be watching whatever I was cooking because she was going upstairs to change.

"The only definition I have for 'snog' is the British usage," said Sawyer. "It's the word for what couples do in a parked car or the back balcony of a movie theater."

"Yes," said Sleeves with a knowing smile. "I'm familiar with the term. There's been a lot of speculation and ultimately disagreement over how and why snog got its name. Some say it's an acronym—S.N.O.G.—that stands for Speed-Night-Option Golf.

"Speed?" Diane Sawyer repeated.

"Yes, you see, what makes snog most unique and exciting," he said, "Is the element of trespass."

"As in illegal trespass?" said Sawyer.

"Very often. Snog began as a backlash. The first snoggers were renegade golfers reacting to skyrocketing greens fees and the suburban sprawl that's been gobbling up municipal courses by the acre. Thanks, in part, to the enormous popularity that begins with the Tiger Woods phenomenon, golf has enjoyed a Renaissance. We have millions of new golfers flocking to the game but new golf course construction hasn't kept pace and now there aren't enough facilities to accommodate them. This demand, coupled with high land and maintenance costs, has driven greens fees up to where they're simply out of reach for the average player.

"Cash-strapped municipalities were caught flatfooted in the rush to build. When the boom came, they'd actually been in the process of closing golf courses, selling them off to commercial developers in order to pay for more essential programs and services. Those not able or willing to pay exorbitant green fees or shell out tens of thousands of dollars for private club memberships had nowhere to play. So golfers—or snoggers—began sneaking onto courses at night."

"How do they see their ball in the dark?"

"Ah," said Sleeves. "That's where the option part comes in. There are balls you can buy that come complete with little glow-stick insert plugs. They only fly about two-thirds the distance of an ordinary ball but can be seen clearly at night. Often a snogger will opt to use one of these luminous balls even at a cost of distance. But these balls are becoming more difficult to purchase. They've been taken off the market in many of the townships in the East Bay because they are thought to encourage snogging."

"Frankly, Dr. Sleeves, for all the press these snoggers are getting, sneaking onto a golf course at night doesn't seem too serious a crime."

"Well, Ms. Sawyer," said the dentist. "If it was confined to golf courses, the authorities might agree with you. Unfortunately, the situation has escalated."

Sawyer leaned forward. "How so?"

"Well, when you have people sneaking onto a golf course at night, the first thing you do is hire security to chase them off."

"And that was done?"

"It was. But that wasn't the end of the problem because snoggers moved into the public parks. The police responded and that put a stop to it for a while but then the snogs got more adventurous—more brazen. They took to the streets."

"The city streets?"

"City, neighborhood—wherever they could get away with it. On any given night they might declare some open car window or garbage can to be the hole and off they'd play. And, if you were a pedestrian walking down that street, you might well find yourself in danger."

"They're violent?"

Dr. Sleeves smiled. "Well… the idea of club-wielding snoggers roaming the streets at night with no regard for property, whacking golf balls indiscriminately. It's not a healthy situation. There have even been reports of home invasions where a ball flies through the window of a home, and some rambunctious snogger climbs in after it."

"Cathy!" I yelled toward the stairs. "You ought to see this."

"Just imagine," Sleeves was saying, "Hell bent snoggers whacking their way through your living room."

"I just ran into the guys they're talking about on the

news."

"What are the police doing to stop it?" asked Sawyer.

"The police can't be everywhere and unfortunately, they're not getting the support they need from people in the community."

"People are apathetic?"

Sleeves smiled thinly, shaking his head. "Worse, I'm afraid. They're *participating*. Joining the rebellion, if you will."

"Joining the snogs?"

"People want to play golf, Diane, and they feel the game has been stolen from them by private interests."

Dr. Sleeves raised his eyebrows for emphasis. "We may be seeing the first stages of a potential epidemic— the most dramatic display of civil disobedience since the war protests of the nineteen-sixties.

"What private interests are we talking about?"

"I'm not comfortable naming names—"

"Charley…" Cathy had come back down. She'd changed into a all-black combination of tee shirt and jeans, and was tying a black bandana around her neck.

"Did you hear any of this?" I asked her.

"I was upstairs, what?"

"Diane Sawyer is interviewing this dentist—"

"Dr. Warren Sleeves—yeah."

I looked at her. "You know who he is?"

"Yeah—the smart dentist—guy who knows everything. You never saw him? He's on TV all the time."

The program cut to a commercial. Two men in golf clothes stood next to a lawn mower discussing whether TifEagle or Ultra Dwarf Bermuda grass afforded gnarlier lies.

"Hey, am I nuts or is there a lot of golf on TV? It

seems like there's golf stuff on almost every channel."

"I don't think it's any more than usual," she said and started for the kitchen.

"Hey," I said. "Have you heard from the kids? I'm surprised Nana hasn't made them call."

She didn't answer right away. Thinking maybe she hadn't heard me, I said louder, "Maybe we should phone up there and see how they're doing." Still no answer. Figuring she'd gone into the kitchen, I got up from the sofa but, when I turned around, she was standing in the doorway, staring at me.

Someplace Else

Cathy's baffled expression was the trigger. My first reaction was to whirl around and look toward the fireplace—the spot directly in front of it. Sara's fawn-colored rocking horse, the one Cathy's parents had brought for her first Christmas, wasn't there now. How had I missed that? But I had noticed the missing refrigerator photos…and Sara's duck painting…

My stomach tightened, and I felt cold dampness on my scalp and under my arms. I ran past Cathy, out of the room and took the stairs two at a time. The door to the kid's room was closed and I saw right away that Sean's Mario Brothers decals and Sara's Dora stickers gone. I'd spent the last couple of nights in the living room and missed that too. I paused there for a moment, steeling myself, but still my hands trembled when I opened the door and threw on the light. A lone, stripped, twin bed stood against a wall, piled high with stacked cartons and old magazines. The sliding door to the closet was open. Inside was a dusty row of wardrobe cartons. A partially disassembled stationary bike occupied the center of the room. There were no Little League trophies, dump trucks or cowboy wallpaper on Sean's side, no stuffed animals, naked Barbies or plastic tea sets on Sara's. There was no trace of our children or any sign that a child had ever occupied that room.

No kids.

No eight-year-old Sean with bright blue eyes that

squinted when he smiled and an untamable amber cowlick—
the image of his mother. No six-year-old Sara—daddy's
girl—with the irresistible laugh who had to be serenaded
each night with "Teddy Bear Picnic" and a re-reading of
Thomas Train before she'd close her eyes.

I slumped against the door jam. "No way. "Not the kids.
I couldn't have dreamt the kids."

"Charley? What is it?" Cathy stood behind me at the top
of the stairs. "What's the matter?"

"Where are they, Cathy?"

"Who?"

"Sean and Sara!"

Her eyes were wide and frightened in a way I'd never
seen. "I don't know who that is."

"Who's got them? Your parents? You said you were
taking them to Shelly and Bob's. I remember that. You were
taking them up to Shelly and Bob's. Call them up. I want
them back here now."

"All right, I'm just going to change and then I'm going to
drive you to the hospital. I'll call Neurology and see if Bill
Wanger can meet us."

She flinched and ducked out of the way as I brushed past
her through the hallway and into our bedroom and picked
up the phone next to the bed. "What's their number?"

"The hospital?"

"Your parents—goddamit—! Bob and—what's her...
what's the fucking number?"

Cathy from the doorway: "Charley, my mother's name is
Jean and my father's name is Peter."

I hung up with a groan and lay down on the bed.

"Charley... you're exhausted and... you're scaring me."

"Oh, I'm scaring *you*?"

"Maybe if you rest a while."

"Tell me something, Cathy. Why does everything take a
while? Can you explain that to me?"

"I don't know but you need to rest now."

"Okay, so I'll rest for a while. And then, in a while when I wake up, the kids will be here, and you won't have that ring in your nose, and everything will back to normal. Do you think that'll happen? Because, if it will, I'll do it. I'll go to sleep right now."

"Good." She covered me with the quilt from the foot of the bed. "Get some sleep and when you feel better, we'll go in and get that head looked at."

"I don't need my head looked at! I need my children. Our children! Whatever this is… whatever you're *doing*… you need to stop it right now!"

"Charley… Charley… calm down. No one's doing anything. You just need to rest. Try and go to sleep."

"Where're you going?"

"I need to run out just for a little bit. But then I'll be back, and I'll come and check on you."

"Cathy?"

"What?"

"Why don't we have kids?"

"Oh, Charley—"

"Didn't we want them?"

"Go to sleep now."

"Was it me that didn't want them?"

"What difference does it make?"

"It was me, wasn't it?"

"Get some sleep."

She stepped out into the hall and pulled the door shut behind her.

Laying there in the dark after she'd gone, frightened and alone, my mind turning in on itself, desperate for any possible, rational solution for what was happening to me, I flashed on a night back in college. It was at a fraternity party, when a guy offered me a tiny handful of what looked like dirt, saying it was magic mushrooms and that they were 'fun.' I'd washed them down with my beer and forgot I'd done it until an hour or so later when I was suddenly swamped with anxiety and disorientation to a degree I'd never experienced. I'd spent the rest of that night, writhing and tossing in my bed, assaulted by an army of hallucinated furies. I'd wrapped myself tightly in my own arms, waiting for it to be over, feeling as if I were holding on to my sanity, afraid to let go or else I would just somehow explode or just be… gone. It was like that now. Only this time, the hallucinations didn't howl and mock and change form. They looked and spoke like real people, familiar and normal, like they belonged here—wherever this was.

Here.

A reality similar but different from the one I'd flown away from last Friday night. Forget Farrow and his dream theory. Sean and Sara do exist. Just not here. This, here, is someplace else. Someplace crazy.

I lay there in the dark, like that other time, wanting nothing more than for this night to be over, terrified it might never be. Then the phone rang.

"Charley?" Dave's voice, sounding wrong—scared or maybe hurt. "It's me, Dave."

"What's the matter?"

"I'm in a jam. Can you come get me?"

"Where?"

"You know the cop station on White Oak? You're gonna need to bring some cash. Can you get five hundred?"

"What happened?"

"Tell you when you get here. Can you get the money?"

I dug into my pockets and came up with three hundred and change remaining from my un-spent Palm Springs stake. There was an ATM on the way. "Yeah, we should be okay," I told him. "Sit tight. I'll be there in a few."

"Charley…"

"Yeah?"

"You recognize my voice, right?"

"Sure. Why?"

"Never mind. Just hurry up."

If You Lived Here…

"So, when I got home," Dave was saying, "I was already there."

I drained my beer and waved Melanie over. "What do you mean you were already there?"

"I was there. Sitting in the living room. It was me."

"Who was you?"

"The guy—me. That's what I'm telling you."

"I get that… you were there. Who else?"

Dave leaned across the table, his voice dropping to a near-whisper for emphasis. "Me."

"*You* were there?"

He nodded.

"Okaaaay… anybody else?"

Dave looked like he was getting ready to augment my concussion but then Melanie appeared, her ample frontage straining against the checked apron.

"Would you gentlemen care for another?"

"Same again," said Dave.

"I'd better not," I told her. "What do you have for a

headache?"

"Scotch, bourbon, vodka…"

"I mean like aspirin or something."

She was looking at my bandaged head. "You been in some kinda accident?"

"Plane crash," I said.

"Oh, my God, are you kidding? Tell me it wasn't terrorists."

I shook my head. "Bankers."

"My God, are you okay?"

"Nasty blow to the head."

She took in Dave's blackened eye and torn golf shirt, covered with mud and grass stains. "So, you came straight *here*?"

Melanie was a mainstay at Earl's Country Roadhouse, the kind of place you almost can't find anymore. Just a big old clapboard white house surrounded by a gravel parking lot. It sat at the end of Cumberland Road, last stop on the way out of Walnut Hill. Earl's was the lone remaining family-owned tavern in Contra Costa County where you could still get a grilled cheeseburger and home-made Tater Tots to go with your cold draft beer. Like Mallard's, Earl's catered to a social cross section. For years, it was our designated pit stop after evening soft ball games, or weekend rounds at Stickley. The only décor aside from the checkered tablecloths and little glass candle holders were the electric beer signs over the bar and the waitresses, like Melanie, in their khaki shorts and cotton aprons, each of them fully capable of tossing you out on your ass if circumstances required.

After she left to get our drinks, Dave started in again, explaining what had happened to him in the thirty hours or so between the shuttle dropping us off and me posting his bail.

"I unlock the front door and walk in. I hear this voice yell, "who's that?" from the living room. It sounds familiar, but I can't imagine who it could be 'cause only me and the manager have the key and I'm not expecting anyone. So, I go into the living room and he's sittin' there on the sofa watching TV, drinking a beer with his feet on the coffee table."

"Who?"

"Me."

"Don't start that again. What do you mean you?"

"Okay, all right—at first I think it's a guy who looks like me. Same face, same hair—he's wearing a coveralls like I wear. Same stains. I ask him what he's doing here and guess what he says back to me."

"What?"

"He asks me what am *I* doing there. And—you wanna hear the real scary part? We both say it at the same time."

"You say what at the same time?"

"He says 'what the fuck are you doing here?' at the exact time I say what the fuck is he doin' here."

"Who was he?"

"Wait—then I say, 'get the fuck out of my house' and he says it too. Is that spooky or what? So, the next thing I know, we're rolling around the floor knocking over the furniture. The manager hears this and calls the cops. But when they get there, they don't know who to arrest because we're both of us claiming to be me. And, by this time, I'm not even sure *I* can tell us apart. Then the dipshit manager tells the cops that this other guy must be the real me because I'm wearing golf clothes and he's never seen me wear anything but coveralls. So, they handcuff me and drag me out of my own place and leave this other guy sitting in my living room drinking my beer in front of my plasma. You believin' this?"

Melanie came back with two beers and a couple of Advil. I gulped them down with half a glassful of beer then sat there letting Dave's unlikely story sink in. Overhead, in the corner behind the bar, the TV showed some announcer sitting in a golf cart talking to the camera. I couldn't hear what he was saying over the barroom din.

"When was this?" I asked Dave.

"Sunday night when I got home."

"They had you locked up all this time?"

Dave shook his head. "I've been talking to some court-appointed shrink all afternoon. Some dude crazier than I'll ever be wants me to explain why I'm stalking myself."

"It sounds like some sort of identity fraud," I said. "Pretty brazen having cops drag you out of your own home."

Dave sighed. "I dunno what to do. The police won't listen to me. They think *he's* the victim. I hate to go back over there but what choice do I have?"

"Don't do that. You'll wind up back in jail."

"What if *you* were to talk to him?"

"Me? And tell him what?"

"Confront him. Tell him you know he's bullshit and that he's got to clear out or you'll go to the cops."

"What if he won't go?

"Then you call the cops."

"What makes you think they're going to take my word for it? You *are* the guy, and they didn't listen to you. We're going to need some kind of proof."

"Ask him a question that only I can answer."

"Like what?"

"Personal stuff. He can't know everything about me. Just trip him up once or twice and he'll be out of there. What do you say?"

What could I say? My buddy Dave was sitting there all red-eyed and grass stained asking for my help. I was certainly in no condition for whatever this was, but we finished our beers and drove over.

Dave's apartment was half of a 70's era duplex on Westmoor. He waited across the street in the car while I climbed the concrete steps and rang the buzzer. I was counting on there being a simple and logical explanation but then the voice coming through the closed door sounded awfully familiar.

"Yeah?"

"Hi… can I speak to you a minute?"

"Who is it?"

"My name's Charley Cotter."

"Holy shit!" the voice said and immediately the door swung open. Dave stood there in his coveralls.

"You're back!" he said.

I couldn't help looking over my shoulder. The Dave I'd come with still sat there in the passenger's seat, partly illuminated by a streetlight.

"Charley," this other—clone Dave was saying. "What happened to your head?"

Clone Dave

There was no difference that I could see.

Clone Dave was identical to the real thing. Right down to the serpent tattoo just above his wrist and the tiny tufts of hair sprouting from his ears. And he obviously knew me, was in fact delighted to see me, slapping me on the back, pulling me inside. I told him first I had to go and make sure I'd locked the car. Then I ran over to the Ford, opened the driver's door and looked in. It was downright bizarre to see Dave still sitting there.

"What'd he say?" he asked me.

"Dave… who is that up there?"

"I have no fucking idea. That's what you're supposed to be finding out."

I looked back at the duplex across the street where the front door stood open. This thing was creeping me out.

"Well, whoever he is, he seems real glad to see me."

"He knows you?"

"Sure acts like he does."

"Who is he?"

"I don't know. Either he's the greatest actor in the world or… he's you."

"Hey—*I'm* me! Shit. That's it—I'm going in there!"

I pushed him back against the seat. "No—wait. Think for a second. Could he be like a distant cousin or something that you didn't know you had?"

"Distant cousin? That guy looks more like me than I do."

"Okay, so a twin. Maybe you were separated at birth."

"He's not saying he's my twin. He's sayin' he's me."

My head was throbbing. "Dave—I'm not sure I'm up to this."

"Charley—the guy's tryin' to steal my life!"

"Yeah, okay. All right. Relax. We'll figure this out."

Dave looked back over at the duplex. Seeing the fear in his eyes didn't make me feel any better.

"Tell him he's got to get out of there," he said. "Or we're gonna have him thrown out. Tell him that!"

"Okay, okay. Relax."

I trudged back across the street, thinking about Cathy, wondering if she was home yet and had found me gone. And what she'd say if she could see me right now. Dave occupied a spot near the very top of her "losers list" compiled almost exclusively from the ranks of my friends. Now here was another one of him for her to complain about.

I stepped tentatively through the open doorway just as a grinning Clone Dave came out of the kitchen with a tall beer in each hand.

"So, Charley," he said, "It's been a while, eh?"

He steered me into a chair opposite the TV and plopped down on the sofa like he lived there.

"How was the desert?"

"You knew about that?"

Clone Dave seemed surprised. "Yeah, sure." Then he grinned. "I didn't think you were coming back."

"Why wouldn't I?"

"You *said* you weren't."

"I did?"

"Don't you remember?"

I shook my head, pointing to the bandage. "Nasty blow to the head."

"Yeah, looks bad. How'd it happen?"

"Plane crash."

"Wow. I didn't hear about it. What airline?"

"Private plane. Didn't make the papers. Doctor says I might have a little amnesia. Listen, ah… should I call you Dave?"

He frowned. "What else would you call me?"

"Sorry, amnesia goes in and out. Sometimes I forget who I'm talking to."

"Does it hurt?

"Off and on."

"I might have some aspirin."

"No, it's okay."

Clone Dave took a long draught of beer and let out a sizeable burp. "Wow," he said. "How long's it been? Gotta be a while."

"A while… yeah."

"Oh, at least." He thought for a second. "How long has it been?"

"I was hoping you'd tell me."

"Tell you what?"

"How long it's been?"

"Since you left for the desert?"

"Yes, exactly how long."

He thought a minute. "Don't you know?"

"Sorry." I tapped my bandage. "Dates are a problem too…"

"Gotcha. Okay, let me think."

Clone Dave leaned back in the sofa, arms folded,

head resting on a Dave's-head-sized grease stain on the wall behind him. "You know," he said. "I can't for the life of me remember when you left." He forced a laugh. "Amnesia's not contagious, is it?"

"Doesn't have to be exact. We're talking more than a couple of days?"

"Days? Oh yeah… more like… "

"Weeks?"

"Sure, weeks. Maybe…"

"Months?"

He was nodding. "Could be months… yeah…"

"Or years?"

"Oh, no, I don't think it's been… well…" He breathed a big sigh and sank deeper into the sofa. I could see it bothered him. He took a long pull on his beer. "Well, however long it's been," he said, "It's definitely been a *while*."

"You think maybe there's a *reason* you don't know?" I asked him.

"Like what?" he said.

"Maybe something you want to tell me?"

He chased a deep sigh with another swallow. "You know, it's strange you ask. It's been one wacky weekend, now with you showing up like this." He shook his head and chuckled. "You wouldn't have believed it last night. Some guy tried to break in here. I'm sitting right here when he walks through the front door. He must have somehow had keys made."

I sunk back into the armchair, feeling the by-now-familiar riptide of déjà vu pulling at me. "Wow. What did you do?"

"I told him to get out. And—you're not going to believe this—"

"He told *you* to get out," I said.

He looked at me sharply. "How'd you know?"

"I mean, what *else* is he gonna say? Gotta keep up the bluff, right? So, he walks right in…"

"Yeah. Like it's his place. And what's even more bizarre—

he *looks* like me. I could be lookin' in a mirror—except he's wearing these golf clothes with mud all over them."

"So, he comes in, pretending to be you and tells you to get out of your own apartment?"

"Exactly. Where he gets the nerve, is what I want to know."

I took a long swallow of beer. "You think it could be something else?"

"Like what, else?"

"You know—more to the story."

"More what?

"Like maybe he actually is you and that you're the phony?'

Dave stared at me; a frown line etched deeply into his brow.

"I mean from where *he* sits," I said.

"Why would he think that? He knows he's the phony."

"I'm just saying… guy's obviously nuts, right? How'd you get rid of him?"

"We tussled a little and then the landlord called the cops and they dragged him away. It was something else." He held out a grease-stained hand. "Get the shakes just talking about it."

"And you've got no idea who this guy was?"

Dave shrugged. "Some *guy*. All I can think of is it might be one of those identity things, you know, where they try to steal your identity for fraudulent purposes."

"Isn't that mostly on the internet?"

"Yeah, you wouldn't think they'd have the nads to barge into your place and try to take it from you in person."

It was time to stop pussyfooting around. Any minute, I knew, the Dave in the car was going to lose patience and show up swinging. That was a confrontation I was in no condition to referee. I stood up, walked over and positioned myself behind a tattered armchair.

"Okay, Dave—or whatever your name is—I think it's about time we came clean, and we laid our cards on the table."

He banged his beer bottle down rattling the empties. "I think I got a good idea what you're going to say," he grinned.

"Uh-huh, you do… well—you do?"

This *clone* Dave stood up came over and put his hands on my shoulders. His eyes were glistening. "I just want you to know, I never lost faith. Not for a minute. I said, 'just give him a little time. He just needs to iron out a few things. Then he'll be back, and we'll get 'er done.'

"Sorry… ah… who are we talking about now?"

"*You*, buddy. I'm talking about you. That's why you came back, right? To play him, right? You want a rematch."

"Rematch?" I said, pointing vaguely toward my bandage. "Rematch with who?"

"Holy shit," said Clone Dave. "You really don't remember?"

Nutville

"What do you mean 'the subject never came up'?"

Dave and I were driving back to Earl's. He'd been grilling me since we left his place—actually, it was starting to seem more and more like Clone Dave's place. I'd spent twenty minutes talking to the guy and at no time had he given me reason to believe he was anybody else but the real deal. Dave was pissed at me for not challenging him, letting the imposter off the hook but I had to tell him I just couldn't do it. I mean the guy never gave me any reason to doubt him. It wasn't like he was hiding anything. He was just *Dave*.

"What did you talk about all that time?"

"I don't know. Just caught up."

"On what? You never saw him before!"

"Of course, I saw him before. I'm looking at him now. It's you—he was *you*. Looked like you, talked like you. He drank three beers almost before I cracked one. Sound like anybody we know?"

"Don't try to convince me it was me in there, Charley. You're never gonna convince me so you can forget about it. You let me down back there. You were supposed to make him clear out, not be drinking my beer while you catch up on old times you never had."

"Oh, right Dave—you expect me to just waltz into a guy's place and inform him that he isn't who he says he is and that I've got the real guy in the car?"

"That's not his place, Charley. And that's what you said you were gonna do."

I felt bad arguing with Dave, knew him well enough to know he was more frightened than angry. I wasn't feeling all that great myself. I was exhausted, emotionally in shock, my head throbbed and that was only part of it—the déjà vu mixed with fish-out-of-water feeling had been growing steadily stronger. Where I'd felt it the most—the real reason I hadn't done a better job confronting this other Dave was that, sitting there in his apartment, I could't shake the feeling that the real ringers in all this were me and the Dave out in the car. But how to explain this now to original Dave or "Regular Dave" as I now thought of him?

We were on our way back to Earl's only because I couldn't think of anyplace else to go. My place, under the circumstances, was out of the question. This new edition of Cathy, I knew, would not welcome the presence of another mental case recuperating in her living room.

It was close to eleven by the time we pulled into Earl's parking lot. The place was hopping for a Monday night; the lot was nearly full up. We grabbed a table in the center of the room next to a table full of league bowlers and started waving for waitresses. I could see Melanie behind the bar serving beers to a couple of yuppie bikers all tricked out in expensive leathers. I remembered Cathy's red biker jacket— the one I'd never seen before and couldn't have imagined she'd ever wear. But then, never in a million years would I have pictured her in that old school nurse's get up either.

Cathy. Just thinking about her and the bizarre scene back at the house roiled my stomach but I needed to set emotion aside for the moment. Answers were closer now. The two Daves, I was sure, were a strong clue toward deciphering the cockeyed reality and general strangeness we'd encountered since coming back from the desert. It was apparent that— whatever had happened—had happened to both Dave and me. We were two fish out of water. Question was how did we get here? Where is here? And what happened to the water?

The weekend's events had taken their toll on Dave. Leta was the comeliest of Earl's waitresses and normally he'd be trying to steer her onto his lap while we ordered but now, he just stared straight ahead, eyes glazed.

"What'll you have, hon?" she asked him.

"Who am I?" he asked her.

"Who are you? Well now—take a minute and I'm sure it'll come to you."

"I need to hear it from you."

"Honey, maybe you could look at your driver's license. I've got orders stacking up in the kitchen."

"I know who I am. I want to know who you think I am."

Leta cracked her gum and looked over at me. "What're you gonna have, hon?"

"Cheeseburger, medium and a Coors. Extra tater tots."

"I'm just asking you to tell me who I am," Dave persisted. "That's not so much to ask, is it?"

"Who are you? Let's see." She squinted at him. "You're… double cheeseburger, the works, chili fries, pitcher of Bud Light and keep 'em coming."

Dave exhaled in relief and smiled for the first time that evening. "Leta," he said. "You rock."

I spent the next quarter hour highlighting for Dave some of the other craziness I'd encountered since he'd dropped me off in the cab Sunday night: Mike and Ron's refusal to acknowledge the golf trip or aftermath, not being recognized at work, non-existence of my children and, of course, Floyd winning the Open. I wasn't sure he heard all of it. He just sat there staring into his beer until I got to the part about Floyd. "Hold it," he said. "Floyd did what?"

"He won the Open. Last weekend at Pebble Beach."

He stared at me. "The U.S. Open?"

"That's the one."

"That's impossible."

"You think?"

He shook his head. "Can't happen. Who told you—him?"

"It was in the paper."

"Okay, forget the guy in my apartment. That's nuts."

"Let me tell you what I think," I said. "Now don't freak out on me when I say this…"

Dave nodded but kind of winced at the same time.

"I'm not at all sure that this place—here—is the same place we left last Friday night."

"What do you mean?"

"I mean this is someplace different. Some other place."

Dave leaned in. "Hell you talking about?"

"Well, you remember the crash, right?"

"Yeah. I was there."

"Well, think about everything that's happened since then. They can't find the plane. Mike and Ron say they don't know about it. You get home, there's some other guy living there…"

"What are you saying?"

"Well…" I shrugged and gave him a look. "Maybe all this strange stuff is not so strange. Maybe you and me—we're the ones not supposed to be here."

"Okay, now you're scaring me." Dave glanced around the bar. "You're not telling me we *died* in that crash?"

Leta appeared with another pitcher. She hadn't finished filling Dave's mug when he grabbed it and gulped it down, splashing beer on the table.

"It's my pleasure to serve you," she said.

Dave looked over at the table full of lady bowlers. "Doesn't feel like heaven," he said. "And it's doubtful they're serving beer and chili fries in hell. I'm sorry, man," he said. "But what you're talking about doesn't sound like dead. More like bullshit."

"I didn't say we were dead—*you* did."

"Well, what then?" said Dave, through a mouthful of

chili fries.

"Haven't figured it out yet. All I know is we're in a different place than we started out in last Friday and I'm also sure, wherever this is, it's got something to do with Floyd."

"Floyd?"

"Think about it. The only person I told about going out to the desert was Floyd. Then I come back and find out everybody knows I went. Everybody except the bankers, who should have known because they went with us. Okay? Then we have the fact that since I got back, everybody and his brother thinks I'm a brain surgeon. But the only person on the planet with any reason to think that is Floyd."

"Why would he think that?"

"Because I told him—long story. Then I arrive back in town to find out that same Floyd Birdwell—a very marginal five handicapper—has run away with the United States Open Championship, beating the best golfers in the world."

"Not in the real world, he doesn't."

"And, for icing on the cake, we have nurses dressing like porn stars and Floyd's dentist on TV acting like he's some kind of Yoda character. Right? And what about all this snogging going on? It's like the whole county's doing it. Who else but Floyd could have thought that up?"

"Okay, but what about the other me in my apartment? What's Floyd got to do with that?"

"No idea," I said. "But *something*."

"What are we supposed to do about all this?"

"I'm thinking, if we can figure out how we got here, we ought to be able to reverse the process—go back the same way."

"Back where?"

"Back to normal. Where we came from."

After last call at Earl's, we drove over to my place.

Seeing Cathy's Volvo absent from the driveway at this late hour was a knife to my heart but, at the same time, a relief. I'd be able to get Dave in the door without an argument. But where the hell was she? What is there to do in Walnut Hill—or Nutville—as I now thought of it—at two a.m. on a Tuesday? I didn't know *this* Cathy. This Cathy was a complete stranger.

Half-stumbling through the front door, Dave had shushed me, saying we didn't want to wake up her and the kids.

A sob caught in my throat. "You remember the kids?"

"You kidding? How many birthdays I been to?"

So much for Dr. Farrow's dream theory. I stopped in the doorway and hugged him. "Thanks, buddy."

"No thanks necessary. I always had a good time."

"Anyway," I said, steering him toward the living room. "Cathy's not home and there aren't any kids."

"What?"

"We're in Nutville, remember? No kids in Nutville."

He squinted at me through blood-shot eyes. "No kids in Nutville?"

"I'll tell you about it tomorrow." I got him onto the sofa and covered him with a flannel blanket.

"Sean and little Sara, right?"

"Yeah. Try and get some sleep," I said.

"Charley…"

"Yeah?"

"Tell me again, what's all this got to do with Floyd?"

As You Probably Don't Remember

"Can I help you?" the security guard said, but he made it sound more like "Are you lost?"

He checked my name against the list on his clipboard, then came out of the gatehouse and gave the Taurus a long look-over, making it plain that the kind of distressed sheet metal I drove was seldom seen inside the sacred portals of Meadowbank's main gate.

"Mr. Cotter… I'm afraid I'm going to have to ask for some i.d."

I dug for my wallet. "Is there a problem?" I asked.

The guard shook his head. "No. But with everything that's been going on, we're taking extra precautions." He handed me back the license. "Thanks for your cooperation."

He directed me to the visitor's lot where I parked under a eucalyptus tree opposite a row of gleaming luxury cars. I was barely out of my not-so-gleaming one, when an attendant drove up in a spotless golf cart adorned with the Meadowbank crest. He wore a crisp white oxford shirt and tie and carried a walkie-talkie.

"Good afternoon, Mr. Cotter," he said. "May I take

your bag?"

The inside of my car trunk generally looks and smells like your typical parking lot dumpster, but the young man reached gamely for my rental clubs and shoe bag and loaded them onto his cart. "Mr. Kelly and Mr. Baxter are waiting for you in the grillroom. I can take you up there."

"Fine." I caught myself whispering. Meadowbank had hushed me. I hadn't seen the course yet and was already awed and intimidated and wondered again, if we were indeed going to play, whether I'd even be able to make contact with the ball.

We drove up the winding driveway past the splendid portico and grand entrance and then around back where a commanding stone terrace overlooked an expansive practice putting green. Beyond it, the sparkling grassy wonderland of Meadowbank waited for me. The attendant caught my expression and smiled. "First time?" he said.

I nodded. "Course looks like it's in good shape."

"Meadowbank," he said, "Is always in good shape."

We climbed a dozen broad stone steps and crossed the terrace into a shadowy grillroom that smelled of burnt firewood, leather, and whiskey.

Mike and Ron sat perched and prosperous over a pair of martinis at the L-shaped bar. Mike was in full-on banker mode in a generously cut double-breasted midnight blue suit that emphasized his height and contrasted with his gray streaked hair. Ron's three-piece gray pin stripe was cut tightly around his middle. A crimson handkerchief billowed from his chest pocket. Starched French cuffs, monogrammed and decorated with gold chain links, flaring from his sleeves. His coiffure had been curried somewhat since our last meeting and now resembled a coonskin cap minus the tail.

"Well, don't we look golfy," he said.

I had worn my "A" golf outfit for the occasion: white Ashworth polo with robin's egg blue collar over pleated khakis. The swelling and discoloration around the stitched-up gash on the side of my forehead had subsided to the point where I'd been able to replace the head wrap with a smaller but still conspicuous square of gauze. And I was glad, looking around, that I'd thought to include a blazer.

"You said we might have a chance to play."

"Absolutely," said Mike. "First, there are some people who want to say hello. He slipped off the barstool and pointed Ron out to the bartender, miming that he'd sign for the drinks.

"What name?" Ron asked Mike.

"Anyone but mine," Mike said, winking at me.

He led me over to a table in the corner of the room where two middle-aged men in sport coats huddled over cocktails with a younger, gray-faced guy in a beige windbreaker.

"Gentlemen," Mike said. "Look who decided to come back."

"Well, I don't believe it," said one of the older men, a salesman type with a TV preacher haircut and too-white teeth. He looked very familiar, like I'd seen him in photos. The other older guy had dark wavy hair, bushy eyebrows, full lips and looked to be somewhere in his fifties. He wore a dark blazer over an open-collared white shirt that set off his deep tan. He had the sure bearing of a guy who came from money then had made more of it.

"Charley," Mike said in the chummy tone he used with his "high-roller" bank customers. "You remember Larry Lerner, Lerner Development?"

The rich guy held out his hand. "I imagine he does. And, if not, I'll bet he remembers the two grand he clipped me for last time. You back for more, Chuck?"

I did my best to return his smile but had no clue what he was talking about. Was he serious? Two grand? Twenty bucks was a big bet for me on the golf course. "You know what?" I said. "I think you might have me confused with somebody else."

That cracked him up. Mike and the TV preacher joined in and even the guy in the windbreaker looked amused.

"He's right," Lerner said. "I was confused out of

two grand." That provoked a new wave of laughter. Mike slapped me on the back and pointed at the TV preacher. "Don't tell me you don't remember this guy."

"Doesn't matter if he remembers me," the TV preacher laughed. "Long as he voted for me."

Now I recognized him. Art Dunphy had been Walnut Hill's mayor for years, since well before Cathy and I moved to the area. I'd seen photos of him in the Gazette and then once in person at a town meeting Cathy had dragged me to but that had been from a row near the back of the hall. This was the closest I'd ever been to the man yet here he was grinning at me like we were old pals.

"Mr. Mayor," I said, taking his offered hand. "I'm pretty sure I *did* vote for you. Twice."

Dunphy's eyes lit up. "Not in the same election, I trust."

That got them all laughing again—Dunphy throwing his head back as if hoping to be photographed like that.

"And of course, you know Roger Stickley," Mike said. The guy in the windbreaker nodded and raised a fore finger. No handshakes for him. This was Roger Stickley, new owner since his old man's death of Stickley Municipal Golf Course. I'd played countless rounds at Stickley but had caught only rare sightings of young Roger slinking in and out of his private office off the pro shop, his low profile motivated, I imagined, by self-preservation. His five-some policy had stirred up much resentment among the local golfing public. Now, with this new plan to allow six-somes, he might want to consider hiring a bodyguard.

Ron came over from the bar and we all sat down around the polished table. A pair of waiters materialized, one clearing away the glasses while the other spread a starched white tablecloth and set out silverware. Refill orders were taken, lunch menus handed out. Stickley and I ordered sodas. The others wanted cocktails.

"So…Charley," the Mayor Dunphy said when everyone had their drinks. "I think I can speak for everybody when I say welcome back." He lifted his glass. The others nodded, toasting me.

"Thanks," I said. "Feels like I hardly left." There was an

awkward pause. Finally, Mike said, "So, how was the desert?"

Only twenty-four hours ago, his question would have infuriated or, at least, perplexed me but now, aware that this conversation was taking place in Nutville, I said, "The desert was… interesting."

"What brings you back?" asked Lerner behind a toothy grin.

"Well, you know—home… family… work."

"Of course."

"Have a chance to play much golf out there?"

The question, for whatever reason, brought to mind the ghostly character trudging through the wind farm with his golf clubs.

"Well, that was the original idea but… not really, no."

"Too bad," said Lerner.

"That's a shame," said Dunphy.

"What happened to his head," Stickley muttered to no one in particular.

Mayor Dunphy cleared his throat. "What I think we're all wondering, Charley, is whether you've done any more thinking about our offer."

"What offer was that?"

The mayor leaned back in his chair, obviously flustered. Mike and Ron looked uncomfortable. Stickley rolled his eyes and mumbled something that sounded like: "You got to be kidding."

Larry Lerner looked up from the martini he was stirring with a sprig of olives. "You don't remember the deal we offered you?"

"Charley's not serious," said Ron. Then he looked over at me. "Are you?"

Out of the corner of my eye, I could see Mike nudge the mayor and point to the bandage on my forehead.

"Sorry," I said. "I had a little accident Friday night. Doctor thinks I might have a mild case of amnesia."

"Well then he's not gonna remem—" Stickley began but Lerner shushed him.

There was a pause while they stared at me and then each other. Finally, Lerner leaned back with his drink. "Well, then I guess we'd better present it to him again," he said.

Mike elbowed Ron who sat up straight in his chair, squared his shoulders and licked his lips.

"Okay, Charley," he said. "Wow, this is really weird. But I'll try, okay?" He took a deep breath. "Okay…phew…you must be aware of the recent incidents of snogging here at Meadowbank."

"I've seen some stuff on the news."

Lerner frowned at my answer.

"Okay, whatever," Ron continued. "Anyway, the situation is much, much worse than they're reporting."

"How so?"

"There's hardly a night goes by when someplace or other isn't getting snogged."

"Ron," said the mayor, indicating a nearby table of diners. "Let's keep our voices down, alright?"

"Sorry." He lowered his voice to a stage whisper. "Meadowbank was hit again just last night. They had themselves a good old time over on four."

Four? That was one of the holes along Hibbard Road. Not far from the spot where I'd fallen through the fence. "Can't the police do something?" I said.

The mayor frowned. "Police can't be everywhere."

"Yeah, but I mean what's the big deal—a bunch of nuts running around playing golf at night?"

All five of them were shaking their heads.

"Charley," said Ron. "This is bigger than that. Way bigger."

"Fellas," the mayor said. "Voices, please."

Ron went back to his stage whisper. "They aren't just snogging golf courses anymore. Or even streets and parks. It's gotten out of hand. Night before last, a foursome snogged the Safeway on Durant Street."

"They played through a grocery store?"

"Shhhh!" said the mayor.

Ron pursed his lips and nodded. "Hacked their way through produce, destroyed the dairy section—cartons smashed, milk and yogurt all over the place. Terrifying. Three people had to be rushed to the hospital."

"They were assaulted?"

Ron shook his head. "Lactose intolerant."

"Where were the cops?"

"I'm sure they were out chasing other snoggers."

"Other snoggers?"

"Snogging is an almost nightly occurrence, Charley," said the Mayor. And the police have been arresting them but—"

"The jails are full," said Mike.

"How many snoggers do you figure are out there?"

Mike looked over at the mayor. Dunphy cleared his throat again and shook his head. "We're not releasing official numbers yet."

Larry Lerner played with his napkin, twisting it into knots. "More than a few," he said darkly.

"Far more than the police are equipped to handle," said Dunphy. "We've gotten reports from as far away as Vallejo."

"It's not only happening *here*, then?" I asked.

"There've been scattered incidents around the county," Lerner said. "But it's mainly around here,"

"Why do you suppose that is?" I said. "Maybe that should give you a clue to who's behind it?"

My lunch companions shuffled around in their seats

and threw sidelong "I told you so" glances at each other.

"These snoggers claim there's no place for them to play golf," Lerner said.

"Tell them to join a club," said Ron.

"They do have that option," Lerner nodded. "And there are public courses." He indicated Roger Stickley. "Stickley Municipal for one."

I couldn't resist saying, "If you don't mind playing six-somes."

Stickley shook his head. "Not my fault," he said.

Mike waved a dismissive hand. "This isn't about Stickley," he said. "Moving on."

"So—Charley," Ron said. "Can you help us?"

"Me? What can I do?"

Stickley rolled his eyes again.

"Charley," Mike said, leaning forward. "Isn't there anything about any of this that rings a bell?"

"I'm sorry to drag everybody through this again."

Mike sighed and gestured for Ron to continue.

"There's this ringleader person," Ron said. "They say he invented snogging. He's the one who inspires the snoggers and gets them to—snog, I guess."

"How does he do that?"

"They have rallies at night, at Stickley or one of the country clubs. They've been here at Meadowbank a few times."

"So, arrest the guy. What's the big deal?"

"We don't know who he is," said Ron.

"So, what we were hoping you'd do," Mike said, "is challenge this Snog person whoever he is and…" He looked around at the others.

"Beat him," said Stickley.

I scanned Mike's and Ron's faces for a signal that wasn't there. "Beat this… ringleader?" I said at last.

"Snog," said Larry Lerner. "That's who we're talking about."

"Snog is a person? I thought snog was the name of the game—night golf. "

"It is but it's also the guy—the ringleader," Mike said. "It's what he calls himself. Snog."

"We need you to out-snog him," said the mayor.

"We're counting on it," said Lerner.

"Odd name, Snog," said Dunphy. "They tell me that in England 'snogging' means heavy petting."

"What's that got to do with anything?" Stickley said.

"I don't suppose there's anything to that?" the mayor said.

"What do you mean?" said Lerner.

"Well, think about it. Men and women… clandestine meetings in the darkness… indiscriminately whacking balls. It could be a sexual thing—some sort of erotic ritual."

"Ooh," said Ron. "An orgy with golf clubs. And we're stopping this why?"

"Let me see if I'm getting this," I said. "You want me to… snog… with this person who calls himself Snog?"

They all nodded.

"And win?"

"He gets it," said Dunphy.

"Somebody give him a prize," groaned Stickley. "Does it bother anyone else that he doesn't remember any of this?"

"Roger," said Dunphy. "Look at his head. The boy's obviously got amnesia. He can't even remember how many times he voted for me."

I thought of the scrawled slogan I'd seen outside the bank building. "This is the guy they say no one can beat at his own game—*that* Snog?"

"That's right."

"But you think *I* can beat him?"

"Let's say we're willing to take the chance," said Mike and winked at the others.

"We've got faith in you," said Ron.

"We're willing to pay," said Mayor Dunphy.

"Within reason," said Lerner.

My head was beginning to throb again and the caffeine in my soda wasn't helping. "I'm still not sure I see the point. Sooner or later you'll figure out who he is and then you can arrest him."

Lerner was shaking his head. "I don't think you understand. The guy's got a cult following. He's like a folk hero. Arrest him you make him a martyr. Somebody's got to beat him at his own game, steal his thunder. People find out he's a loser, they'll drop him fast."

"It's better than shooting him," said Ron.

Our sandwiches arrived then, served with fancy garnish on fine china. The silverware was sterling, each piece emblazoned with the Meadowbank crest. A pair of waiters hovered and missed nothing. Empty plates were instantly snatched away. My water glass was replenished after each sip. When the table was clear and coffee poured, Mayor Dunphy leaned forward.

"Charley, I think we're all in agreement that what happened in the past is past, water under the bridge. What we'd like to do now is make a fresh start. How does that sound?"

"Fine, I guess."

"You see, Charley," Dunphy continued. "We know this snog business is only a fad and, given a little time, it'll die out by itself. We want to accelerate the process. The sooner we can put this madness behind us, the sooner we can all get back to the way things have always been. Walnut Hill is a quiet city, as you know. That's why people come here to live. This kind of disruption damages property and disturbs law-abiding citizens as they go about their daily lives. It needs to stop."

Larry Lerner grinned and jerked a thumb toward Dunphy. "And that's why he keeps getting elected."

"Okay," I said. "I've got it now, but this brings me back to my original question: why me?"

Stickley slapped the table. "That's what he said last time!"

"Last time?"

"Yeah," said Stickley. "Just before you turned tail and ran off to the desert or wherever in hell you went."

"Roger, that's not fair," said Dunphy.

"That's what happened, isn't it? I'm just saying—"

"You're that sure I can beat him?"

Dunphy nodded. So did Mike and Ron. Lerner was occupied with signing the check. Stickley sat slouched back in his chair, arms folded, staring at the ceiling.

"Okay," Mike said. "Now we're up to speed. Do you remember the compensation package, or do we need to go through it again?"

"Maybe, just for clarity." I said.

Mike nodded to Ron who made a show of clearing his throat.

"Well," he said. "As you probably don't remember, we decided against a straight financial arrangement because there's no line for ah, snogging in... ah... anyone's budget. Even if it were posted under 'incidentals' or 'miscellaneous,' it might draw attention so we came up with something we thought would be better."

"Better than money?"

"You certainly thought so the last time we... ah, before your... head thing. In fact, if I remember correctly, you gave me the nicest big, warm hug, even tried to kiss me." Ron blushed. "I suppose I should feel hurt you don't remember."

"Just tell him for God's sake," moaned Stickley.

"All right, here's the deal. We arrange a match

between you and this Snog person to be held as soon as possible. If you beat him—"

"Wait," I said. "Back up. I only get paid if I beat him?"

Ron looked at the others, then back at me. "Well, yes," he said. "But if you beat him… when you beat him… as soon as you beat him… you will receive… are you ready for this…? An honorary lifetime membership for you and your family to Meadowbank Country Club with full privileges. No initiation fee. No monthly dues. All you do is cover your food and bar bills. Oh, and caddies—you have to pay your caddie if you—"

Ron never finished because the coffee cup either flew out of my hand or I tossed it and then—trying to catch it in the air—sprawled headlong across the table, sending cups, tableware and water glasses flying.

"Is that a yes?" said Roger Stickley.

"I'd say we have a deal." Mike said, dabbing at his slacks with a napkin.

"We had a deal last time," Roger Stickley grumped. "How do we know he won't run away again?"

"Charley," Mike said after Ron had settled me back in my chair and was reapplying his lip balm. "I think it would make us all feel better if you could give us some idea why you backed out on the deal last time. It would help clear the air and get us back on track."

"Yes," said the mayor. "We don't want that happening again."

I looked from face to expectant face. The déjà vu feeling was back with a vengeance. In what reality had I had been here before? In this room with these same men looking at me, waiting like they waited now for an answer? I must have said yes. Who wouldn't? A membership to Meadowbank? For a golfer, it didn't get any better than that. I mean, Pebble Beach, Augusta or Shinnecock Hills were equally hallowed but Meadowbank—just a couple of miles from my home!

But how could I explain to them now that I wasn't that guy? That I had no idea why he'd run out on them and split for the desert? This version of me had been someplace else at the time—a place he very much wanted to get back to.

"Well actually," I said at last. "It was a personal thing. Cathy and I had been having our problems and we thought if we took some time off—spent some time apart—we could make a fresh start."

"But we had a deal—" Stickley started to say but Mike cut him off. "Did you get it all worked out?" he said.

"Oh, yeah," I said with a fake grin. "Everything's fine now. Cathy and I are… solid again."

"It would have been nice if he'd said something at the time," Stickley said. "Instead of leaving us high and dry."

Dunphy patted Stickley's arm. "I'm satisfied with Charley's answer,' he said. "We all know that family comes first. And if a situation should arise, I'm sure Charley will come to us before he does anything like… disappear again."

That sort of marked the official end of lunch. Mayor Dunphy stood up, came over and embraced me, saying how delighted and relieved he was that I was doing this for the city. Then he whispered something to Mike, thanked everybody else and glad-handed his way out of the dining room. Larry Lerner shook my hand warmly and wished me luck. Roger Stickley nodded and skulked away.

When they were gone, Mike pulled his chair over. "It's important for you to understand that, whatever happens, all of us—Lerner, especially the mayor, everyone—will need to disavow knowledge of what you're doing."

"I understand."

"Snogging is a sensitive issue," said Ron. "It's only a misdemeanor right now but that could change. And it would be a political catastrophe for Dunphy or any of us if word leaked out that we conspired with you to commit a crime, no matter how trivial. We'd all be in hot water."

As we headed off to the locker room, I remember thinking that I still didn't know where Dave and I had landed or how we'd gotten here but I was more than willing, for the next few hours at least, to set questions and concerns aside.

We were headed out to play Meadowbank.

In Da Hole!

"We can take your party now, Mr. Kelly."

The golf starter beamed at us from behind his gilt-trimmed podium. I thought the tuxedo was a bit much but then decided why not? This was Meadowbank after all, one of the oldest and grandest of grand old clubs. The venerable dame was entitled to her lavishness even if it included a measure of pretense.

And speaking of lavish, Mike, Ron and I had emerged from the sumptuous locker room to find we'd each been assigned *two* caddies, one to drive the cart and suggest clubs and another, a forecaddie, to run ahead and locate our balls. Six caddies for three players seemed like overkill to me, but I supposed a little local knowledge couldn't hurt when it came to gauging distances and reading greens and, anyway, Mike told me Larry Lerner had arranged everything and was footing the bill.

My caddies' names were Raoul and Herbert. Tall and narrow shouldered with large drooping eyes set back in a massive head, Raoul looked like a butler in a haunted house movie. Herbert was younger, somewhere in his early thirties, smaller and energetic. The visor he wore backward with a pencil tucked into it, along with his caddie's apron, made him look like a grocery clerk.

The starter, whose name was Stephen, fussed over us as if we were royalty, managing to kiss Mike on both cheeks then directed us with a flourish toward the first tee box.

Walking onto the first tee was like stepping into an oil painting. It was mid-afternoon by then and the descending sun spread an amber hue. I was so intently gaping down the fairway that I didn't notice the man sitting next to the tee box until I tripped over him, stumbling headlong and rolling over flat on my back in the grass. Raoul and Herbert rushed over and pulled me to my feet. There was a smattering of applause from a small gallery that had gathered around the tee. The man, who appeared to be in his late sixties, had been sitting in a low lawn chair. I apologized and then went over to where Mike was wind-milling a pair of irons with one hand to loosen up.

"Who *are* these people?" I asked him out of the corner of my mouth.

"The gallery."

"Is someone famous out on the course?"

"They're here to see us." He handed the irons to one of his caddies and got a driver in return.

"But we're nobody."

"Charley, this is Meadowbank. every round played here is considered important—historic. That's why a gallery always goes along. It's tradition."

"You mean they're gonna watch us play?"

"They'll be rooting for you. That's what they get paid for."

"They get paid? To be a gallery?"

Mike laughed. "Don't worry, it's on Lerner. You're his boy now."

When it came time for me to tee off my hands were shaking. It wasn't so much the gallery—I'd played in front of people before, back in college and then in the occasional charity fundraiser. It was a nervous reaction to being on those hallowed grounds, beginning a round I never dreamed I'd get a chance to play.

After Stephen, the starter, had presented each of us with a leather-embossed score cardholder and divot spike with pearl inlay—along with a hug—to commemorate our "historic" round, we were clear to tee off.

The first at Meadowbank is a straightaway par four with mature trees set close to the fairway on either side. I managed to semi-top a low, loping drive that somehow stayed in the fairway then acknowledged the gallery's enthusiastic applause with a little wave even though I felt a horse's ass for doing it. I mean I knew they were paid to clap, and they certainly knew they were paid to do it, so how silly was that? Mike and Ron each hit a version of their standard drives, Mike's high, glancing fade followed by Ron's low, curling draw. Neither found the fairway but settled in the lush rough to either side.

Our little caravan struck off then, Mike, Ron and the caddies in carts, me on foot—there was no way I was going to ride on that golf course. The gallery tagged along, keeping a respectable distance. My four iron that cleared a sand trap and stuck on the left side of the green got another nice round of applause.

When my putt curled past the hole, the collective "Oooh!" sounded almost sincere. By the time we teed off on the second, I was actually enjoying our little "army." Before long I found myself playing to the crowd, chatting before a shot, just little comments like "What do you suppose I was thinking, hitting it over here?" or "Anybody got any ideas?" It was the kind of thing I'd seen the pros do to keep themselves loose and the customers entertained. I knew how asinine it was to be strutting around pretending these were genuine fans, but I was enjoying the novelty of having somebody root for me.

Meadowbank was everything I'd hoped it would be, lush and well-kept almost beyond imagining, each hole an architectural and esthetic masterpiece. Unfortunately, the events of the weekend—not to mention the concussion—had sabotaged my game. I bogeyed three of the first five holes and then, on the par three sixth, pushed my tee shot to the right where it bounced off a cart path and kicked into the woods. Hebert found the ball stymied against some bushes and from there it took me four more strokes to get down.

After I booted my drive on seven, I could sense the gallery's fervor waning. Their enthusiasm—one guy had taken to screaming: "in da hole!" a scant nanosecond after each of my drives—had dwindled with each unfortunate stroke into sporadic applause and nervous throat-clearing. I could feel Mike's and Ron's eyes on me and sense their concern growing with each errant shot.

After we holed out on seven, Raoul drove us past the eighth tee box and then cut across the fairway. Mike and Ron, along with their entourage and gallery followed us.

"Where are we going?" I asked the caddie.

"Here's where we skip over to ten," he said. "They're having a do on nine today which means eight green's all fenced off."

"Fenced off? What do you mean?"

"For the dogs," he said. "They're showing them on nine, but they have to fence off the eighth green too or you'll have dogs crapping all over it."

"What are dogs doing on the golf course?"

"Show dogs. Do it about once a month. Lot of the members are dog lovers." He spat tobacco juice into the grass. "Love their dogs."

"Dog show?"

"Yes sir."

"On Meadowbank?"

He nodded. "They use the ninth hole because that's closest to the clubhouse and then you're not trucking dogs all over the place. But when Circe de Soleil comes in, they'll put the tent way out on fourteen and then convoy everybody down there in golf carts."

"They put a circus out here?"

"Couple weeks, every year. You don't hear too much about it outside the club because they do it kind of exclusive for the members, you know."

"Doesn't anyone complain?"

"Who do you mean?"

"The members—the golfing members. What do they say about circuses and dog shows on their golf course?"

"They don't say too much. Golfers're mostly in the minority. Meadowbank—what you have the most of is rich people. Families full of 'em. And I think you'll appreciate what I mean when I say that rich people, when they want it, they don't like anybody sayin' they can't have it. Tell the club manager we want our daughter's coming-out party out next to the lake on number twelve because it's nice out there in May, that's where it's gonna be."

"But I thought Meadowbank was mostly restricted to men."

Raoul glanced at me. "That was once upon a time," he said. "The women have the run of the place now. Make all the rules."

We came up alongside the eighth green. It was surrounded by a four-foot-high, wood and wire fence painted a tasteful green. Beyond the green and the ninth tee box were rows of little green and white striped tents set at twenty- or thirty-yard intervals on either side of the fairway stretching toward the clubhouse. A chorus of barks and howls floated toward us on the wind. Raoul steered us through the rough bordering the tenth fairway. Herbert dropped off the back of the cart and loped off in the direction we'd be hitting.

"We'll just go up here and tee off on ten," Raoul said. "Maybe next time you're here those other holes'll be open for play."

"They're open most of the time, right?"

"How's that?"

"How often do they close holes down for stuff like this?"

Raoul shook his sad lion's head. "You mean how often do they open them. Meadowbank, you almost never get an entire eighteen holes free at any one time. In all the fourteen years I've been here the entire course's been open only once or twice, maybe, that I've seen. One of those was when the president come."

"But this is one of the great golf courses of the world."

Raoul pulled the cart up next to the tenth tee. "So, they tell me," he said, and went to fetch my driver.

Skipping the two holes had tested the staunchness of our gallery. They'd had to hoof the five-hundred-yard detour over to ten and were now untidily strewn across the fairway and in between the trees lining the hole. While we waited for them to clear out of the way, I asked Mike and Ron why, if they were members, we'd had to snog the course that night with Floyd.

"We're not members," Mike said with a laugh. "We're Lerner's guests."

"Oh, God," said Ron. "Can you picture Floyd here in the daytime? He'd want to play right through that dog show."

I said that didn't sound like a bad idea. But I wondered how the bankers could remember, and freely admit, to having snogged Meadowbank but have no knowledge of the golf trip or the plane crash.

"We explained all this when we played last time," said Ron. "Guess you don't remember."

"When was that?"

"While ago. Shortly before you left."

"You really don't remember?" said Mike. "You had a hell of a round going till we ran into those debutantes on twelve."

"The cotillion," said Ron. "You must have been two or three under by then."

I stared at him. "I was three under—at Meadowbank?"

"Yep," said Mike. "You had it going."

"My God, I wish I could remember it. Was that the only time you had me out here?"

Mike nodded. "You're not exactly a big bank customer. We love you, but not at these prices."

"So, Larry Lerner's paying for this?"

"Yep," said Mike. "Same guy who'll make your club membership happen."

"Why does he care so much if people want to play golf at night?"

"He's civic minded," said Mike. "He agrees with the mayor. And the mayor says snogging is—what did he say?"

"An assault on the very fabric of our society," said Ron. "A slippery slope to chaos."

"That's what scares these rich guys the most and turns them into conservatives," said Mike. "Chaos. Disorder. Somebody going against the system. If the status quo breaks down, the big losers are the ones with something to lose. I never met a high roller yet that, after he'd made his, didn't spend the rest of his time hanging onto it."

"What about you?"

"What *about* me?"

"Do you think the snogs are dangerous?"

Mike made a face. "More like a nuisance. Bad for business."

"Was that all true about the home invasions?"

Mike shook his head. "Probably just hysteria.

"People are angry," said Ron. "There's no place left for them to play, except for we privileged few."

"Hey, you know what?" Mike said. "Screw 'em. Golf is a rich man's game, always has been. Land is expensive. There are just too many damn people in this county, new people moving in every day, all of them looking to live the good life. The American Dream. Quiet, safe streets. Good schools where kids don't shoot teachers or vice versa. You live in America, you feel you're supposed to have these things. You work hard, make a living, you earn the right to enjoy yourself on the weekend, play a little golf. Then they find out it doesn't work that way. Golf is a luxury not everybody can afford."

Mike pulled his driver out of his bag and teed up his ball.

"You want affordable golf? Suburban land's a million dollars a half-acre. Keep on going. Get out to the desert where it's cheap—and you know what? Even out there, golf is expensive because there's no water. You want grass and trees, you've got to start from scratch, find the water, truck everything in. I've got no sympathy for these malcontents running around terrorizing the neighborhood with golf clubs whining that there's no place for them to play in the daytime. Who says they're entitled to a starting time? Golf's not a right—it's a *game*. They want to play, they can join a country club, play all the golf they want."

"Hear, hear," said Ron. "Tell us how you really feel."

Mike's little tirade struck me as bizarre because the Mike I knew had always identified with the average Joe. He counted more blue-collar types than not among his associates—Dave being a prime example—and played his golf at Stickley with the rest of us unwashed hacks. Seeing him now, so thoroughly at home at Meadowbank, claiming that golf ought to be restricted to the privileged class was nearly as bizarre as Floyd winning the Open. But this wasn't the time or place to challenge him on it. Nothing—not even a dog show—was going to detract from my enjoyment of Meadowbank.

We played the next few holes in relative silence. The gallery hadn't regrouped since the turn and now straggled well behind.

Fifteen and sixteen, Raoul was saddened to report, were also closed to play. The fifteenth, a pretty little dogleg lined with Japanese Maples was hosting what Raoul described as an old-lady luncheon. There looked to be forty or fifty of them sitting around folding tables under a spacious striped tent like the ones we'd seen erected for the dog show. Raoul and the other caddies gave them a wide berth but even at a distance of seventy or so yards the din rising from the sea of pastel sundresses and gauzy hats rivaled the output from twice as many dogs.

"What are they doing?" I asked Raoul.

"Bingo tournament," he said. "Rich people."

It was late when we finished, after six. A few of the remaining gallery watched us putt out but most shuffled past the green, presumably headed to the paymaster's window. Raoul and Herbert congratulated me on the completion of my historic round, had me autograph their shirts and promised to have my bag waiting for me in the parking lot.

I had carded a sixty-four, which sounds god-like until you remember we only played fourteen holes. When I mentioned what a pity it was that we couldn't play the full eighteen, Mike said we were lucky to get in that many, he'd been out here sometimes when there were only three holes open because of all the birthday parties and crap going on.

"I don't get it," I said. "This is Meadowbank. People talk about this course in the same breath with Augusta and Pine Valley and they're playing bingo out there! Somebody ought to do something about this."

Mike scowled and shook his head. "You get a valuable property like this, Charley, you can't expect it be allocated to just *one* purpose. It's like I was saying— golf is not always the best use of a golf course."

"Anyway," Ron said. "Who says golf has to be eighteen holes? Who determined that? I know I don't always have the time to play eighteen—or even nine holes. What's wrong with playing six holes or three?"

"That's right," said Mike. "Think how many more people could play? You wouldn't need to dedicate such large parcels of land and you could build golf courses on sites where you'd never think to build them before."

"What would be really great," said Ron. "Would be to build courses in conjunction with other things like bowling alleys, parking lots and mini—"

"Why don't we go inside?" interrupted Mike. "Let Charley change his shoes."

Mike led us through the tall oaken doors into the men's locker room. Changing shoes before our round, my first glimpse of the place had nearly taken my breath away—aged oaken lockers and benches, chandeliers, tufted leather chairs and luxurious carpeting. My shoes had been cleaned and polished and were waiting for me on the attendant's counter.

Normally after one of our rounds at Stickley, there'd be a session of bullshitting and bellyaching at the bar while we paid off bets, celebrated our great shots and laughed off everything else. But today Mike and Ron left me alone while I changed my shoes. Afterward I walked out and met them underneath the front portico where an attendant had my clubs and waited to drive me to my car.

I started to apologize for my ragged game, but Mike shook his head. "You're fine. Don't worry about it."

Ron smiled. "We hardly expected you to shoot lights out after a nasty blow to the head like that."

"You da man," said Mike. "We have total faith in you."

"Well, thanks," I said. "How do you want to proceed on this… snog thing?"

"Your own timetable," said Mike. "Sooner the better. And you appreciate that none of us can be directly involved?"

"It's entirely your show," Ron agreed.

"So, I just… challenge him?"

"Yep," Mike said. "First you find him then you challenge him. Then, soon as you have the date and venue set, let us know so we can make sure to have a lot of people there to witness it. We want as many people as possible to see him crash and burn."

Ron clapped his hands together. "It needs to be one of those things that everybody knows but nobody talks about like the gay Supreme Court."

Mike and I looked at him.

Ron gave us a condescending smile. "Get a clue. Those robes?"

"All nine?"

He put an index finger to his lips. "You didn't hear it from me," he said.

Mike waved at the valet and his waiting golf cart. "Looks like they're ready for you."

"You never did tell me why you're so sure I can beat this Snog character."

"Research," said Ron. "We hired a consulting firm—the Sleeves Institute for Personal Golf. They all but guaranteed you'll win."

"Sleeves? Dr. Warren Sleeves?"

"That's the one," said Mike. "You've heard of him?"

"I think he's also a dentist," said Ron.

Dueling Daves

I slept in the next morning, waking around ten. Cathy had gone to work around 7:30. I'd heard the front door close, and the Volvo start up. For a minute or so I considered getting off the sofa but then thought what for? Get up and do what? Give the kids breakfast and drop them off at school? There were no kids. Hurry to the BART station and catch the express train to the city? There was no job in the city. I supposed I might drop by St. Helens—maybe scrub in on the odd brain surgery to see if anything looked familiar. But then, hadn't Dr. Farrow warned me to avoid stressful activity?

By the time I woke again, around noon, my head had stopped throbbing and the exhaustion had passed. The déjà vu feeling was gone too, replaced by a welcome numbness. Lying there in bed I kept replaying the old saw in my head: Today is the first day of the rest of your life. In my case, this was particularly true. I was a blank page, starting over from scratch. With a wife I barely knew, no kids and a profession so entirely foreign to me that I didn't dare practice it lest I kill somebody. And if that wasn't challenge enough, the setting for my new adventure was a world gone nuts, a world where everybody seemed, if not obsessed, well then at least preoccupied with golf. Where fanatical golfers hacked through supermarkets and a driving range psycho, with a five handicap, was the U.S. Open champion and, most nuts of all, a group of bankers and politicians looked to me as the man to beat this Snog person and put an end to his "reign of terror."

There was a note from Cathy taped to the bathroom

mirror that I'd hoped might contain some reconciling words but turned out instead to be an eviction notice. Apparently finding Dave sacked out in the recliner yesterday had been the last straw. She said she had mixed feelings about asking me to vacate the house we'd shared for so long, but that it had been her understanding, when I left for the desert, that I wouldn't be coming back, and she needed to be getting on with her life and that my presence was a 'hindrance' to her plans. But, in view of my head trauma, she offered me a week's grace after which I should kindly clear out.

I read the note again, then found myself staring in the mirror. So, I was a hindrance now? To what? More questions. One thing I was sure of, the Cathy I'd come home to was not the Cathy I'd left. And I sure as hell wasn't her Charley.

My bandage had been changed again, replaced by a large flesh colored Band-Aid that covered the stitches. Apparently, she'd found it in her heart to change the dressing while the hindrance slept. I looked closer to normal now but, under the circumstances, the word didn't seem to apply.

I was downstairs rummaging through a kitchen drawer looking for Dr. Farrow's phone number when the front doorbell rang. Dave stood on the front stoop—both of him.

"Charley," they said. "Tell this guy who I am."

I swore and instinctively covered one eye with my hand. But, no matter which eye I closed, there were still two of them standing there. I tried closing both eyes and opening them again but—no luck. The Daves were dressed alike in well-worn golf jackets and sweat-stained hats. Where they differed was underneath. One wore soiled blue coveralls while the other had on grass-and-dirt-stained golf clothes. Coveralls-clad Dave was clean-shaven while golfing-Dave sported a couple days' growth and a pair of Wayfarer shades.

"Which one are you?" I asked the golfing Dave.

"Three guesses."

"Yeah?" said the other one. "Ask him how come he didn't shave."

"Hey—I know who I am," golfing Dave said. "We're trying to figure out who the hell *you* are."

"Who do I look like, genius?"

They lunged at each other but I stepped between them.

"Guys—let's take it inside. Neighbors don't need to hear this."

We went into the kitchen where the Daves conked heads in front of the refrigerator while simultaneously reaching for a beer.

I hadn't forgotten about the Dave problem. With everything going on, it had just been simpler not to think about it and hope it would somehow work itself out. Bump on the head or no, there was just no good explanation for there being more than one Dave. It was just plain bizarre.

The Daves looked like mirrored images of each other as they popped open the cans, took long swallows and belched. Had Dr. Farrow said anything that could possibly account for this suds-swilling redundancy in my kitchen? I suppose amnesia or even his fugitive dream theory might account for me not remembering how many Daves there were but not why there were two Daves in the first place. Unless, of course, there was a very good reason for there being two Daves but I had forgotten what it was. I'd have to wait until next Tuesday at one p.m. to find out.

"Which one of you flew to the desert with me last Friday night?" I said.

Stubble-faced Dave raised his hand. Then, by way of corroberation, he took off his shades revealing a discolored left eye I'd recognized from the other night at Earl's.

"Yeah, but wait a min—" the other one protested. But I shook my head.

"My kitchen. I'll ask the questions."

I pointed at clean-shaven Dave. "So that makes you the other one—the Dave who *didn't* go to the desert with me."

Clean-shaven Dave nodded.

"But you said you saw me just before I left for the desert. When was that?"

He shook his head. "Gee, I don't know. Gotta be…"

"A while?"

"At least."

"Anybody go with me?"

"Yeah," said Stubble-faced Dave. "Me, Mike and Ron."

"No—not last Friday." I pointed at clean-shaven Dave. "I'm talking about when you saw me go. Who went with me then?"

"Nobody," he said with a frown.

"I went by myself?"

"You said there was something you had to do."

"How did I go, do you remember? Did I fly… drive?"

"You sort of just… walked off.

"Walked off?" said stubbly Dave. "Like into the sunset, huh?"

"Yeah…sorta."

"Sun sets in the west, pal. Desert is east. What'd I tell you, Charley? This guy is bogus."

"Hey—" clean-shaven Dave slammed his beer down in the sink. "You want, we can settle this, right here."

"Nobody's settling anything," I said. "We're just talking, all right?"

We stood there for a long moment while the Daves traded dirty looks.

"Okay, I'm going to ask you both some questions now. And I only want the guy I ask to answer the question, all right? Okay, you first," I said, pointing at clean-shaven Dave. "What do I do for a living?"

"What do you do? You're some kind of doctor, right?"

"Uh-huh. What kind?"

"Neuro-something—I don't know."

"Like a brain surgeon?"

"Maybe, yeah."

The other Dave inhaled some beer and started coughing.

"Who told you I was a brain surgeon?"

"Told me? Nobody told me or…I guess *you* did."

"Wait a minute," stubble Dave choked. "He told you he was a brain surgeon and you believed him? Dude, you are an idiot."

"Shut up a second," I said. "So you're saying that's how you found out? I told you? Nobody else?"

He nodded but I could see he wasn't sure.

"What about you?" I asked stubble Dave. "What do I do for a living?"

"You write television commercials. Ones I've seen suck pretty hard."

"Thank you," I told him sincerely, and felt adrenaline rush into my system. Answers were close.

I pointed to clean-shaven Dave. "How many kids do I have?"

"Kids? Since when?"

"What about you?" I said, pointing at the stubble-faced version. "How many?"

"Two," he said. "Sean and then the little one?"

"Sara," I said.

"Yeah, little cutie."

Clean-shaven Dave watched us with a puzzled expression. "I don't mean to get too personal," he said. "But does your wife know about these kids?"

I could only shake my head. The sense of déjà vu had come back strong. The answer to everything was right here in that kitchen. These doppelganger Daves were a huge clue but—to what?

"Hey," said clean-shaven Dave. "I've got an idea how we can settle this.".

"Yeah, how?"

"Unless," he said, "this phony wants to throw in the towel now and admit he's a fraud."

"Yeah, that's close. Bring it on. What you got in mind?"

Clean-shaven Dave grinned widely, pulling back his gums to reveal some seriously yellow teeth.

"Dental records," he said. "They don't lie."

Of course, neither of them could remember when they'd last visited a dentist or what his name was.

But it did give me an idea.

Golfology

We found Dr. Warren Sleeves listed in the Yellow Pages under Dentists. There was no mention of his Golfology credentials, just Warren Sleeves, D.D.S. The girl who answered the phone informed me the earliest available appointment was "well after the first." Since it was June, I assumed she was talking about July, but she said, no, she meant after the first of the year, late January or February. More than six months away.

When I asked her if she could possibly find a way to squeeze us in—as in right away—she said she was dismayed to have to tell me that not only was the wait list full but so was the cancellation wait list to get on the wait list. Then she confided that I shouldn't feel bad because such luminaries as Dr. Ben Carson, golfer John Daly, Kim Jong Un and former Secretary of State Madeline Albright had been inching up the cancellation wait list for months and had yet to reach the first page.

I was about to hang up when it occurred to me to try something. "That's too bad," I said. "My close friend Floyd Birdwell recommended Dr. Sleeves so highly."

There was a pause.

"You say Floyd Birdwell referred you?"

"That's right."

I could hear some papers shuffling. "Can you be here at two o'clock?"

Dr. Warren Sleeves' office was in a three-story medical plaza on Greenleaf across from the northwest corner of City Park. After a short squabble over whose truck it was and who was gonna drive it over whose dead body we climbed into Dave's Blazer and headed over there, stopping a couple of times to change drivers.

The Daves seemed equally eager for a showdown, each believing the other was about to be unmasked and humiliated. Based on my kitchen cross-examination, I'd already arrived at my own conclusion: stubble faced Dave—I now referred to him in my mind as Regular Dave—was the McCoy, the one who recalled not only the golf trip but the desert afterward and the flight home.

Outside the medical plaza, a flustered parking attendant waved us off the lot. Whichever Dave flipped a U-turn and found a space up the block. We entered the Medical Plaza from the Street side to find the halls and stairways swarming with a diverse throng that might have been scooped up from a Las Vegas casino floor or a Times Square street corner, a cross section of races, creeds, professions and socio-economic groups. Some of them hefted large professional golf bags with logos on them. One of the Daves ran interference for us, up a flight of stairs and down a crowded hall through an open doorway to a reception counter.

Every chair and most of the floor space in the waiting room was occupied. A perspiring, heavy-set man in a floral pattern golf shirt crouched on the carpet and directed a young boy to putt balls at him. In a corner, next to a small aquarium, three men in business suits, snatched a golf club back and forth while arguing in a language I didn't recognize.

Across from them, a lanky Asian girl in a golf skirt huddled with her entourage. Behind them, mounted on the wall was a sign reading: "No swinging of clubs in reception area—this is for your safety." Periodically, the incongruous whine of a high-speed dental drill could be heard coming from the examination rooms.

A Saudi prince swept out from there now trailed by a retinue of wives and flunkies. Off in a corner, an actor from a popular cop show chatted with a British pro I recognized who'd won the previous year's PGA tournament by outlasting Charles Howell III in a playoff. Seated next to them was an older man with a bow tie who might have been a college professor. He sat with his legs wrapped around a contraption that resembled an industrial vacuum cleaner with the handle and shaft of a golf club sticking out of one side.

It didn't take long for the duplicate Daves to get noticed and then stared at and each blamed the other for the unwanted attention. After forty minutes or so, we were ushered into an examination room by a statuesque, blonde hygienist in an impossibly tight nurse's uniform that might have been personally designed by Floyd Birdwell.

Dr. Sleeves, in person, looked very much as he did on the news program, a slight, middle-aged balding figure in green medical scrubs. When we explained the reason for our visit, he hadn't looked surprised or skeptical but just invited the Daves to alternately hop in up the chair for a look.

Dr. Sleeves peered into Clone Dave's (formerly clean-shaven-coveralls-wearing Dave) open mouth like a man looking down a deep well. "Intriguing," he said. "Exact duplicates. It's almost if one had been cloned from the other. You say this one turned up only recently?"

"That's right," I said. "Dave found him in his apartment when he came home from the desert Sunday night."

"Hey—what?" Clone Dave stiffened in the chair. "Nobody found me. I was there all the time—and I don't know who this guy is!" He pointed to Dave. "But I can prove who I am.

Here…" He pulled his wallet out and showed his driver's license to Sleeves.

"Hah!" said Regular Dave (formerly stubble-faced, golf-clothes-wearing Dave). "Any idiot can apply for a duplicate."

Dr. Sleeves sat back on his stool and scratched his head. "You can run a DNA test but I'm pretty certain it'll tell you the same thing."

"That they're the same guy?"

Sleeves made a face. "That's probably not what you want

to hear."

"He's right about that at least," said Clone Dave. Sleeves' diagnosis had further riled the Daves. "Charley—let's get out of here. This dentist doesn't know what he's talking about."

"I know if you don't start flossing, you can both kiss your gums goodbye," Sleeves said matter-of-factly.

I asked the Daves if I could have a word in private with Dr. Sleeves and they said they'd wait in the car, that they weren't going to hang around getting stared at in that zoo of a reception area.

After they'd gone, Sleeves had me climb into the chair. Naturally, being a dentist, once he got my mouth filled up with fingers and tools, he started asking questions. It took some doing, but I managed to tell him about the golf trip and the crash in the turbine field and then not being able to find the plane.

"Just one of them was with you when the plane crashed?"

"Yahb," I said. "Wohn wid da whiskers. Heebbabbin shave tince Hwiday."

Dr. Sleeves selected another instrument from his tray.

"And the other passengers?"

"Goahnnn just lahk a plahn."

"And the crash happened where?"

"Whoonnnhohon," I said.

"I beg your pardon?"

I pulled his hand out of my mouth. "Wind farm."

"You're talking about the big windmills that generate electricity?"

"Rhagg," I said, nodding.

Dr. Sleeves put the probe back in the tray and sat back on his stool. He took off his glasses and rubbed his tired-looking eyes with a waxen hand.

"Well, your teeth look good."

I thanked him and mentioned that I'd been flossing ever since Sylvia, Dr. Miller's hygienist, had scared the crap out of me with her descriptions of bone loss. But I don't think he was listening.

"Those big turbines out there. They're set pretty close together, aren't they?"

"Twenty… thirty yards."

"Not much room for a plane to land. There'd be no way to avoid plowing right into them. Could you see anything?"

"Yeah—propellers. It was raining hard and visibility was pretty bad. At first Ron thought it was the airport—he was sitting up front in the co-pilot's seat. Then he started yelling for Ed the pilot to pull up. But it was too late."

"And you didn't feel the crash."

"Nope. Nothing."

"What was the last thing you saw?"

"Just the propellers—and everyone screaming and hollering and then nothing."

"Nothing at all?"

"Everything sort of went white—you know, just like they say: 'it all went white?' Then, next thing I know, I'm walking down a row of turbines… and that's when Dave found me."

"But not the others?"

"Gone."

"How long did you look for the plane?"

"No time really—I ran into a turbine and knocked myself out. Dave spent a good half hour looking but he couldn't find anything. And then the police did a pretty extensive search. At least they said they did."

"What about the other fellas on the plane? There was no trace of them?"

"Oh—we found them all right. They were home safe and sound."

"I don't follow you."

"Morning after the crash, the sheriff's office called the

wives to notify them about the accident but by then they were already home."

"How'd they manage that?"

"You tell me. But that's not even the crazy part. The crazy part is that neither of them will admit being on the plane—or even knowing about the golf trip."

Dr. Sleeves stared at me. "They're lying?"

"That's what I thought at the time. That they were trying to pull off some kind of insurance scam. That'd be something I could easily see them doing. But then, the more I talk to them, the more it sounds like they're telling the truth. The evidence certainly backs them up."

"But you saw them on the plane."

"Yeah, saw them and talked to them. Hey—*they* planned the trip. The pilot was their buddy.

"So then—?"

"I know it's impossible, but I can't shake the feeling that I'm right *and* they're right."

"That would be impossible. Contradictions can't exist in the universe. The first law of logic. What about your friends—these Daves? You say one of them shared this experience with you?"

"Yeah, Dave. The one with the shiner. He remembers it pretty much the way I do. Of course, he was asleep most of the time."

Dr. Sleeves went over and looked out the window.

"You say there was a thunderstorm that night?"

"Yeah—huge storm. We got nailed."

"I've read where wind turbines are particularly prone to lightning strikes. We are talking about the wind farm in the San Gorgonio Pass outside of Palm Springs?"

"That's the one."

"Each one of those turbines puts out 700 kilowatts per hour."

"You know that off the top of your head?"

I could see his modest smile reflected in the glass. "I'm sure you'll find I'm right. I usually am."

"About wind farms?"

"About everything," he said. "I'm rarely wrong—actually I can't remember an instance where I was completely wrong. I suppose that's the reason I'm asked so many questions."

As he spoke, his voice drifted off. I waited for some minutes while he stared out the window and then began to wonder if he'd forgotten about me.

"Dr. Sleeves—?"

"Funny," he said softly. "I should have it figured out by now. It's pretty clear cut except—"

"Except for what?"

"Your friends—the two Daves." That's the part that doesn't add up. If my deductions are correct, there ought to be two of you as well. Unless I missed something."

I sat up quickly, cracking my head on the lamp and sending the instrument tray flying. "Two of me?"

"That's right. Two Charleys."

"My God," I said. "I thought he was a dream.

A Walking Contradiction

"Are you familiar with the theory of parallel universes, Mr. Cotter?"

"I've heard about it."

"How about quantum physics—String theory or M-Theory or the Eleventh Dimension?"

"Afraid not."

We'd moved across the hall from the examination room into Dr. Sleeves' office. It was a traditional man's library style room with tufted leather chairs, wainscoting, cherry wood cabinets and duck wallpaper. There were half a dozen diplomas crowding the wall along with awards, certificates and photographs of Dr. Sleeves posing with celebrities, heads of state and famous sports figures.

"You see it all begins with the atom, Charley. Ever since scientists got their first glimpse inside the atom— that was eighty years ago—they've been trying to make sense of what they found in there. Little particles— atomic particles. Neutrons, protons, electrons, blinking and moving here and there, twinkling like stars. They could see the particles, but they couldn't place them. Because they were constantly moving, there one instant and gone the next. You could take an infinite number of photographs and never find the particles occupying the same space or even know how many there were because—sometimes they'd be there and sometimes they wouldn't. You with me so far?"

I supposed I was. But then my concentration was disrupted when the hygienist came in to say there were patients waiting in the lobby. Sleeves told her to apologize for him, say that he was in a very important meeting and would get to everyone just as soon as he could.

"Where were we?" Sleeves asked me when she'd gone.

"Atomic particles winking and blinking. Now you see them, now you don't."

"Yes, very good. That's exactly right. Now you see them, now you don't. Every atom, every particle of the universe constantly in flux. But where do they go when they're not here?"

I shook my head.

"No one knows," said Dr. Sleeves. "But we think—that is, scientists think—that they may be visiting other universes. They think that all of us—everybody and everything—can be in two places at once, actually in *infinite* places at once."

Sleeves stood up and began to pace behind his desk.

"Do you grasp the significance? It means possibilities. Infinite possibilities. Einstein, up until the day he died, struggled to find a single theory that would explain everything. A Theory of Everything, a single objective schematic to the universe. But he couldn't do it—even Einstein. And now we think we know why he failed. Because it couldn't be done. Because there is no objective view to the universe. How can there be when everything is moving? Beginning with the smallest sub-atomic particle, nothing stays the same. The universe is subjective, Charley, because its very fabric consists of limitless—infinite possibilities. Now you see it, now you don't."

"But we do see it," I said. "We're both sitting right here in the middle of it."

"Are we? Do you think we co-exist in the same universe, you and I?"

"We're here, aren't we?"

"Sure, we're here. We're both conscious of being here. We're aware of each other and of our common surroundings. But how we perceive these surroundings and the events taking place within them? Is that something we share?"

"You're saying we each have our own point of view."

"Exactly. Our own point of view. Yours most likely differing from mine, wouldn't you say? Our views contrast because we ourselves, like the rest of the universe, are made up of infinite atomic particles, all winking and blinking. Charley, what would you say if I told you that that there is another universe, right now, very close by, where everything is the same as it is in this one with the exception that you are standing here, and I am sitting where you are?"

"A parallel universe?"

"Or another where I am a woman, and you are a… parakeet? Or another where, instead of chairs, we are seated on large pieces of cheese? Or still another where we don't exist at all, where SUV's fly through the air and insurance salesman are venerated as gods?"

"What would I say?"

"What would you say if I told you that there is universe for everything you can think of—and everything you can't? For every variation of every variation? Infinite universes?"

"I'd say… where are they?"

"They're right here, all around us. We're touching them right now, separated by only the slimmest membrane from any one of them."

"Are you telling me this—here—right now is some sort of parallel universe?"

Dr. Sleeves' eyes twinkled. "Parallel to what?"

"To the one I should be in—or came from, or…"

"Considering said Dr. Sleeves, "There *already* was a Charley Cotter here when you arrived…"

"Arrived? You mean the plane crash?"

"Everything seem pretty normal before that?"

I nodded.

"Then that would be my guess."

"But what about the others? Mike, Ron and the pilot?"

Dr. Sleeves sat down on the edge of his desk and picked at a thread on his scrub pants. "Seen any duplicates of them walking around?"

I shook my head.

The receptionist buzzed in with an emergency phone call from Wolfgang Puck. Sleeves apologized, said that was one he needed to take.

I got up and began to peruse Dr. Sleeve's gallery of photos. The first one I looked at was a shot of the doctor in his green scrubs standing next to a grinning Tiger Woods.

"No, Wolfy," Sleeves was saying. "Not lemon—lemon zest… Yes… that's right… half a cup… Yes… big difference. Of course, uh-huh… Not at all. Enjoy." He hung up. "Sorry. He's making up a lunch for Air Force One. Sometimes he gets flustered."

"Wolfgang Puck the chef? He calls you for ingredients?"

"That's right."

"Are you a chef too?"

Sleeves smiled. "Oh, no. Sometimes I just like to fiddle around in the kitchen."

I pointed to the photo. "And Tiger—he calls you for swing tips?"

"No, he's just a pal. We met at the Masters some years back. He was having difficulty with distance control, asked me to have a look."

"Were you able to help him?"

"I like to think so. He won the next four majors in a row."

There were lots of other pictures with golf greats I recognized, past and present: Tom Watson, Dustin Johnson, Seve Ballesteros, Rory McElroy, Jordan Spieth, Nick Faldo and—my God—Jack Nicklaus and Lee Trevino. Some of the photos had been taken right there in the office, others were outdoors on a golf course but, in every one, Dr. Sleeves wore his green medical scrubs.

"How do you happen to know so many famous golfers?"

"I've just met them at one time or another."

"Given them advice?"

"Only if they ask. Some of them had read my book and wanted to meet me."

"Personal Golf?"

"You've read it?"

"Not yet. Doctor Sleeves, don't you think it's odd that a dentist from Walnut Hill who doesn't play golf, writes books about it and counts many of the top players as friends?"

"It seems perfectly normal to me. But we're here to solve your problems."

"But you *are* my problem—one of them anyway. You're just another thing that doesn't make sense—an anomaly. Like the missing airplane or the other me or two Daves or Mike and Ron not remembering the crash or me and Cathy not having kids or me being a brain surgeon."

"You're a brain surgeon?"

"You wouldn't think so," I sighed. "Of course, if you call St. Helen's hospital, there's a voicemail box with my name on it."

"The other Charley, perhaps?"

A few hours later I was sitting with Dr. Sleeves in a deli near his office. He'd asked me to wait while he saw the rest of his afternoon's schedule of patients then join him for an early supper before his speaking engagement that evening.

I told the Daves I'd meet them over at Earl's later, then spent the hours at the public library, looking for information on parallel universes. There were quite a few books that touched on the subject. Most of them were science-fiction novels, but there were a couple of others written by theoretical physicists that mentioned not only parallel universes but also Einstein and his theory of everything. It's not that I doubted what Sleeves had been telling me, but it made me feel better to know there was some actual science in all this.

In the periodicals section, I spotted a front-page article in the Gazette listing the golfers most likely to win next month's British Open. The Vegas odds were listed next to each. Floyd Birdwell topped the list at even money. Koepka and Spieth were at 5 to 1 and 8 to 1 respectively.

We'd ordered sandwiches and were sitting over a couple of iced teas, when I asked Dr. Sleeves, ""How do you get from one universe to another?"

He shook his head. "Normally you don't. At least no one knows how. We're generally stuck in one awareness for the duration. Unless, of course, something impossible were to occur."

"Something impossible?"

"Yes. Some sort of contradiction or anomaly."

Sleeves saw the look on my face and smiled.

"Look," he said. "Just imagine all these infinite universes co-existing side by side, each of them brimming with possibilities yet closed off to one another. When all of a sudden… something completely impossible happens. For just that instant, all the windows in all the universes are thrown open and anything and everything becomes possible."

"How possible is that… for what you're saying to happen?"

"It can't. It's not possible."

"But… aren't you saying that's what might have happened to me and Dave? Something… impossible?"

Dr. Sleeves took a sip of his iced tea. "I wouldn't be surprised," he said.

"Okay, so define 'impossible,'"

"Can't be done," he said.

"You can't define it?"

He shook his head. "Definition of the word—means can't exist. Can't happen in the universe. Can't be done. Doesn't mean whatever it is can't be happening somewhere else."

"So, how'd we get here? Did we do something impossible."

Sleeves squeezed some lemon into his tea then began to spoon sugar on top of it. "You might have. But you wouldn't need to. All you would have to do is be present when the impossible thing occurred. Anything spring to mind?"

"Well—I wound up here."

Sleeves took a sip of his iced tea and grimaced. Then he heaped a couple more spoonsful of sugar into it. "Before that," he said. "Just before."

"Like the plane crash?"

"Plane crashes by themselves are infrequent but hardly impossible. Although… a crash in an energy-producing wind farm." Sleeves' eyes narrowed. and his voice drifted off. "During an electrical storm… You say you never felt an impact?"

"Nope. Just lightning flashes all around. Then everything went white. Next thing I'm walking down a line of turbines wondering what happened."

"You know," said Sleeves, testing his tea again. "It's just possible that your plane collided with a wind turbine at precisely the instant it was hit by lighting."

"Would that do it?"

Sleeves was preoccupied now with some lemon pits that were floating in his glass. "No," he said. "I said it was 'possible' not 'impossible.' It's highly unlikely that both of those things happened simultaneously. The odds against it are astronomical but still theoretically possible. We might have better luck if we examine the result."

"The crash?"

He nodded. "Let's say for the moment that the plane and the lightning bolt struck the wind turbine at exactly the same time. Taken together that would have caused an abnormally large electrical event."

"How large?"

"Well…" Sleeves' tongue lolled slightly from his mouth as he used a forefinger to steer the lemon pits out of the tea and down the outside of the glass to the paper place mat. "Each one of those turbines is outfitted with its own capacitor. That's where the energy is stored until there's enough of it to be released into the power grid."

"The turbine is lightning-protected. It's grounded so that, in the event it receives a massive jolt of energy—like a lightning bolt—that energy is sent into the ground and not into the grid where it might shut down the power supply. Now, just suppose, the plane hitting the turbine interfered with that system, destroyed the capacitor and short-circuited the grounding process. That would send a massive energy jolt directly into the Coachella Valley power grid and would, in all likelihood, knock out power to the region."

"What would that do to the plane?"

"The damage to the plane would be…" Sleeves looked up from his lemon pits. "Significant."

"Wait a minute," I said. "No one mentioned a blackout that night."

"You're right. There's been no power outage," said Sleeves. "Not in this universe, anyway."

"But… if the crash happened in the other universe…"

"That's right."

"And the incredible force of the crash knocked us from that universe into *this* one?"

Sleeves was bent over his glass, sipping through his straw and smiling.

"That doesn't seem possible."

"Exactly. Not possible at all—which is, of course, the only way it could have happened."

"I'm not sure I…"

"The odds against your plane hitting that wind turbine at precisely the same instant as the lightning bolt are astronomical although still technically possible. The electrical charge, however—the by-product of this incredible coincidence—would have been so substantial, so utterly unthinkable in magnitude that it places itself, in my view, well beyond the limits of possibility."

"Just so we're clear. Are you saying it *is* or *isn't*... possible?"

Sleeves slurped up the tea in the bottom of his glass. "You short-circuit an enormous electric power supply and then for good measure toss in a lightning bolt. I'm guessing the effect of the resultant chain reaction to you would be similar to having a thermal nuclear device dropped squarely on your head."

"We're talking impossible magnitude?"

"I would think so, yes."

We sat for a moment in silence before I said, "There's one thing I'm still not clear on."

"What's that?"

"If it's not possible, how could it have happened?"

Dr. Sleeves' smile was patient and kind. "Thank your lucky stars it did. If it was even remotely possible, you wouldn't be here. More than likely, you'd be a small gathering of cinders blowing around a desert wind farm."

That's when the sandwiches arrived. I had a chance to mull this over while Dr. Sleeves attacked his pastrami with a healthy appetite. His remark about the cinders had instantly destroyed mine.

"Then, the others—the real Mike and Ron—you think they...?"

"Dead? Not necessarily. They most likely wound up somewhere else too."

"But not *here*? Why not?"

Sleeves shrugged, gnawing on his pastrami. "As I've described, when an impossible thing happens, the windows to all the universes open up. They could have wound up literally anywhere."

"In some other universe?"

"That's right."

"Which one? Is it just random?"

Sleeves shook his head. "That's determined by point of view."

"Okay, you'd better explain that."

Sleeves put down his sandwich and wiped his hands with a paper napkin. "Let's say you're faced with infinite possibilities; which way are you going to go?"

"You mean I somehow made a *choice* in coming to this universe?"

"As a matter of fact, you did. You may not have realized it, but you made one. And now here you are."

"How do you make a choice without knowing it?"

"Your brain makes it for you. For example, you could even be dreaming when the impossible thing happens, and you wake up in a universe where the people and situations you are dreaming about are suddenly real."

"So, you're telling me that I was thinking about this place when the plane crashed and that's how I wound up here?"

Sleeves finished his last bite of pastrami and turned to his pickle, cutting it into small chunks with his knife and fork. "More or less," he mumbled.

"But it happened so fast—the crash. Even if I'd been trying, I certainly couldn't conjure up an entire universe in just seconds."

"You wouldn't have to," said Sleeves, looking up at me. "I'm just guessing but I imagine that most of what you've seen and experienced in this universe is similar to the one you left. Yes?"

"Yeah, except for—"

"I'm talking big picture stuff. You live in the same town in the same state, I presume? Most people have two arms, two legs, wear clothes?"

"You mean there are some universes where they don't?"

"Absolutely. Infinite universes, Charley. If you'd been

thinking of a universe where people go naked and the president yodels his state-of-the-union speech, that's where you'd be right now."

"And what about you? Would you be there too?"

"That would depend entirely on you. What were you thinking, Charley? At the very last second, just before the crash?"

"Just… dying, I guess. It was pretty obvious we weren't going to make it."

"That's it? No regrets? Life passing before your eyes?"

"Yeah, some of that."

"What else?"

"I was thinking about Cathy and the kids and that my life was going to be over."

"Anything else?"

"And then we crashed… I guess."

Sleeves forked a pickle nugget into his mouth. "That's strange," he said. "If that's all you were thinking, then this universe should strike you as not so different from the one you left."

"Wait a minute," I said. "I'm remembering now… the last thing I was thinking about—the very last thing…"

"Not your wife?"

I shook my head. "No. It was somebody else. This guy I know."

"What guy? Tell me about him."

"He works at the driving range. He's always bugging me to play golf with him."

"You were thinking about him?"

"Yeah."

"Why him?"

"I was angry with myself for letting him get away

with something he said. Something about Cathy…"

"Cathy?"

"My wife. She's a nurse…"

"What did he say? Can you remember?"

"He said I should keep an eye on her because I should know what nurses are like—meaning he thinks they're hot to trot or something."

"So, you were specifically thinking about this guy."

"Yeah."

"And comments he made about your wife?"

"That's right, yes."

"And this is the very last thing before you crashed?" Sleeves eyed me closely. "And how did his comments make you feel?"

"I was pissed. I hated that I let the comment slide. That I hadn't called him on it."

"Why didn't you?"

"I don't know—because he's kind of an idiot, I guess. And a little crazy. And big—not the kind of guy you want to have a problem with."

"But it irked you."

"Yeah, it irked me. This clown making tasteless comments about my wife?"

"You love your wife. And you wanted to—what? Punch his lights out? You were crashing in an airplane. You thought your life was over, yet this is what you thought about."

"Pretty much. I wanted to smash his face in and ask him where he got off saying those things about nurses."

"What was he thinking of?"

"Exactly."

"And then you crashed."

Sleeves was preoccupied now with his napkin, folding and then refolding it. "Well," he said. "That should explain things, I suppose…" He put the napkin aside and stared over my shoulder into space. "I'm just wondering about your friend…"

"What friend? Dave?"

"That's the part that doesn't follow. In order for Dave to wind up in the same universe with you, he'd have to be having the same thoughts—and at the same time."

"Maybe he was."

"I'm sorry?"

"I'm pretty sure I was talking out loud… maybe shouting."

"The plane was crashing…"

"He didn't *know* we were crashing. He'd been asleep. The yelling woke him up… I remember now… he heard me raving about Floyd and—"

"Floyd?"

"Floyd Birdwell. Guy I'm talking about."

"Floyd Birdwell, the golfer… Open Champion?"

"Maybe in this universe he is. Where I come from, he's more your typical driving range psychopath."

"Interesting," said Sleeves. "So, Dave heard what you were saying about Floyd?"

"Yeah… something like who does he think he is or what in hell was he thinking of … I guess."

"You're certain he heard you?"

"Yeah. He even asked me who I was talking about, was looking right at me when I told him. I don't think he knew the plane was in trouble. And then we crashed."

"And then you crashed." Sleeves placed the napkin down with finality. "Well, that's it then," he said and waved for a check.

"It is?"

"We know where you are and what you're doing here."

"We do?"

Sleeves looked at his watch. "Okay, I've got to run but I'll give you a quick summation. Your plane is crashing. You're headed for almost certain death and your desperate mind has become fixated on this person—"

"Floyd."

"More precisely… what Floyd was *thinking* of. Then, something impossible happens. You and your friend Dave, instead of being vaporized in the crash, are propelled out of your universe into another one—a universe that answers the question you posed."

"This…" Sleeves held out his arms. "This is what your friend Floyd was thinking of."

I sat there, staring at him.

"I'll wager this universe is very similar to the one you left, perhaps with a few exceptions? And those exceptions reflect Floyd Birdwell's point of view. This is a universe where people and things exist as he sees or imagines them. A universe—"

I leaped out of the booth. "Where nurses look like exotic dancers. Where everyone including my wife is obsessed with golf. Where Cathy is a biker's wet dream and I'm a brain surgeon and bankers plot to tear down golf courses and replace them with mini malls and where a driving range attendant with a five handicap wins the U.S. Open. And…" I pointed at Dr. Sleeves. "Where you know everything."

Sleeves grinned at me. "Make sense?"

"Yeah—but it's impossible."

"Of course, it is."

My head was spinning. "So, this is Floyd's universe?"

"In a manner of speaking."

"And you live here too. Doesn't that… bother you?"

"Why should it?"

"You don't know him like I do. Suddenly I feel like a character in a comic book."

I followed Sleeves out the door and down the sidewalk to the lot behind his office where he'd parked his car, scanning everyone we passed for Floyd-projected characteristics.

"It's important to understand," Sleeves was saying, "That here, in this universe, I exist as your friend Floyd sees me. But I exist concurrently in an infinite number of other universes. In at least one of them, I am as I perceive myself shaving each morning. In another, I am as a patient sees me. In still another, I am the person my dog sees.

He stopped walking and looked at me. "But in none of those universes am I a fish out of water—so to speak—like you are in this one."

When we got to his car, Dr. Sleeves reached for my hand and shook it. "All these anomalies you've experienced, Mr. Cotter, there is nothing abnormal or strange about them. In this universe, you are the anomaly. Along with your friend Dave."

He turned to go but I grabbed his arm. "Wait a min—how do I get out of here?"

"I'm afraid you don't." He gave me a sympathetic pat on the shoulder. "Unless of course something impossible happens."

Voodoo Balls

"And you bought this?" said Clone Dave. "From a *dentist?*"

We were sitting, later that same evening, at a corner table in Earl's Country Roadhouse where, for the last hour or so, the Daves had been dazzling Melanie with their talent for beer consumption.

"Since when are you twins?" she'd said when they sat down.

"Cousins," they'd said at the same time, and it got her laughing. "Identical cousins? Wasn't that on an old TV show?"

"Never saw it," they said.

Since my meeting with Dr. Sleeves, I'd been gaping around at Floyd's universe with an eye out for what I previously thought of as anomalies but now termed 'Floyd-isms." I suppose I should have despaired to find myself locked in the funhouse of Floyd's imagination, but I was relieved, finally, to have an explanation—however nuts— for everything that had been happening. And, compared to what surely would have happened to me had the magnitude of the plane crash been just a bit less impossible, I counted myself lucky to be there—or anywhere. Inhabitant of Floyd's universe, however goofy, was preferable any time to 'charred cinder blowing around in the desert.' Besides, Floyd's world wasn't really all that different from the one we'd been flung out of. The physical planet seemed unchanged. Only the people had changed, and those differences were mostly attitudinal. I could certainly make it work here if I had to. My advertising career didn't exist of course but that wasn't the end of the world. I'd long since lost enthusiasm for the advertising grind. The prospect of starting over was suddenly exciting. Cathy had been right in saying I needed to explore possibili—

Cathy.

Somewhere in the middle of this galloping delirium, the reality of my situation arrived and smacked me upside of the head. Yeah, I could live here in Floyd's universe but not as Cathy's husband or father to Sean or Sara. Because, in Floyd's universe, there already was a Charley Cotter and he was married to Cathy Cotter. He was a neurosurgeon at St. Helen's hospital and the scratch golfer that Mike and Ron knew him to be. And there were no kids, never had been. Because the Floyd in my universe had never laid eyes on Sean and Sara, had no idea Cathy and I were parents. He'd seen her strictly as this hot nurse whom he assumed was discontented with her life because she was married to a "moron."

In Floyd's universe, Dave and I were the intruders and identity thieves. I might go around impersonating Charley Cotter but, sooner or later, the real deal was going to show up, back from the desert, and reclaim his life. No—happy as I was to have answers at last—the truth was I had lost everything, family, friends, home, career, thrown it all away for a lousy weekend of golf in the desert. I might have escaped death but was nonetheless a ghost.

"What's so impossible about a plane crash?" Clone Dave wanted to know.

Regular Dave slapped his hand down on the table. "It just was, okay? Why do you have to question everything anybody says?"

I held up my hand. "Dr. Sleeves said the plane short-circuited the power grid and then conducted umpteen kilowatts of lightning back and forth," I told them. "It was too monumental to calculate. He just called it impossible and let it go at that." I lowered my voice. "Impossible is the key word here. Whenever something impossible happens, all bets are off and for just the blink of an eye, everything that was impossible before is—just for a split second—totally do-able. The windows to all the universes open and you get bounced out. It's like when you're playing Stickley and your drive hits a power line and then shoots off in some crazy direction you'd never think to look in. What do you do?"

"Declare a voodoo," Dave said.

"Exactly."

We'd been forced to invent the 'voodoo ball' rule at Stickley Municipal where 'outside elements' like low-hanging power lines obstructed play and where it was common for some heedless hack to wander over from another hole and play your ball by mistake. Rather than have our matches loused up with questionable lost-ball penalties, we invented the voodoo designation to cover unexplained ball disappearances. To qualify for voodoo designation, the ball must have been hit well enough to be in the fairway, but is gone when you get there. A ball declared voodoo may be replaced without penalty in the spot where it ought to have been. Everyone in the foursome had to agree before a ball could be declared voodoo.

"That's what we are," I said, pointing at Dave. Voodoo balls."

"But I'm still not clear on what Floyd's got to do with any of this," Clone Dave said.

"This is his universe," I said. "This is how he sees things—what he thinks about."

Regular Dave looked around at the other tables. "I'm not seein' anything different."

"Everything's the same, except now we're seeing it from his point of view. Get it?"

"I got it," said Dave. "I just don't want it. So, what do we do?"

I shook my head. "Sleeves says we're pretty much stuck here. It's impossible to go back."

"I thought he said we could go back but it'd be impossible," said Dave.

"Maybe somebody can explain how those two things are

different," said Clone Dave.

"Some impossible thing had to happen for us to get here," I said. "Some other impossible thing will have to happen for us to get back—which makes it probably twice as impossible. And, even then, a lot can go wrong."

"Like what?" said Dave.

"Just say for the sake of argument that we find ourselves at ground zero at the exact moment something impossible is going down. For us to get back to where we came from, we'd have to be thinking of only that situation and nowhere else—in fact nothing else. If we got distracted right at the critical moment, we could be facing a pretty gnarly situation when we got there."

"What would distract us?" asked Dave.

"Hey, if something impossible is going down," said Clone Dave. "There's gonna be distractions."

"For example," I said. "Let's say, you're sitting at the bar over there and you're ordering a bag of beer nuts from Wendy the bar maid and then—blam!—it *happens*—you're in another universe, except now it's Wendy's universe where—"

"You're her love slave," said Dave.

"Wouldn't be my first choice," said Clone Dave.

"Or maybe you're daydreaming about—I don't know—fishing and you get tossed into a universe where everything is under water."

"Yeah," said Dave. "And you're engaged to a flounder."

"Can that happen?"

"According to Sleeves, it can."

"Wait a minute," said Clone Dave. "What if, when whatever happens, I think about some place where I'm rich—the richest man in the world?"

"Then I guess you would be."

"Really?"

"And for icing on the cake," said Dave. "Why don't you think about being irresistible to women?"

"Okay," Clone Dave said. "I'm sold. What do we have to do?"

"You *do* realize," I said, "that we're talking doing the *impossible* here. And I don't mean like you breaking eighty or getting the grease out from under your nails. We're talking about something that's totally off the wall like—"

"Like pigs flying or talking wallpaper," said Clone Dave.

Dave looked at him. "Talking wallpaper?"

"Why not? That's impossible, right?"

"Right. And when you hear the wallpaper start to say something, you'll want to hurry up and think about bein' rich and chicks digging you."

"We could rent a plane and crash it into the wind farm again." Clone Dave said.

"Impossible."

"I thought that was the idea."

"Forget it," I said. "We'd have to hit the turbine at the exact same time a lightning bolt strikes. Our chances of doing that are non-existent and, without the lightning bolt, all we'd be doing is crashing our plane into the turbine. It wouldn't send us anywhere, only kill us. It's got to be something else— something impossible but still somehow do-able."

"We could swim the Atlantic Ocean," said Clone Dave. "That's pretty much impossible."

"How do you know?" said Dave. "Has anyone tried?"

"You know, Charley," he said. "There's a pretty good chance we're stuck here. You know that, right?"

Easy for him to say. Dave really hadn't left anything behind that he couldn't find here. I, on the other hand, had a wife and two kids waiting for—

Cathy and the kids think I'm dead!

My face went pale I guess because Dave asked me if I was okay. Clone Dave tried to get me to drink some beer, but I just sat there frozen, locked on the image of Cathy, seeing the pain on her face and in her eyes having to explain to Sean and Sara that their dad wasn't coming back. They would have discovered the wrecked plane right away. Everyone between Banning and Indio had probably heard the explosion or been affected by the power outage. Someone would have phoned Cathy. But Charley wasn't on that plane, she'd say. Charley had a business meeting in L.A., Saturday and Sunday. He took a commercial flight. He wasn't going to play golf this weekend. He promised me. He promised me.

Then, just to make sure, but already knowing in her heart he was gone, she'd have called the office and heard Susan tell her that, no, there was no meeting in L.A. Why? Has something happened to Charley? Then she'd have hung up the phone, certain now that her husband, the liar, was dead. She'd pick up the phone again and ask for details and hear that they'd found the plane but not the bodies. *The bodies.* The crash had been violent, electrical, cataclysmic. There'd been an explosion, a power outage. It was on the news. There were no bodies to identify, only bits of clothing, luggage and golf clubs. Cinders blowing in the desert wind.

And then she'd have to tell the children.

"They think I'm dead," I said. "Cathy and the kids."

"No way," said Dave. "Your body wasn't there to recover."

"Yeah," said the other one. "Don't look now but you're sittin' in it."

"They probably think we burned up in the explosion. Even if they wait a few days or even weeks, when we don't show up, they're gonna know we were in there." I wrapped my arms around my gut. "She had to tell them their dad was dead," I said. "I did that to her."

"Aw, Charley," said Dave. "You don't want to think about that. There's nothing you can do about it now."

"I need to go back. I have to explain and make it up to her. I can't do this to her. It's not fair."

"Charley, you know that going back is sounding real impossible."

"There's got to be some way. I mean, getting here was impossible but we did it, right?"

"Sure," said Dave

"Hey—this dentist is supposed to know everything," said Clone Dave. "He might know some way to get a message back to Cathy saying you're okay and not to worry."

"You mean," said Dave, "like 'things are great in the fourth dimension, wish you were here?' If he could get a message back, he'd go back and deliver it himself."

Clone Dave threw up his hands and left to take a leak. Regular Dave leaned over and put his hand on my shoulder. "Charley, it was an accident," he said. "There isn't anything we can do about it. We shouldn't even be alive. We're lucky to be sitting here. If you were dead you wouldn't be blaming yourself, you'd just be dead. I know it's tough, but you can't help what you can't help."

Clone Dave was back. "Hey guys—maybe you want to come see this."

We followed him to the men's rest room where it was carved into the towel dispenser. Someone had used a knife to scratch out: "It is impossible to beat Snog at the game that…" The last words were obliterated where the paint had peeled off, but you got the gist.

"This sound do-able to anybody?" Clone Dave said.

Meet the Press

"You think it's just a coincidence that on the very same weekend John F. Kennedy was assassinated, the first mini mall opened for business in the east bay?"

Cameras whirred, strobe lights popped, and the assembled reporters scribbled. Floyd paused to let the dubious significance of his question sink in. His self-satisfied smirk was the one you saw when he out drove you on a big par five.

The Daves and I stood shoulder to shoulder with twenty or thirty media types in the reception tent for a press conference following what had been billed as "U.S. Open Champion Floyd Birdwell's triumphant return to Mallards." For the last hour, Floyd had dazzled an SRO crowd by crisscrossing the range on his Harley to a medley of piped in biker hits while the range rats swatted golf balls at him. Of course, this being Floyd's universe, none of the shots had come close to hitting him.

Now, the great man sat ensconced in a leather armchair atop a stage riser. "Does anybody but me," he continued, "think it's totally messed up that you've got foreigners running the mini malls in this country but, if you go back where they came from, you won't find a single mini mall anywhere?"

Dave elbowed me and nodded toward the reporters. "They're lapping this up."

"Hey, it's his universe. Everything he says is newsworthy. He *thinks* it today; we live it tomorrow."

A female reporter raised her hand. "What is your reaction," she said, "To the recent announcement that Stickley Municipal will be sending out six-somes?"

Floyd scowled and made a show of leaning over and spitting on the floor, drawing titters from his captive audience.

"Do you see linkage," the reporter continued, "Between that policy and the current mini-mall situation?"

Floyd affected an exasperated look. "Well—duh!" he said.

"Can you elaborate?"

"Look, lady," he said. "Six-somes, eight-somes, twenty-somes—there's only so many chops you can jam onto to a golf course at the same time. More players in a group isn't gonna help anything. What you need is *more golf courses.*" Floyd smacked himself in the head. "Duh—right? What a concept—more golf courses. But the bankers and the developers and the mini-mall operators—they know this too. But they don't want to build any more golf courses. Why? Because you can make more money with a mini mall!"

"What've you got against strip malls, Floyd?" shouted another reporter.

Floyd bristled and flushed as he always did when asked to explain the obvious. "How wide do you think the average car is?" He leaned forward looking around the room. "Anybody know?"

"Five feet?" somebody offered.

"Five feet," Floyd agreed. "And do you know how wide your average strip mall parking space is?" Floyd beckoned to a minion in heavily rimmed glasses who rushed over with a sheet of paper. Floyd scanned the page, letting suspense build. "Four and a half feet!" he shouted at last, waving the paper over his head.

This announcement ignited another round of buzzing and scribbling. It was puzzling at first to see the print reporters outfitted in anachronistic ensembles of rumpled gray suits, trench coats and battered fedoras looking as if they'd just stepped out of an old Frank Capra movie. But then I realized that reporters in old movies were probably the only ones Floyd had ever seen which meant that, here in the universe of his perception, that's what reporters were going to look like.

"They're writing this shit down," Dave marveled.

"What about it, Floyd?" shouted a reporter with a bow tie. "Is Stickley for sale?"

"What am I—a moron? It's a done deal. The ink is dry on the dotted line. They're gonna bulldoze that pasture and put up the world's largest mini mall!"

There was a collective gasp from the audience. Somewhere in the back of the tent, a woman screamed.

Floyd grinned. "You won't be able to play golf, but you can buy a pack of gum at three in the morning—that is, if you can get your car door open!"

A heavily-made-up TV correspondent I recognized from a late news program, stood on her toes and stretched her microphone in Floyd's direction.

"What are you going to do about it?" she yelled.

Floyd flashed his idea of an innocent smile and batted his eyelids like Bobby Sue at the prom. "Who, me? What can I do? I'm just one concerned citizen—who happens to be the U.S. Open champion. What can I do against these ruthless and powerful men?"

This was Floyd appropriating stock dialogue from old movies. This latest I recognized as Don Diego assuring the Commandante' that he had no knowledge of Zorro's activities.

Time to seize the moment… "What about Snog?" I shouted. It was as if someone had tripped a speaker wire. Heads snapped in my direction.

"Who said that?" Floyd's gaze swept the room.

I raised my hand. "Over here."

"Cotter? That you?"

"Hey, Floyd."

He stared at me for a moment then said, "Heard you were back," he said. "Been a while."

"So, they keep telling me."

He nodded, mulling this non-information over.

"How you hittin' 'em?"

"'Bout the same."

He nodded some more, then raised a farewell arm to the gathering. "Okay, then. Thank you all for coming—"

"What about my question?"

"What question?"

"You just said you couldn't do anything about Stickley being sold. I'm wondering if maybe that's what this Snog guy's after—raising public awareness of the need for golf courses."

All the eyes now turned back to Floyd.

"How should I know?" Floyd said. "Why don't you ask him?"

"I would, but I don't know how to reach him. I was wondering if maybe you'd ask him for me."

Floyd's eyes widened. He beckoned to a trembling press aide who came over and leaned into the mic.

"What makes you think—" the aide said, "That Mr. Bird—anybody—knows how to contact Snog?"

"Let Floyd answer," one of the reporters yelled.

Floyd held up a hand for quiet. "How the fu—how would I know?"

"Just had a feeling you might."

"Well, why don't you go have that feeling somewhere else, Cotter. We're all very busy here."

I saw a couple of security guards heading toward me. Time to move things along.

"I have an announcement to make," I said, shouting now. "My name is Charley Cotter. Doctor Charley Cotter. My remarks will be brief as I'm needed back in brain surgery. In view of the fact that our community is being terrorized by a pack of lawless renegades known as snogs and because our law enforcement agencies seem hamstrung in their ability to deal with them, I am hereby issuing a challenge and directing it toward the person who calls himself Snog. I will meet you anyplace, anytime—"

"What makes you think you can beat Snog," shouted a

reporter with dark bags under his eyes. "Conventional wisdom says he can't be beaten."

"Let's just say I have no illusions about my chances."

"They say it's impossible," said the reporter with the microphone.

"That's what I'm counting on."

"But," she said, "If he accepts your challenge, wouldn't Snog be forced to reveal his identity? If he accepts that is."

"I suppose he would."

"Then, why should he?

"Because if he doesn't, everyone will know that all these signs he puts up himself about it being impossible to beat him are just a bunch of headline-grabbing horsesh—excuse me—horse manure he made up."

"You're saying Snog writes those signs himself?"

"I'm saying this match will expose him to the world once and for all as the sniveling, scum-sucking, chicken shit, five-handicapper he really is."

Of *course*, it was Floyd. It was so obvious—to me at least. Who else could the night-golfing, rabble rousing Snog possibly be but Floyd Birdwell? This was, after all, the world according to Floyd, seen through his eyes and imagination. If he could be anybody, whom would he choose to be? What unique situation or status might the Floyd we knew imagine for himself? Certainly, not any sort of authority figure, industry titan or Hollywood 'show dog'. He had nothing but contempt for those 'morons.' And mainstream accomplishments like winning the U.S. Open, while certainly a feather in his cap, didn't jibe with his outlaw image.

No, if Floyd could select an ideal persona for himself, it would be a dashing anti-hero—a hooded avenger like Darth Vader or the Scarlet Pimpernel. Robin Hood with a five-iron, battling oppression in the form of duplicitous mini mall developers from the back of his trusty Harley. The clincher for my theory of course, being my certainty that no one but Floyd—in this universe or any other—

could possibly have dreamt up this daffy scenario.

The Daves and I had already decided that flushing out Snog and getting him to accept our challenge would be half the battle. So far it looked to be working. Announcing my challenge, I had looked directly at him, laying it on thick. Floyd's face had already turned orangutan-ass orange—his familiar preamble to violence.

"What's this got to do with Birdwell?" shouted another reporter. "Are you alleging that Birdwell knows Snog's identity?"

"Why don't you ask *him?*" I said.

Smelling blood in the water, the 'media' turned to Floyd and began peppering him with questions.

"Do you know who Snog is?"

"How well do you know Snog?"

"Who is he?"

"Have you talked to him?"

Floyd looked like he had when the range rats caught him out of his cage, ducking questions like they were golf balls aimed at his head. His little press guy stood in front of him, flapping his arms, shouting, "One at a time!"

Floyd stood up and stormed off the stage, disappearing behind a curtain. Reporters trying to follow him were repelled by a pair of security guards. The rest of them turned on me, thrusting lenses and microphones into my face.

"Who is Snog?"

"Does Birdwell know who Snog is?"

"What's Birdwell's connection to Snog?"

"Who are you?"

"What's your story?"

"Give him some room!" shouted a Dave. "Let him talk."

I held up my hands for quiet. "I wonder how many of you are aware," I began, "that, in England, snogging is a slang term for the passionate exchange of sloppy wet kisses."

Illegal Conversation

"A press conference for U.S. Open champion Floyd Birdwell was disrupted last night," the anchorwoman was saying. "When a Walnut Hill man rose to publicly challenge the golfing terrorist known as Snog to a match."

Then the picture cut to me standing at the back of the media tent. The wide-angle lens made my bandage look especially prominent. I felt a small shudder of apprehension as I cranked up the volume.

"My name is Charley Cotter—*Doctor* Charles Cotter, actually. My remarks will be brief as I'm needed back in brain surgery."

Then the video jumped ahead.

"I am hereby issuing a challenge and directing it toward the person who calls himself Snog. I will meet you anyplace, anytime—" The video jumped again to where I was interrupted by a reporter but, since you couldn't hear the question, it appeared as if I'd lost my train of thought and just stood gaping. Then the video jumped ahead again.

"Our match will prove that all these signs he puts up himself about it being impossible to beat him are so much attention-craving, self-serving garbage."

"Wow," said the grinning anchor, an Asian guy. "Did he say he had just had brain surgery?"

"There was some confusion," said his female co-anchor. "As to whether he was in fact an escaped patient."

"Doctor," I shouted at the screen now. "Escaped doctor!"

"In any case," the co-anchor continued. "He backpedaled from his challenge when he was informed that snogging is illegal and carries stiff penalties."

"Well," sniffed the Asian guy. "I think we can safely draw our own conclusions."

They moved on to another story and I flipped off the TV and, although it was barely noon, went out to the kitchen after another beer. Arriving home to an empty house after my run-in with Floyd and the press, I'd slipped back into the desperation that had lately been my default psychic state. Coming off like a ranting mental patient on the local news did nothing to improve that condition.

I ached more than ever for the life I'd left behind, for Cathy and the kids and the life we shared. Things weren't always great, and we weren't what you would call well off, but we were okay by anybody's definition. We had our health, the kids were great and, while it was true my career had stagnated a bit, I had a good job, and I was good at it. Even Barnett said so. All I needed to do was hang in there. He'd be retiring soon and, as creative director, I was in a good position to wind up with a healthy piece of the business.

I thought again about Sean and Sara and how they'd looked the morning I said I wasn't going with them to visit their grandparents. They'd been disappointed, but just momentarily, the way that kids are when you tell them they can't do something. There's no reason to think next time won't be a different story. Daddy can't go this weekend but there'd be other weekends. My heart ached again as I thought about Cathy having to break the news that, no, there wouldn't be any more weekends with Daddy, not ever. Daddy had died and gone to golf.

I had to get back there.

I spent the afternoon on the sofa, flipping channels, looking for news that Floyd/Snog had accepted my challenge.

It was a long shot, I knew. Dropping that bomb in the middle of his press conference had been a radical yet calculated move. The Daves and I had figured that, in order to have Floyd agree to a match, we'd first need to smoke out his Snog persona—get him to admit he was Snog. If that failed, we'd try to force him into a match under the threat of us revealing Snog's true identity. Except, who'd believe it? His dual identity might be obvious to me but, in this universe—his universe—the Open champ's secret identity was secure.

That evening I drove over to Mallard's telling myself I needed to practice for the upcoming match but really because I had nothing else to do. There was little more than an hour left until closing and a heavy fog lay over the grass and the stalls. A couple of lonely range rats were out there still pounding balls. You couldn't make out faces through the mist, just dollops in a living watercolor, swinging away.

I bought a medium bucket from one of Mallard's interchangeable, aging, bottle-blonde cashiers who didn't look up from the book she was reading and walked out toward the end stalls, near the parking lot. I liked it better down there, away from the teaching stalls and the benches lined with kibitzers. I set up in the second stall from the end and dumped my balls into the aluminum tray, hearing the familiar clatter against the metal, thinking how, only a little more than a week ago, I'd been in the same stall chatting with Floyd about going to the desert. What did the movie poster say? A long time ago in a universe far away? I remembered him asking how long I'd be gone.

A while, I'd said.

The fog had settled in to the point where I could see only about halfway to the back fence. The one-fifty marker was visible but beyond it, the lights stirred the fog into a smoky gumbo. The grip of the eight-iron felt damp in my hand. I wiped it against my pants leg and then tapped a ball out of the metal tray. I normally hit an eight about one-fifty, but I caught this one flush watched it fly over the sign and vanish in the fog. I was reaching for another ball when I heard a familiar engine start up.

A couple of seconds later, a Harley soft tail materialized out of the mist. The rider was Floyd.

"What do you think you're doing, Cotter?"

"Hitting balls." I looked around but couldn't see any of his entourage.

"I'm talking about this bullshit challenge of yours. Even you can't be stupid enough to think you can do something that's been pretty much officially recognized as impossible."

"Who says it's impossible?"

"Me and everybody else. Beatin' Snog is impossible."

"Anybody ever tried?"

"Why would they do that when they know it's a waste of time?"

"How do they know if they don't try?"

"Do you understand that the guy's name is Snog?"

"I understand that."

"His name is Snog and the game is snog. Do you understand what that means? Does that mean anything to you, Cotter?"

"I think so."

"No, you don't. Because if you did, you wouldn't even think about challenging him. It'd be like—hey I think I wanna go bowling so you know what I'm gonna do? I'm gonna challenge a guy whose name is Bowling to a bowling match. How stupid does that sound?"

"Pretty stupid."

"You bet your ass it does, because a guy named 'Bowling' is gonna go out and bowl a three-hundred game 99 percent of the time. Am I right?"

"You're not still working here are you, Floyd? Thought you just signed a big endorsement deal."

He scowled and looked out at the range. "Like to keep in touch with my roots if that's all right with you."

"Sure. I guess."

"And while you're at it, how you gonna get Snog to accept

your dumb ass challenge when you don't know who he is or where he is?"

"I heard he hangs out over at Meadowbank at night."

"Meadowbank," Floyd snorted. "Snog hangs out at a million golf courses. And even if you knew which one, you'd never spot him. He moves like a phantom through the trees—plays right through you before you know he's even there."

Floyd leaned back on the hog, eyes shining. "Feels like a breeze or something went by. His lit-up ball is like a firefly, blinkin' here and there, and then way over there. Be like trying to scoop up moonlight with a beer can."

I hit a little fade eight toward the one-fifty. "Maybe I ought to play you instead."

"Get real, Cotter."

"Why not? As I recall, we never finished our match."

"That was a long time ago and, in case you haven't noticed, things are way different now."

"Since the Open, you mean?"

"You realize that I've only played one tournament and they're already talkin' about fast-trackin' me into the Golf Hall of Fame?"

"That's pretty remarkable, all right."

"Oh, ya think? And did you happen to notice my picture on the cover of every golf publication there is— not to mention Time, Easyriders, Cigar Aficionado and Juggs Magazine? Vanity Fair wants me to eat brunch with some guy wants to 'capture my insights.'"

"Impressive."

"It pains me to say this, Cotter, but my time is way too valuable to waste on grudge matches with chops I used to know." He made a show of looking at his watch. "My business people have me booked pretty much round the clock with tournaments and personal appearances and stuff."

"I'm just talking about a friendly match."

"Cotter, I get paid a million dollars just to show up at a tournament. Don't even have to win. Shit, I could finish dead last and they'd still have to pay me."

"I'm happy for you Floyd. I really am."

Floyd leaned back on the bike, wallowing in his success. "Yep, my agent's got stuff scheduled for me to show up at for about the next ten years."

I hit another eight-iron into the fog. "What if I can raise a million?"

"Give me a break. I just won the Open, and set a record doing it that's gonna stand for a hundred years. They already got me favored to win the Masters next year even though I never saw the course before and now they're talking about calling off the British Open and just handing me the cup so's nobody's gotta play in that shit weather they got over there when they know me winning it is only a formality. You're just a weekend hack. Who's gonna put down ten cents on you beatin' me?"

"Almost sounds like you're *afraid* to play me."

"Nice try, Cotter. And anyway, where are you ever gonna get your grubby hands on a million bucks and I'm not giving you a discount, or anything so forget that right now."

"Let's say I get the money. Then what?"

"What do you mean, then what? Then you lose and go back to oblivion or the desert or wherever."

"Where do we play?"

"Anywhere we want. I call any course in the world right now, they send a ride for me."

"Yeah, but we don't want to draw a crowd."

"Cotter—I sit down to eat waffles a couple hundred people show up to watch."

"I've got an idea. We don't even have to play in the daytime. Remember that night we snogged Meadowbank?"

Floyd's eyes narrowed. "What is this, Cotter? You wearing a wire or something?"

"Just thought we could clear up some unfinished business. Strictly between us."

Floyd's voice dropped to a stage whisper. "Snogging's illegal, Cotter. You just committed a felony just by mentioning it to me. I can have you arrested."

"C'mon, Floyd, you've always been down for a little snog."

Floyd smashed a fist on his handlebars and made a gurgling sound. "I don't have time for this bullshit." He revved the Fatboy's big twin cam.

"But, if I can raise the million, you'll play, right?"

He was already gone, accelerating into the fog bank. I swung the eight-iron and lobbed a ball after him. I thought I heard it strike metal, but I could have been mistaken.

Titanium Teddy

"We need a million dollars."

Mike looked up from his seat next to the drafting table. "We?"

"Floyd won't agree to the match unless he gets a million-dollar show–up fee."

Ron put down the binoculars he was cleaning. "A million to show up? What'll he take to get lost?"

I'd tracked the bankers down to a hangar on the outskirts of the county airfield. The lady at the bank told me on the phone that the two were involved in a "highly sensitive project". The door to Hangar #16 was wide open offering an unobstructed view of a service runway and a grassy field beyond where colored marking posts were set in the ground at varying distances. Just inside the door, a green artificial-turf driving range mat complete with rubber tee had been bolted to the floor.

I'd arrived to find Mike and Ron poring over schematic drawings with a pair of earnest young technicians in goggles and welding aprons. My unexpected arrival was greeted with a flurry of fumbling to roll up what looked like blueprints and drawings and shove them into drawers. Then Mike had asked the techs—he'd introduced them as Dalton and Eric calling them "wonder boys"—to give us some privacy.

"What has Floyd got to do with this?" said Mike after they'd gone. "You're supposed to be playing Snog."

"Floyd *is* Snog," I said.

The bankers looked at me blankly.

"Floyd Birdwell who just won the Open? *That* Floyd Birdwell?"

"By like a million shots." said Ron. "Are you sure?"

"Yep," I said. "He's Snog."

"He admitted it?"

"Well, no. But I can pretty much guarantee it's him. He says he'll play me but only if we can come up with his appearance fee."

"A million bucks?" The bankers exchanged a look I didn't care for. "Charley, darling," said Ron. "We need to talk." He leaned back against a drafting table, twisting a frizzed forelock. "This is awkward. Actually, we were hoping to tell you before you went and challenged him."

"Tell me *what?*"

"We've had to make other arrangements."

"You mean you found somebody else to challenge Snog? Who?"

"We're not at liberty to say."

"But I'm the only one who can beat him. Isn't that what Dr. Sleeves said?"

"Well, yes, we thought that too, until…"

"Until you saw me play Meadowbank? Guys, I was off my game, all right? I'd just been in a plane crash for God's sake."

"And now," said Ron, "that we know who it is we're challenging…"

"Think of it this way," said Mike. "Good news. You're off the hook. You don't have to play him."

"Maybe I don't want to be off the hook."

"What are you talking about?"

"Maybe I've got my own reasons for wanting to play him."

"Oh, say Charley," said Ron. "If it's about the

membership, Lerner would have found some way to back out of it. That man has reneged on more promises than…"

"We have," said Mike.

"Look," I said. "This is something we all need to happen and it's very do-able. We just need to meet his price."

"We?" Ron smirked.

"Okay, you come up with the million, I beat him and everybody wins."

"Doesn't matter if it's a million or ten cents," Mike said. "Beating Floyd Birdwell does us no good. *Snog* is the guy we've got to beat."

"Floyd is Snog."

"So you say. You may be right. But nobody else knows that. We need to beat him publicly. In prime time. Cut this sucker off at the knees." Mike shook his head. "I think you'll agree that your game suffered out there in the desert…"

"You're just not the old Charley," said Ron. "And now we find out that this Snog person is also the best golfer on the planet…"

"Give me a chance, guys. I know Floyd. All I have to do is get under his skin and he'll blow sky high. He'll shoot a thousand. And, anyway, who else are you gonna get?"

Mike exhanged a wry smile with Ron, then shouted toward a closed off section of the hangar. "Hey Dalton, wheel him in."

The "wonder boys" re-appeared and folded back a partition to reveal what looked like a one-armed robot mounted on BMX bicycle wheels. They pushed it over and set it up at right angles to the green mat. Dalton picked up a big-headed driver from a corner and secured it to the robot's arm with a wrench.

"Say hello to Titanium Teddy," said Mike. "He's a refined, state-of-the-art version of the old 'Iron Byron' swing machine the U.S.G.A. used to test golf balls. Why don't you give Charley a preview, Dalton?"

The young technician flipped a switch on a remote-control box he carried. Teddy's head jerked upright and I could see little orange lights shining beneath two eyehole slits.

Eric brought over a bucket of range balls and placed one on the tee. Then he picked up the binoculars and took up a position next to the doorway. Dalton stood waiting for a signal from Mike.

"Let's start with something simple," Mike told him. "Three-eighty-five straightaway."

Dalton dialed the information into his remote, then walked over and stood behind the robot facing down range. "Stand by... armed... and... Fire!" Dalton slapped a large button with the flat of his hand. The robot's sling shot swing was almost too fast to see, just a split-second hum—the sound of the club whipping downward and an almost instantaneous BANG. You couldn't tell whether the ball had been struck or had simply vanished or blown up. But there was Eric in the doorway with the binoculars, grinning as he tracked the shot.

"Three-eighty-five, zero degrees."

"Bump it up another fifty," Mike told him. "And put a little fade on it—say ten yards."

"Four-thirty-five," said Dalton. "Two degrees right drift. Stand by... fire!

Titanium Teddy swung again. This time I was ready and got a better glimpse of the sling shot motion but once again the impact was like a small explosion. Now you saw it, then you didn't.

"Golf shot!" shouted Eric.

"Let's try a thousand," said Mike.

Dalton bent over the controls. "Roger that. Top spin?"

"Sure. But make the thousand all carry."

"How much roll?"

"My God!" I said. "You can control the roll?"

"Yes sir—within a ten-yard margin for error, depending on terrain. Course, if you're landing on tarmac, it's anybody's guess. It could bounce forever."

"Say thirty yards," Mike told the technician.

"Stand by," Dalton yelled again and slapped his remote.

The robot wound up and shellacked another pellet toward the horizon. Eric put the binoculars down and reached for what Mike said was a GPS device. "Each ball is coated with nanopolymer paint. We can track them and measure distance to the inch."

"One thousand thirty-eight."

"Uh-oh," said Mike. "Eight yards long."

"Sorry," Dalton said. "It gets a little downhill out there."

Mike and Ron looked pleased with themselves.

"So that's it? You're dumping me for a robot?"

Ron, still working with the emery board, folded his legs beneath him in the chair. "Dump is such a cruel word," he said.

"It's just business, Charley," said Mike. "There's a lot at stake here. Besides, we didn't think your heart was in it. Not after you walked out on us last time. Anyway, you're off the hook now. Thank you, Dalton."

The techs wheeled Titanium Teddy back behind the partition.

"Listen, Mike, you're making a big mistake. Maybe this pile of scrap can drive the ball a mile but what are you gonna do for a short game?"

Ron started coughing.

"You'd be surprised," said Mike behind his game face. "We've made great strides. Teddy spent a week in Palm Desert with Dave Stockton, and now he's working with Dave Pelz."

"It's coming together nicely," said Mike. "We're over the hump on distance and now all we have to input is speed and break."

"Good luck with that."

"Should be only a matter of days before we have the most awesome weapon in the golfing—"

"Snogging."

"…Snogging world at our command."

I walked over and looked out at the airfield. A breeze had come up and was stirring a stand of tall fir trees on the other side of the tarmac. A line of single engine planes sat, tied down in front of a hurricane fence. What kind of universe had Ed our fearless pilot found himself in after the crash? Or the original Mike and Ron? What, I wondered, had they been thinking of?

"I've been wondering," I said out loud. "Why I took off for the desert instead of playing the match?"

"You're asking us?" said Ron.

"And, if I needed to back out for some reason, why didn't I just do that? Why leave town? Unless…" I said, turning to face them. "Unless I found out about Stickley."

The smile froze on Mike's face. Ron dropped his emery board and gripped the arms of his chair. "What about Stickley?"

"Floyd's right about that, isn't he? What he said to the reporters about Stickley being a done deal?"

"How should we know?"

"You're developing it for a mini mall—you, Lerner and Dunphy."

"Absolutely false," said Mike.

"A vicious slander," said Ron. "No truth whatsoever."

"C'mon, guys, I've seen the plans in your conference room at the bank. 'S.M.G.C.'—Stickley Municipal Golf Course? You're subdividing the land which means the deal is already done or close to it. Am I right?"

Mike glared at Ron. "What did I tell you about leaving those lying around?"

"That's why you care so much about beating Snog. You need him out of the way. Even with the mayor and the town council in your pocket, you still need to put a muzzle on the one guy certain to raise a public stink about it."

"It's not just a bunch of nuts golfing at night in the city streets. You've got the reigning U.S. Open champ— the highest profile golfer on the planet, nipping at your ass, blowing the whistle on your deal to bulldoze the last remaining public course in the county. And you really think that robot has a better chance of beating Floyd than me?"

"It's your fault," said Mike. "When you took off wherever you went, you left us with few options. Dalton and Eric were a godsend. They came into the bank to see about funding for a project of their own."

"A mechanical golfer?"

Mike performed one of his pot-winning smirks. "Keep this under your hat, but they've invented a photo-electric fuel cell that's going to revolutionize the transportation industry and put an end to the world's dependence on fossil fuels."

"Fortunately," said Ron. "We were able to persuade them to put that project on hold while they helped us out."

"We helped them prioritize," said Mike.

"So, it's true, then?"

"Absolutely not." It was hard not to laugh, watching them shake their heads in unison.

"Okay, look," I told them. "We all know that Titanium whoosis hasn't got a hope in hell of beating Snog or anybody else. I'm the best candidate you've got. If you've got doubts, ask Dr. Sleeves again. C'mon, what's a measly million dollars when you're talking about the world's largest mini mall?"

"Let me ask you a question," said Mike. "We already told you that the Meadowbank membership was a non-starter."

"Yeah."

"So—considering the fact that you've walked out on this match before—why are you so hot to play it now?"

"I've got my reasons."

"Personal ones?"

"You could say that."

"Could they have something to do with Cathy and a little score you're looking to settle?"

"I don't know what you're talking about? What score?"

Mike was shaking his head. "Not for a million, Charley," he said.

Welcome to Snog

Two nights had passed since my meeting in the hangar with Mike and Ron. The bankers had refused to fund my impossible match with Floyd and now we figured—the Daves and I—that our best and only option was to catch Floyd in his Snog persona and threaten to expose him if he turned down my challenge. But first, we had to find him.

Cathy was the key. Observing her pattern of nightly comings and goings had me convinced she could lead us to him. Each night after dinner, she'd change into dark clothing and head out, never telling me where she was going—as an unwelcome boarder I didn't rate that information. Some nights she'd return little more than an hour later but just as often, it wouldn't be until well after going to bed that I'd hear the Volvo pull in. I guess it shouldn't have bothered me, not knowing what she was doing, or with whom. This wasn't my wife, after all. This was a stranger. But it *did* bother me. I couldn't help it.

One night I'd gone down and found her leaned against the kitchen counter, a lithe figure in black, sipping tea, staring at the floor. I tried to start a conversation, but she'd brushed past me and left me standing in the doorway, never more aware that I was the wrong guy in the wrong universe.

Later on, I found what I was looking for in the Volvo's trunk. A sleeve of glow-in-the-dark golf balls tucked into a black woolen watch cap in the side pocket of her golf bag. Cathy was one of them—a snogger. Of course, she was—

Floyd would have imagined her that way.

Next time Cathy went out, the Daves were waiting. They had staked out the house just after sundown, and then followed the Volvo downtown. By the time I caught up with them they were parked across the street from a condominium project on Spruce not far from Meadowbank.

"Somebody she know live there?" asked Dave.

"You tell me," I said. "I don't know her any better than you do."

There was a narrow breezeway leading to a garage area and an alleyway beyond. We crept along passing underneath open windows, hearing living sounds: voices, dishes clattering, TV conversations. There was nobody in the garage when we got there.

"She must have gone inside," said the Clone.

Then we heard what sounded like the gabble of cocktail party conversation coming from farther down the alley.

"Somebody's having a party."

We walked down the alley to where it was separated from a dry cleaners parking lot by a rusty wire fence. The store was closed, and the parking lot was not lit but moonlight illuminated a sizeable crowd of people in dark clothing. Ten yards farther, we discovered a broad piece of white linen tied to the fence. Next to it a full panel of the fence had been removed. Just inside the fence stood a guard with a clipboard—the same guy I'd talked to in Mallard's parking lot, same black tee shirt and headset, same attitude.

"Name?"

Mindful of the irony in the fact that we had just crawled through a hole in a rusty fence to be confronted by a doorman, I gave my name making sure to prefix it with "Doctor."

"You're down here, Doc, but it says, 'Dr. Cotter plus one.'" He indicated the pair of Daves standing behind me.

"Uh, they're actually the same guy. Show him your i.d., guys."

The security guard gave me a look but took their driver's licenses anyway.

"There you go, plus one, that's them."

"Same name," he said, frowning. "Same date of birth."

"Same photo," Dave said.

"I don't get it," said the flustered guard. "If they're twins, why do they have the same name?"

"Because they're not twins. If they were twins, the reservation would say plus two."

That seemed to be good enough for the bouncer. He jerked his head toward a big carton leaning against a Volkswagen. "Okay, you're in. Grab yourself a mask out of that box over there."

"What do we need masks for?" Dave said.

"Doesn't matter to me but, if you wind up in a police line-up, you'll be the one gets identified."

We took the offered masks.

"Why do you suppose you're on the list?" Clone Dave said.

"Ask Floyd when you see him," I said, but I'd already figured out that, as one of Floyd's imagined rivals, here in this universe conceived of his pipedreams, he'd want my nose kept available and close at hand, to be rubbed in his success.

There must have been nearly a hundred people milling in the low light, others you couldn't see in the shadows. It seemed a random mix of races and socio-economic groups, almost a demographic cross section, although skewing—as we say in the ad biz—a bit young.

"Jeez," said Clone Dave. "Looks like half the town is here."

You'd assume that Floyd's association with whatever this was would have attracted a mangier bunch, but the vibe was more political rally than biker bash. We saw fresh-faced millennials, twenty-something Berkeley bohemians, suburban 'dink' couples, anxious and smiling and clutching arms like it was Saturday morning at the art fair. I even spotted a few "gray panthers" in sweat clothes and funny hats. Floyd's core "element" was represented too, a motley assortment of range rats, caddies and borderline mental cases I recognized from Mallards. Present also were the ever-vigilant security guards in their black tee shirts and windbreakers, cruising the assemblage, muttering into headsets.

Nearly everyone, including the guards, wore little, black Zorro masks, the kind that cover your eyes and the bridge of your nose. Even so, I had little difficulty recognizing Shortgrass and Hollerin' Hank. You'd need a twenty-five-pound grocery bag to disguise those larger-than-life characters.

But, so far, no Floyd.

One of the Daves tapped me on the shoulder. "Check it out," he said and nodded toward a cluster of black-clad figures nearby. Cathy stood among them, auburn curls falling from beneath her watch cap.

A pair of truck headlights switched on. Screeching feedback from a bullhorn brought whistles, mock screams and laughter.

"Good evening, ladies and gentlemen," The amplified voice was breathy, like a stage whisper. "Welcome to Snog."

This was met with cheers and more laughter but the guy with the bullhorn shushed them. We could see him, standing half-illuminated in the headlights. Dave shook his head in wonderment. "He's *whispering* through a bullhorn."

"This is a very special occasion," whispered the bullhorn guy, "Because tonight we have a very special guest snogger."

"Guest snogger?" said Clone Dave.

"Our guest would be familiar to each and every one of you—were he not wearing a mask, of course." The bullhorn guy handed it now to a gray-haired man in a jogging suit who, even in the harsh backlight, did indeed seem familiar.

"Fellow snoggers," he whispered. "It is indeed a privilege to be with you tonight. You know, people often ask me, 'is it wrong to snog?' Or 'how can there be a law against snogging when it's for such a good cause?' You know what I tell them? I tell them the same thing I tell all my constituents—no, my friend, snogging is not wrong. No more than our Minutemen were wrong in fighting for this country's freedom, no more than—"

"Is that the mayor?" said Clone Dave.

"What's he doing here?" said Dave. "Isn't this illegal?"

"That's a politician hedging his bet," I said. "Lotta votes out here."

"These are the times that try men's souls," the mayor intoned. "And desperate times demand desperate measures. Are we going to sit around on our behinds while private interest groups carve up our golf courses?"

"Noooo!" the crowd whispered back. Their collective voices sounded like air rushing through a tunnel.

"Are we going to permit foreigners to turn our precious fairways into a rat warren of mini malls?"

"Hellll noooooo!"

The hissing crowd was abruptly drowned out by the sound of a motorcycle's approach. A lone headlight raked the huddled mass of snoggers. Without missing a beat, the mayor—if it was the mayor—segued into full throat.

"Ladies and gentlemen, let's have a big welcome for the one the only—Snoooooooggg!"

The crowd gave a huge collective shout, the kind you hear during a major golf tournament when the favorite holes an impossible putt or stiffs an approach shot. Lights flicked on in the condos.

The bike skidded to a stop in front of the headlights. The rider waved and dismounted then strode confident and tall over to where a half dozen excited young nurses in crisp white uniforms and black snog masks, fugitives from the laboratory of Floyd's imagination, clapped hands and jumped up and down. He grabbed one of them, bent her backward and kissed her hard. The crowd cheered again. He laughed as he released the one girl and grabbed another, planting a huge a smack on her as well. Now all the nurses were screaming and pulling at him. It took three security guards to intervene and escort him over to where the mayor—if it was the mayor—shook his hand, hugged him for good measure and gave him the bullhorn.

"Think you can beat me?" The big guy asked the crowd.

"Nooooo!"

"Know anybody who can?"

"Nooooo!"

"What's my name?"

"Snog!"

"What's my name?"

"Snooogg!"

"He thinks he's Elvis live in Vegas," Dave said. "Do you think we're the only ones here who know who that really is?"

"It's so obvious," said the Clone." "Why can't they see it?"

"Because, in his mind's eye, they don't."

"I'd like to thank his honor for that nice introduction," Snog was saying. "I'd tell you his name but then I'd have to kill each and every one of you and we're running short of time."

"Yeah!" from the crowd. Someone behind me let out a big cowboy whoop.

"Now, some of you morons are probably wondering what we're doing here in this here parking lot. Well, listen up and I'll tell you. You see that bunch of condominiums over there? Well those condos and this parking lot right here—this used to be a golf course."

A groan rose from the crowd.

"That's right. Maybe you remember Cumberland

Trail—little nine-hole executive course. Real nice. Not long but lotta trees. In fact, right in this very parking lot—this used to be the third green. Right here. Little pond just over there, where that Mustang is parked. Made for a tricky approach shot."

"And see that section of condos over there? Where the ninth fairway used to be. Green was up at the head of the alley."

"Maybe we oughtta snog it!" someone yelled.

Snog held up a hand. "What the bankers and developers and the 'powers that be' need to understand is that we snogs never forget a golf course!"

Cheers and applause arose now from the assembled snogs, continuing until Snog held up a hand. "And... just because they bulldoze 'em and bury 'em and try to wipe 'em from the earth... we will never... ever... stop *playing* 'em!"

Golf clubs waved in the air, the crowd chanting now: "Snog! Snog! Snog! Snog!"

Snog held his hand up once more for quiet then handed the bullhorn to the original speaker.

"Okay... tonight," the speaker said, whispering again. We've got an extra-special snog in store for you. Starting here in the condos, we take it all the way downtown. Maybe a mile as the crow flies. Take any route you like. First snogger to bounce a ball off the front steps of City Hall wins."

At this point, Snog grabbed the bullhorn back. "Any you morons think they can beat me?"

"Yeah!"

Snog paused for effect, then scoffed into the mic.

That brought a roar of laughter from the snogs.

"All right, losers," Snog shouted. "Time to mount up. Let's do some snogging!"

"Yeah!" shouted the snogs.

I had to hand it to him. The guy knew how to whip up a crowd. The bankers had been right to worry about Snog's popularity. He was a bona fide grass roots hero. This mob was prepared to follow him anywhere, even to the steps of

City Hall where the law was sure to be waiting.

Dave grabbed my arm. "Now's your chance. Get up there and challenge him." But now Cathy was there, standing in front of me, dressed for a snog in black denim jacket and jeans. Combined with her black woolen cap, it made her look like a ninja chick in a caper movie. "What are you doing here?" she said.

"So, this is how you spend your evenings."

"You shouldn't be here," she said. "This is my life, not yours."

"Maybe I want to snog too."

She stared at me for a moment. "You think you can beat him, but you can't. Nobody can." Then she turned and moved off into the crowd. Just as the truck horn blew and the headlights went out.

A Distance Thing

The barrage began with the truck horn blast followed by an enormous shout, followed by the sound of Floyd's motorcycle revving and taking off.

"There goes the great Snog getting a head start on the field," Dave said.

"He rides a Harley and everybody else's gotta walk," said the clone. "No wonder it's impossible to beat him."

We'd missed our chance to challenge Floyd in the parking lot and now figured our best shot was to be there waiting when he got to City Hall. Getting back to Dave's Blazer was tricky business considering we had to cut across a condominium complex that was being snogged. Lit up now, with a medley of frightened screams and angry shouts coming from the open windows, it looked like a small city under siege. Most of the snoggers were headed toward the front side of the complex facing Scott Avenue. Our path back to the hole in the fence was at right angles to that direction which placed us squarely in the line of fire. The volley of luminous balls launched into the night sky was spectacular but also potentially lethal. Balls bounded off cars, ricocheted from concrete, asphalt and brick, smashing glass.

We made it unscathed out through the fence, down the alley and onto the side street where we hopped into the Blazer and drove toward town, stopping at an intersection to look back and see the first snoggers spill from the condos out into the street. Some paused to whack at balls, others came at the dead run pursued by a posse of angry homeowners.

The block in front of City Hall was deserted when we got there except for a few cars parked on the city park side of the street. No sign yet of the great Snog or any of his disciples.

But then, just moments later, we detected the Harley's throaty approach from the direction of the park.

"That'll be the Harley," said Dave. "He's riding cross country."

"How do you know it's a Harley?" I asked.

The Daves shared a professional's knowing smirk. "Nothing sounds like a hog," they said in unison. "Not even close."

We heard something hard hit the side of the Blazer. Dave and I got out and spotted a luminous golf ball sitting in the grass a few yards away. Then the Harley came crashing through some bushes, headlights off, tailing around to a stop right in front of us. Floyd, in his little snog mask, frowned when he saw us.

"Playing through here gents," he said. Then he pulled some kind of mid-iron out of his waistband, strode over to the ball and began lining up a shot toward City Hall across the street.

"All right," he said. "You can go ahead and move that truck."

"Is that legal?" I asked him.

"Maybe after you move it, you'll want to go and consult an attorney."

"Reason I ask—according to the rules of golf, that truck is an obstruct—"

"This isn't golf, Cotter. It's snog. And I make the rules."

"Why's that?"

"Because I'm Snog."

He came over and got in my face. "You got a problem with that?"

"Nope."

"What are you doing here, anyway, Cotter?"

"He's waiting to find out if something impossible is going to happen," said Clone Dave.

"Like what?"

"Like somebody hitting those steps before you do."

Floyd frowned and that made his mask slip. He grabbed at it with his free hand. "That'll be the day," he said, looking around. "Seen anybody yet?"

"Just you, Floyd."

This took him by surprise. With his wild hair, black mask and open mouth he looked like an eighteenth-century highwayman caught holding the swag.

"What'd you call me that for… stranger?"

"Don't worry, Floyd. Your secret is safe with us."

"The name is Snog. Remember it."

"Fair enough, Mr. Snog. But—"

"Not *Mister* Snog—Snog."

"Okay—Snog—but do you mind if I ask you something?"

He didn't reply and that wasn't a good sign. Floyd, I knew, shared a characteristic with aging watchdogs: they are at their most dangerous when silent.

"How'd you know *my* name?" I said.

"Who says I know your name?"

"You just said it. You said, 'This isn't golf, Cotter. This is snog.' Remember?"

Now the stare again, eyes dilated. "I don't give a shit what your name is. Now go move that truck."

"Okay, but first let me ask you something."

"I'm warning you, Cotter."

"I'm just curious—"

"Curious kills. Read the papers."

"What is the U.S. Open champion doing running around playing Lone Ranger with a bunch of candy ass choppers?"

"I don't have time for your bullshit right now."

"If you really want to do something about saving golf courses, why don't you go public with it? You're the Open champ. You can get all the publicity you want—hold a press conference."

"I did that. Remember? People don't listen. You wanna know who people listen to? Terrorists. Because they scare the shit out of them, make 'em think the world is coming to an end. Now I'm going to ask you just once more—nicely—to get that truck out of the way."

"You know what you could do? You could organize a mass protest—a huge display of civil disobedience."

"What do you think *this* is?"

"This? You'll be lucky if this makes the local papers. I'm talking bigger—much bigger—huge!"

"Gigantic," said Dave, picking up my cue. "A giant snog."

"Wait," I said. "That's it! A giant snog for the ages—something all the top golfers in the world will want to show up for—and not just golfers. Civic leaders—world leaders, celebrities, movie stars, the Pope! Everybody you ever heard of."

"Wow," said Dave.

Hold it, I got it, I got it…. you could call it… 'One Giant Snog for Mankind.' How's that sound?"

Floyd was squinting into space as if trying to find sub-titles to this conversation printed in the night sky. "You know something, Cotter?" he said at last. "You're a real moron. The Pope is an old man. He couldn't snog his way to the refrigerator."

"It doesn't have to be the Pope. It could be somebody *like* the Pope—somebody world famous."

"Britney Spears," said Dave.

"No way," said Floyd.

"Okay, how about—?"

"*Britney Spears?* Is this a joke? Are you *trying* to piss

me off?"

"Well, no—"

"Wait a minute," said Dave. "What about the chick on 'General Hospital'—the nurse?"

Floyd's ears perked up. "Which nurse?"

"She's not world famous," said the clone.

"Will you shut up for a minute? Which nurse are we talking about?"

"The hot one. The one with the kid."

"The brother or the kid?"

"The kid. A couple weeks ago, they had her getting out of the shower? When the doctor guy showed up unexpectedly from Africa or someplace."

"You telling me she plays golf?"

"Like anyone cares with that body?" said Dave. "She could keep score or hand out beverages."

"Maybe in a bath towel," I suggested.

Floyd snorted. "Sure you wouldn't rather have the Pope, Cotter?"

"She'd be great," I said. "And we can have anybody else you want. Everybody who's anybody'll be fighting to get in. They'll have to declare it a world holiday like Christmas or New Year's. Re-enact it every year. 'Snog for the Planet,' how's that sound? Then after it gets really going—someday, after mankind migrates off the earth into the solar system— they'll be snogging other galaxies. Interplanetary Snog!"

Even through the mask, I saw concern register in Floyd's eyes. "I'd be on the Senior Tour by then."

"It's something worth doing," I told him. "And think of the stature. You wouldn't be just a cult hero or local crime problem anymore. You'd be…"

"An interplanetary problem," said Dave. "Like Darth Vader or Ming the Merciless."

Floyd's expression turned wistful. "It could be a fifth major," he said.

"Bigger." I said. "Much bigger—bigger than the other four combined. Only question is where."

"Where what?"

"Where to snog. Have you given that any thought?"

"We've only been talking about this for about thirty seconds, Cotter. When would I have time to think about it?"

"I'm sorry. I just thought that—this being such a great idea—you might have already thought of it."

Floyd glared at me. "Oh now, I suppose, you're gonna say snogging was your idea."

"Not at all. Definitely not. That's the one thing I'm absolutely positive about. Nobody but you could have dreamed up any of this."

"Just so we got that understood."

Then we heard a siren coming from the north side of town followed by the sound of shouting. Dave heard it too and gave me a look.

"Venue's gotta be right," Floyd was saying.

"Like Augusta National or Shinnecock Hills," I said. "Or maybe even St. Andrews,"

Floyd slumped his shoulders all at once. "Cotter, I'm the Open champion. I can play them anytime I want. Why would I want to snog 'em?"

"Who says it's gotta be a golf course?" said Dave. "Doesn't that sort of limit the possibilities?"

"You don't want to limit yourself," I agreed. "But it's got to be some place unique—a place no one would ever *dream* of snogging."

"An impossible place," said Dave. "Like Antarctica, Or the Sahara Desert or the Atlan—"

Dave caught my throat-cutting gestures and clammed up. "Those might take too long, Dave. Floyd's got a lot of commitments."

"Wait, I've got it!" said Dave. "The Parthenon."

"What about it?"

"We snog it."

"Why?"

"It's big and I'll bet nobody's done it before."

"Why would anyone want to?"

"It's just a suggestion."

"That we snog an old building in Greece?"

"Greece?"

"That's where it is."

"What am I thinking of—that big thing in Washington?"

"The Pentagon?"

Floyd was looking off into the distance, scratching his bearded chin with the handle of his iron. "I'm thinking it could be a distance thing," he said.

"You mean like how far?"

He nodded gravely. "We play from one end of the county to the other. Along the way, we snog all the condos and mini malls where there used to be golf courses."

Dave was skeptical. "You think they're gonna let you get away with that?"

"Hey man—this is for *mankind!*"

"I like it." I said. "It has a real grass-roots appeal. One simple yet principled man setting out on an impossible mission to bring attention to the plight of our planet. It's like Gandhi takes on global warming."

"Who?"

"Gandhi—skinny guy in the diaper that walked everywhere. Ben Kingsley played him in the movie."

"Ben Kingsley," said Dave. What else was he in?"

"Oh, man, I was afraid you were going to ask me that."

A police cruiser, bubble light flashing, rounded the corner of Park Avenue and sped north on Main Street. When it got to the intersection at the end of the block, the car's siren whooped twice. We watched it race another two blocks then whip a quick left onto Westmoor.

Floyd didn't seem overly concerned with the advancing cops or snoggers. "We'll need to get the word out," he said.

"Very simple. You hold a press conference and issue a challenge—call on the golfers of the world to unite against a common foe."

"Who's that?"

"Whoever is shutting down golf courses. We can help you draw up a list."

"I've got my own people, Cotter. It's all I need is some idiot brain surgeon balling up the works."

We heard whoops again and saw a police car jerk to a stop a block up Main near the corner of Hortense. Two cops jumped out with flashlights and ran into a yard. Then, just a second later, an illuminated golf ball came bouncing down Main Street from that direction, bounding right past the Blazer. At the same time, coming from somewhere in the park behind us, we heard a woman's scream and then raucous laughter. That was followed by the sound of a ball hitting the trees overhead and seeing it drop down nearly at our feet.

"Shit," Floyd said. "Cotter, move that truck, dammit."

"All right, but you've got to promise me something."

"No, I don't. Move the truck."

"Okay, but you gotta let me play in the big snog, right?"

Floyd was looking over his shoulder into the park, anxious now, watching for imminent snoggers. "Damn it, Cotter."

"You don't have to decide now. Just say that you'll consider it."

"Okay. Now, move the truck."

"I can play, right?"

He hissed through clenched teeth and brandished his

mid-iron. "I'm losing patience with you, man."

From off to our left, a salvo of luminous balls came bounding down the center of Main Street. Another ball whistled over our heads, landed in the middle of the street and bounced across the sidewalk into the line of bushes in front of City Hall's south wing.

"Uh-oh." Floyd took a deep breath and, without looking at me, said: "All right, Cotter, this is it."

I gave a thumbs up to Clone Dave in the driver's seat. He pulled the Blazer up a few yards, giving Floyd a wide-open shot at the City Hall front steps across the street. A pair of young snoggers burst out of the park's shadows on the dead run, breathing heavily, looking for their balls. Floyd ignored them, going through his Zen-wannabe pre-shot routine, starting behind the ball, focusing, blocking out the external world then stepping up and wiggling into his stance. A glance up to gauge the night breeze and then once more to see the line. Around and in front of him, snoggers scrambled to locate their balls as patrol cars, sirens whooping and wailing, screeched into the scene.

Floyd drew his club back to about three-quarters of a full swing and punched a low riser that looked at first like it was going to take a cop's head off but then it rose toward City Hall, dropping down onto the concrete steps to bounce once, twice, forward and bang off the front door.

The snoggers milling in the street saw it and let out a cheer. Floyd stepped forward into the light of a street lamp and took an elaborate bow.

"Nice shot," I said.

He nodded, pleased with himself. "Dr. Warren Sleeves taught me that shot," he said.

A Woman's Scorn

"Golfing sensation, Floyd Birdwell," said the TV anchorman, "stunned Tonight Show host Jimmy Fallon and an estimated ten million viewers late Thursday with the revelation that he has been leading a secret double life as the self-styled golfing activist—some say 'terrorist—known as Snog."

The picture on Earl's TV switched to Floyd, in his little black Snog mask, shaking hands with the talk show host.

"The audience greeted Birdwell with thunderous applause, but then grew silent as the golfer declared himself to be not only a snogger but Snog himself— whose identity has, up to now, been a well-kept secret."

The picture switched and showed Floyd in front of a chart, claiming he'd uncovered a direct connection between global warming and the 'great mini-mall conspiracy.'

"Later in the same broadcast," the female co-anchor said, "Birdwell issued a challenge saying he would be taking on "all comers" for what he's calling 'one giant snog for mankind.' Birdwell would not reveal the date or location for the giant snog. But, he confided, some of the biggest names in golf will be competing along with a handpicked assortment of world figures and celebrities."

"This announcement likely comes as an unwelcome surprise to state and municipal law enforcement agencies who are currently waging a so-far losing battle to curb and contain illegal snogging."

"Neither Fallon nor the show's producers," said the anchor, "had been warned that Birdwell planned to drop these twin bombshells during the broadcast."

Now the picture showed Floyd waving at the crowd and then walking off the stage leaving a perplexed Fallon in his wake.

"Oddly enough," said the female co-anchor. "In Great Britain, snogging is a slang word used to describe sloppy kissing."

"Tell me this isn't about me."

I swung around on the barstool. Cathy stood there, pointing up at Earl's TV.

"What isn't about you?"

"This big giant snog for whatever. I assume it was your idea?"

"Hey, slow down a second," I said.

Clone Dave leaned over from the stool next to me. "You know, maybe not a good idea to be talking about this in public."

"Nobody's talking to you," said Cathy.

"Just sayin'."

I hadn't seen her since the other night in the condo parking lot. Her hair was inches shorter and there were other changes.

"Is that a different nose ring?"

"Yes, it is. I suppose you don't like this one either."

"Is it supposed to hook on to something?"

"You know what? Just forget it, okay?"

Dave, on his phone, came over. "Bubba's out," he said. "They just announced it—couldn't guarantee him a courtesy car."

Cathy looked at him and then back at Clone Dave. "What—there's *two* of him now?"

"Identical cousins," I said. "What about the Pope?"

Dave shook his head. "Walnut Hill airport denied him landing privileges. Said the runway's too short for his 747 but everybody knows that's a crock. Guy I know takes care of the hangars told me the manager has a standing order from the city council to refuse landing clearance to anybody showing up for the big snog."

"Including the Pope?"

"Same with Justin Timberlake, Ray Romano and a bunch of other golfing celebrities. Told them fly their movie star butts back to Hollywood."

"Yeah, but the Pope—"

Clone Dave turned around. "What does the Pope care? Catholic Church probably owns a million golf courses. He doesn't need to snog."

"Which one is the cousin?" Cathy said.

By that time, I'd lost track. Either Dave was likely to be thinking or saying the same thing in any given situation. I'd actually heard them argue the same side of an argument—with each other. "We're still working that out," I said.

"We need to talk," she said.

I followed her out of the bar, through the cramped foyer lined with package goods and out into Earl's parking lot. The screen door slammed behind us. She walked over and leaned up against the Volvo. I waited while she gathered herself and then lit a cigarette against the wind. When it was going, she tossed her head back and swept the ginger strands from her forehead. With the warm afternoon light on her skin, she looked… *perfect*… like a movie star. *This is how Floyd sees her.*

"So," she said. "I'm right, aren't I? This big, giant snog is your idea."

"Not exactly."

"No?" She blew out a little stream of smoke and

squinted toward the setting sun. "But you're playing, right?"

I shrugged. "It's for a good cause."

"But that's not why you're playing, is it? Tell me—what do you get if you win?"

"Bragging rights, I guess. Be the guy who beat the great Snog at his own game."

"Big deal. What else?"

"Membership to Meadowbank."

She nodded. "Sounds like your banker friends want him beat pretty bad. Why do you think that is?"

"It's complicated. Has to do with real estate."

"So, it's like last time, then."

"Last time?"

"Don't act dumb. Last time—before you took off for the desert?"

Two guys in baseball shirts came banging out through the screen door into the parking lot. Cathy took another drag and waited until they got into their SUV and started it up.

"Look," she said. "I need you to do something for me."

"Okay."

"I don't want you to play in the big snog."

"Cathy, there's a lot riding on this."

"We both know what's riding on it, Charley."

"We do?"

"Your banker buddies need you to beat Floyd, to humiliate him so that the world will stop listening when he talks about how they're buying up all the golf courses and turning them into mini malls.

"Wait a min—"

"You turned them down once. What made you change your mind?"

"You're saying that's why I left? Because Mike and Ron wanted me to beat Floyd for them?"

"Why can't you be honest for once?"

"Please, Cathy… I *need* to know."

She looked at me and the anger was gone. *Were her eyes always this blue?* "You really don't remember, do you? Poor baby. What happened to you out there?"

"Well…there was this storm—"

She sighed, not listening, and scuffed her cigarette out on the gravel. "When you left for the desert, I knew what you were giving up… your career, your friends, even your home. You showed such… character. That's why I was so disappointed when you came back and just picked up again where you left off."

"I didn't want to be here. Believe me, this wasn't the plan."

"No? Then… what *are* you doing here?"

"Okay but, you were telling me why I left…"

"Well… I guess it was because you agreed with Floyd. It's flat wrong, you said, ripping up perfectly good golf courses just so people can buy chewing gum and toilet paper in the middle of the night. You weren't going to let that happen. And you know something? I was proud of you."

"And that's it? That's all?" I could tell she was holding something back. "Why'd I have to go away? Couldn't I have just stayed here and not played the match?"

"I suppose…"

"What… what is it? Tell me."

"It might," she said softly, "have had something to do with *us.*"

"Us? You mean you and me?"

"Well… this is hard, all right? The night before you left, we were in the living room, you know—on the sofa and I was saying how much I appreciated what you were doing—are you sure none of this sounds familiar?"

"Yes, I'm sure. Go ahead."

"That it was great, you know, refusing to let the bankers use you like that, and that I was proud of you but…"

"But what?"

"But… that, unfortunately somehow… I'd developed these feelings."

"Feelings."

"Uh-huh. Yes. They're hard to describe. I had begun to feel this strong attraction… I mean, it was like… amazing." Her eyes were shining.

"This attraction—you felt it for… some *one*?"

She nodded.

"Who?"

She squinted at the sky. "Charley, do we really have to go through this again? Anyway, what difference does it make now?"

"Floyd," I said.

"What?"

"This is Floyd we're talking about, right?"

"Yes…but it wasn't…I thought you said you didn't remember."

"I don't. It was just a guess. I suppose it was mutual?"

"Was what mutual?"

"Did Floyd feel these feelings too?"

"Well, yes. I mean, I think so. He never actually said. And I never said anything or…you know, *did* anything about it."

"Then how do you know he had them?"

"Feelings?"

"Yes."

She shrugged. "I don't know. I just felt that he did."

"But he never said anything or came on to you?"

"No. It was more the way he looked at me. Always staring. As if he were struggling with—I don't know—overwhelming desire. A woman can sense these things."

"Uh-huh. So, these feelings you both had—that's what you told me about that night on the sofa?"

"Um hmm, yes."

"And what did I say?"

"Not too much. You took it pretty well."

"Really? I didn't ask questions or yell or threaten to do anything or… anything?"

"Not at all. I thought, under the circumstances, you handled it pretty—why are you grinning like that?"

"Sorry—It just struck me funny. Go on—you had these feelings for Floyd?"

"Why is that funny?"

"I didn't laugh when you told me the first time?"

"No. Why would you? Here your wife is confessing she has feelings for another man. It's no laughing matter."

"You know, you're right. What did I do then?"

"Well, you heard me out. And then you got up and paced around the living room and thought about it for a while. Then you left."

"Where'd I go?"

"To the desert."

"Right then?"

"Yes."

"I didn't pack or anything? Just got up and… went?"

"Pretty much."

"That doesn't strike you as odd?"

"Not really. That's how you are—decisive. Surgeons are like that."

"I left my car here, so I must have…what? Just walked off into the sunset?"

"There may have been one. I don't remember."

278

"Wow. So, it must have been a real bummer for you when I showed up again."

She nodded. "I can't say I was happy to see you. I guess I acted badly."

"No, I think, under the circumstances, you did pretty well. So, what you're saying is that the real reason I went off to the desert was because you had feelings for Floyd?"

"I'm not saying that's the whole reason. That's just one of the things that happened. I mean you're the only one who could know for certain."

"I guess that's true."

"So why did you go? Can you remember?"

"Well—not clearly but, I guess it makes sense. You confessed your feelings for Floyd, and I didn't want to stand in your way. So, I just went off to the desert to…ah…"

"To forget," said Cathy. "In movies, people are always doing that. They go off to the desert to forget."

"Sure, like the French Foreign Legion. And that could also explain why I don't remember."

"So, you're not upset with me then?"

"What for?"

"You know…him…Floyd."

"It'd hardly be fair now," I said. "Seeing as how I took it so well the last time."

Cathy sighed deeply and turned away, but not before I saw tears welling. "That's good—"

I moved to put my arm around her half expecting her to pull away but instead she leaned against my shoulder and held a crumpled bar napkin against her eyes. I was aware that this was the first time I'd so much as touched this Floydian version of my wife. Pressed against me like that, she felt familiar. Like Cathy.

"Hey, everything's okay now."

"I know… It's just that I've been worried about you— going around with that bandage on your head acting all crazy, not being able to remember stuff."

"That's all right," I said. "I'm back now."

She pulled away from me shaking her head. "You can't be. Too much has happened." She drew a deep breath that broke in a sob. I felt tightness in my throat. *This is how she looked when she got the news about the plane crash.*

"While I was out there," I said. "When I was out there, you know…"

"Wandering."

"Yeah. I used to have this dream. Still do sometimes. You're in it."

"I am?"

"Yeah. We're married in fact, only…"

"We're happy?"

I laughed. "Yeah. You work at the hospital but—funnily enough—I'm not a doctor."

"You're not?"

"No, I work for an ad agency. I write magazine ads and TV commercials."

Cathy smiled. "That is funny."

"Why?"

"You're so not the type."

"What do you mean?"

"You're so serious and proper all the time. Don't you have to be kind of a live wire to do that?"

"I'm dull?"

"No, but you've never exactly been the life of the party."

"But I'm funny, right?"

She shook her head, smiling. "Not really."

"But we must have laughed sometimes?"

"What else in the dream?"

"Well, you're a nurse and I'm a copywriter and we live in Walnut Hill—"

"In the same house? Our house?"

"Uh-huh. And I take the train to the city every day and you go to the hospital, but you only work part time because of the kids."

"Sean and…?"

"Sara."

"How old again?"

"Sean is eight and Sara is six."

"Who do they look like?"

"Well, everybody says that Sean favors me and Sara's the spitting image of her mother but, actually, Sean's got your hair and eyes. And Sara looks like my Uncle Frank."

"No, she doesn't." Cathy giggled and slapped my shoulder.

"No. But that's what I tell everybody. Then sometimes I pull out the old family photos where Frank looks like a big fish with a cigar in his mouth. And I show it to Sara and say it's a picture of her. And she thinks it's hysterical."

"That's terrible."

"See that? That's what you always say in the dream. 'That's terrible.' Then we laugh because Sara thinks Frank is funny. Sometimes we call her 'Frank Jr.'"

Now, for the first time since we met more than a week ago, this Cathy laughed and, for just that moment, I felt like I was home again. Then she caught herself and stopped.

"Guess I've got a better sense of humor in the dream," I said.

"What does it mean, do you think?"

"Probably just wishful thinking."

Cathy leaned back against the car and peered up at the twist of heavy oak branches that hovered over Earl's roof. "Don't, Charley."

"What?"

"Is that why you came back? So, it could be like the dream?"

"What if I did?"

She made a face.

"Would that be so terrible?"

"I don't know what you want from me."

"We're just talking."

"Yeah, well it feels weird."

"Why? We've talked before, right? We must have talked sometime."

Her expression clouded. "Oh yeah we talked—about how your patients drove you crazy or the administrators didn't appreciate you or how somebody had held you up on the golf course. You were always one of those cup-is-half-empty guys. Then you'd come home, and I'd be all wrong too. My friends were ignorant. You didn't like the way I dressed or the music I listened to or—you know what's amazing? I can't think of a single thing you even liked about me. You'd think there'd at least be something. I mean, why marry a person?"

"That's not me, Cathy. That's somebody else. I could stand here all day and not think of a single thing not to like about you."

"Oh, give it up, please."

"No, I mean it."

"Anyway," she said. "It doesn't matter anymore." She reached to open the car door, but I stopped her arm. "What's the attraction, anyway?"

"What do you mean?"

"Floyd. Where's the appeal? Looks? Charm? Personal hygiene?"

"Don't do this, Charley."

"Help me out, here. I really need to know."

"I don't know… he has this kind of… of…"

"Animal magnetism?"

"Maybe..."

"Which animal?"

"Charley—"

"No, seriously. Which one we talking about? Ask me, I'd lean toward—I don't know—wart hog or jackass. Although, I suppose, you could make a case for horny toad."

"All right." She reached into her bag, fishing for her keys. "I don't need this."

"You want to know why you can't think of anything good to say about Floyd? Because there is *nothing* nice about him. And you don't know why you like him because you *don't* like him. He likes *you*."

"Well, isn't that a reason?"

I shook my head. "You only *think* you like Floyd. You're programmed to like him, just like you and everybody in this nutso universe thinks I'm a brain surgeon and that a five handicapper can win the Open and Ron is gay and some dentist knows everything."

"Listen to yourself. You're not making sense."

I grabbed her arm. "No, *you* listen. You only like Floyd because he wants you to. Because we're stuck here—both of us—in his fantasy world, where he imagines you have feelings for him, so you think you do. But you don't. Not really."

"Who says I don't?" She pulled away from me, angry now.

"I do. The Cathy I know wouldn't be caught dead having feelings for somebody like Floyd."

"Oh, yeah? You think you know me that well, huh? Who should I be caught dead with? You? You think you're better than him? Floyd Birdwell is a good man—a great man. And despite what you think or say, I do too like him."

She reached for the door handle. "Here's another reason for you, Charley. Floyd believes in things. And if he sees something he thinks is wrong with the way things are, he doesn't just sit around wishing for it. He goes out and does something about it. And you know what else? He would never, ever lie to me."

One Giant Snog
for Mankind

"Why not?" said Dave when he heard where the Giant Snog for Mankind was supposed to end up. "You wouldn't expect a Giant Snog to be easy and, anyway, don't we pretty much *need* it to be impossible?"

Even with the starting date, time, tee-off and destination left up in the air till the last possible moment, the Giant Snog for Mankind was the worst kept secret since the gay Supreme Court. Still, what with the 'doomsday' media coverage, numerous postponements, threats from local officials and celebrities bailing out, the Daves and I had expected no more than a couple dozen fanatics to actually show up for the event. But when we arrived a few minutes before sundown at the staging area—a furniture warehouse parking lot on Hibbard Road—we were stunned to find a Super Bowl sized tailgate party amid an ocean of cars, trucks and golf equipment.

Concert-sized speakers mounted on a flatbed truck pumped classic rock anthems to keep the crowd motivated. When we got there, John Fogarty was singing about "going up around the bend." Only a few snoggers wore masks and it was surreal to see all the recognizable faces. Many famous names including Tiger, the Pope, Britney, Kim Jong Un and Oprah, had pulled out citing scheduling conflicts or security concerns but even so, everywhere you looked famous golfers, sports figures, stars from the entertainment world hobnobbed and kissy-faced like they were at a movie premiere or 'save the whales' gala. You'd never dream that these people were preparing to embark on an openly defiant and illegal adventure. The bulk of the crowd—your every-day garden-variety snoggers—appeared also to be out for a lark although you could see where some of them, especially the young ones in their gonzo outfits and painted faces got off on the civil disobedience part of it. I doubted whether anybody but the Daves and me were looking at this event as a chance to switch universes.

I didn't see Mike or Ron and didn't expect to, but it was hard to miss the imposing presence of "Titanium Teddy" lashed to a truck bed. Eric and Dalton, the technicians, outfitted for the occasion in jump suits and mining helmets, stood bent over a map spread out on the truck's hood. A large searchlight was mounted on the roof of the cab.

The rules for the Giant Snog for Mankind were pretty much as Floyd had laid out the night we snogged Meadowbank. Whichever snogger negotiated the "hole" in the least number of strokes would be the victor. Speed was definitely a factor. The first snogger to hole out would have 100 strokes deducted from their score. No provisional balls were allowed, and a lost ball meant returning to the place where you last hit, taking a two-stroke penalty and hitting again. Snoggers were held to the honor system. Every stroke counted and you must count all your strokes. Otherwise it was no-holds-barred, every snogger for themselves.

The tee ground was a bluff behind the warehouse that faced west and overlooked a ravine, beyond which was an expanse of vacant scrubland. It was about thirty yards wide, enough for about ten snoggers to tee off at one time. The tee-off order was determined by the time you arrived. We had pulled into the parking lot around 7:45 pm and been issued ticket number 520. We were distressed to learn that put us in the 52nd group to tee off until yet another guy with a bullhorn—apparently, the preferred form of communication in Floyd's universe—assured us that the staggered tee times would be adjusted at the finish.

About ten minutes before the gun, there was a

collective shiver of excitement as word swept through the crowd that our destination—the designated "hole-out" for this giant snog—was the Hyatt Regency Hotel in downtown San Francisco. Floyd's "distance thing" figured to cover a good 40 miles. I overheard a nearby snogger, a pot-bellied guy in bicycle shorts, remark that anyone trying to make it purely on foot was unlikely to finish before dawn and that snogging his way across the Bay Bridge during morning rush hour was not something he was looking forward to.

"That's why we've got to stick together," said an owlish young man in hiking boots, a knapsack on his back. "It's *not* a race."

"That's right," agreed a woman next to me. She was heavyset and wore a black sweat suit atop yellow sneakers, her hair held in place by a pair of night-vision goggles. "It's a giant snog."

Her apparent partner, a head taller, wore an Oakland A's batting helmet over a ponytail. She carried two golf clubs, a large metal head driver and a seven iron. "Does anyone know what we're supposed to do about the toll?" she asked.

I was familiar with the Hyatt Regency having dined there once or twice with out-of-town clients. It was located at the foot of California Street, a long block off the Embarcadero. The building was memorable for its architecture, especially the soaring seventeen-story atrium lobby and glass elevators. I suppose it made Floydian sense as a destination in that it was big and identifiable enough to be worthy of the occasion. The lobby had been featured in some movies and TV shows making it, in all likelihood, the only San Francisco hotel Floyd had ever contemplated. Our giant snog, the bullhorn guy announced, would take us overland to said Hyatt where we were to hole out in the Eclipse, a large, sculpted orb inside the lobby.

"Whoa—wouldn't want to be the doorman on duty tonight," said Clone Dave.

"I'm thinking a few might slip by at first," said Dave. "You know, the element of surprise and all. But after half a dozen or so, they might not see the humor."

"What about after the first fifty?"

He nodded grimly. "They'll be major league pissed by

then. Charley, maybe we ought to think about this."

"Doesn't matter to us," I said. "It's all or nothing. The only way this works is if we get there first."

We had not known before the announcement where the Giant Snog would take us. But Floyd's "distance thing" idea had led us to assume we'd be covering significant acreage. We also knew that, whatever the set up, he'd be on the Harley. The Daves decided we'd need a bike of our own to keep up with him and next night the clone had shown up with a 'rice burner' borrowed from a garage client with the idea that I should ride on the back holding my golf clubs. I'd said forget it, that I'd ride in the Blazer with Regular Dave. Just because I was attempting the impossible didn't mean I harbored a death wish.

Our plan was to send Clone Dave out solo on the Suzuki to tail Floyd and keep us advised of his progress via cell phone. We knew we couldn't match Floyd for speed or skill but we also knew he was reckless and capable of almost any kind of self-inflicted calamity. We just needed to play conservative and solid, stay in the game, play tortoise to his hare, and seize on any opportunity that came up.

As the last stage of sunset turned red garnet behind silhouetted hills, an expectant murmur rose from the crowd punctuated by whistles and nervous laughter. All around us were eager faces, eyes shining in anticipation, as if a fireworks show was about to begin. The bullhorn voice was back, summoning the first ten numbers to the tee. The edge of the bluff was on higher ground, above our eye level, allowing a clear view of the first phalanx of snoggers, dark figures against the sky, as they climbed up, took their positions and began swinging and stretching. None of the swings were anything much except for a guy at the end who looked familiar.

Bob Seger was wailing about 'Night Moves' when the sound system abruptly went silent. Then, seconds later, the Richard Strauss theme from "2001 A Space Odyssey" came on along with the unmistakable revving sound of a Harley Davidson followed immediately by the accelerated entrance of the self-styled, swashbuckling hero known as Snog.

A spotlight swept the scene and found Floyd just as he zoomed passed us, his handlebar nearly clipping Dave's arm. His golf bag, stamped with the skull & crossbones logo, was strapped to a sissy bar behind his seat. He skidded to a stop at the base of the ridge, dismounted, and then scrambled up the rise to the tee where the spotlight found him again, ringed by the first group of snoggers, waving to his adoring crowd.

"Nice having your own universe," Dave shouted.

Floyd had adopted a sort of Elvis-Action-Figure look for the occasion. Besides his black Zorro mask, he wore skin-tight black studded leathers topped off with a short, fringed cape. A snog roadie ran out and handed him a live microphone.

"Okay, listen up, morons," Floyd shouted. "This is what you came for—the Great Big Giant Snog for Mankind!"

Cheers and screams from the crowd.

"You all know the rules. All you got to do is hole out in the Hyatt lobby before I do." Then he sneered and laughed. "No problem—right?"

More screams mixed with laughter.

"All right then—see you losers in Frisco!"

Floyd then tossed the microphone to a tall, blonde man in a tuxedo who looked like a ring announcer. "And now..." he intoned in a rich baritone: "Let's... get ready to rum-blllllllle!"

"How'd they get that guy?" said Clone Dave.

The sound of engines revving to life drowned out the cheers of the crowd. Off to my right, I saw snoggers scatter as the big Dodge pick-up hauling Titanium Teddy spun out trying to gain the top of the ridge sending gravel shooting like shrapnel from beneath the screaming tires. The truck slid sideways, and it looked for a second like Teddy might get launched before his golf ball did. But after a few close calls and a lot of cursing and shouting from nearby snoggers, the flatbed settled into a more or less tenable position at the extreme right end of the firing line.

Floyd, naturally, occupied the center spot. He appeared confident and relaxed, no doubt expecting this to be a snog in the park. Then, above the din, we heard the wail of approaching sirens and, from overhead, the sound of a helicopter flying very low. I could see the surprise in Floyd's face as he looked up, shielding his eyes with a tasseled gauntlet. Mr. Bullhorn scrambled up to the tee, waving his arms and shouting something I couldn't hear. This prompted the snoggers to fumble in their bags for clubs and rush the tee. At the far end of the tee ground I could see Eric flapping and shouting to Dalton that the flatbed was on a down-slope and that Teddy was aimed straight down into the ravine.

"*Attention snoggers.*" Another amplified voice reverberated now from the street beyond the parking lot. "This is the police. You are trespassing on private property. Secure your golf clubs and leave the area immediately."

More sirens now—closer, heading our way.

"You are engaged in an illegal activity. Secure your golf clubs now and return to your vehicles and you will not be cited. Repeat, return to your vehicles and you will not be cited. If you remain in the area, you will be arrested and charged. This is fair warning…"

Somewhere in the middle of all this, the starting gun went off…and the riot began.

The first phalanx of snoggers, including Floyd and Titanium Teddy launched a meteor shower of luminous tee shots toward San Francisco. The only one who didn't tee off was the guy on the end who appeared dumbstruck, staring up at the chopper.

"Hey," shouted the amplified cop, bewildered by the utter disregard for his previous commands. "Stop that!"

The snoggers who had hit now vacated the tee and a new bunch scurried up to take their place. Titanium Teddy's flatbed skidded off the hill kicking up another torrent of dirt and stones. That, mixed with the chopper's prop wash, created a ferocious sandstorm sending snoggers reeling and stumbling into one another.

The sirens were louder, more insistent and we heard brakes screeching and car doors slamming as half a dozen police cars, maybe more, arrived to block the parking lot exits. Cops jumped out, waving batons, trying to herd the snoggers together. A police bus pulled up disgorging a couple of dozen more in riot gear. These formed a flying wedge and advanced on the crowd.

The snoggers were trapped between the tee ground, a hurricane fence on one side and a slope on the other. With no room to get out of the way, they surged back, swamping the flying wedge in a sea of writhing bodies and flailing golf clubs. The police had clubs but the snoggers had bags of them—longer ones—made of cast steel and titanium. We saw a large, red-faced woman, black mask askew, bopping a cop's riot helmet repeatedly with a fairway metal. His attempts to retaliate with his baton were stymied by her clear reach advantage.

Meanwhile, the queue of snoggers waiting to tee off had broken ranks and now stormed the high ground in a panic. Others who couldn't reach the tee dropped balls where they stood and started swinging. Illuminated balls flew in every direction. Shouts and curses rose from every quarter as people were struck with balls or flailing clubs. If any of the snoggers heard the repeated commands warning them to secure their clubs and leave the area, they made no sign.

As the melee swelled, the chopper descended, kicking up an ever more furious storm of grit and dust. The thrashing snoggers looked like farmers beating back a swarm of locusts.

"What does that pilot think he's doing?" shouted Dave. "He's gonna kill somebody!"

The chopper, hovering now about sixty feet off the ground, shined a spotlight on the teeing area illuminating the guy in the first group who hadn't hit with the others.

I recognized him now—Handsome Freddy from Mallard's.

"What's he waving at the cops for?" said Dave. "He tryin' to surrender?"

"It looks like he wants them to land," I said.

"Land where? They'll cut somebody's head off."

The chopper's side door opened and we saw a guy in a business suit waving a 'come-on' gesture to the golfer. He looked familiar too.

"That's not the police," I said.

On the tee, Freddy readied to hit his ball with what looked like a sixty-degree wedge.

"Look at this!" shouted Dave. "He's gonna hit it into the chopper."

Freddy swung back and let fly. The ball rose, smacked into the side of the fuselage, missing the door only by inches, and dropped back at his feet. The guy in the chopper door leaned out and shouted down to him. The wind whipped his necktie up behind his head and he was fighting a losing battle to keep his hair in place—all the while hanging on for dear life.

"Wait a minute," Dave was saying. "Is that—?"

Ron. Mike in front of him in the co-pilot's seat.

"What do you know?" I said. "Our friendly bankers."

Dave pointed over to where Titanium Teddy's flatbed was fighting for traction in a rut behind the tee. "They already got a horse in this race."

"Must be hedging their bet."

We watched Freddy scrambling into position for another attempt.

"You suppose they're going to fly it over to San Francisco after he gets it in there?" said Dave.

"Looks like it."

"And then what? Chip out, I guess."

"Won't need to," I said. "Don't even have to land, just open the door, bank the chopper and let it roll out. Lower Freddy on a rope. How long you figure the flight time is—once they get the ball in there?

Dave shook his head. "Twenty-minutes tops. Be no contest." He looked at me. "But they gotta get the ball in there first."

Freddy bounced another pitch off the hovering chopper. I guessed that Mike's brain trust hadn't figured on not being able to land or how difficult it is to hit a ball through a small, moving doorway fifty or sixty feet above your head, not to mention doing it in a sandstorm during a riot with a spotlight trained on you.

"That can't be legal," said Dave.

"What do they say? All's fair in love and snog?"

Freddy hit again—an air-ball that undershot the chopper by less than a foot, flew thirty yards and disappeared into a thicket. Bellowing a curse I couldn't hear, Freddy ran to find it. Now appeared another frantic guy in a windbreaker, chasing after him, signaling for the chopper to follow. When the spotlight washed over him and he turned around I recognized Roger Stickley—more animated than I'd ever seen him.

Freddy located his ball in the shrub and began hacking it into position it for another go at the chopper.

"He's wasting a lot of shots," said Dave.

"He's got them to spend. Flying's gonna save him a couple of thousand strokes. He won't have to hit another one till he gets to the hotel."

Freddy had evidently cleared the bush because now Roger Stickley was waving the chopper into position for another shot.

"Be easier if he played over to someplace they can land," said Dave.

"I'm guessing he doesn't have a permit."

I didn't care how much pull Kelly had with City Hall. Even in this funhouse of a universe, no bureaucrat was likely fool enough to issue a landing permit within the city limits for something called the Giant Snog for Mankind.

"Hey—" said Dave. "Tee off. Floyd's building up a lead."

We'd last seen Floyd powder a driver in the direction of the interstate, leap on his Harley and roar into the distance with Clone Dave right behind.

"Forget it," I told Dave now. "He's long gone. Game's over."

But Dave grabbed my shirt and pointed at the chopper. "We can do that!" he shouted.

"How? We don't have a helicopter."

"With a car. We chip in, drive it into San Francisco, park in front of the hotel and then chip out. We'll be having drinks in the bar by the time Floyd shows up."

I thought about it for a second and then shook my head. "There's not enough room to chip the ball out of the back seat. We'll never get the ball out of the car."

"You can open the door and putt out."

I shook my head. "You can't open the door. The car is a hazard and opening the door constitutes improving your lie in a hazard. In match play it'd cost you the hole and since this is a one-hole match, we'd lose."

Dave was shaking his head. "You're thinking like a golfer. This is snog."

"Okay, what do snog rules say about it?"

"Are you crazy? Look around you. Does it look like there's rules to this?"

The donnybrook was in full swing. Not more than ten yards from where we stood, the woman with the yellow sneakers and goggles was alternately whacking at her ball and at the shins of the riot policeman trying to subdue her.

Freddy and Roger Stickley were trying to direct the chopper into position for another shot. The aircraft banked hard, pelting them with dirt and stones.

"Anyway, tell me how we get out of the parking lot. The cops have got it surrounded."

Dave's phone rang. Before he answered, he said: "We'll have to leave the Blazer—pick up another ride along the way."

The clone was calling in. It was difficult to hear him but the gist was that Floyd had cleared the city limits in record time, was on the gallop through the southeastern corner of Briones Park and hacking toward the highway.

Dave snapped his cell phone shut and looked at me. "All right," he said. "This is starting to sound impossible enough to where it might just work. We gonna do this?"

It was Dave standing there, smiling at me but I was seeing Cathy's face that afternoon in Earl's parking lot. 'What do you get if you win?' she'd wanted to know.

"You," I said out loud.

"What?"

"I mean yeah, let's do it."

"Here we go," shouted Dave. "Stay close and keep your head down."

With that, he spread his elbows, got his knees pumping and drove toward the tee like a pulling guard.

The immediate question at hand was which direction to tee off. Most of the snogs had driven their balls, with mixed success, directly into the sunset. That, as the crow flies, was the most direct line toward the target. The Daves and I had plotted out a tentative route that took us west through roughly a thousand yards of scrubland and then into an industrial park where, we assumed, many of the contestants would have vehicles waiting for them. Dave would meet me there in the Blazer and we'd follow a service road south eventually hooking up with Route 24 west. Keeping to the roadways would allow us to ride between shots, saving time and staving off exhaustion. We'd stop just long enough for me to hit, say, a knockdown six iron and jump back in the car. But, with the Blazer gridlocked in the parking lot, all that was up in the air now.

There were also the hazards to think about—militant homeowners, unmarked trenches, unlit swimming pools… dogs. And with every snogger and his brother heading in the same general direction, we'd be dodging state and county law enforcement every step of the way.

By the time Dave had stamped out a spot for us on the teeing ground, a couple of hundred shoving, chopping, scuffling and divot-taking snogs had turned it into an archeology dig. I teed it up in a small hole, still undecided as to which way to hit, thinking I'd fly it west toward the industrial park or follow Dave's advice and punch a six iron south toward the dry cleaner. That way we'd circumvent the crowd, maybe flag down a ride out on Hibbard Road. The cops would have diverted traffic from the neighborhood but at the very least, we could hump it on foot for a while and then call a cab. Oh sure, I said. Some cabbie is going to answer a call to the scene of a riot and then wait while I chipped a ball into his back seat. Dave said I'd be surprised what a driver will sit for if the meter's running.

I stood there, for the longest time, undecided, staring down at my night-vision ball letting my eyes adapt to the glow and seeing everything around it fade into blackness. Behind me, I could hear anxious snogs shouting that I was taking too long.

There weren't a lot of good options. Route 24 was the only direct way to the city. Side streets were obviously not great because that meant having to negotiate unfamiliar neighborhoods. It also meant making turns—not a good idea at night on asphalt or concrete where there'd be no telling how far a shot would run. That'd be like adding a thousand doglegs to an already impossible track. I supposed it would have to be Route 24—unless I could think of some other, quiet frontage or service road that ran in a relatively straight line. Trouble was I didn't drive into the city often enough to have developed any short cuts. There didn't seem to be any point to sitting in traffic five days a week when I could simply take the…

Train!

I fumbled for my wallet and there, inside, was my BART ticket, good for another ten rides or so. I'd purchased it in my old universe but had already used it in this one—just once on my ill-fated trip to the office—so I knew it worked.

"Charley," I could hear Dave saying. "We gotta go."

It wasn't a swing I already had but it was a ticket I already bought and now, all at once, a good feeling came over me that this was more than just an ordinary BART pass. This could be the ticket gonna take me home!

I whirled and set up at right angles to the tee direction, aimed due south toward the BART station.

Hugging my clubs, Dave suddenly found himself directly in the path of my swing.

"Fore!"

He yelped and, along with some startled snogs, dove into a bush. I swung back long and smooth, stayed within myself and konked a high hard one into the southern sky and the sleeping suburb below.

"Let's do this," I told Dave.

We had lots of ground to make up.

The Swing You Already Have

Had this been a round of golf, opting to play my ball onto a San Francisco-bound train placed me in direct violation of golf rule 19-1a: If a ball in motion after a stroke other than on the putting green comes to rest in or on any moving or animate outside agency, the player must, through the green or in a hazard, drop the ball... as near as possible to the spot where the outside agency was when the ball came to rest in or on it.

The train constituted an "outside agency" and golf rules dictated that once my ball landed inside the train car, I retrieve it, wait for the train to pull out, then take a drop on the tracks and play from there. But this was not golf and the rules laid down by the Royal and Ancient didn't apply—a fact clearly demonstrated by Mike and Ron with their flailing-robot and helicopter gambits. The game was Snog—Speed Night Option Golf. Floyd was the lone governing body and he made all the rules.

We eventually found my drive, glowing strong, and sitting pretty, on a patch of brown grass next to Wally's Germ Proof Cleaners. From there I punched a series of five irons through back lots and alleyways behind the commercial establishments that lined Hibbard Road. Off to our left, all manner of public vehicles— patrol cars, fire engines, paddy wagons, ambulances and utility trucks raced back and forth, lights flashing, sirens wailing, along the boulevard. We jogged between shots, Dave humping the bag, me explaining that the trains into San Francisco ran thirty-five minutes apart until around midnight and that, if we played it smart and conservative —no irons longer than five—we'd reach the station in time for the 9:15 which would put us at the Embarcadero station at ten minutes to ten. Even if we missed that one, we could catch the 9:50 and still be downtown long before Floyd had slashed his way out of the East Bay, but we'd call Clone Dave from the train just to be sure.

By that time, Floyd was some twenty minutes gone. I pictured him astride his Harley, tooling down Highway 24 swinging his fairway metal like a polo mallet. He'd be somewhere around Sacanap, riding due west toward the Berkeley Hills.

Floyd was the complete snogging package. He liked to play at night—preferred it in fact—was brazen enough for ten guys, could ride a hog like Ron Turcotte on Secretariat and had no qualms about playing through. When it came to snog, Floyd had game, no argument.

What game did I have? Under normal circumstances— on a golf course—I was what you'd call a 'gifted amateur.' But on a darkened roadway at night? Or in somebody's backyard with the Neighborhood Watch in hot pursuit?

With the authorities occupied elsewhere, playing across town to the BART station had been a cakewalk—if you didn't count a sour encounter with some pricker bushes and then being chased a good quarter of a mile by a highly-strung Dalmatian and her small Terrier sidekick. We declared only three balls lost which, dark as it was, seemed pretty good. In each case, we'd had to retrace our steps as close as possible to where we had hit from and replay. That had eaten up a good deal of time and by the time we got to the station on the other side of Main Street we were laying a no-nonsense 361 at twenty minutes to ten. That had left us with a comfortable ten minutes to get the ball into position on the platform before the 9:50 rolled in. The automatic train doors, by my estimate, opened for a full minute, more than enough time to chip into a car given a clear shot. It would be essential, we knew, to lay up as near as possible to directly opposite the train car door. Problem being of course we wouldn't know where the doors would be until the train got there. If we guessed wrong, I'd have to hit another lay-up. The extra stroke was no problem, but we worried about the time.

We arrived at the station to find that the more immediate and far trickier problem was getting the ball up to the train platform. In laying out the plan for Dave, I'd completely overlooked the fact that the platform was above street level, accessible by two flights of concrete steps. When Dave saw those, he said we ought to call a cab right then and deal with chipping out when we got to the hotel. I told him to hand me the sixty-degree wedge and I'd try to die a flop shot up there.

"Can't be done," he said. "That platform's concrete. Even if you manage to land on it, it's gonna bounce to hell and gone. We'll never find it."

"Then go up there, give me something to aim at and watch where it goes."

"I'm telling you, man. The cab is the better play."

"You call a cab. Me and this ball are taking the train."

We located the ball sitting up nicely in a pile of litter next to a curb. It was a flyer lie if I ever saw one, but backspin wasn't going to help much on concrete anyhow.

The strategy taking shape in my mind's eye had me aiming directly at Dave, maybe getting a lucky bounce off one of his soft parts. Dave voiced some doubts when I laid it out for him but, being a sport, he handed me the wedge with a sigh and sprinted for the stairs, clubs bouncing, making a racket in the bag. He stopped at the bottom to adjust the strap and that was when we heard a 'ding.' An elevator door opened right next to him and couple of ladies came out pushing a baby stroller.

Dave grinned at me and pointed to it. "Great," he said. "This thing's getting heavy." He stepped inside, pressed a button and the door closed behind him.

"Uh… Dave… "

Seconds later, the door opened again. Dave stuck his head out of the door.

"Hey, Charley," he said. "I just had an idea."

Three bump and runs later, Dave, the ball and me were in the elevator and on our way up.

It was exactly nine forty-five by my watch when the elevator door opened onto the platform where half a dozen or so passengers stood waiting for the train. We had five minutes, plenty of time to putt carefully out of the elevator and into position. It seemed eminently do-able but then, as often happens in such situations, complications arose. For one thing, my ball had come to rest up against the car wall leaving me no room to get behind it with a club. That meant I had to come from the side, at right angles to my target and bang it directly into the facing wall. The idea being to give it just enough juice to carom out the door but not enough to send it rolling off the platform.

We had just five minutes till the train arrived, so I got right to it. Dave took a position just outside the door then reached around with one arm to hold it open. My first swipe sent the ball ricocheting off three walls into the corner behind me. The next one put me back where I started. As my caddie, Dave was responsible for keeping score. This he did by calling out the numbers in full voice as I whacked away. "Three-seventy-six… three-seventy-seven." I'd asked him if he'd mind counting to himself, but he said saying the numbers out loud was the only way he could keep them straight in his head. "Three-seventy-eight… three-seventy-nine…"

Advancing that little glowing orb out of the elevator was proving to be tougher than I thought. Sweat poured off my forehead, burning my eyes. I kept at it, slapping at the ball, waiting while it rolled to a stop against the wall and then slapping it again.

"Three-eighty-one…three-eighty-two…"

Dave looked around and said we were attracting attention. Some of the people waiting on the platform had drifted closer to the elevator, intrigued by the man with the golf clubs who stood holding the elevator door open, calling out numbers and the sound of bumps and bangs and muffled curses coming from inside.

Some few bangs and curses later, a little cherub-faced lady in a tan raincoat and sneakers appeared in the doorway and asked Dave if we'd be needing the elevator much longer because a person in a wheelchair was down on the street level and wanted to come up. By then I was in a frame of mind to let her know that, just because I didn't happen to be in a wheelchair didn't mean I didn't have my own problems but fortunately thought better of it and, anyway, by that time needed a rest.

I rode down in the elevator with one eye on my ball and the other on my watch. The train was due to arrive in less than two minutes and I had yet to gain the platform let alone any sort of position for my approach. If we missed this train, it'd be a half an hour wait for the next and then that would be it for the night.

I expected for some reason the wheelchair-bound passenger to be elderly and was surprised to find a guy looking to be around my age in one of those stripped-down chairs you see guys who refuse to be overly hampered by their handicap tearing around in. He hesitated until it was apparent I wasn't getting off, then wheeled himself aboard, spotting the ball even before the door closed and, in the same glance, taking in the golf club in my hand.

"Looks like somebody's out for a little snog," he said. "You know you don't have to play it from in here. You can take an 'unplayable' lie, get relief. Two club lengths ought to get you out of here. Only cost you a stroke."

My mind raced to compute this. If I declared my current lie as unplayable, I'd be entitled—in golf rules anyway—to drop the ball anywhere within a distance of two club lengths. That would put me outside the elevator with room to spare. But that was a golf rule, and this was snog. Floyd hadn't said anything about unplayable lies— had he? If I was going to beat Snog, it had to be fair and square impossible. No short cuts, cheating or breaking of the rules—ignoring for the moment the fact that I was about to deliberately play my ball onto a commuter train. The last thing I needed was to go to all this trouble then have the windows to all the universes not open-up.

When the elevator doors opened, revealing a frantic Dave, the guy in the chair turned around, gave me a wink. "All's fair in love and snog, pal," he said and rolled out.

"Train's coming," Dave said.

"Give me the driver."

"Charley, man, I don't think that's the club."

"Do it!"

Dave tossed me the driver and then backed away fast thinking I meant to somehow blast out of there with the big dog. Instead I used it to measure off two club lengths from the side of the car. That placed me safely outside the door on the platform. The train was just sliding into the station as I turned to retrieve my ball—and walked smack into the elevator door. In the amount of time it had taken me to measure the drop, the doors had closed sending the car back to ground level with my ball inside.

My spontaneous shriek/howl frightened even me. I squandered a few seconds of valuable time in fruitless abuse of the steel door before taking off for the stairs.

"Hold the train!" I shouted to Dave, knowing full well that, in this age of automatic doors and electronic operators, there was no way to do that including hurling yourself onto the tracks. Although, even had there been live conductors willing to hold the train for a late, club-wielding passenger, it's doubtful they'd permit him to precede himself aboard with a golf shot.

Latecomers climbing the stairs ducked over the handrails, making way for the deranged man with a golf club highballing it down the stairs, shouting that someone should hold the elevator. By the time I got to street level, the door had already opened and was closing again. I had just enough time to glimpse a trio of well-meaning senior citizens, groping for the open-door button before it closed in my face. I didn't bother, this time, to vent my frustration on the door but instead took an abbreviated moment to reflect that this must be what hell is like.

By the time I got back upstairs, the train had nearly finished boarding. The elevator had also arrived and was standing open. Dave had his foot wedged in the door and was all but dragging the seniors out of the car.

"Where's the ball?" he asked me.

"It's not in there?"

I ducked into the empty car. The ball was nowhere to be seen.

"Oh, no," I said. "Lost ball… lost ball…"

Had this been golf, the rules were clear. Lost ball was stroke and distance. That meant returning to where I last struck the ball and replaying from there. Since my last shot—my last twenty or thirty actually—had been made in the elevator car that meant we'd need to drop another ball in there and pick up where we left off but, wait— we'd already declared the elevator to be an unplayable lie. Could we drop a ball into an unplayable situation? And hadn't it been an outside agency before it'd been an unplayable elevator? I obviously needed a ruling…

"Where's the guy in the wheelchair?"

But then someone tapped my shoulder. One of the senior citizens was back, a tiny woman with a kind smile. "Is this yours?" She held the glowing ball in her hand. "It was on the floor in there and you looked so—"

"Drop it!" Dave's shout startled her.

"My lord! Is it radioactive?"

Dave grabbed the ball from her hand, handed it to me, then grabbed the old lady under each arm and backed her, heels dragging, out of the shot.

"Right there's good," he said to me.

The platform was empty now, the passengers had all boarded the train. At any instant, the doors would close. The driver in my hand was definitely the wrong club but there was no time even to think of reaching for another. The closest open door was thirty feet away at a near forty-five-degree angle. There was time, I knew, for only one swing and a miss would send the ball bouncing off into blackness.

I held the ball at knee length, choked down to the metal on the driver, and dropped the ball onto the concrete. It bounced to a height somewhere just below my knees and hung shining in the air for just a nanosecond. I got a glimpse, out the corner of my eye of heads in windows—train passengers watching, mouths agape, in disbelief and horror—then I swung and…

"*Charley.*" Cathy's voice. "*What are you doing?*"

…completely whiffed. Must have missed it by a foot.

The doors closed and the train pulled out of the station.

The Impossible Dream

"What's the matter, Charley? Didn't have a big enough audience last time? Now you want to dump me with the whole world watching?"

Cathy was dressed for a snog in a black hooded sweatshirt over jeans and sneakers, hair tied up in a dark blue bandana. It took another moment to recognize the guy she was with, then longer to believe my eyes: the Beaner—way out of context. He was all in black too but with the arms to his hoody cut off showcasing a murky ink montage depicting violent acts. I'd never seen him out from under his golf cap—or cleaned up for that matter. *Cathy and the Beaner*—it sounded like a kid's TV program. Standing next to each other. Knowing each other. Forget your disappearing plane crashes. *This* was crazy. He hung back a few paces in dim light, knit cap pulled low, his presence an unspoken threat.

Across the platform, Dave perched on the end of my golf bag talking to the clone on his cell, keeping one foot on the luminous ball to keep it from rolling off into the rail bed.

"Cathy, what are you doing here?"

"I heard you were up to your old tricks and had to come see for myself."

"Old tricks?"

"Don't play dumb. This must seem *familiar* even to you by now."

Images of the evening's activities flashed before my eyes, the riot in the parking lot, desperate snog to the BART station with canine pursuit and then just short moments ago, my thwarted effort to hit full driver into an occupied train car.

Familiar? No. Ironic perhaps.

"I have to do this, Cathy. It's my one shot at getting my life back."

"Your life back? You mean me?"

"Not exactly."

"You see, I found out about your little side bet with Floyd—the one where I was the prize."

I shook my head. "That's just another thing Floyd made up in his head. Not real."

"Come off it, Charley. Everybody knew what the stakes were. Your banker buddies knew."

"There was no bet, Cathy."

"I know there was no match because you bailed. You decided not to go through with it and took off for the desert."

"There was never a bet to bail on."

"Why? I wasn't worth it? And now you're doing it again."

"Cathy, I keep telling you, this has nothing to do with you."

"Oh, that's right. It's not about me. It's about golf memberships and real estate and mini malls or whether Stickley sends out five-somes or six-somes. And everything else you really care about. Everything except me."

"Cathy…" It occurred to me that I had no way of knowing for certain if, in fact, Floyd and Clone Charley had made such a bet. I—me—the Charley Cotter I knew would never have let Floyd Birdwell get anywhere near his wife, let alone wagered her affection in some fanciful golf match. But that was in *my* universe.

"You know what I don't understand?" she said. "If you're going to keep quitting on these matches, why keep challenging him?"

"Quitting? What are you talking about?"

"Listen to him, Henry. He wants us to believe he's still in it."

The Beaner's toothy grin recalled something furry I'd once seen hanging upside down in a tree.

"Henry?"

"That's his name."

I didn't need to meet "Henry's" hard gaze to understand that I should at my earliest opportunity, delete that particular piece of information from my memory chip.

"Okay, then." Cathy said. "You go right ahead and quit. Only that's it, huh? No more matches. No more showing up in my life. No more you, period. Can you do that for me? Will you promise?"

"Quitting? Is that what you think?"

"Get real," the Beaner growled. "Floyd's in Berkeley by now and you're sucking wind on this train platform."

"And whose fault is that?" I said to Cathy. "If you hadn't yelled in the middle of my backswing, we'd be halfway to the city by now."

She frowned. "You were snogging the train?"

"Duh. What do you think I'm doing at a train station with my golf clubs?"

"I assumed you were running away again."

"Snogging a train's against the rules," the Beaner growled.

"Who says? Show me in the rule book where it says you can't snog a train."

"Rule book?" The Beaner snorted.

"Well then if you can't show me the rule, I'm snogging the train."

I walked over and peered off down the darkened

track to the east. Next one wasn't due for half an hour.

Dave got off his cell phone. "Floyd's just hit Orinda, crossing the county line."

"Game over," growled the Beaner. "You lose."

"What are you really after, Charley?" said Cathy. "And don't say it's about real estate or any of that other stuff or I'm going to tell Henry to bash your head in."

"Okay."

"Okay… what?"

"It's not about real estate or that other stuff." I looked at my watch. "What time does the ten thirty-five get to the Embarcadero?"

"About ten after eleven," said Dave.

"Because…" said Cathy, "if you're trying to win me back—you're not, are you?"

"No—Well, sort of. Not in the way you think."

"What way then?"

"You don't want to know, all right?"

"Why can't you just tell me?"

"Because it's crazy. It's… pointless."

"C'mon on—try."

"You won't believe me and anyway it'll take too long."

"That's a lot of crap, Charley. Just be a man and tell me what you're trying to say."

"All right—I *am* trying to win you back.

Her eyes brightened. "I knew it."

"Except—"

"What?"

"Except it's not you."

"What isn't me?"

"You're not my wife."

"What?"

"Okay, you *are* my wife but you're not the wife I'm trying to win back."

"You're married to someone else?"

"No—I mean, basically, it's you but—"

"What are you talking about?"

"I told you, you wouldn't understand."

"*Basically*, she's me?"

"Yeah."

"What does that mean? She looks like me?"

"Pretty much—except for the haircut and the nose ring

And…" nodding toward the Beaner… "choice of friends."

I could see the outline of her clenched fists pushing through her sweatshirt pockets. She brought out a pack of cigarettes and walked a few paces down the platform while she lit one.

"And she doesn't smoke," I said.

"Charley, I'm gonna ask you a question and I need you to tell me the truth—if you've ever felt anything for me. Okay?"

"Okay."

"What do you get if you win?"

"I get my *life* back," I told her. "Everything goes back to the way it used to be."

"With us?"

I nodded. "Everything. You, me, the kids. Everything."

"That's a *dream*."

"It's the way it's supposed to be."

"So, there was a bet."

"No. No bet. I don't do stuff like that."

"Well then… how is beating Floyd going to make

that happen?"

"I know it sounds impossible but sometimes you just have to… try a thing."

"But—snogging? What does that have to do with…?"

"Nothing—at least it shouldn't. Cathy, all this great big giant snog stuff is just a bunch of garbage Floyd made up in his head. Just like everything else in this crazy universe. It's got nothing to do with two people who love each other and who are supposed to be together."

"Don't you dare tell me you're talking about us." She shook her head. "That's your dream, Charley. That's not how I remember it."

"But you must have wanted it too—once."

"Sure, I guess. Doesn't everybody? The way you talk about it, who wouldn't?"

"What happened?"

"With us?" She looked off, dark eyes reflecting moonlight. "I don't know. I guess we just… lost track."

"Did we see it happening? Try to fix it?"

She sighed. "Yeah, maybe. I don't remember."

"We couldn't fix it? How come?"

She shrugged. "Didn't want it enough, I guess." She saw my face. "Don't feel bad. It wasn't just you."

I looked around at the night. It was quiet on the platform, but we could hear sirens off in the distance. "What are you doing out here, anyway? How'd you know I'd be here?"

She smiled. "About fifty people saw you running from those dogs."

"You thought I was running away again. And you came to tell me what—goodbye?"

"I don't know. I guess I wanted to tell you that if you felt like you had to quit again, I wouldn't hold it against you."

"Why not?"

She wrapped her arms around herself. "I just think we all do what we have to do."

"Maybe you should expect more from your husband?"

"No, that's okay. I know how you are and—why are you looking at me like that?"

"Don't stop," I reached for her hand. "You know how I am and—what? "

"I know how…" Cathy shook her head. "Oh, I lost my train of thought."

"You know how I am and… what? "

"I know how you are…and… it's okay, I guess. Was that it?"

Right then I saw a flash of light and then felt a breeze. More like a draft. Just for an instant. As if someone had opened a door and then, just as quickly, closed it again.

I looked over at Dave. He was sitting on the end of the golf bag, knees pulled up, chin resting on folded arms. The Beaner stood slouched against a railing, not looking at us. If either of them saw or felt anything, there was no indication.

Cathy was staring at me.

"Did you see that flash?" I said.

"Flash?"

"Just a second ago. Like a lightbulb going out."

"You mean in the sky? Heat lightning?"

"No, right here. You didn't see it?"

She shook her head.

"That thing—you started to say. You said it once before. I still remember it as maybe the sweetest thing anyone ever said to me."

"I'm sorry but I don't remember."

"Listen," I said. "Maybe you can help me with something. It's a little experiment I want to try. It'll only take a second."

"Right now?"

"Just take a second." I took her arm and moved her a few more paces down the platform, away from the Beaner.

"Okay, this isn't a trick and I'm not trying to move on you or start anything, but I just wondered if I could kiss you."

"What? Why?"

"Just one kiss. It's an experiment. To see if anything happens."

"What's going to happen?"

"Probably nothing. But I want to see."

"Charley…"

"C'mon, bear with me. It's nothing. It'll be over before you know it."

"Do you want me to close my—?"

I leaned in and kissed her. She pressed her lips into me, and I felt a chill like forever ago. Outside like this but on a lawn somewhere near a lake. I could smell the night jasmine, damp and musty sweet and the fresh wool of her sweater. With my eyes closed, I saw colored lanterns strung in the trees and then another flash, bigger and longer lasting, and a rush of wind that wanted to blow the heart right out of my chest.

When I opened my eyes, Cathy was staring at me.

"Well?" she said.

"Let me ask you something. Don't get nervous but, just for the sake of argument, have you ever considered the idea of maybe somehow, someday you and me getting back together?"

Her eyes widened and then she laughed. "Oh, Charley," she said. "You know that'd be impossible."

Playing Through

"Rockridge is the next stop. Rockridge."

The operator's voice rattled out of the speaker sounding as if he'd been obliged to announce the stop while gargling. I sat in an aisle seat in the second to last row of the train car next to Regular Dave, my luminous ball pressed firmly under my sneaker to keep it from rolling again. I'd had to waste three strokes pulling out of the Lafayette station when Dave had bumped me with the golf bag, sending the loose ball skittering toward the center of the car. It had taken a trio of extremely delicate putts—my 409th through 411th shots—to maneuver it to the spot where it now rested. Dave felt bad about the wasted strokes, but I told him not to worry. With every mile the BART train carried us toward San Francisco, we were saving dozens.

We'd calculated the "practical overland snogging distance" between the tee-off point in Walnut Hill and the Hyatt Embarcadero as being in the neighborhood of one hundred thirty-three thousand yards. Figuring an average shot of say, seventy-five yards that divided out to roughly 1,774 strokes—par for the sake of argument. Barring further complications—e.g. hijacked elevators, rogue Dalmatians, wives showing up—and given a clean exit at the Embarcadero station, we had a decent shot at emerging from the subway at better than a thousand under par—give or take—with less than a city block left to negotiate.

Boarding the ten thirty-five had been—at least compared to our previous attempt—without incident. We were the only ones on the platform when the train arrived. Two short putts got me inside the car with plenty of time to spare. The BART car was deserted except for a couple of sleepy guys near the front. We'd brought along our own gallery—Cathy, noticeably off-balance since our "experiment" back at the train platform and "Henry" who said he wanted to see the look on my dumb ass loser's face when I got beat. We had no doubt that he'd be launching a protest with the Rules Committee, aka Floyd, about our snogging the train but that wouldn't matter if we lost and if we somehow managed to win, we'd be somewhere else.

Dave's last cell phone contact with his clone had been back on the train platform in Walnut Hill. By then, Floyd had reached Orinda and was advancing into the Berkeley hills. Since then we'd been unable to get a phone signal inside the train car. Even with every bounce going his way, we couldn't imagine Floyd reaching Oakland anytime soon. But even if he did, with the freeways and the Bay Bridge still ahead of him, he'd be fortunate indeed to reach the hotel by two a.m. Barring some calamity, we figured to reach the Embarcadero roughly three hours ahead of him with a thousand shot lead—a comfortable margin in a normal match—but, against Floyd in his own universe, with every sign we'd seen declaring what we were doing impossible, we saw our chances as being less than fifty-fifty. Way less.

The BART train dropped down into the tunnel when we reached San Francisco Bay turning the car windows into mirrors. Cathy sat next to Henry in the row behind us. The hole he stared in the back of my head made my ears twitch. From time to time I stole glances at Cathy. My train platform "revelation"—that I was doing this not to specifically win her back but to get my life back—a life that included her—had given her much to think about. She sat leaned against the window, forehead pressed against the glass, brow furrowed in thought.

Back on that platform, I'd been close to just sitting her down and explaining everything—the whole universe-hopping farce from beginning to end. Well there'd be time for explanations later—plenty of time either way. And if, through some miracle we won, I'd be explaining to a different Cathy in a universe far, far away.

The train had added passengers at each stop and now, leaving Oakland, the car was three quarters full. Dave figured a bunch of them would be getting off with us at Embarcadero, so he handed me the putter and had me use a couple more strokes nudging the ball ever-so-gently up the aisle until it was opposite the door getting us into position ahead of time for a quick exit. There were some stares and headshakes from the other passengers, but most chose to ignore us.

When the train stopped, I had only to jab a little "Texas wedge" through the open doors to put us out on the platform. I felt a strong shove from behind, heard: "This is bullshit," as the Beaner tromped past us, toward the escalator.

"Henry—" Cathy called after him but he didn't look back.

She turned to me with a little apologetic grin and shrugged. "Guess I'll hang with you guys, if it's okay."

"No problem," I said.

Dave sidled up to me out of Cathy's earshot. "Has it occurred to you that this is a little strange?"

"Which part, Dave?"

"Here we are doin' this because you're trying to get back to your wife and don't look now but she's right here next to you."

"It's not the same thing."

"I'm just sayin' if things don't work out, at least you've got something to fall back on."

A single stroke with the putter sent my ball halfway down the smooth granite platform toward the Market Street elevator. From there, I played conservatively, stroking the ball with care, making sure to keep it on the platform. The last thing I needed was to be pitching back up from the rail bed when an express train rolled through.

Dave called out the strokes loud and clear. "Four twenty-six, four twenty-seven." The station was nearly deserted, ready to shut down for the night. Just a few stragglers waiting on the opposite platform, but they hardly glanced at us as we snogged along, writing us off as nitwits goofing our way home after a beer-soaked day of golf.

By the time my 429th shot rolled onto the up escalator, I was feeling good about my chances. Floyd had certainly tallied some multiple of that by now. And we didn't expect him to show up anytime soon. It had been little more than a half hour since the last sighting in the east Berkeley hills. Even so, I had Dave ping the clone for a current fix.

As well as this seemed to be going, a whispered voice in the back of my brain kept saying it was all too easy. Even including our little episode at the Walnut Hill BART station, the Giant Snog for Mankind had so far been not all that difficult, let alone impossible. When you consider the other impossible tasks we'd talked about and discarded—swimming the English Channel in ski boots and an overcoat or winning the Ukrainian lottery—snogging into San Francisco on a BART train didn't measure up. I had to remind myself—I'd been doing it all evening—that the snog itself wasn't the impossible thing. The impossible part was beating Floyd. Beating Snog at his own game was our only hope of opening-up all of Dr. Sleeves' "windows."

The escalator deposited my ball on the brick-topped plaza next to the trolley turn-around. Dave had run ahead and when Cathy and I got up to street level, he was straddling the ball and staring at the hulking pyramid Hyatt no more than a sand wedge to the north of us.

Fog had descended on the city, holding the briny, stink of the bay at low tide. A long, misty block to the east, the Ferry Building's tower clock showed 11:20. The trolley had stopped running which meant the plaza should have been deserted but wasn't. Pedestrians hurried past us in groups or pairs, heading toward the hotel.

"Must be a concert or something going on," said Dave.

He had me putt my ball a few yards off to the side where it came to rest against a crowd control barrier next to the trolley stop—at which point he said we were laying a snappy 434. Then he told Cathy and me to watch the bag and went off to reconnoiter the hotel front entrance. That left Cathy and I alone.

We spent an awkward minute looking everywhere but at each other before she said, "I guess I'm still not clear on why you're doing this."

"I told you, I don't have a choice."

"Fine. As long as you realize that whatever happens tonight won't change anything between us."

"Deal."

We stood there for a couple of minutes without saying anything and soon Dave was back shaking his head.

"What's the story?" I asked him.

"There's a hundred cops over there."

"Doing what?"

"And TV trucks and a red carpet running all the way out to California Street. And a band," he said. "Big brass band."

"What for?"

"Charley—there's like a million people. They got bleachers set up. TV news. I just ran into the mayor."

"Dunphy? What's he doing here?"

"Not Dunphy—the *Mayor* of *San Francisco*."

"Oh, my God! Cathy's eyes got big and she bit her lower lip, like that time in the Mark Hopkin's hotel when we rode up in the elevator with Harrison Ford. "I'll bet it's for him," she said. "It's all for him!"

Dave picked up the golf bag. "Yep. They're waiting for Floyd," he said. "They got signs and banners up, hooray for Snog."

"Isn't that something?" Cathy was giggling now. "That's really great."

"Yeah, great." Dave said. "How're we supposed to get in the building now with a hundred cops, the city council and all those people blocking the front door?"

I suppose we should have expected it. Did we seriously think Floyd Birdwell, master of the universe, was going to finish off his Giant Snog for Mankind by slipping quietly into a hotel lobby? This was pure Floyd—cue the adoring fans. Thinking about it, I was amazed he hadn't opted for a larger venue, Levi's Stadium or AT&T Park. It made perfect sense. In Floyd's universe, snogging was illegal for everyone except Floyd. Here he was the beloved scalawag, Dillinger and Robin Hood rolled into one, whose transgressions were not just forgiven but celebrated by the legions of little people who aspired only to be like him.

Dave's cell phone rang, the clone calling. Dave told him our location and situation and then listened for a minute, his eyes widening.

"Okay, come on in," he said and hung up. "Floyd's on 580 going through Emeryville heading for the bridge."

"My God, he's flying."

Dave nodded glumly. "He's got a full motorcycle escort. CHP's bringing him in."

"That's so neat," said Cathy. "Yay Chips! I wanna see." She ran off toward the hotel.

"What's got into her?" Dave said.

"Product of her environment. Pavlov's dogs."

"Whose dogs?"

"Forget it. How much time do you think that gives us?"

Dave looked surprised. "You're not still thinkin' about *doin'* this?"

"I gotta go back, Dave. Sean and Sara think their daddy died in a plane crash and the last thing he ever said to them was a lie."

Dave sighed and looked back at the Hyatt. "I don't know, Charley…"

"I can't let that be the end of it, Dave. It'd always be hanging over me."

He sighed again and then clapped his hands together. "Okay," he said. "Let's *do* this… how?"

"Maybe there's another way in," I said. "A side door.

There's one on this side. I could maybe go in the front door and then come around and unlock it from the inside but that's assuming they're letting people in and anyway, it's gonna have an alarm on it. Where's the loading dock?"

"It's on the other side, off the alley. But they've got it all cordoned off and it's filled with cop cars."

Behind him, the looming Hyatt was looking more and more the impenetrable fortress.

"You know," I said. "There is one bright spot in all this. This is starting to sound pretty impossible."

"That's something, I guess."

I left him to stand guard over the ball and went to scout the plaza. The Hyatt is a twenty-story pyramid, sitting at the extreme southeast corner of San Francisco's financial district, backed up by the Embarcadero and the bay. One side of the triangle looks toward the financial section, one faces Market Street and the third looks down on Justin Herman Plaza and the waterfront beyond.

I wandered back there now, looking for another way in. There were several fire doors at ground level, but these opened from the inside and were no doubt rigged with alarms. Many of the rooms on the upper floors facing the waterfront had balconies while guests occupying the lower floors settled for large sliding-glass windows. But even the lowest of these was five stories up. Figuring each story at somewhere between ten and twelve feet, that put the lowest rank of windows sixty feet or so over my head. Backing away from the hotel, wondering whether one of them would be reachable with a wedge, I bumped into a pair of San Francisco's finest on foot patrol. I flashed them with a goofy tourist grin. One of the cops touched his cap and they moved away.

The volume of foot traffic was increasing by the minute. It was plain that, if window access were our only option, I'd get at most a couple of chances before the cops hauled me away. I thought of Mike and Ron's helicopter and wondered if Handsome Freddy had hit the doorway yet. At least hotel windows didn't move.

I circled around to the main entrance on California Street but couldn't even get close. Dave's estimate of a million people out there seemed only a slight exaggeration. Bleachers had been set up along California Street opposite the hotel drive and front door. They were jammed as were the surrounding street and sidewalks. Office workers pressed against the windows of a facing bank building. I couldn't see the band but could hear them now playing a ragtime tune. I waded through the crowd to where I could see a platform across from the front door that had been set up as a reviewing stand. The Mayor of San Francisco was there along with some other politicos and business big shots I'd seen on TV along with a supporting cast of generic suits, uniforms and wives. You'd expect to see a troupe like that gathered for a building dedication or ship launching—if it were not for the others. Peppered among the tony assemblage and standing out like Hell's Angels at a wine tasting was a troupe of Floyd associates from Mallard's—including Mallard himself. The Beaner was up there too, looking sullen, checking his watch. I saw Cathy climb the steps at one end, stopping to smile at a middle-aged guy in a sport coat who offered a hand. A few feet away from them was a dapper man in green medical scrubs I recognized as Dr. Warren Sleeves. Why not? Naturally Floyd would expect his mentor and personal guru to be present at such a lofty occasion.

When I got back from my scouting expedition, Clone Dave had arrived on the Suzuki. From his expression, I could see that Dave had already clued him to our predicament.

"You see a way in?" said Clone Dave.

"Not really. I was thinking we pitch into an open window except it'd be tough getting trajectory off the bricks."

"Talk about your tight lies," said Dave. "And even then, how can we be sure what room we're hitting it into? We'd never find it."

I shook my head. "What you do is you check in first and ask for the lowest room we can get on the Embarcadero side. Then you open the window and wave to me, so I know where to aim. That's presuming they have a vacancy, of course."

"You really think you can make that shot? You'd only get

a couple of chances before security showed up."

"What other choice do we have?"

"The way I see it," said Dave, "We either find another 'outside agent' like the train or… "He gestured toward the clone. "We go with his idea," he said.

"What's your idea?"

"Start a fire."

"Are you crazy?"

"We ought to consider it."

"We're not setting fire to the hotel."

"Not the hotel. Just a tire or something, create a lot of smoke—enough to set off the alarm. Then, when everybody runs out in a panic, we snog our way in."

"So, all we have to do is smuggle a tire and what—a can of gasoline into the hotel? Don't you think that might be at *least* as difficult as a little glowing ball?"

"Okay, then we look for another outside agency. Something already going into the building we can land a ball on."

The clone snapped his fingers. "I got it. We call and have a pizza delivered to the hotel. Then we grab the guy on his way in, slip him a few bucks to let us chip on to the pie and then he carries it into the lobby for us."

"Right up the red carpet, huh?"

"Hey, they'll let him in. People gotta have their food."

"Forget it," I said. "That's not an outside agency. That's just us paying a guy to carry the ball into the hotel. Anyway, I'm not chipping on to a pizza."

"Well," said Clone Dave. "We'd better think of something fast. I figure Floyd's on the Bay Bridge by now. We're running out of time."

"Okay," I said. "Then I guess we've got no choice."

"What do you mean?"

"Give me the seven-iron."

"What for?"

"I'm going in."

The Daves looked at me in horror.

"Going in? You mean the *front* door?"

"Charley, they're expecting Floyd. They see anybody else comin' up the carpet with a golf club, they'll eat 'em alive."

Dave was clutching my golf bag to his chest. I reached in and yanked out the seven. "Hey, we're snoggers too. They can't keep us out of there."

"Charley," said Dave. "This is Floyd's party. He's the one they came to see. We're just crashers. We get two feet up that carpet we better hope the cops grab us before the crowd lynches us."

"He's right," said the clone. "We gotta sneak in somehow and drop a ball into the Eclipse before anyone notices us. Then whatever happens, happens."

"Nope," I said. "No more pussyfooting around. I'm going in the front door this time, right up the red carpet and let 'em try to stop me."

"Charley, that's crazy—"

"You mean like *impossible?*" I grinned. "You might want to stick close to me. We pull this off and there's a good chance we'll be going places. Where's the ball?"

Dave moved away from the post where he'd been shielding it from view. Even in the lit plaza, and after four hundred plus whacks, it glowed strong.

"All right, now," I said to the clone. "Clear a path with the bike. Your cousin's with me."

Clone Dave kick started the Suzuki. "Hey…how'll we know when it's happening?"

"Everything sorta goes white," I said. "That's when you want to start thinking about where you want to end up."

The brothers exchanged a look. Clone Dave shouted over the engine: "Maybe we oughta think about the same thing so we can all be together?"

"Don't worry about it," I said. "Anywhere we go, we'll all

be there. It'll just be different according to who thought of it."

That seemed to be good enough for them. The clone pulled his goggles down over his eyes and revved the engine. From around in front of the hotel we heard the band strike up a cover version of ZZ Top's "Legs."

"Okay, here we go," shouted Clone Dave. "Playing through!"

Fore Gone Conclusion

Just getting to the red carpet seemed impossible enough with Clone Dave out front, revving the Suzuki, blowing the horn, parting the crowd for me and my seven iron and then Regular Dave behind us, humping the clubs and shouting out stroke numbers as we went. Progress was slow and painful—slow for us and painful for the bystanders my shots bounced off. Most of the crowd had their backs to us, facing the reviewing stand, a situation that presented me with a formidable selection of posteriors to negotiate.

"Four sixty-one… Fore, please! Four sixty-two…"

My little chip-and-runs ran scarcely more than a few yards before hitting somebody in the butt or leg and then skittering off into some equally unpleasant situation wedged up against a foot or a curb.

"Four sixty-six" … "Ouch!" … "Four sixty-seven…"

Dave and I fell into a sort of "good cop—bad cop" routine, Dave all business, pushing people aside and me smiling and apologizing for the inconvenience, then swatting another shot toward an unsuspecting butt and moving on.

"Four seventy" … "What the f—k!" … "Four seventy-one…"

The crowd, by this time, was so dense that neither the cops nor hotel security saw us coming and the indignant yelps and curses were, for the most part, drowned out by the band.

I was profusely apologizing to a crimson-faced spectator after my ball had gotten hung up underneath his date's skirt, when up ahead I saw Clone Dave break through the crowd into the traffic lane that fronted the hotel driveway. He pushed a wooden traffic barrier aside, then turned and waved us up. Dave saw him too but then grabbed my arm. "Hear that?"

The band had quit playing and now we heard sirens—dozens of them—howling from the Mission side of Market Street.

"That'll be Floyd's escort. Gotta move."

The crowd surged back as a rank of policemen in riot gear double-timed it up the drive and formed a cordon for the approaching motorcade. A big guy in a raincoat backed into me and booted my ball. Dave and I chased after it and found it nudged up against a small advertising kiosk, almost back to where we started.

"This is nuts," I said.

Dave said we were entitled to a free drop back in the lady's underwear and that from there our best play was a flop shot over the gallery onto the red carpet. We wouldn't be able to stop it, of course, but he figured security would chase it down and from there we'd be able to get a ruling. I told him there was no way I could slide the club head far enough under the ball to get the ball airborne and that the best I could do was work at ankle level but, if we kept on hitting people, it'd be only a matter of time before the crowd turned on us.

Now Cathy materialized out of the throng wearing a luminous necklace made from the same stuff as the glowing golf balls. I was taking dead aim at a pair of easy-fit Gap jeans when she said: "I've been thinking about…what you were saying."

"Oh yeah?"

"Yeah. And I think I understand what you mean about me not being the real me and you not being the real you and—you're not going to hit that, are you?"

I chopped a little runner that missed the jeans but then bounced once on the pavement and then dodged through a thicket of legs, footwear and bicycle tires.

"Four seventy-six…" Dave pushed after it, beckoning for us to follow.

"Sorry," I said. "Missed that last part."

"I just wanted to tell you that this—what you're doing—isn't necessary."

"This? You mean snogging?"

"Yes. You don't need to do this."

"No?"

"What you said before about the other you and trying to get back to the other me—"

"Yeah—?"

"I suppose we have changed. I guess we all do and it's not always for the better, but—*what are you doing?*"

"Sorry, I just have to—hold that thought—" *Whack!* "Uh-oh!"

"Four seventy-eight…"

"Oh, my God! He's not happy—don't look at him."

"Sorry!"

"Maybe you should be using a putter."

"I can make my own club selections, thanks."

"Hey—" She grabbed my arm. "Stand still a minute. I'm saying something here. It doesn't matter to me whether you beat Snog or Floyd or anybody else. It's not going to change how I feel about you."

"I didn't think you felt anything about me."

"Well…I mean… of course, I have feelings for you. After all, we were married."

"Still are married. Hang on, I have to hit this."

"That's not a good idea. Charley—they're looking right at you!"

Whack! "Oh, my God!"

"Four seventy-nine..."

"Sorry! What kind of feelings?"

"What?"

"Those feelings you say you have..."

"Oh, well, I'm... certainly fond of you."

"Fond, eh? That's nice."

"And, of course, I respect you."

"Respect too? Wow."

Whack! *"Sorry!"*

"Four eighty..."

"Well, what do you want me to say? And what do you want from me, anyway?"

"What do I want from you? Well–I... respect is one thing." Whack!

"Hey—what the hell?"

"Sorry!"

"Four eighty-one..."

"Oh, for God's sake. I *said* respect."

"And... love and patience and understanding and— see if you can get the guy in the shorts to move out of the way."

"Excuse me. Excuse me, sir...could you just... thank you so much."

"Four eighty-two..."

"Hey, what do you think you're—!"

"Oops, sorry! Charley, if you wanted those things, why didn't you ever say anything?"

"Cathy, when you're married, you're not supposed to have to ask for that stuff. It's part of the deal."

"Oh, I see. You mean take each other for granted?"

I stopped in the middle of a swing. "Yeah...I guess. Trust is a better word. I need to trust that you'll be there for me. I need you to be a pal."

"A pal? I see. And when wasn't I there for you?"

"Oww! Hey—watch out with that thing!"

"Four eighty-three…"

"Sorry… What, you want dates? All the time—that's when. I needed you to be there for me all the time."

"You're saying I wasn't?"

"Were you?"

"I thought I was."

"Well, you weren't."

Whack! "Four eighty-four…"

"Oh, yeah? Name a time when I wasn't there for you."

"Only one?"

"Oh, I'm sure you think there are thousands, but I'll settle for one."

Whack! "Four eighty-five…"

From off toward the Mission district, we heard approaching sirens. The gallery in front of us shifted its attention to the right, jumping and straining for a first look at the arriving champion. The band struck up a big brass version of "I Fought the Law." There was still a good forty yards of humanity between the hotel door and us. Clone Dave and his Suzuki were somewhere over near there.

"What do we lie?" I asked Dave.

Before he could answer, we heard a loud crack like a rifle shot followed by screams. A wave of cheers rolled toward and then past us. A young guy shinnied halfway up a lamppost shouted: "That's his ball!" Near us, a girl sat hoisted on her boyfriend's shoulders screaming and twisting her hair. *"Snog!"* she screamed. *"Whoooooo!"*

"I was *always* there for you," Cathy was saying. "What about the night you got sick at Scoma's on the Wharf? Who drove home and took care of you?"

"Big deal. I guess anybody else would've left me there."

"What about all those boring golf tournaments I let you

drag me to? Do they count?"

"Four eighty-five…"

"Sure, and don't forget the time you passed me the salt."

"Four eighty-six…"

We were slowly making our way up to the front of the crowd where it lined the red carpet.

"Will you listen to yourself?" Cathy was saying. "You don't sound like you even like me. And this is what you want to get back to?"

There was activity now up where the driveway ducked under the hotel entrance canopy. Cops were pushing people back, clearing a circle. It looked like someone was down on the pavement. Then, from behind us, we heard a whoop-whoop and a horn sound. A paramedic wagon crept its way up the drive.

"Floyd's shot hit somebody up there," Dave told me. "That crash we heard was it bouncing off a windshield."

When we reached the front row, we found Clone Dave and his Suzuki just a few yards beyond the carpet behind a rope and surrounded by police. He shook his head and splayed his arms out in a gesture of hopelessness.

Dave turned to me. "What do you want to do?"

The words were scarcely out of his mouth when there came another, much louder, crash. People were pointing up at a balcony eight or nine stories above the street where something had struck with enough force to shatter the glass door. We could hear screams coming from inside the room. Then a man in pajamas came out on the balcony, held up a luminous golf ball and shouted something I couldn't hear. This new impact galvanized the authorities. A troop of cops grabbed the mayor and rushed him into the hotel. Others shouted urgently into radios or drew their weapons, forming a defensive perimeter around the platform.

"What monster hit that shot?" said Dave.

I grabbed Cathy by the shoulders. "Okay, you want

to be a pal? You want to be there for me? We need to get into this hotel now, *with* the ball."

"You know, Charley, it's always something with you."

"I know… and I'm sorry, but will you help?"

"Give me one reason why I should."

"If this works then I can come back to you."

"So, we can go back to being the way we never were? Gotta do better than that, Charley. You want me, you take me the way I am."

"I would if—I mean I will." I grabbed her shoulders. "Listen to me, Cathy you don't need to change. You're perfect. You're beyond perfect. You're fabulous just the way you are."

"Nice try—"

"No, I mean it. Look at you. What's not to like? You're all he ever wanted. Why would he want you to ever change?"

"Who's he? Who're we talking about now?"

"Your husband—me. If anybody needs to change, it's…

it's—"

There was another flash, just then. Everything going white for a second, Cathy fading out then back in again.

"Charley," she said. "You look weird."

"Like how?"

"I don't know—you went all pale."

That's when a helicopter rounded the side of the Hyatt and began to hover no more than a hundred feet or so over the reviewing stand. The cops pointed their guns at it, shouting to each other. Clone Dave cupped his hands over his mouth and yelled for me to hit the ball.

"C'mon," said Dave. "This is our chance."

Cathy was staring at me.

"This is it," I said.

Holing Out

"Well," said one of the Daves, raising a beer. "Guess it wasn't impossible after all."

"We might have a case for false advertising," said the other one. "Failure to deliver on claims as advertised."

We were sitting at a corner table in the Hyatt's lobby bar. The noise from Floyd's victory celebration boomed out from the grand ballroom and echoed across the hotel's main floor. It had been less than an hour since the conquering hero—preceded by his illuminated golf ball—had arrived on his Harley with CHP escort to a thunderous ovation. He'd been greeted by the mayor of San Francisco along with other Floydian dignitaries including Charles Barkley, Golfer John Daly, Robbie Knievel, ZZ Top, porn star Alexis Texas, Senator Bernie Sanders, the "General Hospital nurse chick," golf commentator Verne Lundquist, actor Mickey Rourke, Mallard, the entire Fox TV news team, and Dr. Warren Sleeves.

By the time Floyd had rolled up the red carpet on his Harley, the Daves and I had been ready to concede defeat. But then Titanium Teddy's approach shot (we were to find out later it had been made from a distance of two hundred yards but Dalton, in the heat of the moment, had mistakenly set the robot's distance control at two thousand yards and that had accounted for Teddy's ball's hyper-velocity impact) had shattered the hotel window causing security officials to take action.

Even at that, the situation had remained relatively stable until the arrival, moments later, of Mike and Ron's much-delayed helicopter. (Freddy, we would later learn, had squandered nearly three hundred shots——more than half of them incurred as lost ball penalties—before managing to drill a skulled gap wedge through the open door that ricocheted off two interior walls, the pilot's helmet… and Mike. That episode, along with subsequent delays including a harrowing encounter with a Homeland Security attack helicopter followed by a confrontational interrogation and insensitive strip-search in a holding cell at the Oakland airport accounted for their late appearance on the scene).

The chopper's arrival was an entirely unexpected development that prompted the police unit below to hit it with a spotlight. The blinded pilot had banked sharply, causing various items including Handsome Freddy's ball—and Ron—to roll out of the open side door.

Freddy's ball plummeted some hundred feet or so and might have bounced halfway back had the San Francisco police chief, by sheer coincidence not been standing directly under it. (We read later that the chief's earlier decision to support his men by donning a riot helmet most likely saved his life. The impact did, however, stagger him to the point where he lost his footing. Officers nearby, believing someone inside the helicopter had shot their leader, were quick to return fire).

Ron was lucky too, managing to grab onto a skid and hold on for dear life while the chopper dipped and yawed.

The crowd, by this point believing that the hotel was under terrorist attack—panicked and scattered. In seconds, the 'gallery' in front of us vanished leaving Dave and I with an unrestricted angle past the reviewing stand to the front door. Clone Dave was up there, waving his arms.

"Don't make a big deal about it," Dave was saying. "Just tap it toward the door, real casual."

Moving slowly and just a few feet at a time, we worked our way toward the door, me nudging the ball along while Dave whispered stroke numbers. And no one—certainly not the police, busy with the "terrorists," or the city officials and visiting dignitaries cowering inside the building, noticed us. In fact, as we approached the door, a pair of hotel doorman actually swung the door open and then held it while we strolled through rolling our little luminescent ball.

There was a large crowd milling inside the foyer, but all eyes were either distracted or glued to the unfolding action outside. We drew not a single glance as we moved to the escalator and rode up to the lobby. With one Dave leading and the other covering our rear, we sauntered, golf clubs and all, past the front desk to a garden area adjoining a restaurant where "The Eclipse," a circular sculpture, sat situated inside a reflecting pool. The carpet surrounding it made for a tight lie, but we figured a fifty-six-degree wedge would do the trick and I made the shot on my first try, holing out from about four yards away.

Of course, it wasn't quite as simple as that. When I was ready to make the shot, the Daves and I took a couple of moments to discuss the ramifications of what we were doing. Dave pretty much reiterated what he'd said earlier about wanting to stick around now that he'd finally found someone who he felt understood him. Clone Dave said pretty much the same thing—at pretty much the same time. They were a little anxious about how it was going to go once I made the shot and the impossible thing happened, wondering whether they should think about staying where they were or do their best to just think of nothing and hope they'd be left with status quo. (The danger, of course, in thinking about nothing is that rather than winding up someplace where nothing had changed, they might find themselves instead in a universe consisting entirely of nothing— except of course for the two Daves).

In the end, we decided that the safest tack would be if, when the windows opened up, they simply thought about each other and then, wherever they wound up, they'd at least both be there.

Mine was a different story. There was only one place I wanted to go and that was back where I'd come from, back to Cathy and the kids. I had no idea how it would pan out with me already having been pronounced dead, but I'd deal with that when I got there.

We'd said our goodbyes and I was touched to see the

Daves get a little teary-eyed when we realized that, if I did manage to get back to my former universe, only one of them would be there to greet me. Then Cathy had rushed in to tell us that we'd better get it done because the situation outside had stabilized to the point where Floyd would shortly be making his way to the lobby accompanied by the dignitaries and press for the final, ceremonial, stage of the Giant Snog for Mankind. I wanted to say something to her—a parting word or a last look but I needed to concentrate on the task at hand—especially, the destination. Once the windows opened, I knew, one little slip of focus, just a single maverick image in my head could scuttle me and send me off to God knows where.

"Okay, guys, this is it," I said.

I had locked my eyes on the ball, blocking out everything around it. Then, more deliberately than I'd struck any golf shot or done anything in my life for that matter, swung back and through—keeping my head down throughout the shot—seeing the ball disappear at impact, not seeing it pass through the sculpture but then hearing it drop into the water.

"Did it go through?"

"Yeah," said a Dave.

"Yep," said the other one.

"Did anything happen?"

"We're still here if that means anything."

"And you're sure it went through?"

"Yep, right through."

"No question."

"And this is where we're supposed to hole out? The Eclipse sculpture in the lobby?"

"That's what they said. Want to try it again?"

"Charley—" Cathy gestured toward the escalators. "Here they come."

We'd withdrawn at that point, Cathy, the Daves and me, to the lobby bar to sort it all out and to witness Floyd's march to the Eclipse. Following a short invocation by someone in priest's garb that looked a lot like Samuel L. Jackson,

Floyd said, "One flop shot for man, one giant snog for mankind," and chipped his ball through the eclipse to enthusiastic applause.

"Look at that," said a Dave. "It happened again."

"What?"

"*Nothing.*"

"Nothing was *supposed* to happen," said the other. "He *is* Snog. It's not like he gets anything if he beats himself."

We sat and thought about that, sipping our drinks, while Floyd and his retinue —including now a gaggle of strippers in nurse's outfits—drifted off toward the grand ballroom.

"Aren't you going to tell anyone?" Cathy asked me.

"Tell them what?"

"You beat him! We all saw it."

"It doesn't matter."

"Of course, it matters. You *did* it. You did the impossible. Don't you want to be famous?"

"Not for beating Floyd. Anyway, it obviously wasn't impossible."

"But all the signs—"

"I'm guessing he puts those up himself," said a Dave.

Cathy stood up from the table. Her cheeks flushed with anger. "I don't get it. You're sitting out here like a bunch of losers while they're in there celebrating. If you don't care so much, why did you even bother?" She looked at me. "And if it doesn't matter to you, then why did you say those things to me?"

The Daves said we probably ought to tell her.

So, we did.

The One You Already Love

A few nights after the Giant Snog for Mankind, I was hitting balls late over at Mallards. It was getting close to nine and most of the regular range rats had called it quits for the evening. The Daves had been there earlier and wanted me to drive over to Earl's for a couple of beers, but I had half a bucket of balls left and said I might stop by later. I really wasn't in the mood for practicing, but the night was clear, and a cool breeze had wandered over from the ocean bringing some aid for my damaged spirit.

My eyes must have been closed for a few moments, because when I opened them, Cathy was there in the next stall looking at me. I hadn't seen her since the other night at the Hyatt when we'd coughed up the whole unlikely story about how an impossible plane accident had flung me and Regular Dave into Floyd's universe. She'd sat sipping her drink, eyes moving from one of us to the other, waiting for a punch line that never came. We brought her completely up to date, right up to my shot at the Eclipse.

When we finished, she hadn't said much except that she was tired. The trains had stopped running so we'd taken rooms in the hotel for the night—separate ones. The Daves had bunked with me. Next morning, when I phoned Cathy's room, she'd already checked out.

Now, seeing her again at Mallard's, I had to smile. *Cathy at a driving range.* Even in Floyd's wacky universe and despite everything that had happened, she still seemed out of place. That made two of us—*voodoo balls*, way out of context.

She'd come from an afternoon shift at the hospital and wore the red leather jacket over her retro nurse's uniform—

art direction by Floyd, I guess. I'd gotten used to her hair short like that, now almost preferred it. It seemed to suit this heartbreaker version of my wife—dazzling, independent yet vulnerable with just a dash of 'can kick the crap out of you if I care to.'

"One thing I can't figure out is why you never became a golfer."

"What—go pro? You gotta practice all the time."

That got a laugh. "Think the pros practice as much as you used to?"

"I don't know. Maybe a couple of 'em."

"So, did you always want to write ads?"

I shook my head. "Thought I was gonna be a golfer, but I didn't have what it takes. Or maybe the desire."

"That's funny, you know."

"What?"

"Coming from the guy who just went out and beat the best golfer in the world."

"That wasn't golf."

"Same difference."

"Okay, but in my universe—or any normal universe—Floyd isn't the greatest golfer in the world. He only thinks he is."

"And how good are you—in a normal universe?"

"Just fair. How about your guy?"

"Charley?"

"Yeah. What did he always want be?"

She thought for a moment and then shrugged. "He never said, and I never thought to ask."

"He might have surprised you."

She walked over and sat down on the bench and looked up at the stars. "What am I like where you come from?"

"Mostly the same. A little different."

She laughed. "She's prettier?"

"Nope."

"I'm prettier?"

"You're more—striking I guess you'd call it."

She grinned. "I'm hot."

"Yes, you are."

"Because Floyd sees me that way?"

"I guess so."

"But *you* don't."

"I didn't say that. You're different. Cathy'd never cut her hair like that or get a nose ring or wear a sexy outfit to work."

"So, you disapprove and that's why you want to go back?"

I laughed. "No, that's not it."

"How else? Is she smarter? Sweeter? What else is your Cathy that Floyd's Cathy isn't?"

"It's funny. I thought there were a million things but when I'm with you, I can't think of one. You're just… she's my best friend. It's like we've known each other forever. I can't imagine us not being together."

"Do you make each other happy?"

"We did. I think now it's mostly the kids do that for us."

Cathy smiled. "Sean and Sara."

"I guess we're the kind of couple you expect will stay together, who are supposed to grow old together. That's how I've always thought about it anyway."

"That's nice."

I joined her on the bench, and we sat there for a few moments not saying anything but just listening to the evening, until the big range lights switched off leaving us in semi-darkness. Outlined now by the spill light from the parking lot, she turned and ducked her head into the breeze, letting it push the hair away from her eyes.

"I'm wondering …" she said.

"Yeah?"

"Well… we know Floyd thinks you're this high-powered, successful guy with a totally hot wife and a golf game good enough to challenge the U.S. Open champion, right?"

"Okay…right."

"So, my question is why don't you think that?"

"Thinking something doesn't make it true…"

"I think it helps."

"…especially when the guy thinking it is half-crazy."

Another gust of cool air rushed between us. She shivered and pulled her knees up to her chest. "Sometimes it's good to be a little crazy, don't you think?"

We watched the last of the range rats shove clubs back into bags, slip into sweatshirts or windbreakers and amble off toward the parking lot. Out on the range, Floyd's replacement was tooling around in the cart, sweeping up the remaining balls. I couldn't see the face inside the cage but wondered what kind of universe he or she might be thinking of.

"Maybe that's why nothing happened," Cathy said.

"What do you mean?"

"Well, you beat Floyd, and nothing happened, right?"

'Uh-huh."

"Then he's not Snog."

"Of course, he's Snog. Who else would it be?"

"Well, think about it. Here, in this universe, you're brilliant, successful… hold the human brain in the palm of your hand…"

"Do it every day."

"And you're married to Floyd's dream girl."

"That's right."

"So, doesn't that make you the one *he* has to beat?"

She looked just like my Cathy now, shivering as another gust of cool air rushed over us. We sat there for a while longer, looking up at Floyd's twinkling canopy of stars. They seemed to shine extra brightly.

"The other night," I said. "On the train platform, you started to say something. You said, 'I know how you are and…' then you stopped. Do you remember that?"

"I think so."

"I thought you were going to say something you said to me a long time ago. I'd done something stupid and was too bullheaded or embarrassed to apologize and you said, 'It's okay, Charley. I know how you are, and I love you.' Just like that— 'I know how you are…' It's the sweetest, kindest thing anyone ever said to me."

She slid over and leaned against me, her breath warm and familiar on my neck.

"How long are you going to stay out there?" she said. "Aren't you ever coming back?"

"Sure, I will. I never stop thinking about you. You're all I think about."

"Why not come home, then? What're you doing out there?"

"I want to. I'm probably just lost without you—and maybe a little scared. But I'll be back. You don't have to worry about that. I'll say I'm sorry and ask you to forgive me and then you'll say…"

She said it then and I kissed her, and she kissed me back. And it was a real lover's kiss, the kind I'd almost forgotten, like the first time or the first night, when you're a teenager in a car or back row of the movie theater, breathy and trembling.

"Umm," she murmured. "Sloppy kisses."

The Man in the Mirror

"Mind if I play through?"

It was like the first time seeing my reflection in a three-way, department store mirror. I must have been seven or eight years old and, by that age, had a pretty good fix on my appearance—or thought I did—the straight-on view in the bathroom mirror, when I brushed my teeth and combed my hair for school. The same crooked-tooth grin captured in my annual school photos.

Seeing myself from a new angle had stunned me. This, I realized, was how others saw me.

Now, here, walking around in the desert, was the living, breathing, talking embodiment of that off-angle perspective. And, like that first time in the department store dressing room, I stood and stared.

He'd appeared, as before, coming over the rise, humping his sticks, shoulders curled, bent to the raging wind. He recognized me too—I could see it in his glance—but, even so, didn't stop, and didn't say the words until he was nearly past me. Half of me—the chicken shit half—wanted to say nothing and let him go. But I'd come this far and had brought my clubs.

"Hey, wait," I said, half-choking the words out. "I was thinking, if it's all right, maybe I could join you." He stopped then, turned and smiled and, I might have been mistaken but, I thought there was relief in his eyes. Like he'd been hoping I'd show up and afraid I wouldn't.

It was easy to see why I'd originally thought him a ghost. His windbreaker and slacks were faded and, like his hair, covered with a layer of sand-colored, dust. Even so, I recognized the clothes as the ones I'd worn that night at Mallard's when I told Floyd I was headed for the desert.

He led me to a small bluff where a pair of spinning wind turbines hovered like desert sentries, tall and half-lit by the low-hanging moon. From there, we launched our illuminated orbs into the night sky where they mingled and interacted with an infinite canopy of winking and blinking possibilities, there one instant, gone the next.

"Which way is the green?" I asked.

"Out there somewhere," he said. "I'm guessing we'll know it when we see it." Then he grinned. "Although I've been doing this a while now and haven't spotted it yet. Thought I did, once or twice but, when I got there…" He shook his head, sadly. "Was always something else. Wasn't it, at all."

"How are we supposed to know what direction to hit?"

"What I've been doing—play the shot that seems right. Trust it'll eventually take me where I want to go."

That's how we played that night, lugging our bags through the desert, stopping only to hit a shot. Sometimes they came off as planned. Other times a gust came up and blew them far off line into a situation we couldn't have imagined, where the lie would seem impossible at first but then you'd take a second look, or see it from another angle, and it'd be all of a sudden do-able. Then, on to the next shot and the next.

The other Charley was every bit as good as Floyd thought he was. But I was good too, matching him shot for shot, falling into a rhythm, not pressing or even thinking, just one swing after another, remembering the swing I used to have, always had. Along the way, we talked. Having so much in common, there was plenty to talk about. He loved Cathy, he told me, but the marriage had never gotten on track—not for lack of effort on both sides. The two of them had just, for one reason or another, been always at odds with each other, making the prospect of kids pretty much a dead issue.

He still held out hope, though, that they could somehow, someday, get back together and make it work. He said he'd always felt that the two of them were somehow fated to spend their lives together.

He also confessed to being unfulfilled by his job—something else we had in common. Never had any real desire, he said, to be a physician. He'd been "cursed" with book-smarts, routinely aced his chemistry and biology courses and managed to fall into a medical career. Aside from his dysfunctional marriage, he said, his greatest regret was not pursuing his early musical ambitions. He'd played tuba in the marching band at Cal Berkeley, but the rigors and demands of medical school and the long internship had required he give it up. More than once, he confided, he'd be scrubbing in for the odd bi-frontal craniotomy when his mind would drift and he'd picture himself in a Bavarian restaurant, playing polkas with an oompah band. When he got back from the desert, first thing he was going to do—after squaring things with Cathy—was take up the instrument again.

"What about you?" he asked. "What did *you* always want to do?"

"Play golf," I said, laughing to hear myself admit it.

"Touring pro?"

"Yeah, but it wasn't a serious thing. More a pipe dream, really."

"You never gave it a shot?"

"Thought about it in college. But…" I shook my head. Didn't believe it, I guess."

We played on into the night, with only the stars and the hulking outline of distant mountains to guide on, playing out beyond the wind farm into open desert where we took relief from the relentless wind behind a pile of rocks. It occurred to me, then, to ask this other Charley why he hadn't seemed fazed by a carbon copy of himself showing up out of nowhere. Why it almost felt like he'd been expecting me.

"Thank my dentist," he said, laughing. "He warned

me something like this might happen. Hang around on that desert wind farm long enough, he said, and you never know who'll turn up."

"What are you doing out here, anyway?" I said.

"You know, it's a funny thing. I came out here to forget. And it must have worked because I can't seem to…"

"Maybe looking for something?"

"Like what?"

"I don't know… the Answer maybe?"

He shook his head. "No. No, I found that a while ago."

"You did?"

"I think so," he said. Then he smiled. "It's not that big a mystery. Comes down to something that dentist used to say about swinging the swing you already have.'

"Personal golf," I said.

He chuckled. "Didn't really need to come all the way out here to learn that."

"Well then, if you can't remember what you're doing here, why not go home?"

"I think about it now and then."

"She wants you to, you know."

"She say that?"

"Uh-huh."

His expression brightened. "Sometimes I imagine how it would be to just show up out of the blue some morning, surprise her."

"I know she'd like that," I said. But then, over his shoulder, I saw the mountains to the east now outlined with the pink of approaching dawn and said we needed to hurry up and finish our match because I wanted to get home too and couldn't do it until something impossible happened.

"Like what?" he'd said.

"Like beating you."

"Me?"

"Yeah. You're Snog."

He creased his forehead like we do when we're perplexed. "I am? Since when?"

"Aren't you?"

"News to me. Isn't it Floyd?"

I shook my head. "I've already beaten him. Wasn't even close to impossible."

The other Charley was staring off. "Maybe it's not *anybody*," he said. Then he stood up and stretched. "All I know is," he said. "Snog is a *game*. And, while I guess you could make a case for its being sometimes impossible— *inevitable* might be a better word—like fate, that's not something you're ever gonna beat."

"Then what's the point," I said, "of whacking your ball through the desert and not ever getting anyplace? My question caught him mid-swing. He grinned and pointed his club back the way we came, telling me to have a look.

And, still visible in the pre-dawn glow, I saw our star-crossed, haphazard, wind-blown trek through desert scrub land now clearly defined as a golf hole—not on the desert floor but in the night sky where the stars had somehow aligned into a wondrous, twinkling fairway.

"I don't get it," I said. "It looks like we knew where we were going. But we've just been wandering."

"Yeah," he said. "It does seem that way."

Then, looking ahead, we saw only barren desert and starry darkness, random and infinite. "What I do," he said, "is, every so often, look back over my shoulder toward where I came from and then guide on that. Keep heading the same way. Swinging within myself, like the books say to do."

"The swing you already have."

"Uh-huh." Then he pointed again, back over my shoulder. "Take a peek back every once in a while. That should tell you all you need to know."

He grinned and shook my hand, and in that instant,

I was swept up once more with the fish-out-of-water meets déjà vu feeling, and I stood again in the department store mirror, facing three Charleys, all grown up now. Reflected in the middle glass was me, as I saw myself. Next to that, in the left panel, was Charley as others saw me. And in the right panel, there he was—from my dreams of Meadowbank and sometimes Riviera—over the course of a thousand frustrated nights—crowding me, blocking me, the guy always at my ear, insisting that what I loved most, had always done best, remained forever beyond my reach…*impossible.*

"Hey, Dude," I said to him now. "You're in my way."

That's when Dr. Sleeves' windows and doors must have opened up because everything went white, and I felt a rush of air and the wind take me and…

…I was gone.

Cathy

As I write this, I'm sitting on the balcony outside a Los Angeles hotel room on a luminous August morning. From here, I can see the tops of the towering eucalyptus trees that line the fairways of Riviera Country Club just a short drive to the west down Sunset Boulevard. Cathy just left with the kids for a couple of hours at the beach, but she's promised they'll be at the course in time for my match this afternoon.

It's been nearly a year since I got back from Floyd's universe and much has happened. Barnett was stunned, of course, when I gave my notice but also, I think, relieved to hear I wasn't jumping to a rival agency. When I told him my plans, he'd laughed, said he wasn't at all surprised, knew it was just a matter of time.

Then last spring, after some intensive months of training and preparation, I entered and won the San Mateo County Amateur Championship and, a few weeks later, took the Lompoc City Championship in a walk. In July, we packed Cathy, Sean and Sara into Dave's RV and drove down to Bakersfield for the U.S. Amateur qualifying where a pair of sixty-eights secured me a spot in the championship field this week at Riviera.

Cathy made sure Sean and Sara were on hand for the final eighteen. They rooted hard for their dad from the gallery, cheered me every step of the way. It's amazing how sometimes all you need to accomplish something is someone besides you thinks you can do it.

Floyd's been a champ too. Had him caddying for me all these weeks and it's gone so well we're talking about making a permanent arrangement. He's a demon at reading putts and a look from him can hush even the most raucous gallery. I suppose you could also say he inspires me with his single-minded toughness and seeing how hard he takes it when we lose. Fortunately, we haven't done a lot of that. Dave's been great too, driving the RV, getting us to the course on time, making sure I get enough rest and practice—running interference for me like he did back in you-know-where. And I've got to say it's a welcome relief to have just one of him again. One of these days, over a couple of beers, I might be tempted to tell him about the 'cousins' I left back in Floyd's universe, but probably won't. He'd only think I was nuts. And who knows whether he'd be right?

At the risk of jinxing myself, I'll go out on a limb and say I've got a better-than-even chance of coming away with that Havemeyer trophy this Sunday. Mike and Ron are certainly counting on it. The U.S. Amateur champ, they keep telling me, gets an automatic invite to The Masters, both the U.S. and British Opens and all sorts of tournament sponsor invitations. They've gone ahead and scheduled a press conference for this coming Monday morning where they're hoping I'll announce that I'm turning pro. And they've already dredged up a raft of investors from among their dodgy roster of bank 'clients' with ready money, enough they say, to fund a year's worth of tour expenses. We'll see.

As you might imagine, it's a relief to have escaped the funhouse of Floyd's imagination but it's increasingly clear that this is *not* the same universe I started out in. My first clue was when nobody seemed surprised to see me alive, or ask where I'd been, or how I got back. In fact, no one had noticed I was gone. There'd been no golf trip or impossible plane crash. True to my word, I'd flown to San Diego on that business trip and returned home that Sunday night.

Here, the kids are happy and healthy. Their parents love each other, enjoy each other's company and are presently living out their dreams—I've already told you about my budding golf career. And Cathy, who I'd always known was brilliant but assumed was content with motherhood and a nursing career, has graduated with honors from medical school at Berkeley and begins her residency this fall at UC

San Francisco Medical Center—in *neurology*. We'll have a real brain surgeon in the family. How's that for irony?

Sometimes, out on the course, I think about that impossible match in the desert; about infinite possibilities, and how the choices we make and paths we take can seem windblown and random, yet still, somehow, we manage to wind up where we're supposed to be.

That night, when Dr. Sleeves' windows opened up, with all the possibilities winking and blinking, I'd barely had enough time to think about anything—except Cathy. *My Cathy*. About how much I loved her and Sean and Sara and that there'd never been anything I'd ever wanted or needed beyond the life we shared.

Mostly, though, I thought about Cathy, and wondered what *she'd* been thinking of all those nights at the opposite end of the sofa.

I might have known it'd be something like this.

Acknowledgements

Sincere thanks to the friends and early readers whose observations, suggestions, and encouragement kept me going:

Bob Levin, Casey Mortensen, Jeannine Canter, Michael Braverman, Michelle Harris, David Tate, Denny McArdle, Mark Rowland, Richard Taylor, Mark Ragonese, Mary Ann McArdle, Marian Sloan.

And to editors Jonathan Starke and Lynn Hightower for their insight, expertise and unflagging reassurance that there was a book in here somewhere.

About the author

C.P. Mortensen has written and produced more than one hundred film and TV documentaries including The Unreal Story of Pro Wrestling and biographies of Mike Ditka, Kobe Bryant, Andre the Giant, Joe Cocker, Field Marshall Montgomery and Bodacious, the Rodeo Bull.

At the age of eleven (pretending to be twelve) he caddied at Winged Foot. Sometime later, he produced a David Leadbetter infomercial in exchange for golf lessons.

As a boy, his favorite golfer was Cary Middlecoff—who, strangely enough, was also a dentist.

www.ingramcontent.com/pod-product-compliance
Lightning Source LLC
Chambersburg PA
CBHW071152100726
47908CB00002B/349

* 9 7 8 1 7 3 3 3 3 5 3 0 0 *